BY PAUL HORGAN

THE THIN
MOUNTAIN AIR

THE THIN MOUNTAIN AIR

by Paul Horgan

£222413 .

THE BODLEY HEAD

LONDON SYDNEY

TORONTO

This story is concerned in part with political events as
they might have occurred in New York State in the
1920s. I have chosen the period arbitrarily to serve the
established time frame of the sequence of the novels.
As my politics are imaginary, so are my politicians.

P.H.

Copyright © 1977 by Paul Horgan
ISBN 0 370 30081 5
Printed in Great Britain for
The Bodley Head Ltd
9 Bow Street London WC2E 7AL
by Redwood Burn Ltd, Trowbridge & Esher
First published in Great Britain 1978

For
Martin Griffin

Contents

There is only one kind of love—but there are a thousand different imitations of it.
La Rochefoucauld

A man can either be himself or not himself— he doesn't necessarily coincide with himself.
Walker Percy (in an interview)

CHAPTER I

❀

The Niagara

"IN EVERY LIFE, RICHARD, THERE IS SOMETHING, great or small, to be ashamed of," said my father with more force than necessary, and with reference to a concern unknown to me then; for we were simply conversing in general. But the priest hidden in every Irishman was being eloquent in him, and his eyes flashed, even as he smiled with scowling charm. "Just as there is something noble. Never fail to be ashamed of the first, and never take credit for the second. You'll remember this . . ." He paused. Then, "I've tried to."

He looked at my mother for confirmation. She gave him a glance and held her embroidery hoops away to look at them with a blurred gaze, judging the effect of what she was making so deftly. In her lovely expression there was a hint of reserved wisdom which briefly brought the conversation to a halt.

"Rosie," said my father, "it's a little unnerving when you put on that look."

"Oh, really?" said my mother lightly, in a way which could have been either ominous or meaningless. My father sighed comically at the old mystery of marriage, and said to me,

"Come on, Doc, let's take a little walk to Park Lake and back before bedtime."

In my youth I was a cultural migrant. Unexpected events came my way instead of my seeking them out, in places or conditions far from my native moral climate.

When my father was acclaimed in public, I was there to witness the crashing homage; and I wondered if I contained worthiness as his son. But my undoubting mother, rosy with excitement, strenuously took my hand and cried above the clamor,

"Oh, Richard, aren't we proud of him? He has never looked so handsome— My dear, my dear!" she called suddenly, not to me but to him, across the teeming convention mob below, as if he, there on the platform which was gaudy with bunting and harsh with light, could hear her.

His first words, accepting the nomination, had set off the great crowd, so that he could not speak again for a quarter of an hour. The delegates, marching and colliding in their struggles to dramatize their joy, looked like microbes aimlessly darting about in the lighted field of a microscope. My father had to keep nodding and smiling, his arms high, his eyes roving the vast hall, searching out and recognizing his particular blocs of supporters, lighting upon an individual or two in the front rows to trade flattering public confidences with them, finally looking up to us in the balcony over the rostrum. When he saw us, his eyes seemed to go bluer and to send out light. We called to him, and though he could not hear us, he knew what we gave to him and it filled him with still more joy. A few people in the crowd saw this exchange between the nominee and his family and redoubled their acclaim. The air was full of a sense of propitious fortune.

There had been a long and exhausting struggle for my father's nomination as lieutenant-governor of New York State; and, coming after an acrimonious, even an ugly, fight to nominate Judge Pelzer for governor, the protracted business of the Democratic State Convention had worn everyone out, so that when the matter was finally resolved the relief was explosive, and my father was the heroic pretext for letting go. As he stood waiting for silence in which to speak, and even as I exulted in his share of public glory, I was ashamed to feel something heavy in my breast—was it doubt of an unknown sort? Was I disconcerted to be the son of a man approaching the first step of a success which "could lead anywhere," after this, as everyone predicted?

Nothing was clear, but if my father was about to become a great man, what would I be? Why should seeing him newly that night at Niagara Falls in the early 1920s make me obscurely troubled about what I was like myself, in my second year of college, and why should I even wonder? Even as I rejoiced for him, I was ashamed of being conspicuous as part of his new prominence. He seemed to know himself so well—myself I hardly knew.

My mother pressed my arm.

"To think that we belong to him!" Her happiness in her loyalty was so great that it made me blush, with love and anger, the one for her, the other for myself that I could not be as free as she in the tumult of our feelings. My father had a gold watch with a hunting case inside of whose back lid was an engraved testimonial. (I have it still.) It reads, DAN, COMMAND OUR WHOLE CROWD, ALWAYS WITH YOU, ALWAYS FOR YOU. It was unsigned, for there were far too many names to fit within the golden disk; but they all knew who they were, and so did my father. They were those men in Dorchester— professional men, bankers, business leaders—among whom he had steadily emerged as the most articulate spokesmen in the community. Whatever in life they were confident of, they believed in it entirely, and because my father did too, but could speak for it better than any of the others, he seemed to embody that bright time, after the First World War, when victory, prosperity, and unlimited progress rose as a vision beyond the fact of that mortality to which many ideas, and all men, were subject.

But so new in college as I was, optimism had come to seem to me naïve. I would not then have said it just so; but an immemorial melancholy, something like the leaf smoke drifting out of the ashes of summer in our street in Dorchester, where yardmen in fall piled leaves to be burned along the curbstones, appeared to be inseparable from any aspect of life. The strongest thing, I would say to myself, was to face this with love for any beauty of statement about any subject, knowing that human fallibility would at last be left visible, ashen and black, like the fallen leaves in the yardmen's burned-out bonfires.

❧

During the convention there were many hours when there was nothing to see. My father would be invisible with committees. In order to have some family privacy, we were staying in a hotel on the Canadian side of the Niagara. My mother would sit in her bay window writing letters about the excitement of the week. Left to myself, I would go across to the American brink of the falls, which always filled me with many strands of feeling. The strongest of these was a fascination terrible in its hypnotic power as I watched the constant yet ever-changing brink, and I felt a resigned fury at the impossibility of truly describing in my notebook what I saw there at Prospect Park.

What I saw was of course what the world saw—the other tourists, the traditional honeymooners, the children who seemed abashed at the power before them—but there was something more which drew me back again and again. It was the memory of my first sight of the falls, and the rumor of them even before I saw them when I was a very small boy. Dorchester was near enough to the falls and their city to be convenient for a day's "outing." My fear of the heavy power of the river as it fell persisted as much from ancestral memories as from my own sight of it, for we had family legends connected with it. One of my mother's brothers, out canoeing with a friend, had been drowned upstream in the rapids and his body had never been found. The tragedy was talked of so often in my presence that the falls, the river, the lake behind them, all began to mean more to me than simply bodies of water to be seen by anyone. My uncle's body could have vanished on only one course, and I knew enough about this on my first childhood day there to imagine its journey over the brink into the chasm below. This uncle was young, with—so everyone said, sighing—a wonderfully fine singing voice. A serious career awaited him. They used to speak of how splendid he was as he stood by the piano singing "Die Beiden Grenadiere," handsome and martial, and I saw a heroic manliness in him, for I knew his oval photograph on my mother's dressing table, and I was often thoughtful about the drowned song and the fine body sweeping by in tumult.

My grandfather used to go to the falls on every anniversary of this son's death. He would go alone in his famous Panama hat, with his gold-headed stick, and his notebook and Waterman fountain pen, and, as we were told, he would write "reflections," sitting in a grove of birch trees near the bank, making a picture which later I related to Brahms walking in summer fields, or Goethe seated meditating on a Roman ruin, or Beethoven lost to nature in a woods clearing— the stuff of romantic German culture sternly imposed by my grandfather. It turned out that his riverside "reflections" were poems in German which he later published in Munich (he had emigrated from Germany as a young man) under the title *Am Niagara*. Not all of them were elegiac, but all made reference in one or another way to the falls, and the book's embossed binding showed a stylized image of the American brink. Staring long enough at the cover, if no one was around, I could make the image seem to move, in its eternal fall.

And, too, in early years, I was pinned in imagination to the ordeal of certain men whose boat of heavy timbers was wedged into a cluster of rocks hardly a hundred yards above the falls. I heard how—three of them on a sporting expedition—they had threaded their way through the upper rapids, knowing just where to turn toward shore and safety after challenging the current with the high spirits of young fellows who knew how to manage the natural powers of life to their own advantage. But even in their certainty they miscalculated. The rapids seized them and threw them forward and sideways out of control, while people on the banks watched in horror. The men cried out, their voices thin and distant over the clamor of the water, as they staved away from rocks trying to turn their boat, while the mist and the roar of the cataract came closer with terrible speed. They could see the rainbow lights of the mist clouding upward, and they must vanish into it like my uncle, and I voyaged with them to their very fall of disaster—but in a wild turn, the boat headed for almost concealed rocks forty feet offshore and suddenly lodged among them.

Would the stay hold?

The river's driving power was at its greatest just there as it approached the falls; but as it swept by the boat, it drove the hull into the rock formation more deeply. The wedging held, though every now and then a strike of the current would make the boat shudder and slip, as if to come free and bound ahead into the tumultuous foam. Darkness fell before rescue crews could be brought, while the men wondered when the river would break the boat free again and throw them to their doom. Lanterns and bonfires, cries of encouragement from the bank now and then reached the eyes and ears of the men in danger, one of whom could be seen praying.

All night long, as the boat gave its periodic lurches, with what outcome they dreaded to think of, the men awaited their death. At daylight the boat was still there, lines were shot across to it, the men were brought ashore, and everyone in the rescue party marveled to see that the hair of one man's head had "turned white overnight"—

so it was reported to me by an aunt who used the phrase as proudly as though she had coined it.

All of this had happened before I was born, and the boat was still there on my first picnic at the falls, and it was there still all those years later, a sodden hulk, when we went to the state Democratic convention, and I gazed at it with an old respect. The rocks, the violent sameness of the current, met in a terrible nicety to preserve the evidence of the river's mighty nature and man's folly. In my boyhood I sometimes had nightmares about being on that boat and hearing the cries, and the sound of the falls, and seeing figures moving in the shoreline groves by lantern light with desperate hopes which they were unable to enact. When at about five years old I awoke from the first of these nightmares, I went to see in the mirror whether my hair had turned white. It had not, and then I slept easy.

All such information added richly to the physical fact of the falls.

On that latest visit, I found changes in the fixtures added for the convenience and safety of the visitors. There was a long, narrow platform built as close as possible to the brink, so that leaning on the barrier of three iron bars which was elbow high, you could stare almost directly down at the great curve of the water as it swept over its shelf of rocks to be lost in the clouds of mist rising from so far below. A wooden stairway, turning back and forth with many landings, led along the face of the chasm a little way to the right of the platform, and I went down several of its flights to recognize, if I could, the rocky face and the slippery ledge where Chateaubriand, in his early twenties, as I then was, had let himself down by twined creepers, only to lose his grip and fall. He was saved when he landed on that ledge, though he broke his arm in the act. It was a relief, reading about this a year earlier in my French class, to know that a friendly Iroquois Indian had managed to rescue him, in the story he had to tell of wild America in 1791.

But nothing man would do to the place could diminish what was to be still the open mystery of it, every time I went there free of my father's affairs in the convention; and that was the river's sudden and fearsome change of character. With the vast, calm reservoir of Lake Erie behind it, it placidly enough entered into its channel and went downstream, yet with something ominous in its glassy progress. Even so, riding, as I did once or twice in boyhood, I could bring my hired pony close to the bank, coming through the birch groves of my grandfather; and I remember bone-deep pleasure in hearing mingled the sounds of the river washing along and the steady, slow strikes of an ax biting into a live tree trunk somewhere deep in the groves. The river went levelly along and I would parallel it as closely as I could through woods and brush. And then it became agitated as it met rocks. The rapids boiled noisily; yet still the river was level with the earth—true to its gradual lowering, until out of the inscrutable distance came the first pounding upon the air by what the river was soon to do. Abruptly the stream was divided by little islands. The distance was cut off by towering clouds of mist, and suddenly the river left its level way and with mightiness all unsuspected fell tremendously, transformed, it seemed, into an entirely different phase of nature.

Yet given the hidden edge of the chasm, how could it do otherwise? I stared by the hour at the instant of transformation, which now brought all strange analogies and metaphors to my thought—for like many students I was in search of meanings of change, and the word "fall" became heavy with these the more I thought about it, when I then had nothing to attach to them beyond my groping wonder. In the presence of the vast slide of endless water beyond its lost bed, I was, like everyone, unable to reach much of any meaning except the stupendous beauty and menace of that shining emerald-green curve which below the brink turned into iridescence and vapor. How take my eye off it? For my inner eye was as fixed as my outer.

So it was that I almost always became unaware of the people around me who came to marvel, and then to go away to buy post-cards. On certain days there was a strong wind over the falls when voices were driven away which otherwise if shouted might have just sounded above the booming of the endless heavy plunge. But on that last day of the convention, when I leaned my chin on my arms on the railing of the barrier and lost myself in looking, the falls thundered, but the day was calm, and I heard people a few feet behind me. Their voices were heightened to reach each other. A woman cried out shrilly in an accent I was not used to,

"Now do come, Pamela, silly girl. You'll not see the like of it again."

A little girl's voice cried out tearfully in reply,

"No, I don't want to, I don't *want* to!"

"You really are such a silly. Look, Christopher isn't afraid. —Christopher, come back here, not too close, you can see quite well from here!"

I turned to see them. They were a small boy of four or five, a little girl who was surely his twin, and a tall, bony, middle-aged woman who wore a sort of blue uniform which included an elbow-long cape and a bonnet tied with a ribbon under her chin. The girl was half hiding behind the woman's ankle-long skirt. They were an English nanny and her charges. The boy stood leaning forward with his hands on his bare knees. He wore woolen shorts, long socks, and miniature brogans. He and his sister had identical camel's hair top-coats, though the day was warm. His pale-yellow hair was topped by a small round cap with a shallow visor. Looking at the falls from his little distance, his eyes were huge, bright blue, in his healthy pink face. Both children were as freshly shining and beautiful as new apples.

Without warning, while the nanny struggled to force Pamela around to give at least one glance at the terrible falls (a matter of discipline now), Christopher bolted forward, running in glee, and struck the barrier of iron bars with a force of a projectile right next to me.

He scrambled up the fence like a wild young kitten. His cap flew off into the river and there was a glimpse of it sailing over the brink. He threw his leg over the top railing, and then, like someone using too much energy in mounting a horse, he could not keep the rest of him from going over the railing which he had meant to straddle, just above the water, which seemed to slide faster as it was about to plunge.

I flung my arms across him. The nanny screamed. For a long moment I held Christopher where he was, most of his body on the far side of the fence; and then slowly I pulled him back toward me, across the rail, and into my arms. He pinned his arms around my neck and the force of this knocked me off balance and together we fell to the wet planks of the platform. I was on my back. His small, brilliant face was close to mine. We were making the nursery game of owl eyes at each other. We were both panting. He did not yet know what to think.

The nanny shrieked,

"Come here, come here at once, you wicked boy!"

His sister burst into sobs.

I rose to my feet as the child clung to me, and with his sturdy legs dangling, he tightened his arms around me in a hug, so that I held him even more closely. It was one of those small instants of the present which seem to open into the common, unknown future. As I held him, I felt for the first time the meaning of potential fatherhood, in a rush of tenderness so great at his trusting hug that I was amazed to feel it edge over into a love which stirred in my loins— the first coupling of the idea of sexual joy with procreation. The vital stir of the little boy in my arms brought powerful intuitions of beauty and purity at the same time, as if I held the infant god Eros in my arms, and knew all his hot little life.

"Well," I said to him, "that was rather close."

"Yes, wasn't it, rather," and now that he could speak, he lost his composure. Looking ruefully over my shoulder at the falls, he turned pale.

"Come on, let's go to the others," I said.

We started toward the nanny and Pamela. Halfway to them, he began to struggle in my grasp, to avoid being delivered over, for once we were at a safe distance from the falls, the nanny darted forward and in a rage of relief began to berate Christopher. She reached across me to slap his face and pull at him, Pamela's sobs turned to shrieks at the commotion, and Christopher himself caught their fear and began to howl. His face was pressed against my ear, his grasp grew tighter than ever. No matter how furiously the nanny tugged at him, he would not let me go. What had been an adventure, a near calamity not understood by him, now became a crime for which he must suffer. He began to shiver and shake. Hysterically he cried out through his tears, "No, no, no, let me alone," and successfully kicked at Nanny until she had to retreat a little.

"Don't you know," she trumpeted, while people all around stared in curiosity at how the scene of the little death they had just missed observing must end, "you could have been drowned? Killed? Oh, wait until I tell—"

"No," he wailed, "you shan't tell my father!"

"Oh, won't I just!" she cried. Her face was naturally pale and now it was as gray as stained ivory.

"I didn't do anything! I didn't," but an image powerful in his small world returned, and he cried, "My cap, my cap!" and again he saw it sailing terribly over the brink, and he redoubled his howls, seeing himself gone with the cap.

[13]

"You nearly went over the falls, that's all, if this young gentleman had not caught you! Come!"

But he would not leave me, and as her heartbeat began to subside, she suddenly became efficient. She said,

"Would you just carry him to the car, sir, if you don't mind? I must get him back to the hotel and pop him into bed and give him something hot to drink."

With Christopher still clinging to me, I rode with them to the Royal Canadian Hotel across the river where the English family also were staying. The little boy soon enough recovered himself, though he refused the nanny's orders to leave my lap and sit properly on the jump seat of the hired limousine driven by a fresh-faced young Canadian. When we came to cross the highway bridge, Christopher craned to see far away the churning rapids below the falls. He pointed.

"Is that where I might have gone?" he asked in the offhand tone of a miniature Englishman abroad.

"I'm afraid so," I said.

"You wicked boy," said the nanny automatically.

At this, Pamela, who had almost done with her abating sobs, broke out again and the nanny had to give all her efforts to consoling her in the atmosphere of terror which was too fine to lose. Pamela's tears only made her great blue eyes more brilliant, her exquisite flower-like little face and her gleaming pale hair more appealing. Her brother leaned to pat her wet cheek. They looked so exactly alike that they seemed to be two parts of one life. Nanny pushed away his little paw and said to Pamela,

"There, my pet. —*Oh, you wicked boy*. —Now, now, Pams, *we're* all right, aren't we. —*Oh, just wait till I*—"

"You cannot see my father. You *shan't* tell him!" cried Christopher. "He is gone for the day with Mummy."

"There is always the evening," snapped the nanny grimly.

When we came to the great white wooden hotel with its shingle turrets and whipping flags, Christopher at last had to yield me up.

As he was dragged across the lobby he kept his rueful gaze on me, and just before the elevator doors closed on him, he made a good-bye, repeatedly opening and closing his extended fist to me.

※

My father returned early from the post-convention committees. He was tired, he said. My mother put out her hand to his brow.

"Are you hectic?" she asked. "You've been overdoing."

"That is politics," replied my father. "You get nowhere under-doing a campaign."

"I hate it all," she said.

"Now, Rosie."

But there was an undercurrent such as sometimes flowed between them in my presence—something so private as to exclude me even as I was with them. At such moments I would think of them not only as father and mother but as husband and wife.

No, all he wanted now was a hot bath, and an early dinner, before a short evening meeting with Judge Pelzer, to discuss final details of the rest of the campaign. My mother and I were to go along, as the judge had asked for us to be introduced to him, since we were all going to be one great happy family. My mother shuddered comi-cally. Judge Pelzer, said my father, was in a high state of elation at his nomination for the governorship of the Empire State, and my father's designation as his running mate. "An unbeatable ticket," Judge Pelzer had said to everyone. My father made his comic face at this—George M. Cohan's lower lip stuck out—and said to us,

"We'll wait and see. *He* has something to live down, all right."

For only last year the judge had been accused of accepting a bribe from a powerful client in a civil suit involving millions of dollars, and by only a narrow margin had emerged from the scandal with safety. No proof had been produced against him, but his political opponents would be making the most of it, even so, and it was generally understood that my father, after a fierce floor fight at the convention staged by certain industrial interests, had been chosen to head the ticket with the judge in order to lend the Democratic campaign an air of honor, disinterestedness, and enlightened progress.

"Of course," my mother said with her habit of outspoken loyalty and even flattery, which my father had come to enjoy as his due, "*you* should be the governor, Dan. I cannot imagine why they don't see that."

"Oh," he replied, "I have no political base as yet. —But just wait."

And he embraced her and rasped the fine line of his jaw along her temple, at which she seemed to wilt a little with what I used to regard as simple pleasure, but now saw in my emerging maturity as love and desire. But these could wait, as it was early evening, and I was there, and it was time for the hot bath and the early dinner.

I roamed about the hotel until they joined me in a little while. The Royal Canadian's porches were wide and rambling, as they echoed the white façade with its many bay windows which culminated in the turrets with the flagstaffs. Its many decks, like the rooms upstairs, held much white wicker furniture. The public rooms downstairs were paneled in mirror-dark mahogany. The main dining room was long and narrow, with a side of windows giving on the view of the Canadian Horseshoe Falls, which at night were illuminated by green floodlights. Something about the establishment had that air of shipboard—the trimly uniformed pages, waiters, and maids, the brisk service, the majesty of senior employees who took their manners from the distant example of royalty—which the British so often imparted to their civilization wherever it might be encountered. The hotel, long since demolished, was, also, a tightly knit establishment, so that any news traveled fast throughout the ranks.

We were about to finish dinner at eight o'clock when a man and a woman came toward our table with a slightly inquiring, hesitant look to them. The man was only about ten years older than I, a slender, pink-faced person with a blond mustache brushed sideways. He held himself smartly, as though in uniform, though like my father he was wearing dinner clothes, as people regularly did in those days. He had neatly carved features and a lively blue eye. His wife was almost as tall as he, very slender, and beautiful with a pink and white delicacy set off by her auburn hair and an evening dress of frost-blue lace. As they came still closer, and then paused, my father looked up in some surprise.

"Yes, excuse me, please," said the man, addressing my father by name, "I am Hugh St Brides, and this is my wife."

My father said,

"Good evening, Mr St Brides," rising, and I rose with him.

"We simply had to come," said St Brides, "to thank your son for what he did for us today."

My parents turned to me and laughingly my mother said,

"And what did you do, if you please?"

I wanted to be gone. St Brides went on,

"My wife and I have been away all day—we went to Dorchester to the Historical Society Museum, where there's a portrait of an American ancestor which I've never seen. He fought in the battle of Lake Erie. I had an American grandmother, you see. When we got back, we found out your son had saved the life of our little boy—" and the whole story was quickly told.

My mother gasped in quick sympathy, putting her hand out to the young couple, not so much for the danger which was now past, but for the anguish which they must feel as parents, even in retrospect. To me she exclaimed,

"But you never said anything!"

"No, I suppose he wouldn't," said St Brides, smiling at me with warmth. "I cannot tell you," he continued to me, "what we feel for you in thanks. There's no way, really, to say much when a thing like this—so final, or potentially so—is the thing. Anyhow, sir, we are grateful beyond measure, and to hear Christòpher talk, Niagara Falls are nothing, and you are everything."

"—Nothing," I murmured.

"No," said the lady, "not to embarrass you. But really"—her voice was lovely, the words shaped, each perfectly—"what to do?"

"How is Christopher?" I asked.

"Oh, of course he is now appallingly smug."

"And Pamela? She was really the frightened one."

"Fast asleep as we came down."

"And Nanny?"

"Shocked to the marrow, and absolutely loving it," said St Brides.

"Yes, but you see," continued the lady, "we did want to do something, and do so hope you don't mind, so my husband asked me if I would give you, for us, a little memento of today."

With that she took from her small satin bag a long, flat, gold cigarette case and held it toward me.

It was a fine object, gleaming richly, with a heraldic device engraved on it. Instinctively I put my hands behind me and said,

"Oh, no thank you, I couldn't."

My father nodded at me with approval.

"No, really," urged St Brides, "we are immeasurably indebted to you, and this is not a reward, heaven forbid, but a reminder, however trifling."

"He doesn't smoke," exclaimed my mother radiantly, as though this would settle the matter in good sense.

His wife looked at St Brides inquiringly, and he shrugged.

"I daresay he is quite right," he said. "I wish there were some other way we—" and then saw that he must give up any effort at recompense, and knowing that chance encounters must end, tried to end this one with a little further idle friendliness. "We are on our way to our ranch in Alberta, we come over every year to spend a while there. It is a working ranch, you see, we all work like fury. The children love it all, riding Western saddles, and the rest. —Perhaps during the summer you might like to have a taste of ranch life?" he said to me. "We'd be so delighted to have you . . ."

"That would be a treat," said my father, "but I have commandeered him for my campaign. —I'm running for office this year."

"Oh, yes, I know," declared St Brides. "I am in politics, back home, in a mild sort of way, and your American campaigns do fascinate me. We've been going to your convention hall for part of each evening, I heard your speech last night. It was absolutely first class. I do wish you well in the election. November, isn't it? We shall be home by then, but no doubt we'll be reading about you."

"What an extraordinary man the other man is," said his wife, referring to Judge Pelzer.

"I say, Phyllis, perhaps we should keep out of that."

My mother laughed with forgiving charm.

"Many people think him more than extraordinary," she said, clearly meaning it not as a compliment, and looked at my father as if to nominate him.

"Hush, my dear," he said, laughing. Then he looked at his watch, and said with polite regret, "You make us proud of Richard, and we are tremendously glad your little boy is safe. But we have an appointment with 'the other man' and I'm afraid we must ask to be excused. It was kind of you to come to speak to our son."

St Brides took his gold case from his wife, slipped it into his pocket, and made their goodbyes, saying,

"Well, we're off early tomorrow, but we'll never forget today and what we owe your son, and neither will the twins. Good night, and all fortune in your campaign."

After shaking hands all around, they turned toward their table.

"What a beautiful dress, Mrs St Brides," exclaimed my mother, in farewell. Then, as they receded, "What an attractive couple. What are the children like?"

"Just like them, but of course in miniature. Such clear, tiny, lovely features. Twins."

"Sometimes I wish you were twins," she said, so fondly that I knew what she meant. If one of me was good, think of two! I felt a small rise of irritation at this, which subsided at once; but outright love was then difficult for me to accept, for reasons obscure to me, except that a few years earlier I had fallen in love only to be sent away after one encounter with love in the flesh. I thought of it so much—its brief amazing joy and the denials which followed—that it seemed to me more real than actual later opportunities, and it seemed to seal me off from feeling in return for what was sometimes offered to me, even such love as my mother offered to me daily, in small, ingenious ways. But in this she reminded me too much of my childhood, for it was her nature to please, and her reward came in how she imagined others must admire her sweetness, never allowing for their self-absorption.

As we were leaving the dining room of the Royal Canadian, the headwaiter, who clearly cultivated a long-cherished resemblance to King Edward VII, bowed us out with more than his usual remote grandeur. Struck by his manner, my father assumed it was a tribute to his new political eminence.

"Thank you," he said with the cordial modesty which served him so well in his campaign. "Good night."

But the headwaiter's respect had its own origin.

"I did not know that you knew His Lordship and Lady St Brides," he said.

"Oh: is that who they are?" asked my mother. "Good heavens, I called her Mrs."

The headwaiter with an air of privilege made a subdued announcement.

"The Earl and Countess of St Brides, and their children, Viscount Covington and Lady Pamela Covington, have been our guests here for three days."

"Ah!" murmured my father. "So his mild politics are in the House of Lords. A charming pair," he added to Edward VII, who leaned slightly backward, elevating his grand front, to indicate that this was an inadequate American estimate. As we left the heavily draped archway of the dining room, my father turned and waved to the St Brides', confident that they were watching us go, and they waved back.

"What a pity we won't ever see them again," said my mother; but early next morning as I was out to watch the first sunrays through the rising cloud of the Canadian Falls, I saw Christopher running toward me. When he could be heard, he asked, with his precise air of tiny adulthood,

"Are you going to take care of me from now on?"

I laughingly shook hands with him and answered,

"No, Christopher, I'm afraid now we go our ways. But what a spectacular time we had meeting!"

"Oh! ever so spectacular," he cried. "Goodbye, then. We have all spoken most gratefully of you."

He sounded like his parents. They were calling to him from the steps of the hotel—"Come, darling—" and he turned and ran to them. They all waved to me from there. Some invisible fiber joined us all. I thought with regret how I would never see any of them again. Some vague, new knowledge of myself remained with me as they went. What if Christopher were my little son?

Judge Pelzer received us in his hotel suite on the American side. His wife was with him in their bird's-eye maple sitting room. I had seen him only at a distance and only now realized how tall a man he was. Distance gave him, because of his large features and frame, a heroic, almost noble aspect, so that facing a crowd he made a sculpturesque impression. Near to, his proportions seemed coarse, and the smile which carried like a shaft of light over space now looked up close like an arrested guffaw. He leaned out of his armchair with heavy, bony energy when we came in. With a sharp U-shaped smile he greeted my father loudly, pounding him on the shoulder in a sort of public fellowship which I had seen in summer camp meetings upstate, where in my pre-college days I used to go to examine what I defined as "religion in the interior of America."

"Well, Dan," he intoned from deep in his cavernous chest, "we're off and running!"

"Yes," replied my father, "and here are my magic charms—" introducing my mother and me.

The judge took my hand and held on to it with a huge, moist grasp, never looking at me, but keeping his eye on my mother as he spoke—the old political trick of detaining one constituent while addressing another.

"This is a fine boy. Just like his sire. He will go far. Far"—still holding me but gaining my mother's "vote" with flattery. "Miz Pelzer and I would give a 'pretty' to have a son like this, wouldn't we, Mo?" and he turned to her, still holding my hand, and said, "Thiz my wife, Mo, the long-suffering cushion of my doubts and the inspiration of my days."

Mrs Pelzer nodded vigorously at this portrait of herself. She was short and so enormous with flesh that she did not seem fat but molded immensely of hard substance from without. She gave a hearty little burst of laughter, twisting her head aside in monstrous coquetry. Her hair was graying white, pulled so tight in a topknot against her skull that it drew the skin of her brow and cheeks taut, until, for all her smiles, she appeared to have a chronic headache. Her arms were bare and as large as thighs. At that age I saw matters romantically as well as in caricature, and I thought that beside her tall, lean husband, she made a farce out of marriage. He gazed down at her with his fixed scowl—for his eyebrows were thick as mustaches, and as coarse as iron shavings, and their outer ends were trained to curl up and outward to give a satyresque look to his face, in which his dark eyes held a piercing yet unfathomable stare. His merest glance from the bench when he was trying a case was said to make all defendants and witnesses give up hope. Despite all this he had a sort of egoistic appeal whose vitality drew many people to him. The lower part of his face, with perpetual smile creases, and the velvety trumpet sound of his voice on which he seemed to breathe forth his words through his great black nostrils, gave his remarks a confidential sound which flattered many a listener, and made him a plausible candidate, despite the public damage done by his earlier indictment for bribery, and his escape from it. But he was evidently well separated from that now, though his support for the present campaign came from huge sums of money invested in it by some of the state's greatest corporations, including the coal and steel interests which ran fleets of the splendid ore and grain boats on the Great Lakes. His air of genial, almost fierce, confidence, was in fact awesome.

"My, Judge," declared his wife with tremors of agreeability animating her vast surface, "such a dear little family"—making anyone of ordinary proportions sound underfed. "We must get t'be just such good friends! After all, we're going t'be seeing such a lot of each other, en't we?"

She could never have been a girl, I thought, but the unnerving thing about her was that she still behaved like her idea of one. Everyone knew sooner or later that she had been a schoolteacher in Binghamton, where Henry Sabin Pelzer as a young law-school graduate had first practiced law. His inclinations drew him toward corporation law; he prospered, some thought too rapidly to be explained; his wife Emmeline Moberly (hence "Mo") Pelzer gave herself conspicuously to public good works and the more arcane works of the Order of the Orient Sands, of which she became Grand Orphic Sibyl; and both husband and wife presently outgrew Binghamton. The judgeship at Albany followed, thanks to Pelzer's personal formula of how to mix politics with expedient prosperity. His later recovery from almost certain ruin was so astonishing that in an odd result it drew a certain admiration to him.

Now, with practiced but clumsy amenities out of the way, he took my father to chairs in the bay window to talk of campaign plans and personalities, while his wife and my mother set out to charm each other while taking each other's measure. My mother was over-polite, leaning forward like a lady to show interest in the cottage affairs of someone less fortunate, and Mrs Pelzer countered with aggressive heartiness, asking how many jars of plums her visitor expected to put up this year, while in her small pale eye a needle of light betrayed her resentment of my mother's beauty and kindly prattle. I sat apart, watching them all, wishing I were on the way to Alberta.

The conference did not last long—the two nominees would meet in New York in ten days, and in the meantime would return to their homes to dispose of personal affairs before spending the rest of the summer on the hustings. I was an unpaid aide to my father "for the duration," as he put it. When we said good night, Judge Pelzer put his great gray hands on my shoulders, looked down at me with his hairy glare, and said,

"When we *get in,* we must keep this young man in mind for something rewarding!"

"But he's still in college," explained my mother.

"College doesn't last forever," said the judge, blinking both eyes at me like a welcome conspirator, again with his U-shaped smile, which resembled the habitual expression of a mature male goat. When he let me go, he turned to my father and gave him an important afterthought.

"And, oh yes, Dan: we could do with a little less of Woodrow Wilson in your speeches. You quote him quite a lot, and of course he was our great party leader for a while, but what brought him down? Idealism, that's what." He blinked his eyes again persua-sively. "Let's stay with the practical interests of the voters. They want to know who gets what. Am I right?"

Mo gave her vigorous supportive nod, but my father turned his face a little sideways and, with his jaw forward, replied in his most quizzical Irish manner,

"Well, Judge, the strength of our ticket lies in its variety. You stick to your line and I'll stick to mine. In that way we'll catch everybody."

Pelzer could only give his loud hollow laugh at this, and clap my father on the shoulder as if he were a "card," and send us off with false pastoral geniality.

Once back safely in our rooms across the river, my father would have preferred to say nothing about the encounter, but my mother would not leave it at that.

"Was there anything to that old accusation?" she asked.

My father sighed fondly, as if to say that she would never learn to leave well enough alone.

"We Democrats never talk about it," he said. "The Republicans would yell 'foul' and score off us."

Outside of marriage—their kind of marriage—this would have been a snub; but I marveled at the true meaning of their intimacy, which could agree or disagree, attack or defend, give and receive endearments, with the same abiding love, and, if overshadowed for a moment by a mood, would soon again make itself known by some small attention unrelated to the passing withdrawal. I looked at them now with a stir of reassurance in their beauty together, in contrast to the Pelzers.

My mother really looked like her name, which was Rose—a rose whose petals, pink, edging toward gold, were just fully opened. She had light-brown hair, which she wore loosely dressed. Her face was a classic oval, her eyes a deep blue, her mouth slightly open to her ardent breath. All this was relieved of vapid sweetness by her energetic spirits, her shrewd if uncomplicated mind, and some impression she gave of laughing stubbornness under her outgoing manner. She knew how to dress to bestow both elegance and modesty on her trim figure. She was never idle. Her fingers were always busy—writing notes at her desk in her sunlit upstairs window where so often I saw her edged with light; embroidering, knitting, making gifts (many of my early toys were her handiwork); sewing to improve her various dresses; assembling packages for orphans at Father Raker's famous orphanage across town, where, if I were a bad child, I was always threatened with exile, so that I hated the very sound of Monsignor Raker's name and I thought of his children's home as a set of dungeons under the huge dome and twin towers of his baroque basilica.

All my life my mother had gone to any length to please me, in the way of effort; for priding herself on proper economies she dealt mostly with unextravagant trifles. Her particular grace was to put herself out—exhaust herself, really—to do something for someone else. The result of this was now and then a day or two of "sick headaches" and silent darkened rooms. Her weakness used to frighten me when I was small, as by a sense of strength withdrawn; and I would sigh with restored confidence when Dr Breuer, departing from a visit to the silent front bedroom with his black bag, which he sometimes let me open for a glimpse of instruments and rows of beautiful little phials of colored liquids and pills, and shut with a click which sounded professional, even when I caused it, would say under his large sandy mustache, "A day or two . . ." meaning that all would come well. Because I so admired his powers, to which I assigned no limit, I early decided to study medicine, and at five I was known as Doc to my father, who fixed my ambition more firmly for himself than I did for myself.

When a momentary irritation in either parent, from a cause which might have nothing to do with them, put a distance between the two, she always ended it with a little "surprise" which required thanks; thanks brought forgiveness; and forgiveness secured my world again for me. Why, I would wonder in these youthful years, was I so often put off by my mother's great love for me? What would give me again my freedom to return it in the feeling I actually had but disdained to show?

My father could dominate her, and as they both knew this, he rarely tried to do so. Sometimes he mocked this power by quirking one eyebrow at her, which made her laugh and say his name with a scoff. He was tall and finely, sparely, built, holding his head high, and his chest too. He was something of a dandy, which meant that he was glad of his distinction of body and face, and he loved occasions to wear formal clothes, which he knew showed himself at his best. It was an innocent enough vanity, for he had risen, as they used to say, from a poor boyhood as the son of Irish immigrants, was self-educated, read valuable books late every night, and had the Irish knack for quickly assimilating the best taste and style as he found prosperity. People always thought him a very rich man, which he was not; but he had the easy air of one. Something about him made rich people feel less rich near him. Among his deep simplicities was a strong religious spirit. He often went to weekday Mass and Communion but never referred to it. Our pastor, Monsignor Tremaine, could never understand why, with all his devotion, my father continually refused to join parish organizations and committees and the Knights of Columbus. With a kindly nod he would tell the old priest, "We'll leave all that to the others," indicating that lesser worthies could do all that the parish required. As he could not be faulted in faith, and was a friend of the bishop, he was never disciplined for his fastidious exclusiveness. He had a way of showing that he meant what he said. This was a way of smiling with his mouth and eyes, and at the same time scowling with his brows, which gave a striking intensity to his presence. He used it on me either playfully or sternly, as game or reproof might suggest, and now, in politics, it became a powerful trait suggesting his public integrity. Blue-eyed, like the rest of us, he often used his quizzing look on people. It was an expression which seemed to say, not "What are you hiding?" but "What makes you so interesting?" Most people responded quickly to his unarranged charm. Until I was old enough to know why, I would wonder that some of my mother's women friends would gaze at him, half closing their lids speculatively.

My mother was not through with the Pelzers.

"Well," she said as we sat in our white wicker chairs for a bed-time chat, "if we are elected, I know one thing."

"Yes?"—my father.

"We are not going to move to Albany and have to see those people day in and day out. —We can go for the assembly months, and stay at the Ten Eyck Hotel, and you can preside over the senate; but we won't close our house in Dorchester."

"Are they that bad?"

"Dan!"—*you know they are.*

"He has an excellent mind, despite everything else."

"That may be mechanically true. But I think he will do anything for money. —And she would do anything, poor thing, for a flirtation. The difference is that he will receive offers. She never will."

"God knows, you can take people apart," he said, laughing at her. "God help them when you do."

She leaned forward and stamped her foot in imitation of the tyrannical fury of the outraged Gibson Girl type which had been the model of her youth, but she, too, laughed, and added,

"Then I hope the excellent mind will manage with decent means for the sake of the public. Have you any influence with him, Dan?"

"No. And he has none over me—though he thinks he has—as he'll discover when I get to work in the senate. He's the kind of very stupid man who got high grades in college. With all his famous shrewdness, he sees only himself in people."

She regarded him for a long moment, then asked,

"Why did you take it, dear?"

"Not for Pelzer, I assure you. But the fellows all kept after me."

"Civic leaders," I said, " 'Our Crowd,' " and though I meant it ironically, it sounded more disagreeably superior than I had intended. My father gave me a straight look which made me feel small for mocking his values.

(Something which happened a few weeks later in Utica during the campaign falls into place here. I was with my father at a confer-ence held in the Fort Schuyler Club. Pelzer was also there, and at one moment he converged with us during a break in the meeting. He said to me,

"Dick"—which no elder ever called me—"you just wait outside here. There's something quite confidential I have to take up with the lieutenant-governor."

He took my father into a nearby card room and closed the door. I waited in the hall. Ten minutes later my father came out alone. His eyes were burning like blue fire under coals. His face was brick red. I never saw him before or since in such a fury. Whatever Pelzer had discussed with him must have violated my father's every principle. In response to my open-faced stare of inquiry, he shook his head, roughly turned me around, and walked me out of the club. For a long time he did not reveal what had happened, but as we rushed by cab to the railroad to leave for a speech in Buffalo, he said,

"Never trust a man who trains his eyebrows!" and he campaigned for the rest of the summer as far from Pelzer as he could be, though necessarily they met on a few scheduled public occasions.)

From Niagara Falls, after the convention, we made a leisurely return to Dorchester in our old high-decked Packard, which rocked as though on long waves. I was permitted to drive in the country. It was an open car. My mother wore a broad motoring hat with veils. We lunched in Batavia at a favorite family tearoom inevitably called The Copper Kettle. My father was asked to autograph the menu. I was generally silent. At one moment my mother leaned over and felt my brow for fever, found none, but kept her hand there a trifle longer for love, while she made an impatient little breath at the ways of youth. I wished I were ten years older, with a wife and two children, preferably twins, and well beyond the uncertainties and contradictions, the broken ease, of my age; and I deeply luxuriated in the romantic pessimism which, like my friends, I regarded as proof of high intelligence. At the same time, I longed to be back in college, where this philosophy, though generally esteemed, did not preclude driving physical activity.

CHAPTER II

❦

The Fire Ship

THEY CALLED ME OFF THE SOCCER FIELD during a varsity practice game. I was not a natural player, but I was determined to play, though I was lighter than my mates, and my scrawny obsession impressed the coaches enough to land me on the varsity back-up squad. There was a great matter at stake. We were training for a college match in England to which we had been invited for play during Easter vacation. Six days at sea, each way, on the *Aquitania,* three days in England. A high prospect. Perhaps—in fantasy—I would meet the St Brides' again. I was working hard to be among those chosen for the trip, and the head coach kept encouraging me to try, at the same time making it clear to me that he considered me not only rather light for hard scrimmage but generally under par in other ways— "run-down," as he put it. "Do you study too hard?" he asked. "Get enough sleep? Let yourself alone in bed?" There was no way to answer him with dignity and yet not force him to put on his tough, anti-academic face, and write me off as "a nut," which would hurt my chances for the *Aquitania* and the British adventure. I kept "trying" harder than ever.

It was a cold, violet-gray day in early March. We played harder and faster for the sharp air off the river beyond the town below the university. I played, too, for more than the game. All things merged in a great oneness which was like a disembodied well-being, even though its medium was physical—breaths of spring under the wintry airs, silvery streaks of light in the long, gray New England clouds, bite of cold on our bare legs, running pattern of our bodies edged in light like golden liquid along our flanks, back and forth in sudden shifts and turns like those of birds over the rye-green field, joyous insult of the impact when with all our impersonal might we collided with each other, ball sailing fast and straight and taking us after it, freedom from everything but the fierce intention of the game, on whose outcome nothing depended but a finally unserious victory: in sum, thoughtless joy of our own making. That, we were sure, was what all life ahead must be made of.

During a scrimmage I heard the coach's whistle and my name being hooted from the sidelines. I turned my head as I ran, and a flying elbow struck me near my right eye. A classmate at the edge of the field was jumping up and down and waving both arms at me. His urgency, the fact of his interrupting play, were serious. The game stopped, and with a signal, the coach summoned me to run to the sidelines.

An emergency message at the dean's office, I was told. "They want you right away."

❦

So it was that I was on a train that night bound for Dorchester. My father was seriously ill, at home, though I had heard nothing of his having left Albany, where since January he had been presiding over the first session of the new senate. My mother had been unavailable to talk to me when I tried to reach her by phone from the dean's office, but my father's legislative assistant, a young law graduate named Samuel Dickinson, had gone home with my parents, and he gave me the message tersely and without many details.

As most of the night I pondered it in the sleeping car which would let me off at Dorchester at six-thirty in the morning, I reviewed incidents of the campaign and after. Some of these, though not alarming, had seemed too odd and frequent for comfort. My father's nature had always led him to "overdo." He spent his energy with such focus and drive that this habit was what had brought idler men, men perhaps less surely ambitious, to create a following around him: Our Crowd, who in a kind of instinctive aggregate lodged their undefined goals in him, with such large visions for him that he was finally persuaded to step out in front for them—and for himself. He went at life as we went at soccer.

In late summer, as the campaign drew toward its close, he had tired more rapidly with each day, and he made some people impatient by leaving them early after the speeches and the little local caucuses were done with. He said he had his homework to do—and with a flattering hand on a shoulder, a glimmer of his blue eye, which confidentially made an accomplice in intelligence of his listener, a general wave of the hand which told them all that he would never forget any one of them individually, creating the emotion which always reaches forth from great actors, he would leave for his night's lodging. Not to study, not to write, but to sleep. Behind his fine smile, his dark gaze, which at will he could make sparkle with interest in the light under his quizzically furrowed brow, I sometimes saw a wincing sort of fatigue; and sometimes his voice became as hollow as straw, though when necessary he managed with main force to make it reach through all the municipal halls and hotel ballrooms where we made our nightly stands in town after town. From any distance, he always looked vital, powerful, and charming, standing below the great banners which bore the two huge oval portraits.

Midway in the summer he would ask to be left alone for half an hour before having to give an evening speech. He said he had to collect his wits. Only I was allowed to break in, and then only if something important required his notice. One evening in Glens Falls, I knocked and then went into his hotel bedroom. He was sitting in an armchair facing out into the high summer twilight. The room was shadowy. He was looking at nothing. I spoke his name. Without turning, he said almost under his breath, "Violets."

"What?" I said.

"Ah. It's you. —Nothing. What've you got?"

I handed him my copy of his speech, which I'd typewritten from his beautiful handwriting, with its strong down-curves and its classical spacing—he used his flexible Waterman fountain pen as an instrument of visual artistry. In some assumed animation, to convince me that his odd lone utterance had been without meaning, as it then was for me in any case, he asked.

"How does it read?"

"Great, I think. I like the line from Wilson."

"That'll show the old goat," and suddenly with his vigor and charming mischief he was on his feet ready to go to the rally as if impatient to put something behind him.

Was there anything? What could it be? I was depressed, even somewhat cross, at what seemed to me an undertone of abstracted melancholy in him, as though he might be sorrowing for something. I had theories. Did he think himself unworthy, after all, in what he was doing? Was he thinking his ticket might lose? Did the thought of internecine battles with Judge Pelzer exhaust him? Was he sorry he had taken on the nomination? And then I would feel disloyal for holding such unsympathetic thoughts at a time when he, or any man, must be tested to the limits of his natural strength by elation, real to start with but more and more simulated as the work went on at dreary banquets, endless reception lines, eager interviews, the result of which for the most part was honest misrepresentation of what he actually had said, and the shameless egotism to be maintained in full view of the public if they were to believe as he must about himself, and the image he made stronger by the day in the huge state over which we campaigned. With him I came to know possessively the Mohawk Valley, the Hudson Valley, the Batavia flats, the Adirondacks, Lake Champlain and Lake George, and the shores of Lake Erie and Lake Ontario; from farms, to wooded mounds, to granite mountains, to the placid canal way, to the Finger Lakes and their classical towns; and rocky gorges and chasms. Such variety was exciting, and I would think my father as stimulated as I by it.

But again my qualms would seem justified when at home on weekends I would think I saw concern in my mother. One Sunday evening she said,

"Dan, where are you?"

He looked sharply at her, almost apprehensively, but he said with comic patience,

"Right here, in the bosom of my family. Why?"

"Oh—sometimes you seem so far away. Of course, there *are* days of that, literally. But I don't mean just the campaign"—for she had declined to travel most of the time along the election trail—"and of course I hate all of it."

He shrugged.

"I suppose I'm rather tired."

"Poor darling. Yes. But sometimes I wonder if you're running *for* something, or *away* from something."

"There we go, Doc," he said to me, not unkindly, but with mockery and a blue fire of suppressed anger in his eye, "a laboratory specimen of woman's intuition." Then he turned to her and added, "I don't know what you're fretting about, Rosie. Running away! Not from you, not from you, you may be sure. Come here."

She went to him.

One night at Binghamton, he was feverish, and we called a doctor, who ordered him to rest for a whole day and night. When the next rally was canceled, an irate phone call from Pelzer ordered him to be up and about their furious business; for the campaign was running uncomfortably more close than anyone had expected and

[34]

the judge was beginning to fear his defeat as the old charges against him were, after all, shouted by the opposition. Wearily my father obeyed him and reconvened the canceled appearance, and from some mysterious source called forth enough strength to make one of the best speeches of his life. Again he commanded all his Irish ingenuity of rhetoric and every device of the magnetic appeal he could assert even against the cleverest of hecklers, whom he either won over with laughter in which they could honorably join, or failing that, genially made fools of, so that everyone laughed at them, and with him.

But the cost was considerable, and luckily a weekend followed in which he could rest. He slept off and on for thirty hours during the next two days. My mother said to me with a shrugging sigh,

"Richard, is it worth it?"

She asked me with her eyes whether we were losing him, had perhaps already lost him; and I had at moments the notion that she was with difficulty holding some knowledge away from me. But then she would dismiss her underthoughts, wafting with the backs of her hands the loosely caught waves of hair at her temples as if to brush away doubts which would only trouble if left in possession, and I would swallow questions which I could not ask because they had no final form.

On the Monday after that weekend, he went forth like his old self. I was astonished that day to notice for the first time little feathers of whitish hair at his temples. They must have been coming gradually (not overnight—where was his night of terror in the rapids?).

During the mid-year holidays, with the election safely behind him—Pelzer and he and their whole ticket won by a comfortable majority after all; my father was editorially credited with the victory; Our Crowd told him, and each other, with words and souvenir gifts, that they knew he would bring it off—my mother had plans for a celebration at our house in Dorchester for the closest family friends, and some of my friends from college, who were expected to stay for the best of the holiday dances at the big houses and the clubs of the city. But two days before the party, my father suddenly woke up with a high fever, the party was off, the guests were sent telephone and telegraph messages of regrets, and the papers were notified that the lieutenant-governor-elect was confined to his home with an attack of influenza—an ailment dangerously prevalent throughout the country. The inauguration was not long away: the press asked daily whether the lieutenant-governor would recover in time to attend the inaugural ball and the swearing-in ceremonies of the day after. They were continually obliged to report that the attendant physicians gave them every assurance that he would be present.

My mother was indignant when Mo Pelzer telephoned her from New York to ask her what color dress she would wear at the ball. On being told that it was American Beauty satin—a pun on her own name which my mother and father had arrived at with measured merriment safe enough for the sickroom—Mo Pelzer did not ask her, but ordered her, to change to something else, as that was the color and material she herself had chosen, it had always been her color, she had worn it at her installation as Grand Orphic Sibyl years ago, the new dress was already finished, and after all, she was the First Lady of the state, she should have been consulted in advance about the issue, and in her position she felt she should have her way. My mother made a high, cool reply without committing herself and flew to my father's dark bedroom about the matter. He laughed so hard that he coughed, which hurt him badly, but he managed to say,

"Rosie, if you wore a flour sack for her sake, nobody would look at her anyway."

She took this to mean that she was to keep her American Beauty plans, which gave her satisfaction, and telling me about the affair, she said,

"Do you know that thousands of people voted against Pelzer because of her? 'Imagine that "washtub" in the Governor's Mansion!' they kept saying—I heard it everywhere all summer!"

We all went to Albany, escorted by a great delegation of my father's associates and supporters—Our Crowd, which now had many new recruits in honor of achieved success. By their possessive admiration, they made him their creature, and he responded to their comradely love with a show of health. They could never follow a weakling. His energy returned—perhaps in too great measure, and his cheeks were heightened by high color under the eyes. His brilliance seemed to burn as he entered into all the convivialities of the train ride to the capital; and there, afterward, into all the incidental meetings and the big parties at which he and my mother were obliged to make appearances. The Pelzers were always present. There was no denying the magnetism of the governor when he was observed across a room or from greater distance. All his features, his size, were larger than life, and carried conviction deep into crowds; but while talking to him, you felt all was exaggerated and assumed, and were uneasy with him.

There was a small incident at the ball of which my mother was the heroine, showing an unsuspected gift for political adroitness. Photographers asked for a picture of her and the governor's wife together. When they were brought to stand side by side, resembling a slender vase beside a tub, a reporter spoke of the similarity in their ball gowns, both of satin, weren't they? in American Beauty crimson? Was this an accident?

As Mo Pelzer turned dark red herself, my mother quickly said,

"Oh, no, not at all. The First Lady and I intended to show a spirit of the new harmony we have all brought to Albany. We thought if we wore the same color, this would be evident!"

And she put her arm through Mrs Pelzer's with a lighthearted smile. Mo nodded her strange topknot in agreement, though a shiver of fat woman's rage went all over her under her skin, and she gave forth her deep, rapid, fellowship laugh from her great sloping bosom, and the press had its picture.

Later, leading the grand march to open the ball with the governor, she made an impressive show of dignity, which was enlarged by her bulk. Like many heavy people, she was light on her feet, and when she danced the first dance with her husband (a slow, stately waltz), she even conveyed the romantic satisfaction which the usually envious girl within her felt on an occasion so splendid. My parents, following their lead, were less visible on the ballroom floor; but I saw them—slim, elegant, and beautiful. With my grim analytical mood upon me, I watched it all, examining all the details of the event, which, with a posture of ironic disdain and embarrassment, I classified as a folk ritual of fixed recurrence. A persistent image was that of Mo Pelzer, vastly gleaming in her red satin, dancing with the new secretary of state—a man so small that when the waltz turned them with Mo's back to me, he was totally eclipsed, and she seemed to be treading a mysterious measure alone; then slowly veering, she gradually revealed her small partner again.

On the following day my mother and I sat in the guest rows of the outdoor tribune to witness the inauguration. It was a clear winter day. The men sat in heavy topcoats but uncovered, the ladies in furs and every variety of enormous hat garnished with dead birds, sprays of feathers, cloth flowers. At the head of the steep front flight of capitol steps, the platform stood against the Renaissance doorways and fenestration of the ornate gray stone façade, all of which sprang oddly from a ground-story base of heavy Romanesque arches. Even as he rose to take the oath of office, my father turned to us a swift glance proclaiming our own unity—rays of blue light, conveying an almost liturgical power of style and spirit to us, and to those who saw him do it. My mother, with that ageless and formless foreboding which women harbor for those they love, said in a half voice,

"Oh, I hope he's all right . . ."

I thought his mere unspoken appearance was more eloquent than Governor Pelzer's in the inaugural address which horned forth in that strange tone of his and seemed to resonate from caverns of nasal cartilage. Pelzer trumpeted a fearless call, supported by oddly uncoordinated gestures of hand and arm, proposing that the great commonwealth of New York should stand as a model for the federal government at Washington. He promised that with his first budget message on February 15 he would astound the people, through their legislative branch, with certain innovations, economies, guarantees of integrity never before offered to them by their highest elected state official. Glaring deeply at his audience, his eyes took accent from the long, twisted, black hairs of his eyebrows with their upswept Mephistophelian ends, as he called his hearers to righteous battle. I said to myself that he knew all the same tricks as those of the itinerant evangelists whom I had sardonically studied in the summer-heated towns and valleys when the teeming nights combined with practiced eloquence to turn the listeners' hearts at first toward God and later, secretly, in the heavy-shadowed, rank bushes of rose of Sharon and lilac and rhododendron, toward sweaty, hungry love. Could high feeling, I began to wonder, turn from one expression to another without losing its energy? Of Pelzer, I believed, and it turned out to be true, that it would not be long until a struggle would begin below the surface of the administration between him and my father: between the governor's office and the state senate: between differences of visible style and invisible character.

After I returned to the university I would see newspaper stories and editorials—*The Albany Times-Union, The Dorchester Chronicle*—marking these emerging differences in terms of specific issues, and occasionally my father would send me a clipping with a hasty penciled note on one of his memorandum forms with some such comment as, "Keep your eye on this one—there is a very interesting principle involved. We'll see. Government is an iceberg, and the part that shows is labeled Good Faith, but the part below! etc. Sometimes I wish I were a sea lion and could dive deep enough for a real look. Tear this up. Liked all your grades but chemistry—should be better for incipient M.D. Love, D."

All night long the train to Dorchester kept company to my thoughts, for I slept almost not at all, reviewing the previous months, and the puzzling alteration in my father's health, and even state of mind—or heart. Of little help to me all night long in the wakeful secrecy of my green-curtained Pullman berth was that personality which in common with my intimate fellow students I cultivated under the fashion of the times. It was a personality of grinning hardness which we expressed in all possible ways. We dramatized our youth and health in violent exercise. We closed our minds against all persons and ideas which our fraternities did not represent in membership. Fanatical about bodily hygiene, our vanity was saved from effeminacy by our rough tweed suits, our expensive, colorless cravats, our short haircuts, even our shoes, which were heavy brogans with extra-thick soles and solid, hard leather heels which made our steps, crossing the bare parquet floors of clubs, sound loudly like those of a race of young giants who trod the earth heedless of anyone who was not a young giant. If our frivolities were alcoholic, they were always unsentimentally so. If we had talents of an unusual sort, the thing to do was mock or conceal them. Hard men had no talents. They had powers. My hardness was counterfeit, but I gave a fair impersonation of it when not alone. But alone, now, in the train as it passed through hushed towns where few lights showed, and the crossing bells rang a rapidly descending scale as we raced by, and the occasional boarding or leaving passengers made dreamlike sounds as we stopped at stations where steam rose in comforting hisses alongside the car, I was filled with weakening qualms, wondering what awaited me at home. How fared my father—the thoughtlessly accepted tower of our family strength—in the illness which Sam Dickinson had described on the long-distance call to the dean's office as serious—serious enough to call me home? I turned my face into my pillows and felt like crying—for the first time since finding love and losing it three summers ago. But I was afraid that someone else might be awake, and might hear me if I wept. Instead, I began to say a prayer for us all, which summoned up images of the past, even from my earliest childhood, in the company of saints, sacraments, and guardian angels; the banks of lighted candles at Mass far away where the figures at the altar moved in all their gold and color representing powers which had nothing to do with hardness, but with hope, and a way to hope. Yes, I said, yes, God's will be done—but it was my will I was praying about.

The nearer we came to the Great Lakes and Dorchester, the more heavily a snowstorm developed; and when at six-thirty I descended from the train, snow was everywhere, showing through the darkness under the clouded lights of the train shed. Faithless, I had slept after all, and had awakened only in time to dress and, unshaven, hastily combed without a mirror, to be greeted by Sam Dickinson.

"Awfully early—thank you, Sam," I said.

"Your mother wanted me to tell you how things are before we get home."

We moved out into the grand Roman hall of the station waiting room, where the early-morning electric light was golden and melancholy. Sam laughed, looking at me, and said,

"You've got quite a shiner there."

I put my hand to my eye, wondering about a vague ache I felt.

"The other one," he said. "Brawling again?"—which was lightly sarcastic, and possibly rather hopeful, as the idea was so foreign to my nature. I suddenly remembered the elbow in my eye on the field.

"Soccer," I said.

He nodded gravely at an honorable wound. Sam was a small man between twenty-five and thirty, neatly made, with a clever face full of charm. His small black eyes, like cloves, behind large-lensed spectacles, gave him a look of amused awareness which he was too well-bred to assert. In an odd way, the glasses made good looks out of his neat, regular features. He was one of those people born to look clean all their lives in any circumstances. He had a law degree from Harvard, his father was president of a small, distinguished New England college, and Sam, too, was destined for an unemphatic career of distinction and public usefulness—an ordained supporter, not an innovator. He was devoted to my father, and brought to him a dimension of witty and intelligent advice which in their blind fealty Our Crowd could not equal.

Outside the station, Sam took the driver's seat of our car and we started home in the snow-muted dawn. If he had ominously been sent to meet me, I was afraid to hear what he had to tell. As we left the station, I caught a glimpse of the frozen harbor with its grain elevators, moored lake steamers, and the ice-covered breakwater far beyond. A faint peach-colored light drifted up from the lake horizon. On Iroquois Avenue the great houses were still asleep, the street lamps still alight but paling. We came into the park, where the little lake was under ice and snow. The shoreline pavilions looked like black brush strokes against the white, and in the falling snow the white marble museums of the Historical Society and the art gallery were made visible only by their shadowed sides and classically shaded porticoes. Sam was silent but for trivialities until we had passed Yates Circle with its great fountain and basin, where I had played for so many childhood hours with little boats which, in the way known only to children, I inhabited even as I pulled them along the pond by strings. Finally,

"Your mother wanted you to be pretty much ready for how things are with your father."

"Why did you say emergency?"

"Because that's what it is. —He has been home ten days, though this is not publicly known. I was with him in Albany when—"

They were alone, the two of them, working late one night in my father's inner office in the capitol, when about midnight my father seemed to choke, and when he coughed into his handkerchief, the white linen was heavy with blood. Sam at first thought this was caused by a nosebleed; but my father shook his head and put his hand on his chest. Sam made him lie down on a black leather settee while he ran for a glass of cold water, thinking to cool the blood and stop its flow. It was a hemorrhage. It seemed to come from below the throat—from the lungs. The flow stopped, and after he had rested for half an hour, during which my father and his aide said almost nothing, but, said Sam, told each other serious conclusions with their eyes, both thinking of what might be happening, Sam carefully, carefully raised him up, took him by freight elevator down to the car, unseen by anyone, and home. My mother was waiting, as she always did unless my father advised her not to. When she saw how pale he was, how frightened, she automatically did all those things which an experienced wife and mother did for sickness in the family; and only when my father was quietly in bed did she hear from Sam what had happened in the office. Her cheeks seemed to go hollow at the information—she said she had been dreading something for many months, but not this, after all the little warnings of the campaign and since. And so had I, without knowing quite what. If I had felt that extra, unknown drain on his resources, had she not also? She telephoned old Dr Breuer, who had taken care of us all my life. He said the matter was surely grave, but nothing sudden could be expected before morning, when he would come with Dr Morton Frawley, a chest specialist, to make a first examination. After several days in the hospital for X rays and other tests, pulmonary tuberculosis was firmly diagnosed. My father was returned home. Bulletins were issued saying that he had suffered a relapse of the influenza and was threatened with pneumonia. Meantime, the temporary president of the senate presided in his absence, and Governor Pelzer reigned alone in Albany.

"What is the emergency now?" I asked. "Is he worse? Is he going to die?"

"No," said Sam. "He is not going to die—if he does what Frawley and the rest of the doctors say is flatly necessary. But your mother needs you because of all that."

"What do they want?"

"They want him to be moved as soon as possible to a high, dry climate, take a leave of absence from his office, and have nothing on his mind but getting well. They say that last prescription is the most difficult *and* important. Evidently tuberculosis has a high relation to emotional states. I never knew this."

"You mean leave Dorchester?"

"Probably for quite a while. Nobody can say how long. Every case is unique; but all seem to share a general course."

"But where will they send him?"

"They think New Mexico. They think Albuquerque. There are specialists there, sanatoriums, altitude a mile high, sunshine. —Frawley (you must meet him, he's quite a specimen of the fashionable medico) says the disease is the leading industry of the city."

"But what will he do? He is so active."

"Too active. We all saw it in the campaign. We should have arranged matters better for him. Anyhow, he will do nothing for some time; then he will get back to things a little at a time, until— until he is well again."

"Sam, have you talked to the doctors yourself?"

"Yes," he replied, without expression, and his restraint told me much.

"How is he now?"

"You'll find him changed. He has lost weight. He is fighting to remain cheerful and be a good patient. Your mother is frightened, tries not to show it, but it shows, and it upsets him, for he is frightened too, and trying to hide it. One day I came upon her weeping in her upstairs sitting room. She has a thousand things to talk over with you."

We reached the house and went up the long driveway at the side. There was a rich mantle of snow on the fan-shaped glass canopy above the door, and on all the shrubbery, the roofs, the trees, rounded beautifully at the edges. Hating through fear to know what was within, I had a flash of thought about my father, seeing him as he raised his glass in a toast during the inaugural party. He was alight with gaiety and power. His evening clothes fitted so well that his raised arm did not disturb the elegance of their line. His smile of the moment seemed like an unending statement of what life was really like, and it persuaded me, I thought, forever. His high color, his shining brushed hair, the rays from his eyes, the light, far-reaching pitch of his voice, and his words of victory, joyful in tone and magnanimous in style, seemed to stand for something which could never die, though I could not define it, sure as I was of it.

※

My mother was watching for us and opened the door as we came up the outside steps. Light poured upon us from the vestibule. She was ravaged by fatigue, which strangely gave some new loveliness to her face. We embraced. Blinking her eyes and shaking her head quickly to hold back the tears which started up, she said with lightness meant to postpone what we must speak of,

"Why, look at you, darling. You have a paint-box eye"—using the phrase out of my childhood which used to greet me when I would come home from play or fight with an eye all yellow and purple—a phrase meant to diminish self-pity and suffering. It was like her to summon strength from the trivial, if harder trials had to be faced.

Smiling, she took me to have breakfast at a little table set up in the sun porch, which was filled with green plants against the winter. Sam did not join us—went up "to see the Governor," as he always called my father. Our cook, Marie, embraced me with old privilege out of the nursery, saying little, and then brought breakfast. Until

[45]

we were alone, my mother spoke of the sudden return of winter, the effect of this on the lilacs in the deep garden behind the house, the way the house had "deteriorated" while we were away in Albany, so much to be done, and what to do about my eye? Was soccer worth it? Yes: of course: battle wound: she supposed I had had no raw beefsteak to hold to it all night on the train to "draw out" the inflammation. And wasn't I rather thin? Had I been working too hard? I must keep my weight up, get more sleep—

The association of this struck suddenly at her withheld concern. Unable any longer to hold back, she suddenly put her hands over her face and began to weep. It was some minutes before she could speak above incoherent murmurs.

So sudden. The change was hardly to be believed. A lifetime built together so gradually, so surely, advancing so steadily on course, was now like a ship dead in the water. They had the best care, nurses day and night. Morton Frawley was not discouraged, but was fearfully firm about his orders. The sooner the better.

"Richard, we need your help so much! Oh! Plans? Plans? What to do with everything? How can we? What is that desert going to be like? But what does it matter, if only it will make him well again!"

"How long?"

"Nobody knows. —We don't know a soul out there, though people here have written to friends who have gone there before us for the same reason; they say it's odd how the place casts a spell after a while, you know. But how can I manage it all . . ."

She meant *alone*. She looked at me so longingly that I knew what she could not bring herself to ask me. I thought of college, and all my ties there, the game waiting to be played in England, which at once, and newly, became all-important to me. She gazed away from me, out into the falling snow, and at last I said,

"Do you think I should go with you?"

Knowing what this would demand of me, which unkindly I had

not concealed in my hesitation, she again gave way to tears, and silently nodded.

"Does Father?"

She nodded again, and said in a broken voice,

"But he was not sure we should ask you to leave school this way."

I put my arms around her. She grasped my hand and kissed it, and postponing her urgent hope for fear of a disappointing answer, she said,

"I think you can go up now. The nurse probably has him ready."

—Has him ready: my father: a great child.

Uneasy, reluctant, dreading the encounter, I said,

"Should I shave and bathe first?"

She shook her head. She touched my black eye and said, "Oh! Will you ever get over getting yourself beaten up!" and sent me away.

※

My father lay against a low bank of pillows. A bed light was dimmed by a large manila envelope pinned to its shade. He was in shadow. How thin he was; colorless; how lighted his eyes. When he put his hand to my sleeve I felt his fever. His hand rested there in smooth, bony beauty, like a carving. He ground his jaws together in the old smile he used to have for me, and said,

"Well, Doc, here's a fine pickle of fish," and I replied, in our game of "mixed-up sayings," "Or a pretty kettle, hey?"—for we were all hungry for even the idlest reference to more confident days.

He suddenly began to cough, a rapid, liquid sound, as shallow, it seemed, as he could keep it, in order not to strain the fiber of his lungs. His mouth filled with who knew what particle of his flesh.

Taking up the utensil called a sputum cup, which had a light aluminum frame, handle, and lid enclosing a disposable paper container, he discharged the disturbed mucus into it and with a sigh set it back on the bed table.

"Excuse how I look," I said, explaining about the eye and my generally disordered appearance.

He nodded.

"Heavy practice? A heavy schedule coming up?"

"Pretty heavy." Should I tell him? I told him. "We have an invitation match in England next month."

"England! Have they picked you to go?"

"Not yet. But I'm on the squad."

"Well. That's—that's really great."

Despite his smile, and the forced sparkle in his eyes, I saw why this bothered him. I was sorry to have told him. I did not know which emotion should stay on top.

"Yes," he said, "well, you'd better get bathed and changed and shaved. And put something on that eye. You look like a dog with one black spot. Can you twist your head sideways and let one ear flop and the other stand up? Cute? Go on. I have to rest now, but when you're ready, Sam will let me know, and if Miss Cleary"—the first nurse of the day—"will let me, I must talk things over with you. Your mother has been *suburb* but she can't go on alone much longer."

In our exchanged look we both knew what he was talking about. He added huskily,

"We're going to lick this thing after we get away. That'll be the worst part for us all. Leaving."

With a slight movement of his jaw, and a drift of his gaze, he made me see the whole fabric of our life where we had lived it and all that had gone to make us. For the first time, I felt not my emotional need of him but his of me. I felt my childhood tugging at me. I knew it must be cut away. My middle was hollow, hearing him, seeing, remembering him, and I said,

"I'm going with you, of course."

With relief so great that it weakened him, he closed his eyes and pressed his lips together until they were pale. Unwilling to show me further feeling, he nodded against his pillows, and faintly motioned to me to go.

When I found my mother downstairs, and told her what I had just said, she put her hands on my shoulders and remarked so endearingly that I felt unworthy and therefore cross,

"You do look more and more like your father . . ."

I scowled.

"What's the matter? Don't you *want* to?"

I scowled, not because I didn't want to look like my father, but because I didn't believe it, and wished it were true. If it were true, I could be more at ease with my new manhood.

❧

Knowing I must leave it against my will, I fell awarely in love with my city then, even though its furious lake-blown winters and exhausting hot summers must have contributed to my father's susceptibility under strain to the tubercle bacillus. I had many duties at home in helping my mother and Sam. My father's office secretary, Lillian O'Rourke, came daily to work at packing, and at lamentation, at which she was expert, and to cheer my mother with bright, pious words and swimming eyes. Miss O'Rourke had the image for me since childhood of a plump parrot which could say more than a few words. Once, during my mimicry phase as a boy, I twisted my neck and rolled my eye out of sight, and pronounced her name, "O'Rour-r-ke," in a grainy squawk imitating a parrot, for her name sounded like a parrot's natural utterance. This made my parents scold, telling me it was wrong and unkind to make fun of so good a soul as Lillian. They sent me into exile upstairs; but as I lingered on the mid-stair landing, I could hear them laughing after all. My father said, "He's a scandal," and my mother, "Yes, but it was just like her." I felt righteous, then, even in my caricature of a person we all thought so good, so self-sacrificing, so devoted to my father and to the Sacred Heart of Jesus. We often spoke of her as "poor soul."

Still, she did have a parrot's beak in the form of her nose, which rose between her pouched little pale eyes and curved out and downward above her small mouth, which it almost concealed. Her chin receded toward her heavy throat in tremulous folds. When I was little she would clasp me to her hungry, rolling breasts, for she was a spinster, filled to overflowing with love to give, but unable in her catechetical chastity to bestow it upon any man and, therefore, upon children of her own. She believed in God the Father, God the Son, God the Holy Ghost, and—my father—God the Unattainable. In this she was happy. Her body was numbed, I concluded, to the idea of sex, and I was sure she met it only in dreams, which she confessed to the priest as mortal sins. Meantime, she became almost part of the family. Her worship went on daily in my father's local office in the Iroquois Building, where she ruled with intolerant exactitude over the office staff. At daily Mass she renewed her blessèd state in thanksgiving. She was to go West with us as companion to my mother, and to deal with my father's forwarded business mail. Oddly, she was openly jealous of Sam Dickinson and his confidential access to my father. Though she was unaware of this, Sam understood it, and took every occasion to give her precedence in the sickroom, which filled her with suppressed fury so that she would thank him with her idea of queenly dignity for favors which were not his to extend.

My own preparations for leaving were simply managed. I telephoned my roommate to pack up my clothes and books and express them to me. The dean granted permission to drop out for the rest of the semester, with the privilege of returning for the fall semester. The head soccer coach said this was a fine time to tell him, when he had his squad all picked out, including me, after all; and with the athlete's single-mindedness dismissed me with a word about how loyalty ought to work both ways.

Now that we were about to abandon it for nobody knew how long, I grew more acutely sensitive to our house. The cook, Marie, and her husband would live in it until we should return. They had been with us since the death of our old servant Anna, whose melancholy and innocent realism had played a great part in my early education. I was sensible of the individuality of the house—any family's house, and how much what was often unnoticed gave character to its atmosphere. I had always taken for granted the comforts and the mild beauties which my mother had arranged; a sense of how the rooms downstairs glowed with light, silvery through wide windows in the daytime, golden in the evenings, with curtains drawn and exactly convenient lamplight playing over soft colors of pale rose and ocher and gray, and firelight, gleaming wood, pictures and mirrors, walls of books, and prevailing little tyrannies of order in the events of meals, parties, and quiet times alone. What contrasting moods, too, left their lingering tones in the atmosphere of memory. Intimacies. Health and illness in their seasons. The odors of the body—our bodies—in the common humanities of physiology; the density of bedroom air after the night; the coffee-in-the-morning kisses; petty estrangements and patient misunderstandings, and occasional ruefulness drifting in the shadows of the house, to be dissipated by the fresh winds of joyful moments scenting the drafts of air all the way from the open cellar door to the living room, and up the stairs to the upper halls, and into the attic itself, from which the mystery of the unused was never quite dispelled. The times of my wickedness and punishment, the festivals of birthdays and holidays; the gaze-widening, bowel-changing, greedy ecstasy of Christmas in childhood gradually giving way to the calmer satisfactions of "thoughtfulness" in useful gifts of later years. Above all, a house as a garment habitually worn but consciously owned as the most protective and precious of all possessions. To keep busy now seemed my mother's source of strength, even as she mourned each object she must leave behind, and with it a fragment of our lives.

※

Aimless with waiting, I began in a sort of anticipated nostalgia to revisit places which I had always valued, once idly, now with purpose.

When in good conscience I could leave the house and its living questions, I went to the white marble palace of the Historical Society. There, years before, I used to go idling along the exhibits where mementos of Dorchester and upstate New York and the Great Lakes were displayed. I knew the battle of Lake Erie in terms of its uniforms, its cutlasses, its (model) frigates, including the *Niagara,* which was Commodore Oliver Perry's flagship, a little ship barely a hundred feet long carrying twenty-two guns. I had belonged in its longboats, manned by sailors in ribboned caps and striped jerseys. The *Niagara's* fiery broadsides matched exactly the color of the orange pan in my watercolor paint box, which had less exact colors for the great pearls of battle smoke above varnished green waves.

Again, for hours, in an aggregate of many visits, I would linger a few feet away from the catafalque on which the coffin of President Lincoln had been laid in state during his funeral train's pause at Dorchester in 1865 on its way home to Springfield, Illinois. The cloth which covered the catafalque was black and musty, faded (like a coachman's coat) to dusty green in places. Unseen moths had done their work. The bier slanted upward toward the head. I made my eyes see the coffin and within the coffin the famous face as it looked in my school book, only with the eyes closed instead of looking at me with printed sorrow, which was expressed throughout the whole figure—how long it was! judging by the bier—in its loose-hanging frock coat and rumpled trousers. Here he had been. I wondered many times whether I might touch the catafalque; and one day, when I was sure nobody was watching, I did so, and shivered, implicated in death and history. Now, with thoughts of my father, I touched it again in an obscure filial rite.

To be exorcised of ultimate thoughts, I sought out the narrow gallery where portraits of local heroes were hung. I was looking for a certain one. I must have seen it many times without particular attention. Now I wanted to see Hugh St Brides's American naval ancestor. I found Commodore Perry easily, and then three portraits down the line I stopped before a young ensign in blue and gold, beardless but for silky sideburns, bare-headed, pink-faced, with the lake wind blowing his pale-yellow hair forward above his brow. His eyes were as blue as the sky above the gold-lighted clouds behind his head. They looked directly at me, and I said, "Christopher," for the young officer was the child grown up, and once again the present was the child of the past. I leaned to read the gold label on the frame, to document my recognition. It read only, *Portrait of a Young Naval Officer, Battle of Lake Erie,"* by Thomas Sully, 1783–1872. But I knew what I knew, and was satisfied, for I was searching for the mortal upon the mortal which eventually reached the present, and gave mortality its quietus. In their continued life, I said goodbye again to the St Brides . Pointing heroically with arm outstretched toward a painted battle on the lake where fire and smoke from twelve-pounders, and burning shrouds, and fallen spars, celebrated both victory and defeat, the young ensign was like an anonymous prophet. Through the truth of the past, I was consoled by a sense of the actual immanence of a future. No story existed only in its single moment of the present. I was surrounded by the history of my birthplace, whose great men and events were kept in honor. Surely one day the portrait of my father, some of his possessions, the marvel of his once having lived, and worked, and been lifted up by his fellows, would rest here with the ensign, and the dead President who had passed by, and the men who had created buildings, parks, streets, and colleges?

꽃

Even though I was virtually alone in the museum, I felt too exposed to feeling which might be observed. The truth was, I didn't know what to do with my emotion. It would be no help to those at home if I let them see my fears and discontents. To be unknown—to see what I loved without knowing I must lose it as if it had never been mine, I went from the history of Dorchester and the lake and the *Niagara* to the inactive docks of Dorchester harbor under ice. I spent the rest of the afternoon walking by the piers to look out into the basin within the breakwater. Here and there I found a shed which when I sat in its shadow protected me from the wind. The great ore and grain freight ships were winter-locked. Against the gray sky and the pale ice their immensely long, black hulls—empty now and riding high above the ice—their white castles at the stern with their dead funnels, their delicately etched masts, their helpless imprisonment in the very element which in the warm summer months they could command in majestic, leisurely progress, had some heroic quality of endurance obscurely comforting to me. I went there to think over my problems, but actually was trying to escape them, as I soon discovered at the frozen harbor.

In the inner harbor the lake excursion boats were also tied up for the winter, with their decks and their stacked deck chairs covered by lashed tarpaulins. One ship, the old wooden *Inland Queen*, was the largest, most famous, of the summer steamers. The lake ports, Canadian or American, all the way from Dorchester to Toronto to

Cleveland, were proud of her when cloud-white against lake blue she steamed into view bearing passengers whose idea of joy was to sail with her on an "outing." There she lay, now, at her dock, with her stilled walking beam, her two tall, black, cable-braced funnels, her semicircular wheelhouse. I could hear her faintly creaking when the icy wind blew my way. Moping against a pier shed that afternoon, I saw a young man and his girl come across the dock to the gangway, unlock it, and climb to the first deck and disappear behind an overlapping fold of lashed canvas.

Did they live on board?

That first glimpse of them was like a jolt of freedom to me. I did not define it at the time, but my strongest desire was to find a way to evade the responsibility of a witness to suffering, and the duty owed to the family godhead. I was greedy to enter the lives of others, any others, to any degree.

The winter evening fell early, and I saw a light begin to show in a forward porthole of the *Inland Queen*. There the young pair must live. The black water lapped and sucked below cracks in the ice. Built for gaiety, the old ship faintly moved with the life of some under-ice current; and the round glow of light inside her, and the thought of the two people of my own age, secure and alone together, aroused in me my latent treason. I wanted to be in that weathering old steamer, snugly removed from our troubles of the time. I wanted to belong to another life: an unseen partner of those two whom I invested with beauty until my thought became hot with lust. I wanted to embrace them, even at the risk of denial and shame—for in my settling adulthood the body was ordinarily turned away in constraint from chance persons, strangers, while in childhood, in a life of close-ups, it had been given freely and in innocence.

How did they live in the forward cabin? Or did they come only occasionally, to love each other, to leave the ship, and to disappear into the city where others knew them? Perhaps he was a watchman? If so, he had not seen me, loitering by my shed. On certain days perhaps she came alone—why I could not think. But I was hot with desire to belong to them, he a comrade, she a lover, both needing me as I needed them. The emotion of home in which I felt so helpless was turning over in my breast into another which had nothing to do with good sense; only with power which drove me toward new wants—for protection, assuagement, removal; and the key to these seemed in imagination the life of those two in that secret space beyond the round lighted porthole of the excursion steamer, vessel of seasonal gaiety, now locked by ice and privacy.

I watched to see if they would return to the world; but soon, mysteriously, the porthole light went out. They were there to stay. The knowledge pierced me, and so, suddenly, did the cold, the dark, as evening fell; and so, like shock, sanity fell again upon me, and I was shivering, not only with winter, but with realization of my foolish desires, which had the aftermath of sin committed. I turned from the docks and walked uptown. Snow was beginning to fall again in flakes so huge they seemed to descend slowly, each in a spiral, which, multiplied infinitely, dazzled my vision against the blooming street lamps.

Going against the storm with turned and lowered face, I began to know the full meaning of my private betrayal; and secure because I was alone, I was not diffident about looking for forgiveness and strength when in my homeward walk I saw looming through the lamplighted snow the white marble Cathedral of the Holy Angels— the scene of my rescues from earlier visions and betrayals. Prayer stirred in me without words, but with an urgency loftier than what I had felt in childhood whenever I asked God for a particular toy after which I imperiously lusted. What had I just done but ask the impossible of chance?

The immense bronze doors of the cathedral were still unlocked. I let myself in, making an echo far away and above as I stamped off the snow which clung to my galoshes. I went up the long central aisle and knelt down before the deserted but not empty chamber of the sanctuary. From its high shadowed arch came the lofty gold chains which suspended the crimson glass of the eucharistic lamp, whose tiny flame burned without a flicker in the stillness. I brought clear to mind my contrition for my thoughts of folly and treachery; vowed not to entertain them again, to put away forever the life of the young man and woman of the *Inland Queen* and all they called me to. Again I was grateful to be alone, now because I was afraid of being seen at prayer, especially by someone of my own age.

But the next afternoon, going by my watch with the anxiety of one who is committed to a crucial appointment, I was at the dock again. The snowstorm was over, the sky was overcast with gray color which matched that of the lake, and I waited to see if they came back at the same time.

They came, entered the ship; their light slowly became visible, making me think they must use a kerosene lamp whose wick caught flame slowly, and I felt both chagrin and hot comfort at this regularity. There was that world again. I was that young fellow whom I longed to be: a working man, with my scarred black lunch box, which I would carry by its frayed leather handle. There was my girl, whose job observed the same hours as his, so they could come and go together. The shipping line must pay them for living on board, guarding the ship. It was now clear that it was their daily habit to return to the ship toward evening. It was their home. A new thought struck me. What if they were married? Why had I not thought of this before? With a rush of feeling, I hoped they were not married, for if they were, how might I expect to enter their lives? The idea was tormenting. How foolish of me to have come back, after my deeply meant vow of the night before. A sense of urgency came alive in me. We were, the family, to leave in a very few days. Until I knew more of the lives I hungered for, how could I leave? Waiting and watching to see their light go out, I made another vow—one I knew I would keep.

Tomorrow I would return. I would be waiting for them. When

they approached the gangway and were about to disappear into their privacy with all its imagined joys, I would come out of the shadow of my shed and intercept them. I would have ready a few apologetic general questions about the ship, the harbor; and with diffidence, which made my heart beat even in thinking of the scene, I would ask if they might let me see the ship's interior. Did they live on board? How lucky they were. Lucky? they would ask in honest puzzlement. Yes, I would say, to have such a life to themselves, away from the usual habits of the city. How I wished I were as lucky. They would look at each other, silently asking whether this stranger was to be taken seriously, or dismissed as a nuisance, possibly as someone dangerous to their matter-of-fact comfort. But my sincerity would win them. They must not see my hunger just yet. They must remain as uncomplicated as I must seem. If they were not people of many words, they might just shrug and make small smiles, and let me come on board, and after a brief tour of the shrouded decks, when they would be ready to have me go, I would ask where they lived—they would pause to consider again, and then won by my earnest liking for them, they would tell me where, and lead me there, and light their lamp, and out of common decency would have to ask me to sit down for a moment, perhaps to have a cup of coffee, warmed over from their pre-dawn breakfast. Soon we would have more to talk about than we could use, for we were all young, and wanting to stay beyond time, I knew I would soon have to leave the city, and when they heard this, they would become fonder of me than ever, and as if to defeat time, we would exchange news of our separate lives, an act which would give us to each other . . . I would not leave them until it was clear that I would be welcome to return; and with that, and a disarmingly worried look at my watch, which made clear that I was late for an urgent event elsewhere, I could go. They would walk the deck with me to the gangway and close the canvas after me and padlock it through the brass grommets for its lashings and I would say, "Until tomorrow!"

I felt there was now another dimension to my life. It gave me energy. Early the next morning I was up and about, out to the snow to rescue the morning paper before it was dampened through. I went to the kitchen to brew coffee for myself and, while the water heated, opened the paper and glanced at—

But what I saw was hardly a news event to me; it was a private calamity. In the middle of the front page a four-column photograph showed the *Inland Queen* burning by night. Against the wild blaze of her flames, the huddled figures of firemen were silhouetted. Their hoses sent great arcs of white water over the ship, but to no avail. She burned like any wooden house. Through smoke, sparks, dazzle, I could see parts of the ship as if they were broken and hanging in air—the forward wheelhouse, the funnels, the walking beam, masts, lifeboats dangling at crazy angles, great sheets of fallen canvas like curtains open on a theater scene.

"Fire of unknown origin," said the news story. Officials of the navigation company which owned the ship declared when interviewed that a young man—they gave his name—was employed as a watchman who stayed on board at night, after his daytime hours as a student (senior) at Dorchester City University. He was working his way through college and was regarded as a thoroughly reliable young man. So far as could be determined at press time, he had been on board when the fire broke out. Efforts to find him, or his body, were prevented by the intense heat and rapid spread of the flames. Further photographs would be found on a later page. I turned the pages until I found them. The ship from several angles; the fire chief calling commands to his men through a white megaphone; and a photograph of Jay William Drew, Jr., taken from his high school yearbook. He was posed leaning slightly forward. The photographer told him how to cock his head, and to smile, which he did evidently with some unwillingness, and to look right into the camera. His hair was brushed glossy and flat, dark in color. His eyes looked very dark under thin black brows which met just above the bridge of his nose. He had large ears and square bony jaws. I had never seen his face, but I had seen him moving. There was no mention of anyone else on the ship. The fire had broken out at about 2 a.m., and was first seen as glow in the sky by the motorman of a streetcar making its last run of the night two blocks away. He turned in the alarm. His name was Herman August Winckelmann, of 233 Rohr Street.

By the time my father called for the morning paper, I was composed enough—inscrutable, I believed—to take it to him. But when I handed it to him, he asked,

"Are you all right, Doc?"

"Oh, yes. —I didn't sleep very well. I read till very late."

"You must get your sleep. It's important for later"—he was thinking of resources against tubercular breakdown.

As soon as I could I went to the harbor to see the ruin. Was his body found now that the char had frozen under the hose water? A small crowd stood on the dock gazing, mostly in silence. I heard someone answer my silent question, telling someone else in the crowd.

"They never found him, but the fire evidently started in the cabin he lived in. Nothing was left there but the kerosene stove. The chief had it taken out an hour ago."

The *Inland Queen* lay half sunken and at a sharp list away from the dock. She was like a burned-out house, with icicles bright against her blackened superstructure. She would never again sail the Great Lakes to Toledo, Toronto, and Cleveland. Down, now, in the slow current under the ice, she shifted now and then ever so slightly —or was this my imagination, as I stared at her so intently that I made her move? My loins shrank, at a general loss of love. A part of my secret life was over in tragedy; and I was ashamed that for a while I mourned this more keenly than I did the threat suspended over the lives of my father and the rest of us.

When I reached home later in the day, my mother said,

"Everything is settled. I cannot believe it. We go on Saturday. Sam says so. The train and all."

Her wondering look was replaced now by a brave lift of her neat, small head, as if to say the worst was over.

"Yes," I said, delivered in my way from the obsession which had taken me for those few days from the emotion proper to a member of any family; and in my way I asked that from our trials we would emerge as safely, under that disembodied mercy forever addressed by mankind.

❉

Departures and arrivals were occasions I disliked because they required visible emotions and ardent, often false, demonstrations. We were at the railroad station early, because of the special arrangements needed for bringing my father into the train. He did not want to be seen by other passengers as they boarded. His ambulance was allowed to drive along the wide concourse at track end long before the passenger gates were opened. At the farthest track, standing alone and clouded with steam from temporary connections, was the combined gesture of fealty by Our Crowd; for to make my father's three-day journey to New Mexico as comfortable as possible, they had, without telling him until a day ago, "chipped in" to charter a private railroad car to take him all the way West. It was called the "James Buchanan." In the dusky, cold train shed, the yellow-shaded lights within the car looked inviting and reassuring. Polished wood paneling showed within, and a round-vaulted ceiling painted a soft green. Horace, the steward of the car, stood waiting on the rear platform with its shined brass railings and deep, overhanging canopy.

As my mother and Lillian O'Rourke, Sam, and I stood watching, the ambulance attendants brought my father on a specially narrow stretcher and lifted him across the brass railing, through the rear door of the car, and to the first stateroom down the corridor. It was then that I fully understood how ill he was—that he was not allowed to take even one step. My father remained silent, guarding himself, but he nodded and gazed keenly at each stage of the arrangements. Dr Morton Frawley arrived and made rapid bedside tests, said all was stable, and departed without further words, but glancing at each of us as he left the car to note what we thought of him, on his way to more urgent matters. My father's favorite of the nurses from the house was going with us—Mrs DeLancy. In no time she had the intimate Pullman stateroom established as an efficient hospital room: lights, window shades, pillows, blankets, racks of medicine, bedside table, placed pillows, just so. My father sighed in the contentment of the moment, which was the best, now, that he dared do with respect to time and the future. The door of the room was left open as the rest of us found our quarters. The car had six staterooms, a dining room, a galley, and, occupying the last third of its length, a sitting room with sofas, easy chairs, magazine racks, and little tables.

I was looking at our departure time on my watch when we felt a gentle jar. A switch engine had coupled itself to the "James Buchanan" and now pulled us to the end position on another track, and there by particular permission (since limited trains were not supposed to pull private cars) the famous flyer called The Wolverine slowly backed into position until with jets and screams of steam, and metal clinchings, train and car were attached.

Ten minutes before the station gates were to open for the public, a sizable crowd of men came to the train from another entry—Our Crowd, who had to see my father off, as they said, and also inspect the private car which at great expense they had provided for him. They filed through the car from the rear platform, each pausing a second at my father's open doorway to say a word to him, while he waved back in silence. I was moved and therefore irritated at the open show of emotion which so many made—I saw more than one man trying to pretend he was not in tears.

My mother was equal to the event. She stood on the platform outside at the rear steps by which Our Crowd came down from the car. She shook hands with them all, and from a few of the closest friends she accepted a kiss on the cheek. Over the cavernous, contained noises of the high train shed, heightened words of encouragement were said, bright promises of early return and gleeful reunion, offers to do anything possible in the way of help back home while we were so far away.

"Yes, thank you, oh, we do thank you, yes, you are a dear," my mother would say, holding her fur collar to her cheeks against the cold air scraping on a long draft through the shed. "Of course we will write, yes, postcards, do keep in touch. Dan is so grateful. We are going to be perfectly fine."

But underlying much of their good cheer, Our Crowd felt uncertainty and disappointment. They had relied on so great a return for their belief in my father that they could not help wondering if all might not now be endangered. They had persuaded him to run for office when he had at times shown a strange, almost angry reluctance, they had helped powerfully to elect him, they knew that in politics he would be as brilliant and reliable as in business; and to the extent of his success they would be entitled to feel success in themselves. As they left the car, they gathered by my father's stateroom window at the offside of the car, hidden from the platform along which passengers were at last hurrying to their numbered Pullman sleepers. There followed one of those pauses when it was time to go, but when nothing yet happened, and Our Crowd were obliged to stamp their feet against the cold, and in pantomime send messages and sentiments through the steamy window, whose shade Mrs DeLancy had agreed to raise, and one or two clowned a bit.

Two interruptions took place toward the end. The first was the arrival of a florist's delivery boy bringing a huge basket of American Beauty roses from the Governor and Mrs Pelzer, with a silk ribbon saying in gold letters, GET WELL QUICK FROM JUDGE AND MO. The bouquet was so large that it attracted attention, and created the second interruption. The reporter from *The Dorchester Chronicle* regularly assigned to the daily departure of The Wolverine followed the basket of roses, discovered to whom it was going, who had sent it, and asked for clarification.

Sam Dickinson met him on the platform before he could board the car and gave the desired statement: *The lieutenant-governor had been ordered by his physicians to take a vacation of a few weeks in the warm Southwest, where the sunshine and the dry, high altitude would help to dispose of the influenza and the mild pneumonia which had plagued the lieutenant-governor earlier in the year. It was not possible to see him as he had gone straight to bed on boarding the train. No, the private car was not chartered at public expense. Yes, the lieutenant-governor would continue to keep abreast of affairs at Albany, and in fact, to make that official routine possible, he, Samuel Dickinson, the permanent legislative assistant, was accompanying the lieutenant-governor, who was taking along also his personal private secretary. Yes, there were others in the party—the lieutenant-governor's wife and son, and a registered nurse. No, it was not at this time advisable to release the party's destination, since publicity would result in activity which would make demands on the lieutenant-governor and impede his rapid convalescence. No, regrettably, a photograph was not possible—*and just at that moment, the conductor gave the long cry of "All aboard." The engine bell began to toll in its arch. Deafening gusts of steam came forth from the great pistons far ahead, and The Wolverine began to draw slowly out with all doors clanged shut, as Our Crowd, led by one of their members, broke into a chorus which rose almost unheard into the high steel girders overhead, "For he's a jolly good fel-low." From the observation platform at the rear I watched the train shed recede.

It was a scene in black and white, with smoked girders, and drifts of steam, dark empty engines and cars, and lines of frozen snow tracing the perspective of the tracks which so steadily narrowed. Our Crowd were now soundless but still singing and waving, and like a child gravely obedient to custom, I waved back.

CHAPTER III

※

Laughter in the Desert

ON THE THIRD DAY we came to Albuquerque in a state of general blindness whenever we looked out of the windows of our car. For hours the land had been obscured by a vast dust storm which threw desert earth, almost gravel in size, against the "James Buchanan." Eager to see the new country, as if seeing it would give us the power to foresee our life there, we were denied sight of those features which such great names stood for—the Rio Grande, the Sandia Mountains, the mesa at Albuquerque, the volcanoes on the horizon west of the river valley. Though we kept all windows tightly shut, the dust penetrated the car. Mrs DeLancy laid wet towels along the windowsills in my father's stateroom to keep him from breathing the choking air.

"Whiii!" cried my mother, brushing the air away from her face. With a finger she traced patterns in the dust on the glossy furniture of the car, as later she would do so often when the dust blew into our house in the Rio Grande valley; and for her the dust (the stuff, I wrote in my notebook with gloomy literary relish, of our promised mortality) remained ever afterward my mother's main image of the new land.

But to me it showed something else—the very energy and scale of the storm spoke of vast spaces and movement. Now and then when the storm thinned for a moment, the sun, a great pale-blue disk, showed like an omen and then vanished before it could be read. At Albuquerque the "James Buchanan" was shunted off from the California Limited of the Santa Fe line to which we had been transferred in Chicago.

We waited, so it seemed, for over an hour on our side track, expecting a visit from the doctor to whom Frawley had sent us. My father was apprehensive until the doctor finally arrived; and then he found extra energy, assumed a mask of confidence and all his old charm in an imposture of health. The doctor went into the stateroom, retained Mrs DeLancy, and closed the door, while the rest of us waited in the rear sitting room.

"What do you suppose is taking him so long?" asked my mother after a few minutes.

"God have mercy," murmured Lillian.

"It's rather early for that," declared Sam, with an excusing grin, and just then the doctor in long, swooping strides came along the corridor and into the room with us.

"Well and good," he stated generally, and shook hands with us all. "My first, cursory observation tells me that the patient must remain here in the car until the air clears. We're in our third day of it. Probably the last day. Then we'll have an ambulance ride to Saint Anthony's Sanatorium. Have you time? Let me sit down with you for a few minutes," sweeping us all with a glaring smile.

Dr M. Jamison Birch was fiercely amiable in order to deny his own precarious health. He was himself tubercular—an arrested case, as they said in that colony of consumptives. He had been a classmate at Cornell of Dr Morton Frawley and ironically had become, in laboratories and sickrooms, a victim of the very disease in which he had chosen to specialize. Tall, stooped, skeletally thin, he had a skull-like face which constantly wore its fierce bony smile, as if without his volition. His head was small for his long frame, and across its dome a few black hairs were brushed flat, though several at the rear stuck out like feathers. His eyes were sunken in their sockets and his nose resembled a hawk's beak between them. He had a way of standing with his bony hands loosely furled together before his concave chest. His coat hung on him as on a hanger.

"How is my old friend Frawley?" he asked in a thin, throaty voice. "We used to call him T.L.P., which stood for This Little Pig, he was so round and pink, you know, as a student, and he was so sure of where he was going, you know. —How is he?"

"Oh, splendid," replied my mother, astonished that we would not immediately discuss my father's condition. "He was—most professional."

"Haa. You didn't like him."

"Oh, no, no. —I simply meant *brisk*."

"Yes. But he knew what he was doing."

Dr Birch was attempting to establish a kindly social atmosphere for us all, and succeeded then, and even further, in the days following, until he became a friend who rejoiced whenever he could escape in conversation from the morbid ingredients of which his professional life was made.

"I have not seen T.L.P. for years," he went on. "He remains quite perversely healthy. I think this is because he feels it more fashionable to be well than ill." He laughed hollowly. "However, we speak frequently by telephone, and lately, quite often about your husband."

At last my mother's anxious concern was recognized openly.

"Yes—how do you find him, Dr Birch?"

"I shall be making detailed examinations during the week. I'll know more then. I expect we will be able to move him tomorrow."

He suddenly turned his eyes on me—they gleamed remotely but hotly, I thought, like anthracite coals, as in a long silence he seemed to penetrate my being, almost in a trance. But he was concentrating so fiercely that he made me feel like a specimen, which, I was to learn, was just how he saw me. Then abruptly he became social again, smiling with winning charm. He leaned toward my mother and said,

"You are quite naturally worried. But let me say this: the more you worry, the less you can help your husband. Your own health will be the best medicine he can have, once we establish him in a proper regimen."

My mother could not help asking,

"Oh, *is* he going to be all right?"

"Madam, I am an eternal optimist. Look at *me*. I was sent out here twenty-one years ago to die, as it was believed more seemly for me to die in a beneficial climate than that of New York. And now the tubercle bacillus gives a faint shriek of alarm every time it sees me."

I laughed, and so did Sam. Lillian shook her head at such a marvel. The doctor turned again to me.

"That's *better*," he remarked genially, and the emphasis set him to coughing—the liquid, shallow, self-sparing cough of the tubercular. Covering his mouth, he shook his head to discourage alarm. In a moment, "Please come to see me in my office tomorrow at the sanatorium. Four o'clock. We will know more to talk about then. Meantime, don't pay attention to the dust. It is merely an irritant. Above all," he added, again piercing me, now accurately, "do not take it as a metaphor."

With a lanky bow, he left the "James Buchanan." Watching him go, Sam said,

"We are going to like that man."

"If only he can help," said my mother, as though he was now the controller of our lives, which to a degree he was.

※

"They're all so cheerful," remarked my mother after a week's acquaintance with the staff and some of the patients at Saint Anthony's Sanatorium. Even my father's spirits seemed to rise now that he was settled in his hospital room, facing the mountains a dozen miles away across the mesa. A sliding glass door opened on to a little balcony where in discreet doses, to begin with, he could be moved into fresh air and sunshine.

Mrs DeLancy had gone home on the same train which took away the empty "James Buchanan," and the sanatorium nurses now managed my father's needs.

They were Sisters of Charity, whose order had come to New Mexico in the nineteenth century to establish hospitals and orphanages. They were now assisted by registered lay nurses whom I thought of as civilians, as against the nuns. There was at first the kind of little flutter of extra interest, at which the nuns were innocently expert when their lives were heightened by anything at all unusual, when they identified my father as a public man; for the newspapers by now had the full story of who he was and why he was there, the news of which had been released over the wire services by Governor Pelzer at Albany. "We hope he will soon be back with us," the governor was quoted as saying. "His leave of absence is expected to be reasonably brief"—but Sam had private reports of maneuvers and speculations about what shift of power in the state senate might follow upon my father's absence, and whether the governor would now gather all control for himself. My father smiled sardonically and said,

"Well, Sam, Pelzer seems to have the luck of the Devil himself."

"He doesn't look like that for nothing," replied Sam. "We can watch him fairly closely from here. I've got the office all set up to telegraph us daily."

But as yet he was not supposed to show my father any reports which would require extended concentration. Rest, rest, was the order of the day. Time itself had to be the dosage which if properly used would cure my father. Even certain kinds of thoughts were prohibited by Dr Birch. No dwelling on the past, or on what had to be relinquished for the time being, or particularly on what opportunities for a brilliant future might be endangered now. Live for each day; for each breath.

"Sam," said my father, "I don't know what I'd do—any of us would do—without you. How can I thank you for what you've left in order to be with us?"

For Sam was engaged to marry the daughter of a dean at Harvard, and it had been his habit to go to Cambridge from Albany. They had not set a date for their wedding, but the assumption was that it would come in either June or October. Now no date could be set until certain conditions became clear at Albuquerque. Joanna was unwillingly patient; thought she would spend the summer in Europe and see how she felt about things on her return. Even though there was no question of a permanent breach, she could not resist this hint of a threat. Sam was more worried than he admitted, and spent a great part of his salary on long-distance calls to Cambridge, from which he took enough reassurance to keep his gleaming good nature visibly intact. He suffered no impairment to that one trait which most pleased my father. This was a smiling irony well this side of cynicism which used the skeptical to dramatize the actual. It made him politically valuable and a fine companion responding to the daily shape of life.

"Governor," he said, "it is rare enough to be able to serve principle as embodied in a member of *Homo sapiens*. I should be thanking you."

It was never spoken between them, but their bond lay in Sam's belief in my father's great public potential, for which almost anything—Joanna, even? I wondered—could be sacrificed, and in my father's thankful acceptance of the loyalty of this young patrician whose quick mind, selfless charm, and good manners were so effortless and reliable.

The sanatorium was a long, three-story, red brick building which looked as if it had been bent from the straight into a shallow angle at the center. It had white pillars at its central entrance, and a grand curved driveway which gave a manorial calm to the front, while at the rear, a stark cement deck and wide folding doors served the emergency entrance. At the north end the manorial air was displaced by a small, added Gothic wing whose two-story windows of stained glass, tented slate roof, and slender gold-leafed steeple announced the hospital chapel, where my mother spent a supplicant hour every day. The main lobby, and all its corridors, had floors of brown linoleum which were polished daily to a high gloss, giving off a pungent smell of faintly sour wax, which came to seem, for me, like the very odor of illness; but when I mentioned this to others, they had not noticed it, and said I was too morbid, especially for someone who was to become a medical doctor—for this vocation was still tacitly agreed upon in my family, having been established in my childhood by my first toy doctor's bag with candy medicines in little phials out of which I cured the greedy illnesses of my playmates until the brightly colored pills were all gone.

The rear of the building had a long sun porch. There the ambulant patients went to drink the air and sunlight. Waiting there sometimes for my father to be made "ready" for the day and visitors, I saw the patients in their long deck chairs and made the acquaintance of a few, and saw enough of others to recognize what they had in common—an acute awareness of their physical states at every moment, and their almost furtive but zealous care of the moment's evidence: taking their own pulses, counting their respirations, inhaling with deliberate measure, exhaling with luxurious caution. They held their hands forward to see if the color beneath their fingernails showed a trifle more pink today, indicating new red corpuscles.

When they changed position they used slow gliding motions so as not to disturb tissues in tender suspension between healing and hemorrhage. They observed a programmed gladness in their greetings of each other, since any admission of their constant concern would express pessimism, which Dr Birch had said was an enervating state of mind.

Cheerful under eternity, the nursing sisters of Saint Anthony's, with death postulated all about them, established an early intimacy with us all; and when we came daily to see my father, we were recognized and welcomed as if we belonged to their family, as in their professional eyes and actual faith we did.

Among the rather large circle of the staff which seemed to take form about my father as they felt his interest in them despite his own state, one nun in particular became a family intimate. This was Sister Mary Vincent, a nursing sister, who supervised the floor where my father lived. On duty, she was a stony-faced tyrant with a restrained and awesome temper; but when she was free for a moment from professional pressures, she was an amusing woman who loved harmless gossip (the hospital was full of all kinds of gossip) and had to be the first to know and tell it. Her countenance was bright pink, plump, naturally full of gleams, which were doubled by the flash of her enormous rimless eyeglasses. These reflected light in streaks as she swiftly turned her head to catch every facet of any possible interest in the life about her.

My mother, who had always had a feeling for nuns, in early times would now and then infuriate my father with an idle speculation about why she had abandoned her girlhood dream of becoming a nun herself, and whether after all she had done the right thing to change her mind. "You simply grew up," my father would say, scowling, and add, "Do you think it altogether kind to the rest of us to bring that up *now?*" And she would be flooded with comic remorse, as all along it was just this response from him which she had been playing for. Observing this, my father would be more cross than ever, so that my mother was forced into the delicious duty of winning him over again, and calming my fright at imagining the loss of her.

Now, at Saint Anthony's, my mother could not resist claiming affinity with the nuns on behalf of gaining their special attention to my father's needs. One day she confessed her schoolgirl vocation to Sister Mary Vincent, who replied,

"I had a feeling you understood us; but you obviously did what God wanted you to do, and now: your lovely family. You must not complicate matters by having any regrets."

"Oh, I don't, I don't! —How do you think he is? You have seen so many—"

Sister Mary Vincent folded her scrubbed, capable hands within her bloused sleeves and pledged with her eyes that my father's case would have her special attention.

She was particularly interested, too, in knowing everything about me, which led to my unexpected involvement in the hospital life. As I could never give an account of myself, my mother did this for me, usually forcing me to leave the room when my attainments were recited. Now,

"Exactly the one," declared Mary Vincent, as we soon began to speak of her, and then address her. "We need someone for the volunteer library, and since he is idle"—it being too late in the year for me to enroll in the university on the mesa beyond Saint Anthony's—"we shall put him to work."

She made a wagging command and promise with her forefinger; and within a few days, I was spending three hours a day as librarian at the desk in the indoor solarium, where ranks of donated books ran along the shelves facing the opposite glass wall. My working hours were in the morning, since the patients had to rest all afternoon.

On my first day two patients became individuals to me.

One of these was a young man of about my own age. He idled along the shelves, glancing my way when he thought I might not notice. When he saw me smile dutifully at him, a library patron, he took heart and came to my desk, holding a book which he asked about. It was a battered blue volume called *Memories of an Ambassador's Wife,* by Mary King Wallington. I had never heard of it.

"It has things about life at the Imperial Russian Court," he said in a light voice, cadenced with italics and deliberate refinement, and carrying an emphasis on the sibilants. "I think I would like to read it."

I took down the title and author, and asked his name.

"Carlton Gracey?"—as though I might recognize it.

I recorded him as the borrower.

"Have you just come here?" he asked. "Have you chased the cure very long?"

"Oh: I am not the patient in our family. It is my father." I told him the name.

"Oh: the New York governor. *Oh my!*" impressed.

I explained my father's actual status.

"*Still,*" said Carlton, needing to hold on to any distinction when he met it. I was somewhat startled that by my appearance he had assumed me to be a tubercular like himself. Surely I had none of his visible symptoms? He was skeletally thin. His face was pointed and narrow, with flushed cheekbones, and eyes, sunken under blond brows, with something of a bird's look about them. Under his carefully neat, pale clothes his body seemed to be working to remain upright. He moved with conscious grace. When he coughed he closed his lips to contain politely a rude sound which might offend others. When he spoke he tossed his head faintly as though demonstrating pathetic courage in the face of a hard world. "*Thank* you," he said, and with elegant steps made his way out of the library, holding his book curled into his shallow chest with one hand, and balancing his steps with the other in a restrained sway.

If he made me want to smile at his airs of excessive refinement, he also touched me with his desire to show himself as a superior person. In repeated visits, he began to feel my uncritical friendliness, and I was soon given his history. He grew up in Rolla, Missouri, conducting a longing search there for *the finer things of life,* without much success. In Rolla, there was no accounting for him, and he was made to feel this. His high school years were *torture,* for his difference from all the rowdy students. When he could, he escaped to Chicago with a small inheritance from his maternal grandmother, who died just as he was graduated from high school. He went to the Chicago Business College, training for secretarial work. Chicago was the great lodestone for those of the Middle West who starved for the cultural life. Carlton was so happy there he thought at first he could hardly *stand* it. I nodded. The Art Institute; the magnificent mansions of Lake Shore Drive; the Chicago Symphony Orchestra; most wonderful of all, after all the years of reading and wanting, the great Chicago Opera. He knew the names of all the artists, and suddenly released from his cultural loneliness at Saint Anthony's, he would spend as much time as we both had in describing them, their roles, and their world, which, from his top balcony seat when he could afford it, he entered like one coming home. The music, yes, but above all, it was the *ballet* which entranced him, and of the ballet, it was one dancer who became his *idol.* She was not the female star, but even so, for him, in her second leads, she outshone everyone on that vast distant stage. He watched the playbills for her name, and saved his ticket money for her nights onstage. Her name—he pronounced it with a sound which seemed Russian to him—was Stasia Rambova.

He looked about. If nobody was in sight, he would show me how Stasia Rambova stood alone in a spotlight as the curtains parted. He asked me to notice how the line of the left leg was continued in the upraised right arm, and was countered by the sharp turn of head. Glancing down, he would call attention to the perfect placement of her feet—the heel of one set into the instep of the other, both turned wide at a stylized angle. Best of all—

He was about to show it, when another patient came from nowhere into the library. Carlton's world collapsed. Coldly, he took up some books and walked out with his left shoulder raised.

"Getting a free show?" asked the intruder.

This was Lyle Pryor, who read two or three books a day. He too spent time talking to me in the solarium. In his way, he too was hungry for a world denied him by the disease. He was a New York journalist who lived at Saint Anthony's, but his case was close enough to a cure to permit him to come and go, as though from a hotel. "General activity in moderation," as Dr Birch had said. Tall as a heron, and built rather like one, he had a bony pink face, pale eyes, huge eyeglasses, and a high braying voice in which he rapidly spoke comic insults under the privilege of genial cynic—a role he had created for himself. As soon as my father was permitted visitors for a few minutes at a time, he made habitual calls on him, asking rapid-fire questions like an interviewer, and offering opinions which were deliberately provocative. He would tire my father with his energy, and then, with a scratchy laugh, he would go away. Under the pseudonym of T. B. Crabb he contributed gratis a weekly column to the local morning paper in which under the guise of humor he made biting comments on local and national affairs. One day he remarked to my father,

"Politics, eh? Albany, Chicago, Albuquerque, Santa Fe—there's no difference, y'know? A vocation for poltroons"—H. L. Mencken was his model—"and here, locally, for small-time crooks. You're lucky, Governor, you come from the land of big-time crooks. I'm glad to see you have overcome the temptations of the gaudy life."

This was too much for Sam, who was with my father, sifting the morning mail.

"The Governor," he said with smiling mouth and angry eyes, "has already done more than any other man to begin cleaning up the leading state in the Union!"

"And they got him for it, didn't they?" cackled Pryor, beyond logic. "Look where he is now, out here with the rest of us lungers and social parasites!"

My father, weary of this fevered irony, simply shut his eyes, and Lyle Pryor had to go.

But Carlton Gracey had no one to guard him against Pryor, who stared after his scornful departure with a snicker that day in the solarium.

"No, not a show," I said, "he was explaining things about ballet."

"Stasia Rambova, eh?—I got it all a long time ago, when he first got here. The poor little bastard."

"You don't really sound very sorry for him."

"Oh, hell, I feel sorry for him, and for everyone, what's more, but there's no use moaning over it, is there? One day when he was raving to me about his Stasia Rambova, trained in the Imperial Russian Ballet School, who escaped just in time from the Bolsheviks, I said, Oh hell, kid, she was probably just Bella Feinblum of East Side Chicago. He turned white and said he for one was not to be addressed as 'kid,' and that I was never to address him again."

"You're pretty rough on him."

"What else can you do with a Missouri Exquisite? —They tell me you want to be a doctor, eh?"

"Who says so?"

"Oh, Mary Vincent, for one."

"The two of you are the town criers here, aren't you?"

"We trade items. —But you're always writing in some notebook or other. What about?"

"Not medicine."

"Clams up, don't he." He laughed. On principle, he liked an adversary. He drifted away.

The next time Carlton came about books, he said,

"If you ever see *that creature* coming while I'm here, I'll be *grateful* if you will give me a word of warning."

I promised.

"Look," he said, "here is her picture. I cut it out of a program. She does look Russian, really, don't you think?"—for something of his

[78]

belief in his fantasy about the Imperial Russian Ballet School had been damaged in spite of loyalty by Pryor's grinning skepticism.

"Oh, yes. Black hair and Tartar eyes. She is beautiful."

"Thank you," he said soberly, as though he could take credit for the opinion. "I *was* going to show you her most wonderful gesture: her curtain call."

With that, once sure nobody else was watching, he drew himself up nobly, lifting one arm with his hand upward and its fingers curled open to receive the world, the other arm cradling an imaginary spray of roses, then turning his head slowly from side to side to sweep the great balconies, the boxes, the orchestra, as though inhaling the ozone of glory; and when he had surveyed the whole house, he slowly sank with bowed head to one knee in grace and humility. The illusion he created was startling. When he returned to himself,

"Wonderful," I said.

"You *see* why I love her?"

"Oh, yes."

He sighed.

"The late spring season opens very soon. Perhaps I'll be there."

Was this the optimism of the tubercular?

Actually, it was the very opposite.

Soon afterward Lyle Pryor said to me,

"We're losing the Missouri Exquisite."

"How do you mean? Is he worse?"—for I had not seen him for some days.

"No. He's leaving."

"Good Lord, why? He's not all that well."

"No. Mary Vincent told me. His money is all gone. He can't afford to stay any longer."

"Oh, no. Can't anyone help with funds?"

"It wouldn't make much difference. Matter of fact, I offered a little something on the sly to the san. But Birch says he might as well be let go." The first note of sympathy came into Lyle's voice. "Incurable."

"Do they really think so?"

"Listen, kid. I'll tell you something about this disease. Physically, the poor little idiot is far gone. But he's dying of more than t.b. Can't you see that? Some people, when they're denied what they most want, die of the denial. That's what's happening to the Missouri Exquisite."

"You mean, he's actually dying of love for Stasia Rambova?"

"Not quite as you mean it. He wishes he could *be* Stasia Rambova. He can't. He's dying of it, with t.b. to help it along. We'll never see him again. Nobody will, for long."

The revelation was so startling to me that at the time I saw nothing beyond it. As Lyle left me, I felt, though, that I had judged him too simply.

The next day Carlton Gracey came to say goodbye.

"This is quite sudden," he said, with simulated high spirits, establishing his version of his news, "but I simply decided I *can't* miss the spring season at the ballet. I'm leaving this afternoon. I'll be on *tenterhooks* till I have my reservation."

"For the train?"

"No, Richard. For the *opera house*. Oh! To see her again!"

I put an enthusiastic face over what I knew now.

"You lucky dog!"

"Yes, thank you, aren't I?"

He straightened himself up in rickety vitality. Pallid, sand-colored in various shades, skin, hair, neatly pressed suit, he held himself gallantly until the effort made him cough; then he slumped protectively until the spasm passed. When he could, he said,

"You've been very kind. I *really* oughtn't tell you something, but for some reason I want to. You know that *dreadful* thing that *dreadful* creature said about Stasia changing her name? Yes. Well, of course she didn't. But actually"—he leaned confidentially closer—"*I* changed *mine*. My real name is Homer Morper and I couldn't stand it after I left Rolla. I thought and thought on the train all the

[80]

way to Chicago the first time, and by the time I got there, why, I was *Carlton Gracey*. Don't you think I was right?"

I reassured him energetically. I wished I could tell him what Lyle had tried to do for him. Everything was impossible. We shook hands. His hand was moist and trembling, holding on to what he must, for as long as he could, which had nothing to do with me. I was sorry and relieved when someone else entered the solarium to return books. With a face suddenly real and woeful, Carlton Gracey silently took leave of me with all his mortal information secretly intact—so he thought, in his final bravery.

※

From the first, Dr Birch had said that as soon as it seemed prudent he wanted my father to be moved to a domestic atmosphere. He would let my mother know when to start looking for a house. In the meantime, she and the rest of us stayed at the Fred Harvey hotel beside the railroad tracks which bisected the city.

At that time, the hotel, called the Alvarado after a Spanish captain of the early explorations out of Mexico in the sixteenth century, was the social center of the town. It was a long, low, stucco structure in what was called the "Mission Style," imitated from the California foundations of the Franciscan monks of the eighteenth century. There was a patio with a fountain, there were arcades with low arches and tiled floors, the lobby was amber-lit, the main dining room with its arched windows was furnished in heavy dark woods amid which the starched white linen and the shining glass and silver promised excellent service, and the best—the only good—public food in town. For us it was a temporary home, much as a resort hotel might have been. We had our fixed table in the dining room, and always the same waitress—a hearty girl named Della, who seemed to enjoy her work. Now and then she would lean against my back, serving my dishes, and I would think that she might have an even more enjoyable life after working time. She had loose, bright-orange hair and she put rouge high up under her eyes on her ivory-white skin. Lillian disapproved of her on the basis of her appearance. My mother said,

"Oh, Lillian, nobody is always what they look like. —Say a prayer for her and be done with it."

But her smile excused any hint of offhand impiety, and Lillian, summoned to charity, lowered her eyes. When next Della came round the table, my mother favored her with a specially bright smile of thanks.

Sam asked one evening,

"Are all these people going to be a problem, or a welcome distraction?"

"It depends," said my mother, "whether they play a good hand of contract."

For letters from home were beginning to bring callers—people who like us had migrated from the East and now lived in Albuquerque. Some of them were already easy members of the local population, others kept their faraway origins visibly present in manners and styles. All of them shared a fraternal sense of victory—they had survived the bacillus, and had decided to live where they had won. All had begun their local life at the sanatorium, which, like Lyle Pryor, they called Saint Tony's, in his same spirit of deliberate lightness. The first new friend to call on my mother, introducing herself, said,

"First the traders, then the railroaders, and now the lungers," after which she gave a loud, husky laugh, which spoke more of cigarettes and whiskey than of tuberculosis. She was Eleanor Saxby, a large, white-haired widow whose lung disease had long been considered arrested; and she remained in the Southwest because, simply, she had nowhere else to go. She had money, she needed no interests beyond evening bridge games and afternoon movies and her skillful gathering of local gossip. She knew before anyone when a celebrity came to town—a curiously large number of these drifted in and out of town every year—and she was often at the railroad platform beside the hotel as the California Limited paused, going east or west in those great days of transcontinental railroading when a dozen trains by day and night went by with their huge Mallet locomotives. Early movie stars were often to be seen striding the platform during the stopovers while the limited trains were being serviced and Pueblo Indian vendors sat in the sunlight with their pottery and turquoise set out for sale on native blankets. Mrs Saxby never hesitated to introduce herself to any one of the travelers whom she recognized, and always brought away anecdotes, reproducing every word of the dialogues she enjoyed with the lustrous film stars. Under her white hair and black eyebrows she had eyes as brown as chestnuts, a short nose with widely cavernous nostrils, a thick-lipped mouth heavily painted, and a heavy throat, where she fingered her pearls for comfort and attention. In her coarseness she was the opposite of my mother, and I would wonder why they rapidly became such friends; but her robust curiosity, her heavy voicings of her comic view of the world, had such vitality that I think my mother found her reassuring as a lesson in how well one could recover from an often fatal disease. "My Gahn!" Mrs Saxby would cry when animated by joyful shock or true dismay.

She spoke her credentials from friends in Dorchester, and also introduced the man who came with her the first time—and every time afterward. This was a slim, dark, hollow-cheeked Spaniard who was spoken of as Count. The convention was that he was truly a Spanish nobleman named Jaime d'Alvarez y Cuesta, Count of Alarcante. But in the circle of friends who grew up around us, his title was always used as though it were a nickname. He did not mind, so long as it was used. His narrow brown face was thinned further by his glossy black hair, brushed straight back close to his skull. He wore pince-nez and trim suits. I remember his bending forward constantly to ingratiate himself, uttering extravagant compliments, which he would affirm excessively by saying, "No, *really!*" in his correct but oddly stressed English. This gentility did not conceal the fact that he was mercilessly clever at bridge. Eleanor Saxby was heard to say that he made his living out of his winnings, even at a tenth of a cent. When she won a hand, or a round of Mah-Jongg, she regarded it as a personal victory over him, and expertly snapping her cards or loudly rattling her tiles, she would cry charitably, "My Gahn, Count, I never thought I'd see the day when I took a trick from *you!*" He would take her thick hand and kiss it, gazing at her four or five heavy diamond rings. They were invited as a couple to the bridge or Mah-Jongg evenings in our hotel rooms, though nobody thought of them as lovers.

As it took more than those two for the table games, since neither Sam nor Lillian played, and I was present as little as possible, another pair, and Lyle Pryor, whom everybody knew, became habitual guests in various combinations. Lyle brought a couple whom he introduced with his rapid bray as "high-toned, if you go in for high tone"—a gibe which they themselves passed over with concealed satisfaction at being properly recognized.

They were Percy and Serena Sage, who came from a then fashionable part of Long Island, where the Sage family money had been gathering itself for several generations. "Sage Paints for the Wise" was a slogan known nationally. As one sometimes did over maddeningly trivial matters, I speculated whether the second word was a noun or a verb, and when I asked Percy Sage, he smiled stylishly and said, "Both," with an air of achievement. He was deeply tanned and bony, easily elegant in tweeds. His bronzed, sharply chiseled face in profile was almost a medallion of a purebred Mohawk Indian. Speaking of others, he often adverted to the general idea of being "well-bred," and Mrs Saxby would adjust her deep bosom, which she comically called "my bust," and say she was content

[84]

enough to be "well fed." Percy was full of the idea of being a Founder in the colonial American sense, for if his fortune went back only three generations, his remote ancestors had taken part in the Revolution of 1776—some even on the King's side, as he would admit with falsely modest amusement in his confident gravelly voice.

His wife, Serena, often wore suiting materials matching his. She had a plain, lumpy, droll face and an air of dowdiness somehow beyond and better than fashion. She had brought her own great fortune to her marriage. She and her husband kept their Eastern seaboard accents, spoken in lifted, clear sounds, through excellent teeth, and an effect of almost clenched jaws. Lyle would often pretend not to understand what they said.

"Y'know, I'm just a hayseed, I don't always get your lingo. —What did you say?"

"You know peefectly well," Percy would reply with a little laugh which ignored any false appeal.

The fevered irony which, spoken or unspoken, seemed to filter its way into the group personality of the ex-invalids was accepted by them all. All having had a glimpse of fatality, they suffered each other, locked in a knowing, and outspoken, comradeship. I wondered how, when he was well enough to join us all, my father would respond to the general manner of my mother's evening circle.

After one occasion of provocative mockery, Lyle Pryor said,

"Oh, think nothing of it—it's just laughter in the desert. Y'know? All those bleached bones out there among the mirages. Silent laughter, in the end, of course, kid, y'know? because a skull hasn't anything to laugh out loud with any more: only a few teeth. Y'know?"

And they would all think of themselves, and perhaps a small silence would fall, except for the snapping cards, or the clatter of the pretty Mah-Jongg tiles with their ivory faces and carved, painted characters.

One day, when my mother, Lillian, and I were all spending an hour with my father on his balcony at Saint Tony's, he asked for more information about the established circle of the "Inevitables," as Lyle had dubbed the finally winnowed group of the Alvarado evenings.

"Oh, in their various ways, they are a comfort," said my mother.

"But what do they *talk* about?" asked my father. He disliked table games, thought them inane, and had no interest in the mental ingenuities they required.

"Mostly about how that last trick should have been played," I said.

"But after all, we don't gather to *talk*," murmured my mother.

"Why else?" asked my father irritably. "They sound rather silly, all of them, except Lyle, who drops in on me here rather often. —At least, he thinks some of the time."

"Yes, they're silly, mostly," agreed my mother. "Richard mimics them."

"Do me somebody," ordered my father.

I pretended then a rapid entrance from the bedroom on to the balcony, eagerly bending forward to ingratiate, a swift glance around through pince-nez, which I sketched in the air by removing and replacing them with my fingernails, and I kissed my mother's hand in a flattering crouch, making her laugh, and say, "It *is* Count!"

But I did not enact all I knew about him. One evening when I went to fetch ice from the pantry of the apartment for the depleted drinks of bootleg liquor at the table, he followed me and, with careful, rapid looks over his shoulder, asked me in a hurried whisper, dried by an excitement which I half understood and disliked, whether I would go with him the following weekend to Juárez, at the Mexican border three hundred miles to the south, where he went every six weeks "for sexing." Nobody else knew of this, but after all: a man had his needs: if I went with him people would think it just for the "sightsees," and in a way it would be, for he knew every place there was to see in Juárez, where "a bery good time" was to be had in any way one might enjoy. His rising inflection was like an ambiguous inquiry about my own tastes. Taking up my ice bucket, I thanked him and said I was too busy. He felt my disdain and drew himself up with a flare of pride, as if it had been I who had made an unseemly proposal. But I wondered if corruption was everywhere, and if it was a characteristic of the disease all about me.

My mother, lightly drawing conclusions from my performance as Count, said,

"What a little snob you are. Of *course* he is not a count, we have all decided that, but if he wants to be, what's the harm? Even Eleanor Saxby won't gossip about him. —Besides, he *looks* like one."

Sam joined us with the daily papers.

"Are you playing the animal game?" he asked.

"No, but let them do it," said my father. "I'm trying to get a view of the gambling den operated by my wife."

"All right," I said, "I am a cow who has been first to the beauty parlor, and then to Tiffany's. Who am I?"

"Mrs Saxby!" cried Sam.

"Correct. —Your turn."

"I am a tailored monkey who leans forward all the time to prove that he never committed mischief. Who am I?"

"Count!" exclaimed my father, confirming my dramatic art.

"You're all dreadful," said Lillian, "talking about your guests that way."

"I am an elegant bird," announced my mother, "and I turn my head this way and that because my brain is a little small for my hat."

"Dr Birch," answered Lillian brightly.

"No, no, someone else."

"Percy Sage," I said.

[87]

"I see," said my father. "Sam?"

"I am a little pony wearing a heather-colored cardigan and pearls."

"Too easy," said my mother. "Serena Sage."

"That's darling," said Lillian, touched by the word "little." Then she darkened ominously, like a prophetess, and said, "But they're troublemakers. I know their kind."

"Who?" asked my mother. "For heaven's sake."

"Those Sages. They always do the *wrong* thing. They never think anybody else knows the *right* thing."

"Why, Lillian. Whatever put those ideas into your head!"

Lillian, in her great soft bulk, gave a momentary impression of stern hardness, and said,

"They don't believe in God. Besides, they're rich, and they don't work."

"Now, Lillian," said my father, "we're never serious when we play the animal game. —I can finish this round. Here's one": and he gave us Lyle Pryor as "a plucked, hyperthyroid crane wearing large spectacles."

"Yes," said Lillian, "but how do I know you don't say things about *me* when *my* back is turned?"

And we all had to work for a few minutes to convince her that she was our treasure, our indispensable Lillian, who kept everything together for us.

"Oh, I don't know," she said with a heavy squirm, but so pleased that her eyes welled, which relieved my mother, for she now counted on Lillian's usefulness and good temper.

My mother amazed me with the strength with which she covered her fears. I had always considered her, if not frail, so delicate that she must be given every protection which my father and I could offer. But now I began to see that the prettily wondering, slightly abstracted air we had always known in her was a contrivance meant to make my father, and me as I grew older, feel bigger and stronger than we were, as guardians. Now she was the stronger one, and her playfulness, once like that of a kitten of many moods, was a form of power by which she kept our spirits up. Now, in any situation, she "reasoned" like my father of the old days, while he listlessly acceded. The power of decision had passed to her.

⚘

Privately instructed by the doctor, my mother was looking for a house to rent "for a year" where we could all live when my father would be allowed to leave Saint Anthony's. For fear of arousing hopes which might have to be deferred, she was not to speak of it yet. But in his daily visits to my father, Dr Birch, often nursing one eye with a curled forefinger to ease what seemed to be a chronic pain there, used the other eye to pierce my father's moods; and sometimes to stare at me as though to make a case out of me, too, which made me uneasily feel like one.

But he had just the mixture of sardonic humor and professional realism to distract my father from his periods of lengthy regrets, uncertainties. For someone who had been so affirmative as my father, these were new traits. Dr Birch dismissed them as integral parts of the disease itself.

"I am like the recovered drunkard who can help another to sober up: I've been there," he said in various ways and times. "This room won't be your world forever."

My father gave him back a Birch-like glare of ironic comedy, indicating that the room would cease to be his world when he was carried from it to the grave.

"No," said the doctor, "given a prolongation of what is now going on, which will depend on several factors, of which the psychological is highly important, you will make a more fortunate escape."

"How do you telescope time?" asked my father.

"Time is *not* being wasted, even though many patients think so. It is working for you. It is literally medicinal."

"Why do I feel—"

"Some mornings you wake feeling like cracked ice in sunlight; brilliant and cooling. Other days you can hardly open your eyes. Some mornings you feel like the cleverest man alive. Others, you wonder at your vacant head." My father smiled at having his feelings so exactly understood. "Sometimes in the afternoon, late, after your nap, you feel hot and angry, but it is only a rise in temperature. Some evenings you feel almost well enough to dress and go down to the Alvarado and meet people in the lobby and go outside and watch for the trains to go by. Often when you wake up at night, you feel you contain all the sorrows in the world, and nobly, perhaps, you decide to assume them for the relief of all suffering humanity. You are Christ on the cross, until, as soon as this notion becomes explicit, you have to laugh at yourself, and turn over cautiously, and define the act of falling asleep again as the ultimate pleasure and goal of all life."

My father stirred and laughed like a child in its bed. He nodded, nodded.

"Then I am not unique," he said.

"Not in all that. But don't forget the ways in which you *are* unique. There is a terrible democracy about a disease common to much of humanity. If you let it, it can slowly edge out of mind everything but itself. What you should now do—for you are recovering steadily if slowly—is begin to think about developing some sort of continuing interest in something productive, if still physically restricted. I think you might now consider what this is going to be, and you should be ready to take it up when I release you from the sanatorium. That day will come."

He turned to me.

"What are you doing these days, Richard?"

I said something about the patients' library, and the errands I did for my family.

"More."

"Well, I like to go rambling out to the river. It is still wild along most of its banks."

"Good. I think you should use this climate, too."

My father made an inquiring sound. The doctor said,

"He's rather run-down, I'd say. —What *are* you interested in?" he asked me. "You seem to spend much time alone."

My father answered for me.

"We think he's going into medicine. —Besides, he writes."

The doctor nodded ominously at me.

"I understand. I've heard it before. *Medicine is a splendid way to examine human nature, which is the writer's stock-in-trade*. Hey?"

There was a note of harsh sarcasm in this. It extended my silence. My father said with spirit,

"He knows what I wish for him. If he must choose otherwise, and if I am here to know it, he will have my confidence."

Dr Birch shrugged, lifting his great bony arms and settling them again, like an old eagle on a rock from which—the foot of my father's bed—he rose and declared,

"Yes, you see, one sees one's youth so often in others." This was mollifying, and he turned to me and added, "One of these days I want you to come round to see me. I want to look you over."

"Yes, sir."

"Why?" asked my father with anxiety. "Do you think there's something—"

"Nothing serious. Simply a generally good idea, in his case." He turned back to me. "Meantime, stay with your river as much as you can," and left.

"Odd," said my father. "I always thought him so direct, and now he turns out to be a laminated character. —I suppose there is no such thing as a tubercular without his finally accepted disappointments. Not," he added, grinding his jaws in his familiar amiable mockery, "that I have accepted any, just yet."

We had bought a Ford touring car, black, like all the Fords, in which Sam or I or Lillian (who learned to drive with the same reckless competence with which she attacked the typewriter) drove my mother on her errands and visits. For myself, they had given me a new bicycle, an Indian Flier, which gave me independence in my explorations of the city, the great empty plain of the mesa between town and mountain, and the Rio Grande. Lillian bought me a klaxon horn for my handlebars "for safety" and I demonstrated the sound for her—"oo-ah, oo-ah."

There were three parts to the town. The central part was built in a grid about the Santa Fe tracks, and in fact, the main street was called Central Avenue, which cut across the tracks at right angles. In its middle section, for several blocks, the main commerce of the town went on in shops, movie theaters, offices. Above, to the east, rose the residential town into the sand hills which led to the mesa, at whose edge the university marked the city limits. Ten miles away, in a grand arched profile, lay the Sandia Mountains, pale rocky brown by day, with blue clefts and inky cloud shadows over their many faces. To their south, another range, the Manzanos, dwindled away in fading blue ridges. At evening, the mountains were washed by a deep rose glow, and at night, during the full moons, they abided in a sort of silvery dark wall against the pale moonlit sky. The other end of town to the west reached from the twentieth century into the eighteenth, when Central Avenue arrived at the original settlement beside the Rio Grande.

There, the oldest houses were still made of the dried earthen bricks—adobes—which the Pueblo Indians and the Spanish-Mexican settlers both used for building. The streets were unpaved in Old Town. The original plaza still stood, with its church and convent at one corner, and old adobe houses with deep *portales* along their fronts casting cool shadows out of the great glaring light of the sky. Closer to the river, and reaching north and south along its banks, were small farms along the dirt road which paralleled the river course. Between the fields and the river were thick groves of cotton-wood trees and willows into which straggling paths led here and there to reach the riverbank.

I rode everywhere to see the town and to watch the people. As everyone discovered, there were three distinct orders of people—the Indians who came into town from their pueblos to sell their pottery and weavings; the Latin descendants of the first conquerors; and the Anglo-Americans, like us, who represented the third occupation of the land, and now dominated it, in all material ways.

Abstractly, I found myself apologetic for this domination, not on behalf of the Indians, who lived self-sufficiently in their unchanged ancient ways; but to the Mexicans, as everyone called those Ameri-cans whose ancestry was derived from the Latin Americas. Some Anglos used the term with condescension. Consequently, the Mexi-cans resented it, though they used it themselves, thinking of it in terms of their heritage instead of their position. The fact was, their position under the moneyed energy of the Anglos was subordinate in their own land, and in many cases, close to menial. They were laborers, servants, lesser employees in business and public service. Most of them spoke English with a lilting misplacement of accents, in their trials at joining the society of their employers.

"But," said Lyle when we were talking about the laminated so-ciety one evening, "it will be a long time before they will be allowed to join it."

"But why?" I asked. "They were here before us. They even have the very look of the land."

"True, true, kid, but it's all a matter of who has the power, meaning the money and the know-how. You know who. You, your father, me, the Anglo bankers, railroaders, doctors. And like all colonists, we bring our style of life with us, and we make it prevail over the old life we find here, and the two don't yet mix, or if they do at all, they mix on *our* terms."

"Sam says they resent us—he has read all he could get about the Southwest, and he says it goes way back to the Mexican War and the American conquest."

"Don't you feel it?"

"No, the Mexicans I run into are polite."

"Spoken like a true colonist. The natives know their place: how convenient: and they damn well better, y'know? —Isn't that the usual attitude?"

"I suppose it is."

"Well, let me suggest that you avoid getting caught alone in Old Town, or up in the sand hills, if there's a gang of Mexican kids around. You and your nice shiny red Indian Flier bike. —They like bikes, too."

"They won't bother me."

"Don't give them the chance."

"I don't feel hostile. Why should they?"

"You don't have any reason to. They do."

"But why?"

"Have you ever been an underdog in your own back yard? —See how you'd like it."

I heard newcomers talk of how outlandish the place seemed to them, with its grinding dust storms, its distance from everything that mattered elsewhere, its searing sunlight, the bad roads, the Spanish/Mexican language and its speakers; and I would be reminded of our first impressions of the desert where fate had brought us as a family.

But as the months went by, I felt a spell coming over me; and, in my mind, I claimed possession, like an explorer, of a whole empire where I spent all the free time I could. This was the east bank of the Rio Grande for a stretch of two or three miles where nobody lived and nothing was cultivated. Instead, a wonderful wilderness of cottonwood and willow groves cut me off from everything but the wide, shallow, brown stream. By bicycle, I went as far as I could along a certain broken path in the groves, and when the footway almost disappeared, I dismounted and chained my bike to a young cottonwood trunk and put the elastic cord with my key around my neck and went on toward the river on foot, thrusting away branches and changing the daylight branch by branch. For a hundred yards or so I was closed in by my woods; and then I came into a small clearing, like a green room, whose trees had been washed out by flood, so that only seedlings grew up against the older thickets. The fourth side of the room was open upon the river. The water flowed past only a foot or two below the cut sandy bank. The flow was hardly three feet deep, and it reached out into the riverbed for only fifteen feet or so. Then came a long, dry spit of pale, fine-grained silt. Beyond that was another, narrower trickle, and still farther, another long, dry island where a few willows clung by precarious roots. Where the water was not shaded, it reflected the sky in a cool bronze blue. The opposite bank of the river rose away in gravelly slopes which eventually reached a wide mesa, stretching away westward for miles until a black facing of centuries-dead lava rose abruptly. Far away beyond that cliff, the profiles of three extinct volcanoes rose and fell like a melody against the sky. Their old cold craters were edged with burned-out fire color above their tawny sides.

In my glade I was alone and lord of that immense sweep of light, heat, water, and vision. To the north in the searing heat of the desert afternoons, impossible continents of cloud towered—by a rude triangulation I made in the dry sand with a stick—to a height of seventy thousand feet. Against the intense blue sky they shone with white radiance broken by every imaginable sculpturesque form. Every dimension there was lordly; and when I threw off my clothes to idle in the warm, clinging, brown water—swimming as such was difficult in so shallow a stream—I felt I must possess the land by its river with my whole skin. There were hot muddy shallows in which to roll sensually, from which to rise and fall again into the river flow to be cleansed. There were hours to lie on the bleached dry islands and embrace the sky through the empty air, made sweet by the hot scent released from the cottonwoods—a scent which mingling with the rich rankness of the river mud brought a drowsiness under eternity filled with the faraway drone of insects and the tiny, crackling commerce of unseen woods creatures and birds. I heard and saw beavers, herons, high-sailing hawks with tawny undersides; and now and then, as far away as memory, came the occasional sound of a railroad engine's steam whistle, or when the wind was right, the musical chord of the sawmill's whistle, which brought to inner sight its tall stack and the white banner of smoke which it released against the blue mountain screen at the ends of the earth.

When done with the water and the sand for the afternoon, I would return to my encircling green and lie drying, while reading slowly the book which had been assigned in one of my classes in preparation for the following year. This was P. D. Ouspensky's *Tertium Organum*—a book much talked of at that time in the intellectual mode. Often I fell asleep over it in luxurious indifference.

※

"We have a house, my dear!" exclaimed my mother on an important morning at Saint Anthony's.

My father scowled.

"I know nothing of this," he said.

"No—the doctor wanted to be sure."

"So I did," said Dr Birch, appearing like a stage figure at that moment in the doorway. "You are pleased with it?" he asked my mother.

"Oh—it is so charming. So right for *here*." (But later when people praised the house, she would say, "Yes, but it's not *my own*.")

She described it. It was on the Rio Grande road a little north of town. A hacienda, really, set in wide fields of alfalfa belonging to neighboring farmers. It was an old house, one story high, made of adobe, with a front patio flanked by a living room and dining room and kitchen, and a rear patio enclosed by half a dozen bedrooms and a glassed-in sun porch which was like a long gallery, with tables, chairs, and bookcases. There was a little fountain in the second patio. The mechanical fittings were modern, but the original flavor of the Mexican style was carefully maintained. The interior walls were lime-washed with painted dadoes. Dr Birch nodded. Some floors were tiled in a terra-cotta from Mexico. The ceilings were held up by beams—*vigas*—each a single tree trunk left in its natural color stripped of bark. Navajo rugs and wall hangings were scattered here and there. Paintings by Taos and Santa Fe artists of immense thunderheads at sunset, vistas of mountains in the always mystical blue, adobe huts enlivened with strings of red chili peppers, Indian drummers—the art slang of the time—were on the living-room walls. From the road a hundred feet away you could not see much of the long, rambling house, but it was proclaimed by a wonderful grove of very old cottonwood trees towering almost a hundred feet, like a great bouquet, shedding faint bittersweet fragrance and bounteous shade like blessings over the house. Behind the house were thickets on an old dried course of the Rio Grande, and farther yet was the live river itself. No other houses were visible, though others were scattered farther along in the riverside groves.

"It is like a piece of the past!" exclaimed my mother, hoping with enthusiasm to stir my father's pleasure.

"But precisely that is what it is," said the doctor. "I know the place," and told what he knew.

It had been built in the mid-nineteenth century by an early Santa Fe Trail merchant importer of goods from the East and Europe. It had remained in his family for two generations, and then had been sold to later comers, and sold again. The latest owners, who now rented it out, had restored it to its original quality. The founder's family had many descendants, some of whom were Dr Birch's patients. Their name was Wenzel. Very well-off Mexicans.

"But that sounds German," muttered my father.

"Yes, but the first Wenzel married a Mexican lady. The *raza* absorbed the Teuton."

"Oh, you will love it, Dan," said my mother, taking his hand. "From the back patio, you can see the mountains through a lovely opening in the big trees. A lovely place to read, and rest, and get well!"

"When do I go?" asked my father.

"Whenever your new place is ready," said the doctor. "A few days, I gather. —Now, let's have a look at you," he added, politely nodding to my mother that she could leave the room now, and with a jerk of his head indicating that I should stay and observe examination techniques, for he soberly pursued the convention that, as I was to be a physician, the more I saw of practice the better.

The philosophy behind the move from Saint Anthony's to domestic surroundings was clear. The hospital atmosphere, necessarily suggestive of illness and reminders that death was never far away, would henceforth work against my father's cure, now that various clinical mileposts had been safely passed. He must no longer be confined by sanitary white walls and gleaming aluminum and enameled vessels and regimented hope. Freedom in his thoughts must come to prevail. The vague sounds from far down the spotless echoing halls and the nearer and more explicit sounds of suffering need no longer raise speculations in his mind. The signals of death when rapid steps went past his door accompanying the little creak of wheeled stretchers must no longer let him place his imagination at the center of these events.

But as the doctor went over him with the stethoscope, my father plainly had qualms.

"What is it?" asked the doctor.

My father wondered—intent as he was on swift recovery—whether his progress might be slower "at home," where professional care day-long would be missing.

"You will rapidly adjust to freedom," replied Dr Birch with his cavernous, sardonic grin. "You will now follow on your own the regimen I will prescribe for you in detail. I will see you there as often as necessary."

Still oddly reluctant to yield up the enclosing reassurances of Sister Mary Vincent and her shifts of nurses, my father said,

"But my shots?"

For he had to have a daily hypodermic injection of a clear fluid whose name I never learned.

Where he now sat on the foot of the bed, Dr Birch swung his crossed leg, which was so thin it looked like something whittled out of wooden slats hinged at the knee.

"Anyone can give them to you at home."

"I don't want to ask my wife—she has enough to bear."

"There are others."

"Not Miss O'Rourke. She is so modest she would faint if she had to pinch my bare flank and jab it."

"Others."

"That is not what Sam is for. He is already giving up much to be with me, without making a male nurse out of him."

The doctor looked at me.

"Why not Richard? I'll show him how."

I flinched visibly. My father scowled. Would I not do so little a thing for him?

"I'd bungle it every time," I said.

"Nonsense. Come here," said the doctor, for it was time for the daily shot. He signaled my father to turn on his side. He then took the hypodermic needle from its nest of sterile cotton and found the ampule in its white japanned box, filled the needle to the proper level, expelling air bubbles, and then said,

[99]

"Observe closely."

He took a thick pinch of flesh at my father's bared hip and with a darting throw set the needle in, and with slow, steady pressure emptied the contents into the pinched flesh. Whipping the bed-clothes back over my father, he asked,

"Did that hurt?"

My father shook his head.

"Very well. You see? The first time you do it, I'll be there to help and watch."

My father reached for my hand. He knew what troubled me. I could not bear the idea of giving him physical pain.

"Never mind, Doc. I promise you it won't hurt."

So it came to be that every day before lunch at the river house I gave him the injection; but I could never do it quite the same way every time. I never knew when I was going to hurt him—for I hurt him often, and try as he might, he could not always suppress a wince when the needle went in wrong. One day he said irritably,

"Don't try to be careful. That's what makes it hurt. And if it hurts, don't be upset. The point is, you are helping me, and I love you for it."

But I never became easy about this life-making duty, and I would sometimes see a grin on my father's face when after I had done my worst he would say, mocking his hope for my entire future,

"Thank you, Doctor."

※

The owners had named the house "Casa del Rio" and we kept the name. Newcomers took to the Latin style as joyfully as they did to gift shops full of Mexican importations. Once we were settled, the game evenings were resumed at Casa del Rio. Lyle said, "Here come the Inevitables," and once again on two evenings a week, when my father now watched until his bedtime, even occasionally taking a hand at poker, which was his only game, the snap of expertly dealt cards or the rattle of tiles and chips simulated merriment at the duty of killing time, as I priggishly thought.

The Sages sometimes came to dine. Their own house was farther down the river. Percy had built it when his cure indicated that he should remain in New Mexico, taking only a few brief trips to the East every year for his directors' meetings and Serena's shopping. They were amiable and detached, and though as Republican as they were Episcopalian, they had a sort of connoisseurship about my father, the Democratic Catholic politician from Upstate; and they seemed to share a never-spoken secret about how "second-rate"—one of Percy's words—the other guests were who gathered for the evenings. It was a secret which my father recognized and repudiated with humorous attentions to Eleanor and the others. Serena Sage would watch these with her plain, contented face, and in her wide smile, and her expensive dowdiness, made kindly excuses for him. Every time Mrs Saxby shouted, "Oh, my Gahn!" Serena would wince slightly, and look about for some object to point out as "pretteh."

When my father would leave those evenings early, there would be protests, but he always said he had "work to do." It was a fine joke, and they nodded, knowing that the point of it was rest, rest, this side of eternity.

But they were wrong. He always had a certain amount of reading he must do before going to sleep. The household knew that his work was pursuit of the health-bringing preoccupation which Dr Birch had advised my father to develop. During hours alone at Saint Anthony's, he had long thoughts about what this might be. He was happy when he decided that he must write a book on *Woodrow Wilson's Theory of Government*. He believed that no man since Jefferson had brought so rich an intellect to the idea of government as his hero, though he admired others for their human intuitions and—Lincoln—a sense of individual compassion for the anonymous citizen which in Lincoln's acts seemed to see the whole nation as one man, to be understood and honored in all degrees of need, suffering, and dignity.

Accordingly, during most mornings, while Sam was going over bulletins from Albany with my father, which was now permitted by Dr Birch, I went to the edge of the mesa where the university was, and spent hours in the library taking notes on Wilson from books and periodical files. These would later be copied on her typewriter by Lillian O'Rourke with a rattling virtuosity which made the profusion of cheap rings she wore dance with light. She had fine tremors of fulfillment in reflecting on my father's gifts—"Such a mind, all this information, he is a marvel."

Sam obtained books and other material from the state library at Albany and himself made the first rough references and classifications which my father would leaf through while his book slowly took form in his thought. He kept a color reproduction of Sir William Orpen's portrait of Wilson in a standing frame on his bedroom desk. The white margin on the picture showed a facsimile of President Wilson's signature, and I quickly learned to make a fair forgery of this, and took to signing my library notes with it, or with "Okeh, W.W."—the pedantic rationalization of "O.K." which Wilson had once given, declaring that it was an early American Indian locution (Choctaw) and thus a correct American usage. It was a proper undertaking, this book, since it forecast a long future for its realization; and a future was most of all what my father needed to believe in. He believed it would not be long before he would be ready to begin dictation of a first draft with, but only with, the approval of Dr Birch.

So the Wilson portfolio grew, and after going over the regular reports from Albany every morning with my father, Sam would bring out the material for the book and they would discuss the pattern which began to show. In the afternoon, after his nap, my father saw Lillian, dictated short replies to personal or private mail, and then spent the long twilight in the back patio, reading Joseph P. Tumulty, Colonel House, Champ Clark, Admiral Grayson, H. H. Kohlsaat, Walter Hines Page, Herbert Croly, Elihu Root, and others whose public life and personal contacts with President Wilson at various periods fed my father's imagination. He would mark the margins, Sam would evaluate the markings for extracts, and Lillian would transfer those approved to working cards.

The systematic procedure soon became a vital factor in my father's pursuit of his health, as the doctor had expected. When it was interrupted for any reason my father fretted: a few days of unusual fatigue, requiring total rest; or a diversion on Sam's part when his fiancée, Joanna Winthrop, came for a brief visit to see with her own eyes what so fascinated Sam in the outlandish Southwest that he chose it above attendance upon her at home; or—most disturbing—a series of bulletins from Sam's "spies" at Albany which made my father scowl over his enforced absence from his duties in the state senate.

※

For Sam received, first, hints of suspicion, then, confidential statements of fact that Governor Pelzer was running all too true to form. Certain metal and coal-mining interests, along with Great Lakes shipping lines, were building up a large secret fund for the governor's personal fortune, in return for his sponsorship of legislation which would show leniency to those businesses in regard to taxes, franchises, and raised transportation rates. The information about all this was not yet public, and Pelzer's advisers were working hard to keep it from ever coming out. Some, in fact, had urged him to return the money (by now in the hundreds of thousands of dollars) before the legislature would be acting on new bills already introduced to gain the favored ends. There had been veiled hints in the *Albany Times-Union* which meant something to those who knew how to read them.

What could the lieutenant-governor do, so far away, so unwell, so devoted to nothing but recovery until he could return in full strength to Albany, and there, in person, carry on the struggle for integrity?

He and Sam spent hours discussing alternative actions, and in the end, Dr Birch had to be invited into the matter. How far should my father try to enter into the affair to save the New York State administration from scandal, and the people of the state from being legally robbed?

The doctor wasted no time.

"The answer is simple," he said on that morning in the patio, "if you intend to recover completely, you must not interrupt your present regimen. You must concern yourself with nothing but what is right here." He gestured to the half-shaded patio, the house, the desert, the mountains beyond, the world of light above.

"But this matter is gathering force all the time, like an infection," protested my father.

"So will yours, if you provoke it."

"But *when,* then, do you think I might count on—"

Going back to stay: it was a question which no one had yet asked. Birch was silent for several long thoughts while my father, Sam, and I all watched that saturnine hawk's face for a hint of a reply. Finally,

"Has any limit been fixed to your leave of absence?"

"No. It is left to me, so far. I am on leave—without pay, at my request. *But I am still in office.* One feels responsible, you see."

Another long silence. Then,

"Nobody can predict with accuracy. One always considers the possibility that wisdom might require the patient to spend the rest of his life in some such place as this."

"Is that the case with me?"

"No certainty. One watches the course of a given case and finally one comes to a decision."

"Then I must be thinking along the lines that possibly I may have to decide on permanent exile?"

"You should, without despair, consider it a possibility. Not a foregone conclusion."

"Percy Sage," declared my father in a bitter voice, while an image of that agreeable idler roved between us all.

"There are others," remarked Dr Birch dryly, "who have led useful lives in this most beautiful of landscapes."

"Oh, yes, yes, forgive me," said my father hastily. "I meant nothing personal!"

"This is, quite understandably, a disease more self-centered than most," said Dr Birch with an ironic note of forgiveness.

"I've been wondering," said my father. "Is it possible that there exists a predisposition to it which can be detected early and might help prevent it?"

"There are certain typical physiologies and temperaments, yes, which suggest a vulnerability."

Without looking at me, my father said,

"He seems healthy enough, but I know you've suggested giving my son a check-up. Is that what you had in mind?"

"I can hardly say so. But I share your concern for every possible precaution." He turned to me. "Come to my office at the hospital tomorrow at three, if you are not otherwise engaged?"

My father nodded at me.

"Very well, sir," I said, so angry that I left them.

❦

For the next few days, we were like a household of strangers, polite to each other, but unsuccessful in concealing our separate miseries. My father saw himself as if under life sentence, my mother was almost at the end of her good nature at the prevailing gloom, I was withdrawn into reproachful dignity at having had to endure Dr Birch's physical examination, whose results would be reported when the tests were all analyzed. Most trying of all, Sam was torn between his duty and concern for my father and his longing attempts at mollifying his fiancée. Joanna Winthrop was staying with us, and Sam had to spend more time with her than suited my father, though he granted the reason its emotional purpose.

Joanna did her best to show interest in all that went on, but this amounted to little more than a display of overeager good manners. She disapproved of us all, and therefore was overly pleasant in her use of the charm in which she had been drilled at the Mayhill School in Virginia and Wellesley College in Massachusetts. She would write little cheering notes to my father and send them to him by me in the mornings. Her writing looked like little square boxes all leaning to the left—a hand much favored by Mayhill girls, several of whom I had taken to dances at home.

"Dear Guv," she would write, "Golly-day, I am having the most *superb* time since I don't know when. How lucky you all are in this divine house and this absolutely *adorable* little town! I'll simply *loathe* leaving when I have to. I have a *frightfully* funny story for you at dinner tonight. Be well! Joanna."

Sam was in love with her even as he resented her patronizing and mannerly indulgence of the household. She was slender, tall, handsome rather than beautiful, very good with horses like all Mayhillies, and she spoke in a stylized drawl which put to shame the one we had always heard from Serena Sage. When she spoke, her head and neck moved in small not quite involuntary shifts, from side to side, from short to tall, like a bird with a long, exquisite, and expressive neck. She was taller than Sam. It was clear that she adored him, but so possessively that even in company, when speaking to someone else, she looked mostly at him, as though to keep their intimacy inviolate and privileged, shutting out those others present. His sparkling intelligence, his perfectly neat, symmetrical, strong, small body, his unassumed good manners coupled with his lighthearted but direct ironies, all fascinated her. She saw herself as the perfect career wife whose cool good sense included a willingness to snub unsuitable or useless beings, while bestowing favor for Sam's advantage where appropriate. How she longed to wrest him away from this house of the sick, this land of dust—for during her visit another great dust storm blew for three days, obscuring all vistas like dry fog, stinging the face if one ventured out of doors, and reducing my mother, a proud housekeeper, to misery at the hopeless task of keeping the dust out.

"Why don't you go home with Joanna when she goes?" I asked Sam one day in a low temper affected by the abrasive storm.

"Two reasons," he said without his usual excusing smile, which beguiled men and women alike. "She will wait. Secondly, I think your father worth anything anyone can do for him—assuming I am doing anything for him."

In this he was both real and ideal. My selfishness was pinned like a specimen to my self-image.

❧

"So it's off to the ranch, eh, kid?"

This was Lyle Pryor as he noisily shuffled the Chinese tiles between games. During the patio supper earlier when he sat beside my mother he learned that during the afternoon Dr M. Jamison Birch had reported on my examination and had made firm recommendations regarding me. The tests showed an old tubercular scar healed from my time of infancy, which signified nothing, as probably 90 percent of the population showed similar evidence of completely healed lesions. But I was looking "run-down." I was too thin for my age and height. Despite being tanned by the desert sunlight, I showed something about the eyes Dr Birch did not like the look of. I needed to be "built up." Physical labor was wanted, somewhere, away from this atmosphere of illness and fretful concern. Dr Birch told my mother he thought he had an ideal solution.

There was a prominent ranching family who had great land, and sheep and cattle holdings, in the western part of the state. He had seen to some of their medical problems for many years, and in fact had made ranching investments on the advice of the head of the family, Don Elizario Wenzel, who lived here in town. He would ask Don Eli (as he was often called, pronounced in the Spanish way) whether I might be given a few weeks' summer job at one of the Wenzel ranches. No favors asked. I was to be worked as hard as anyone else. It would build me up. I was too introspective. It would be infinitely good for my later life if I could base my interest, which was likely to be that of the study rather than that of the strenuous world, on a strong physique. Dr Birch spoke now both as a friend and a physician. He would, if my parents agreed, promptly speak to Don Eli about me and report the response.

Much of this dismayed my mother. Should she start to worry about me? She had been so attentive to my father that she hardly saw others around her except in a smilingly absent fashion. But a ranch. Did that mean cowboys and steers, dangerous creatures both, surely, for someone so young (I was over twenty) to live with?

No, at this season, it would most likely be a sheep ranch. Sheep were mild enough, in fact, safely stupid at worst. As for ranch hands, some were rough and some were gentle; and that was how the world ran, and it was not too early for me to discover this. Don Elizario Wenzel himself was an old man, shrewd, generous; too old for his age, thanks to certain earlier prodigalities, but still actively working on the ranch during such times as that coming soon—the season for dipping the sheep, which was hard work for everyone.

Dipping the sheep?

Yes, every season before time for shearing, the flocks had to be driven together and brought to the ranch headquarters to be disinfected of ticks and other parasites. Ranchers often took on extra help at such a time. Don Eli might well be able to use someone like me. It was a rough job, but a newcomer could learn his part of it soon enough. Every young American ought to have a taste of ranch life. It had played a great part in our history, our economy, and the health of those who had the privilege, don't you see. Look at Theodore Roosevelt. It made a man out of a weakling. And thus and so.

"I would miss him so," said my mother.

"Yes. Properly. But you have Mr Dickinson and Miss O'Rourke to help out. Richard won't be gone for more than a few weeks. He wants toughening. I saw it as soon as he arrived here."

"Yes," mused my mother, my father had often said as much to her.

"A man can be strong and sensitive, both," said Dr Birch.

At that moment of their talk, so I was told, I came home, and my mother said,

"Richard, darling, Dr Birch has something wildly interesting to tell you."

I then heard the whole proposal. In glum intuition I had been expecting some sort of doom, because of the conspiratorial emphasis on my medical examination, but not precisely what I now heard. Before I could make any comment, Dr Birch looked at his thick, heavily chained watch and said,

"I have only a few minutes. Let us discuss it with Daniel."

My father listened without interruption, but, in his familiar little gesture of rumination, set his jaw slightly sideways; then turned to me.

"Would you like to go?"

"Not really." I disliked having plans made for me. I reached for an excuse which would involve my father. "How am I to drop all the work on W.W.?"

It swiftly appeared that Sam could manage all that would be

wanted by the book project while I was away. What persuaded my
father in his concern that I must be physically fortified against his
own disease was the doctor's insistence on the benefits of toughening
hard work in the open country. He said,

"Yes, please, go ahead and ask your friend Mr Wenzel. I am sure
Richard will see the wisdom of this in the end."

Later, then, at supper, my mother, who always thought that in
order to keep conversation going almost anything should be talked
of, gave Lyle Pryor next to her an animated account of the family
plans for me.

"Make a man of you, buster," resumed Lyle with his whinnying
laugh. But he looked at me with an odd waft of sympathy across his
face, and despite my dislike of his slanging ways, I saw that he was
no fool, and that he covered both his thoughts and his feelings with
abrasive mannerisms—the only way he had of defying the mortality
approaching him on the evidence of X rays and other clinical tests.

The evening party adopted my topical importance. The Sages
were alert at once to the excellence of landed labor.

"Some of our best months," declared Serena, "have been spent on
one of the ranches—Percy's fathay was clever enough years ago to
buy those places in Montana, Wyoming, and northern Mexico.
When we're there, at any one of them, I become such a clever
housewife, cooking, baking, *all,* you see."

"Serena adores being Marie Antoinette," remarked her husband
with a stylized arching of his slim black eyebrows. "She even wears
an apron when she gives her orders to the head ranch cook."

Count was interested in something else.

"Wenzel," he mused. "I have met them. First I met him, then I
met her, after he married her." He gleamed through his thick pince-
nez, which reduced his pupils to a tiny focus, giving a signal that
scandal was to be had. Eleanor Saxby was greedily alerted by this
and cried,

"Tell us about them, you wicked thing, my Gahn, is there *any-*
thing you don't know about *any*body?"

Count shrank into himself with the effect of bowing to a compliment. Then, recovering, he told us all he knew about the Wenzels. In a small city—Albuquerque at that time had fifteen thousand people—there was no difficulty in learning anything you wanted to know, if you asked enough searching questions of barbers, waiters, barmen in speakeasies, newspaper people. Elizario Wenzel he described as a "rich peasant"—a statement which reassured some as to Count's own title.

"I will tell you something remarkable," he said. "This very house was built by Don Elizario's grandfather. Your house, where we are playing Mah-Chongg."

"Our house?" exclaimed my mother. "Of course: I thought I had heard the name before—Dr Birch mentioned it when we found the house."

My father, who had to keep early hours, indicated that he would let the last round of the game go by if Count would go on with his history.

※

Old Heinrich Wenzel—the ancestor—was the German merchant trader who had come to the Southwest over the Santa Fe Trail in the 1850s, like others of his countrymen. Some had settled at Santa Fe, others at Las Vegas, he at Albuquerque. In time, he prospered, bought great reaches of river bottom land from Mexican families, and built his hacienda. Originally it was about half its present size, but when he married a local Mexican girl—one of the Apodoca family—his household grew as children were born and rooms and servants were needed, and he then added the rear section with its patio. His youngest son, Elfego Wenzel—for as the whole tribe assumed the Mexican style, the German flavor of the founder disappeared except for the surname—married a Margarita Montoya, whose father was a sheep rancher with big properties in the west toward Arizona, where great peril from Apache raiders continued for decades. Their oldest son was our man, Don Elizario Wenzel. When his time came, he married a daughter of one of the Basque sheep-ranching families near Vrain, New Mexico, and so more sheep-raising country was added to the already considerable Wenzel holdings. The wife of Elizario, Rosario Ybarra, bore him two sons, Lorenzo and José, and two others who died in infancy. Two still lived. Each operated one of the ranches, while Old Don Elizario managed the whole empire—a holding of some hundreds of thousands of acres. When he was fifty-eight years old, his wife Rosario died. Count was already in town at the time, and he would see the lonely old man, heavy in the middle, who walked like a cinnamon bear in the mountains, looking for something he could not name. He would drift into the Elks Club at Sixth and Gold Streets to drink an illegal bottle of corn whiskey with anyone who would talk to him. People paid him respect because he was well-known, and rich, and politically influential. But when his back was turned, the Anglos made fun of him—so simple, so old, and a Mexican, with all that money.

"He spends money like a peasant," said Count, "throwing it around to show that he was always some*body*," and Percy Sage nodded in recognition of his truth that some people simply ought not to be rich.

And then, last year, said Count, the old fool astonished everyone by marrying again, at sixty-five.

"You see?" trumpeted Eleanor Saxby at having her general view confirmed—that sex would have its way regardless. She rolled her wide-open brown eyes and flared her nostrils, which always looked as though they took more breath than she could use in her great chest cavity. "Who was the bride?"

"Ah." Count now had his moment. He removed his pince-nez, polished them with maddening delay, and smiled provocatively.

Then in a wide arc of gesture replacing them on this thin nose, he said,

"She is the, but *the* most beautiful girl—"

"Girl! But he was sixty-five!"

"—girl in the world. She is eighteen years old, and now she is Señora Elizario Wenzel and has all *that* money and fifty milliard sheep, and sousands of *square* miles, and an old man, and that's all."

"But why haven't we ever met her? Or him? Or seen anything of them?"

"I'll tell you," said Lyle Pryor harshly. "Because she is a spic, and he is an old Mexican with a German name who goes around without a collar on his shirt and his collar button showing, and a sad look on his old face, with a walrus mustache, and all the money in the world wouldn't do them any good at getting in with people like you, y'know? and the rest like you, because they're Mexicans, and we're Americans, y'know?"

"Oh, Lyle, how unpleasantlay you put it," murmured Serena.

"But it's the fact, and you know it. Here's their land, and we came and took it, and made second-class citizens out of them. They hurt every day because of it, and we take it for granted that we are simply superior."

"But we *are*," said Percy Sage. "After all, education, and where-withal, and a certain sophistication, and manners really ought to go together, don't you think?"

They were both touching on facts, though one was sourly sympathetic and the other frivolously snobbish.

"How do you know so much about them?" Eleanor asked Count.

"*Sí, sí,* I have *a* lot of ways," replied Count archly, and I said to myself, "Here? as well as in Juárez?"

My father sat listening and turning from one to the other, like a judge weighing evidence.

"Why do you suppose she ever mahrried him?" wondered Serena.

"I know why," said Count.

"Yes?"

"She was from poor people, she wanted position more than any-thing, she knew she deserved to be with all the other girls in society, she thought the money would make the difference. —The wedding present he gave her was that house on Copper Avenue, you know? the one with the tiled tower, and the conservatory, the slate roof, three stories high, the biggest house in town that was the house of the old mining engineer millionaire Macdonald, who came here before 1900? *The* grand house. Concha was going to be *the* grand lady. Everybody was going to come to call on her and leave cards, and invitations, for Mrs Wenzel, eh? Nobody came."

"But what does she *do?*" demanded Mrs Saxby.

"But nothing. She rides around all day in the big Cadillac he gave her."

Now I knew. I had seen her. Count was right—her beauty, at eighteen, was something you could see from far away. In her bright-yellow touring car, with the top down, she was one of the familiar sights of town. She was usually alone, or if anyone sat beside her as she drove, it was likely to be one of her small nieces or nephews. Nobody ever saw her parents. They were poor, and though Don Elizario had bought them a new brick house far away from their old adobe riverside hut, with its animal yard, and the wrecked tonneau of a Model T Ford out front, and half-dressed grandchil-dren and loose chickens and somnolent dogs and foraging cats ob-scurely aimless below the cottonwoods, they could not take up their daughter's new life. They stayed home in a sort of exile in their small modern house on the uplands, where Concha went to see them daily during her ceaseless roving by motor. All she could have of the new life she had thought so desirable was the ability to move around and see from the outside what was going on everywhere in town. She was caught halfway between the ancestral ways and the newly imposed ways of the invader. She seemed never to know that by her constant visibility in her lumbering yellow car, which she drove sulkily, she had made of herself a kind of personage—exclusive and virtuous—in that small, intimate, isolated city, which, with its Indian, Spanish, Mexican, and American traditions, was only a stopping place on the great transcontinental railroad where passengers were fed in the Harvey House and the mighty Mallet 2-4-2 engines were refueled and watered, and the Pullman car windows were sponged clear of their desert dust.

Her face was a perfect oval. Black with blue highlights, her hair was pulled smoothly back and fixed by combs. Her eyebrows were black, and almost met above her exquisite small nose, and her lips had the curves of perfectly carved scrolls. It was her eyes which brought all these features together in a splendor of loveliness which was visible at a distance as though in a theater. Her eyes were darkly and luxuriantly lashed, around their pupils of lilac gray. It was the unexpected contrast between her palish eyes and her dark coloring of hair and her dark creamy skin which made her beauty so startling. She had what I later thought of as a theater of the eyes—there were shadows and brilliances, hazy starings, and sudden flares of interest and excitement which revived old desires out of their earlier lives in those who saw her for the first time. When I was younger I had been taken to see great actresses who in their world glory would come to Dorchester on tour; and in their artifices of personality enhanced by every theatrical aid, they conveyed across hushed dark spaces the inner life of the characters they assumed, while retaining boldly their own surface beauty as almost a thing apart. Like everyone, I was their self-forgetful subject. I thought that if Concha only had talent, instead of the puzzled innocence which I soon came to know, she might become a great actress herself. The spirit within her was unquiet, questing after something she could not define.

Meanwhile, her theater was the town, or whichever of the ranches she went to with her old husband when seasonal work called him. But wherever she was, she was the most lonely person I ever saw.

She lived only on glimpses of the complacent life which was denied her by the local immigrants and no man could come near her for the watchfulness and the jealousy of Don Elizario.

"Of course," said Percy Sage, "now I remember. I have seen them both—I have seen him at the Sandia State Bank, they say he owns almost half of the shares; and I have seen her out in her car, but I never knew who she was. How would I? But she even drives down our river road now and then. I wonder if she knows this was her grandfather-in-law's house?"

"She wouldn't like it, y'know?" said Lyle. "It is the most beautiful house in this valley, but she wants brick, and stained glass, and that tile turret and that cement carriage block that says 'Macdonald,' y'know? with the cast-iron little nigger groom and his iron ring for the reins? Yes: she ought to have a victoria carriage in Mexico City, and a coachman on the box, and she ought to be riding around the Alameda there every afternoon, with *caballeros* beside her on their horses, scowling bloody murder at each other, because of her, so beautiful, and so disdainful, eh?"

"What she needs," declared Eleanor Saxby, "is a good, hearty love affair, *all the way,* in spite of that old man." She rolled her large brown eyes. Lyle called her the Wife of Bath. She went right on. "I tell you something: she's going to have it, too, sooner than anyone thinks."

Saying this, she smiled conspiratorially at Sam and Joanna, as if to nudge them with her understanding—mistaken as it was—that, unknown to everybody but herself, they were lovers.

Joanna with her bird-like stretchings became erect at this, and with fastidious lifts and turns of her tall, lovely neck, said to my mother,

"I hate to leave all this fascinating information, but something has given me a blinding headache, and if you don't mind—" She stood up.

[116]

Mrs Saxby answered for my mother.

"Sure enough. It's the altitude, of course—they blame everything out here on the altitude and the freight rates."

At this everyone laughed in reassured recognition. It was comfortable to have access to any local mythology, so long as enough people believed in it.

Sam took Joanna to the far wing of the house, where her bedroom was. I followed to say good night, and before they were aware of me, I heard Joanna say,

"What perfectly terrible people. —Oh, Richard. Hell-a-o. *Good night.*"

※

Two days afterward, obedient to a telephone call from Dr Birch, I went to meet Don Elizario Wenzel and his wife at their house on Copper Avenue to arrange my job at the sheep ranch beyond Magdalena in western New Mexico.

The front door was set into a corner of the house under an overhang which rose to a pointed turret of oxidized copper and blue tile. The upper half of the door consisted of a heavy mosaic of cut and faceted glass of many colors, depicting a peacock with its feathers all spread.

I was admitted by a housemaid in black with white cap and apron—a young Anglo girl who held out a silver salver and asked for my card. I had none, and told her my name. She said, "Please wait," and disappeared down a long, dim hall heavily laid with Oriental rugs. Nobody else in town carried on with such airs. I saw a little silver dish on the hall table which held several calling cards. I glanced at them. Of varying size, they bore only the names of the Wenzels. They were bait for other cards, which they had never attracted. In a moment the maid returned and brought me to the living room, which opened into a large glass conservatory filled with heavy green plants.

Old Don Elizario, in a black coat, with a necktie, and loose gray trousers, came forward to meet me. His courtesy was instinctive. He had a stubble of beard, his white hair was awry, his hands were horned with the color and roughness of hard work. His drooping gray mustache hid his mouth, but his cheeks rose in a smile and his dark eyes smiled amid their heavy wrinkles as he said, in a Mexican accent,

"Come in, come in, welcome, you are the friend of my friend the doctor."

We shook hands.

He led me to a sofa draped with Spanish shawls, in the center of which sat his wife, Concha. She raised her hand languidly, but her state of mind, with no change of expression, betrayed itself through her eyes. They seemed to ray with light. In a plain silk dress, she was being grand for my benefit and, without speaking, waved me to a heavy, square armchair of bright-blue cut plush. As I sat down, the maid came with a tea tray and set it before Concha on a low brass table inlaid with bits of ivory and colored glass. Her husband watched her with pride as she poured tea into china cups, each of which was nestled into a sort of gold filigree cage with a handle. The maid handed around the cups and passed a dish of macaroons and then at a nod from her mistress withdrew.

Silence fell. Don Eli wrinkled his eyes almost shut, the better to see me. He inspected me thoroughly and frankly. Concha drank her tea with delicate movements, but when I saw her saucer tremble slightly, it was plain that she was undergoing a private ordeal. I looked about me at vases of peacock feathers, stands of cattails— *tules*—from the river, paintings bought for their frames. The silence had to be broken. I said,

"What a fine place you have."

Don Elizario waved his hand dismissively as if to say, "Why not?", but Concha came alive for the first time, and with a smile asked,

"You like it?"

"Oh, yes."

"She did it all herself," said her husband, transferring his heavy gaze from me to her.

Having made our first sounds, now we could talk. Concha ceased her trembling. Don Elizario was not discouraged by what he saw of me. The work at the Magdalena ranch, which was called the WZL after the brand which for two generations had marked the ranch animals with letters of the family name, would begin in about ten days' time. He would have a month's work for me. I must go by train to Socorro on a certain day, and there change to the freight train with one coach which went west to Magdalena. There I was to wait to be picked up by the ranch foreman, who would be coming to town for supplies and mail. Someone else employed for temporary work would also be waiting. We would be driven forty-two miles farther west to the ranch headquarters and the work would begin the next day, when the sheep would all be gathered from the pastures and from the Wenzel ranch farther to the south. Had I ever been on a ranch? I would not need much in the way of clothing. Did I read? I should bring a book, as there were none at the WZL ranch. There was a small bunkhouse where I would sleep. Another young hand would probably have the other bunk in it. Most of the ranch hands were older men, some from Mexico for temporary work, others from the distant Wenzel ranches. They would live in the larger bunkhouse near the corral. The main house was occupied by Mrs Wenzel and himself.

"It is a good life. A good life," he said, in his clouded old voice, and through him spoke the oldest of man's work. He had dignity and the dormant power of confidence in his wealth, his position, and his heritage. I thought he liked me on sight, but found me a somewhat comic creature, in my youth, my alien style; and that, without avowing it, he would if necessary keep a protective eye on me if I should meet with any trouble at the WZL.

"It is hard work, hard work," he remarked with satisfaction. "Have you got the muscle?"

He lunged heavily out of his chair and came to feel my biceps. With a slow, subdued laugh, "Not much now, eh, but more after!"

"Oh, Don Eli," exclaimed Concha in reproof of such intimacy, preening herself to show detachment from it. Her voice had a low flute-like tone which made me think of how nuns sounded—obedient to decorum and deprecatory of the body.

Somewhere in the ornate, stifling house a telephone bell rang. The maid came to say that Mr Wenzel was wanted. He excused himself, and as he went, he pulled off his black coat and the necktie he must have been instructed to wear for the social occasion, and he disappeared. Concha let him go in silence while she eyed me to see what I thought of him; of her; of their marriage; of their race. I looked at her with clear admiration.

"This is your first time in New Mexico?" she finally asked. "Will you take more tea?"

"Yes. No, thank you. I'll tell you something I think about it."

"Yes"—with a hint of suspicious alarm.

"I hated it to begin with. Now I am in love with it."

"I am glad. Will you like the ranch, though?"

"Why not?"

"Oh, you're so different."

"Yes, I will like it." I gave her a flattering look, at which she scowled and raised her head. "It is very kind of your husband to take me on faith."

Did I mean it? She lowered her head, keeping her eyes on me.

"Such an important rancher," I continued. "He can't take risks with ignorant strangers."

"You know he is important?"

"Certainly. Everybody has told me. He is one of the great men of the whole state. They all say that."

"They do? —Yes, he is, I know it." She added sharply, "He is a very kind man," as if to justify her marriage.

"I can see that. I feel very lucky."

It was a long telephone call. We could hear Don Eli's voice but not his words, shouting far away as though to make his voice carry across the implausible wire. Concha asked,

"How is your father?"

Dr Birch had given them our history, then.

"We think he is better."

"He is a governor?" —*Was this a governor's son who sat in her parlor?*

"No—not quite." I explained. She did not seem unduly disappointed.

Suddenly a strange sound came from somewhere in the green undersea light of the conservatory, whose glass doors were open into the room. It began with a low, ominous ruffle, and then, in a series of shrieks leaping wildly free of the proper pitch, but unmistakable in what it meant to declare, a voice sang, amidst the ferns and the vines of *copa de oro*, "O-h-h-h-h, the sun shines BRIGHT on my-old-Kentucky HOME!"

At my astonishment, Concha burst into laughter, putting her hands to her mouth like a child in an effort at polite concealment which failed.

"What in the world—" I said.

Suddenly she was a girl instead of a stiff impersonation of her idea of a grand lady. Still laughing, she rose, took my hand, and pulled me to the glass doors and pointed. There in its polished hoop was a great green parrot, hanging upside down by one claw, and giving us one eye which blinked lightning fast its granulated lid as though to invite an opinion of its performance.

From that moment Concha Wenzel and I were friends, at ease with each other in our years, and without pretense.

I soon made a move to go, but she detained me.

"You will say goodbye to my husband?"

I sat down again and we talked of her yellow motorcar; the heat which was already on us in early summer; the mountains which I would see west of the WZL ranch; how the nuns treated us while we were attached to the hospital.

"My friends are nuns," she said, and looked around idly as if to see what was detaining her husband, for the remote yelling had ended, but he did not return. She was afraid I would leave. She was lonely. She felt obliged to entertain. Her eye caught a pile of albums on a wicker table in the bay window which was cloudy with two layers of heavy lace. She could now entertain me.

"Let me show you."

She brought the albums to the sofa and seated me beside her. She was drenched with a strong perfume.

"What are these?"

They were mementos of her days as a pupil in the local convent academy of Saint Vincent, which she had attended for three years. It was conducted by the Sisters of Loretto, who had taught her how to be a lady of polite accomplishments.

"They know everything," she said.

She demonstrated. How to pour tea, had I noticed? How to sit down like a lady, first leaning forward, then placing one foot slightly to the rear, the other a little advanced, the hands upon the front of the skirt to hold it modestly in place, and then with a graceful and slow bending of both knees held together, to settle upon her cushions without suddenness or a rush of air. More: in addition to reading, writing, arithmetic, cooking, manners, and piety, they had instructed her in embroidery, piano, working designs with colored yarn on heavy paper, "Italian" painting (madonnas with distant landscapes), walking properly, and, best of all, living pictures.

"What are living pictures?"

She patted the albums.

"I can show you."

Every year at commencement, the academy exercises included "living pictures" directed by the sisters and enacted by the elect of the year's graduates. Concha opened the first of the albums, and there she was, in tinted photographs, portraying some of the nuns' favorite subjects. She was heavily made up as if for theater, which masked her own beauty. In the first picture she appeared in nun's robes, with a full-sized harp leaning upon her shoulder. Her hands were daintily spread upon the strings and her eyes were cast aloft to heaven. To see what I thought, she looked sideways at me, leaning close so that a strand or two of her shining black hair tingled against my ear.

"Saint Cecilia," she explained. "Patron saint of music."

"Beautiful."

She turned the stiff cardboard pages. There were many pictures from different angles of each pose. Now she was Queen Isabella of Spain, in a pearl crown, with a high-standing lace collar, in full robe edged with cotton ermine. She held an exposed Rand McNally map of the United States in one hand, and with the other she extended a sword toward an imaginary Columbus kneeling at her feet. A great queen, her head was held haughtily high, even as her imperious gaze was cast down toward him whom she commanded to find the New World. The gallery continued.

"Spanish Dancer," she announced, and showed herself in high comb and mantilla, with one arm high in front, the other low behind, her hands clutching castanets, her red bodice high and tight, her flaring yellow skirt, her little feet set together in purple slippers, an expression of defiant provocation on her face.

There followed "The Shepherd Girl," "The Madonna and Child (a female doll whose golden ringlets were not quite concealed by a pale-blue baby blanket), and finally, "The Bride of Christ," all in white lace, with white prayer book, rosary, gloves, and veil and with downcast eyes whose dark eyelashes on her dusky cheek called for kisses, all depicting the image of a novice about to take the nun's lifetime vows.

"I almost became a nun," she said. "The sisters said I had a real vocation."

"Why didn't you?"

Shrug.

"He did not want me to."

"Who?"

She made a silent, very Mexican, gesture, of her chin across her shoulder, indicating the far part of the house where Don Elizario must still be.

"Oh. —Did they ask him?"

"Yes. So did I. They understood."

"Understood?"

Well: it seemed that when she was thirteen years old, Don Elizario, recently widowed, saw her one day when he came to hire her father for some small spell of work. He was struck by the already special beauty of the child, and seeing her again on any pretext, he proposed to her father that she be placed in Saint Vincent's Academy to receive a proper education. Don Eli would pay the tuition. The family were doubtful, but Don Eli was a powerful man. He prevailed. He saw her through her years at the convent. She became an interest greater to him than his absorbing affairs with sheep and cattle and banks. He made two conditions with Concha's father— one was that she was to be told that the nuns had offered the family a scholarship for her with no mention of where the money came from; the other was that when she was graduated she would be given to Don Eli in marriage. She was doubtful when the time came for the second condition to be met. All of this I later heard or deduced for myself. I could reconstruct the reasons, and also the persuasions which overcame her. He was a kind old man, but oh, that tobacco-stained mustache, that heavy belly, that old black coat smelling of sour tobacco. She and her father had a fierce quarrel, during which the secret of the first condition was betrayed. She owed all her years of learning to him, then? He was rich enough for that? Her father told her how much richer. She would be as rich as any of those Americanos in town. Her eyes were opened to opportunity. In the academy she had been condescended to by the Anglo pupils. For years she had seen their world and been denied it. Only the nuns were continually kind to her. If she married the old man, she would be in a position to buy that other world. She went to the altar with him in the old Jesuit church of San Felipe de Neri in Old Town, acquired her splendid house, and settled down to await her social success, which never came.

She remained a perfectly proper convent girl, still longing for what everyone else believed in aside from God. She said, in a mixture of ruefulness and anger,

"I told my husband, I said, 'I'm go'g to have that house, then they'll come.'"

It was time for me to leave, having nothing to say to comfort her. Feeling me move in advance, she reached for more albums—"my wedding pictures"—but she did not take them up, for her husband returned, walking heavily but softly on the thick rugs. He looked severely under drooping brows at me, as I stood up and away from Concha on the couch. Why had I been so close to her? With weary dignity she waved her hand at the albums in explanation. He nodded and slowly lost his suspicion. But he had seen enough of me, and so, he thought, had she. He put out his hand to shake mine in dismissal. His handshake, like that of most Mexicans, was soft and loose. He saw me to the peacock door, which from the inside was dazzling. As I walked off, I glanced back, and now Concha stood with her husband watching me go. In a remarkable illusion, the tiny space of air about her eyes sent forth a hazy light which conveyed the sense of her deep and confused emotions, reaching to me like a message from a theater stage. "Such puzzled virtue," I thought. "Such longing beauty."

When next the evening crowd of the Inevitables came for their game, Eleanor Saxby set herself to inhale whatever information she could force from me, saying,

"They tell me you have been to the Wenzels'?"

"You h'have been in that house?" asked the Count of Alarcante, with a face stricken open as though I had unbelievably beaten him in a race.

"I am sure it must be entirely Grand Rapids throughout," murmured Serena Sage. "My deal, I think, dawling."

Her husband gave over the cards, saying,

"Nao, more probably pure Juárez."

Count cringed in suspicion at this.

"You h'have been to Juárez?" he said, wondering if anyone but myself knew about his disappearances there for sexing.

"Once. It was enough for a lifetime."

"No, but tell me," demanded Mrs Saxby. "You haven't told me!" I heard myself defensively describing the Wenzels.

"Well, first of all, it is what they want and what they think is beautiful, and as far as they are concerned, that is enough. It does not concern anybody else."

"Are you a young prig, dawling?" asked Serena.

"Better than a young snob," I replied.

"Then you *are,*" she said in an amused drawl and leaned to pat my cheek.

"Oh! you're impossible," exclaimed Mrs Saxby. "What we want to hear is what it looks like, and how they are together—that child, and that scruffy old man."

"She is the most beautiful girl I have ever seen," I stated without emphasis.

"Yaa," jeered Lyle, "you'd better watch youself, buster."

The knowingness all around me seemed like prurience. I said, now with feeling,

"He is formal, she is respectful. They belong to a world of manners we know nothing about. I do not speculate."

"No, but tell me," persisted Eleanor Saxby, "what *do* you think? Do you think they really—? I mean, they *are* man and wife, after all. But can you imagine—?"

I was outraged. But that was decades ago; and until very late in this chronicle I wondered about such matters, never without a qualm of chagrin mixed with an ironic admission that so the world ran, in its curiosities and conclusions about private lives—probably more often untrue than true. That very evening, they all looked at me (except my mother, who disliked intrusions behind the face of things) and they hoped to read the Wenzel history behind my face. There was something to tell—the ardent unhappiness of Concha, the possessive and suspicious pride of Don Elizario; but I did not tell of it, even by significant evasions.

"Of course I have seen her now and then at the movies," sighed Eleanor, having to fall back only on what she herself knew. "She always sits as far down front as she can, just as if she wished she could jump up on the screen, actually, my dear. Sometimes after I have seen the whole feature, and she has too, and I am leaving, my Gahn, she doesn't get up to go. She wants to see it all again."

There were two motion picture theaters on Central Avenue, a couple of blocks apart. They were shaped like large shoe boxes, with nothing of the gilded and draperied opulence of the great picture theaters in the big cities—those palaces of the people where popular dreams were enacted for them amidst every elaboration of plaster splendor. We had no huge Wurlitzer organs which rose on electric platforms into amber spotlights, or symphonic orchestras in the pit with glamorously advertised conductors who led grand overtures before the film and accompanied parts of it until the organist would take over. On Central Avenue, our movie accompanist to the silent films was a single operator who presided at an upright player piano which went automatically through its paper rolls of music selected for general suitability to the theme of the picture—love, or horror, or fast-riding adventure. The operator augmented the automatic music by working a wonderful set of percussive effects—drum and cymbal, rattles and bells, gun shots and train whistles, each set going by a pull on a rope with a wooden handle for which the player would reach when the screen action called for it. These added some old excitement to the mechanical pictures—live human play of the saltimbanque reaching as far back as the history of the theater. When I went to the picture shows, I was as much fascinated by the percussionist at the player piano and the rack above from which dangled the pull cords as I was by the aching and overrapid motions of the chalk-white and stark black figures filling the grainy screen with their stock gestures—not to forget the worded subtitles which gave us dialogue or pressed home meaning. It was a transporting experience; and when Eleanor Saxby saw Concha coming out of the movie matinees now and then, I could imagine the drained look on the girl's longing, beautiful face, and how painful it must be for her to stagger back to life after hours in the fulfilling if untouchable dreams in the humble darkness beyond dimension. Who was she, of those whom she had been with for that hour or so in the dark—Louise Glaum? Clara Kimball Young? Mary Miles Minter? Bessie Barriscale? selves all too quickly banished by the pitiless reality of the New Mexico sunlight and the hot sidewalks of Central Avenue.

Count asked peeringly,

"Did she wamp you?"

(For vamp was then both noun and verb born of the movies: the fatal woman with rings of black around her eyes who destroyed men in the act of maddening them.)

"Well, I know one thing," remarked Eleanor, "the old fool would be a fool to leave those two alone together. —*Did* he leave you alone together?"

I pretended absorption in my cards and she gave a rasping laugh which ended in a coughing spell. Count mistook my diffidence.

"*¿Usted es virgen?*" he asked with his head tilted at what he thought a beguiling angle.

"Oh, come on, Count, leave the kid alone," said Lyle roughly. His intervention was a surprise.

Mrs Saxby leaned to give me a probing look, and, satisfied, settled back in her chair and declared,

"No, I don't think he is."

Count shrugged in guilt, as though to ask me for absolution, which must be in my power to give, as, perhaps, it was, considering his emotional addiction, and my youth and remoteness. Something in his plea—monkey-like in its self-absorbed appeal—gave me compunction; and I smiled at him on general principles. At once he took this for encouragement; raised his eyebrows at me; breathed happily and became arch, cringing toward me in bodily flattery; and then, in haste, added Eleanor and Serena, as women, to his homage.

My father glanced at the clock, and stood up.

"Bedtime," he announced. "You can cash in my chips."

Percy Sage flushed darkly under the unnatural health of his heavy tan.

"I've barely begun to reap my just rewards," he said irritably, looking at his depleted pile of chips. Like many rich men he was mindful of the pennies. "Don't you think you might give me just another half hour?"

"Good night," said my father genially, as though Percy had said nothing, and made his way to his bedroom. Bad feeling, gathering all evening, openly fell upon the rest as they prepared to leave. How sensitive those half-people were to each other. What a maimed society it was. Their disease had forced them back to the self-regard of children. Every frustration, however trivial, was magnified. I would soon be going away. My departure for the first time looked to me like deliverance and I exulted privately like a young pharisee, for I was not as they; and I remember thinking how this was treason, and how pleased, a spiritual criminal, I was with it.

⁂

"Here," said my father, handing me an open book, "read me the paragraph I have marked."

We were working in the patio on the Woodrow Wilson material. I began to read while my father listened with his eyes closed under the shadow of his visored cap.

Here muster, not the forces of party, but the forces of humanity. Men's hearts wait upon us; men's lives hang in the balance; men's hopes call upon us to say what we will do. Who shall live up to the great trust? Who dares fail to try? I summon all honest men, all patriotic, all forward-looking men, to my side. . . .

It was a message from Wilson's first inaugural address. By the look on his face, my father was living these words for himself. He could hear his voice speaking them. His thought was animated by them. One day, again a well man, strong and resonant before the great crowds whom he had learned how to reach, he would be saying words like these.

"I remember," he said, awakening to me and the patio, "exactly where I was and what I was doing when he died. It was February 3—almost six months ago. I was in the office at Albany. The ticker was sounding out in the big room. I was at my desk, working on new wording for a bill that was coming up—it had to do with taxes on some upstate counties for farm roads. Suddenly Sam came in. His face was white. He said, 'Boss, you'd better come out and read the ticker.' I got up, went out to the big room. The secretaries were crying. 'What is it?' I asked, and went over to the ticker, where the tape was clicking out from the glass dome. I read: *Former President Woodrow Wilson died quietly a few minutes ago at 11:15 this morning, in his home on S Street, in the nation's capital.* It is odd how we react to tremendous emotion. Right then I had resentful and uncharitable thoughts about Mr Harding." (My father was never heard to refer to him as President Harding.) "Also, in that moment, I felt so numb that almost as if to prove I was alive I did a most prosaic thing. I took out my watch to see what time it was, though the office clock was right on the wall facing me. —Do you remember what you were doing then?"

"I was in class. Someone came in and told the prof, and the class was let out. They had a concert that night by the Boston Symphony Orchestra on tour. Before the regular program, they played *Siegfried's Rhine Journey* in memory of the President, and the orchestra and the audience all stood during it except the little man who played the glockenspiel. People cried. The next morning the university had a memorial service in the chapel—he once taught there, you know, as a young professor."

"No! He did? I didn't know. —Did you go?"

"No."

"What did you do?"

"We—we had a little soccer scrimmage, just a few of us. It was snowing a little."

He sighed.

"No, I suppose the world never stops, no matter what. —Read me some of the other places where I have put slips."

We can have no sympathy with those who seek to seize the power of government to advance their own personal interests or ambition.

I knew whom he was thinking of.

"Go on."

I know that you will appreciate the scruple upon which I act.

"There: that's the word: *scruple*. This is from a letter he wrote denying his support of a certain bill sponsored by a good friend in the Senate. —Did you know Wilson was the first man to go personally before Congress since John Adams? He said he would do anything in his power to free business from control by monopoly and special privilege. That is what I preached all through our campaign."

"I remember."

"He called his program the New Freedom," said my father, and fell silent. I thought he was brooding upon the idea of freedom in his own case, longing for escape from the captivity of his disease. Presently he said,

"Take a little note for the book: title for a chapter heading: 'Progress with Honor.'"

I thought he was seeing his own future in the phrase.

It was late in the morning. There was a slow breeze off the river half a mile beyond our house, bringing the sweet scent of warm cottonwood boughs and pollen, and the lazily inciting odor of the riverbank mud, where decay mixed with fresh growth, and the rank earth was released into the air by the slow-flowing brown stream. Our very house made of earth gave off a breath of ancient life and renewal, and the great shadow of our huge tree fell and stirred over us like a benediction. All of it made me feel lazy, drowsy, aware of the power of sexual desire. It was heady to breathe deeply of such clear, thin air. Through the wrought-iron patio gate showed the blue of the far mountains—pale where the sun was direct, inky where the cloud shadows drifted over the immense rocky faces of the distant heights. It was country which cast a spell like no other, as I had already discovered. How could our vast peace ever be disturbed?

We knew soon enough.

Sam arrived with the morning mail. As usual, he had read all of it which was in any way official, and was ready with summaries for my father. At such times, in case confidential matters might arise, I usually withdrew. Today, Sam, with a brisk nod, indicated that I should stay. He was unsmiling—an unfamiliar state.

"News?" asked my father.

"Three things," said Sam, in demonstration of his mental ordering of matters.

First: there was now clear evidence that the earlier charges against Governor Pelzer would undoubtedly be reopened and brought to light along with new suspicions as yet unexposed.

Second: there was a letter this morning from Governor Pelzer, the gist of which was that constant questions were being asked about the lieutenant-governor's absence from his duties. It was becoming most awkward to respond to such questions with sympathetic evasions. The governor felt obliged to ask for some definite indication of a date when the office of lieutenant-governor could again be actively filled by the official duly elected to it. If it were impossible to fix such a date, then, however painful it must be to consider, the alternative of resignation would have to be seriously weighed. Signed, "Yours ever admiringly, Judge."

Third: behind this, of course, lay a real and brutal desire to eliminate the lieutenant-governor and his "scruples" from the scene. Sam had discerned earlier that there was a new partisanship beginning to form in Albany around my father, even in his absence. Pelzer could see this only as a threat. If he was to meet the growing danger of alignments against him in the accusations of corruption which were impending not only in rumor but in new evidence, then he could not afford to have forces organized against him within the administration.

Sam's exposition was clear and without emphasis; but its burden was charged with emotion. My father listened impassively until Sam finished. All implications went through my father's mind as he looked from one to the other of us. He knew what Dr Birch would say if consulted. He knew by now that we had taken the Casa del Rio on a year's lease. Above all, he knew the state of his own health.

He was at a crossroads. At last, in a husky whisper, he said musingly,

"Resignation?"

The question hung in the air. But we all knew the answer—we had known it, actually, for some time before Governor Pelzer's letter arrived that morning. My father reached for his watch in the little breast pocket of his sweater-coat. He did not look at the face of it, but at the engraved message on the back. What would Our Crowd think? He smiled with a tough, youthful expression, and said,

"Sam, prepare a draft of the resignation letter. I will go over it with you this afternoon. —No: no need to say anything at all to me now. We all know how we feel."

He wanted to be left alone. I picked up my W.W. materials and retreated with Sam. When we were out of earshot, Sam, with almost a catch in his voice, said,

"He's probably seeing a parallel between his breakdown and the President's—great things thwarted by the body giving out."

"But he must get well!"

"He must get well. There's still plenty for him to do when he can."

In a few days, then, Sam left for Albany to gather my father's personal possessions in the capitol office. Joanna left with him, visibly suppressing an air of victory. In a coolly sympathetic voice, she had pointed out that now, since there was nothing "official" for Sam to do for my father once he had cleared the office, they were free to set a date for their wedding. If Sam returned to us, it would be only for a brief interlude to report, to help outline plans for the future of my father's intention to return to public office—two years? four years?—and to say goodbye for the meantime. The wedding would take place in Cambridge.

As I finished giving my father his daily injection, he took a few breaths to subdue the pain I had caused him, and then regarded me quizzically.

"Doc, will you do something for me? I've been thinking about it for some time, but now that you'll be going off to the country pretty soon, I want to speak of it. —Find my key ring in the top drawer there. Go to the storage room behind the garage and open the big blue steamer trunk. In the second tray on the right, you will see several large black leather envelopes. They have brass locks in their flaps. Bring me the one which has my initials on it in gold and the words *Personal and Private.*"

When it was in his hands, he turned the envelope over several times, as if musing whether to open it. He seemed to be looking through it at another time and place. Finally, taking the smallest key in the ring, he unlocked the portfolio and took out a sheaf of letters fastened with a broad rubber band. These, too, he regarded with some uncertainty—would he release them from the retaining band and read the letters, or hand them to me to read? But no. Without disturbing the packet, he replaced it in the leather case, which he locked. He then removed the small key from the ring and gave me both envelope and key.

"Go to the Sandia State Bank. Ask for Mr Ramsey, introduce yourself, and tell him you want to rent a safety-deposit box, *in your name*. He knows who I am. Have him charge the box rental to my bank account. When you have the box, put the portfolio in it. After that, I want you to keep the two keys—the box key, and the little key—yourself. I don't want anybody else to know about this. Not even your mother. It is a private matter and I am ready to trust you with it. If the time comes to do something about the safe deposit, I will tell you what to do. If anything should happen to me before

[135]

then"—I found the hackneyed euphemism brave and touching—
"destroy the contents of the box, envelope and all. Is this all clear?"

"Yes, Father."

"Off with you."

He sank back against his pillows with a long breath of relief,
closed his eyes, and nodded me, and whatever concerned him, away.

The business was done within the hour, after which I retreated to
the riverbank and my willow glade with my notebook, from which,
and many others· like it, much of this chronicle has been assembled.
I was puzzled but proud that my father had given the confidential
task to me instead of to Sam. I lay in the leafy play of light, and
wondered what I was now custodian of.

❦

The Wenzels had gone ahead to the ranch some days ago. My
train would leave Albuquerque at ten o'clock at night and arrive at
Socorro about midnight. There I was to change trains—to a freight
train with one passenger coach attached—for Magdalena, arriving
during the forenoon. One of the cars from the ranch would come to
pick me up. The other newly hired hand was to be there also,
coming from El Paso. I had no idea of the country where I was
going. I thought of some ancient map with unexplored blank spaces
where a legend was hand-lettered in brown ink: *Terra Incognita
Hic Sunt Leones*.

"Will Sam stay a while when he comes back?" I asked.

"I doubt it. Have you seen this?"

My father handed me a letter from Governor Pelzer acknowledg-
ing my father's resignation personally, and enclosing two official
things. One was the formal acceptance of the resignation from the
little Secretary of State of New York; the other was a file of news-

paper clippings announcing the resignation, which included several editorials. *The New York Times* deplored the loss of a new public servant whose great promise had scarcely been tested. "It is to be hoped that his health, fully restored, will soon permit his return to political life, perhaps in a greater capacity than that which ill fortune obliged him to vacate." There with febrile determination my father saw his future.

"Ah," he said suddenly, "I almost forgot. Here is a present which Lyle left for you this afternoon." It was *Prejudices, Fourth Series,* by H. L. Mencken. "He is reviewing it for the *Journal*. He says it will keep you from going native out on the ranch."

"Does he like it?"

"Mencken is his God. Lyle thinks you need disillusioning. He means it kindly. Fact is, he himself is afraid of *not* being disillusioned. It explains much about him—and t.b. or any chancy disease. You must write and thank him."

It was odd to think that Lyle, in his abrasive, grinning mistrust of sentiment, should have thought of me. On the flyleaf he had written, "See essay on 'The Husbandman,' if you get romantic about your bucolic role. L.P."

When I said goodbye to my mother, I saw the signs of her endurance which I had not really noticed before—the suffering which she had concealed, which I had been too self-absorbed to see. Her delicate, wistful, mischievous prettiness—so much of it lingered from her girlhood when she had been called "The Kitty" by her brothers and sisters—was marked by changes. When she smiled, it was to mask the weariness in which her face was set. Permanent shadows were under her eyes, giving them an intensity which was not impulsive, as before, but constant. Lines faintly showed between her eyebrows. Her cheekbones were more prominent, her cheeks a little hollow. Slightly parted, her lips seemed to permit the silent escape of words framing the worry which she must not let be heard. None of what lay behind these changes would she acknowledge openly. She

[137]

was as active, ingenious, and original as ever in making the household one of grace and comfort. It was her courage which made tears come to my eyes when I said goodbye to her. In her selflessness, she misread them, and said, in a family idiom as though I were still a small boy,

"Richard, my darling, it will only be three shakes of a lamb's tail until you are with us again."

Then in a gesture out of my childhood she made a tiny sign of the cross on my forehead.

My father, who was now taking daily walks with caution and humorous pride, went out to the car in which Lillian would drive me to the train for Socorro.

"You see?" he said, indicating his feat of strength.

As we drove away, Lillian, with her voice as always misted with worship, declared,

"He is a marvel."

When I was leaving her, about to shake hands, she threw her heavy arms around me and hauled me into her deep-cushioned bosom and kissed me, and, through me, my father.

So I went away blessed by many loves whose images of me I thought it would be impossible ever to betray: my father, my mother, the gods of my river glade. Who has ever managed to express enough love in saying goodbye?

CHAPTER IV

The Animal Creation

THE SILENCE: only an immeasurable emptiness, a prehistoric solitude, could have held such quiet. What sound came was an occasional animal call, remote and pathetic in its meaningless statement. A sheep, "Nbla-a-a," far away. A sighing mutter from a dozing sheep dog. Now and then a creak or a singing waft on the night stir of air from the windmill cutting the silence with its canted sails, which looked like the petals of a single great flower against the sky. The very silence, against which the broken night sounds carried, seemed foreboding. I was removed from every aspect of my supporting world, and for much of my first night at the ranch I traveled again in wakeful dreams the journey to this other country.

At Socorro I had waited from one in the morning until about six, when a freight train hauling empty coal cars departed for Magdalena. I rode in the caboose. The exciting smell of coal smoke blew back from the stubby, toiling engine far ahead. It was a run of about twenty-seven miles, which took two more hours, during which I dozed, for I had sat awake in the wooden station at Socorro watching for the other new hired hand to appear from El Paso; but he was not on the early-morning train which went north.

I was again dozing in the Magdalena station—a shack by the

black water tower—when someone roughly shook my shoulder and asked my name.

"Yes?—yes," I said, coming awake in a lunge, to see a tall, bony, weathered man more than twice my age.

"Come own. You're comin with me out to the Wenzels'. My name's Tom Agee. I'm the foreman."

We shook hands and sleepily I followed him out to a Ford touring car in the dust outside. "We'll get us a cup of cowffee and I'll pick up a few things Miz Wenzel wants from the general merchandise before we get goin."

He drove through the earth streets raising veils of dust which the hot south wind blew forward upon us in the open car. There were few streets, and at the end of each one was the immediate country. Rolling, abrupt, bare hillsides rose at the west side of the town. Tailings added to the hills all about the timbered entrances to old mines, where little activity showed. Wilted trees—cottonwood, tamarisk, mulberry—sparsely edged the streets. Most of the houses were wooden, some unpainted, with here and there one made of brick or stucco. None was over one story high. The morning light gilded the sunward faces of all things, and promised a beating heat as the day advanced. We came to the Marigold Hotel, which stood a few blocks from the station.

The hotel was a long, two-story, red brick building with a white-railed balcony along its whole front and far end. It was a fading remnant of the years when the little town had first been a thriving center for silver and coal mines. In its size, the Marigold spoke of old aspiration, when men had come to grow rich, and to bring every expensive comfort alive when the gold should begin to pour in. Now, even from the outside, it was evident that the hotel was mostly empty. One or two cars and a wagon with two mules were drawn up to the entrance porch, at one end of which a window showed the word CAFE in an arc of gold leaf.

There we went for breakfast. A cup of coffee turned out to be three cups, with ham, gravy, eggs, biscuits, lick (a heavy molasses-like syrup), and a piece of pie made from canned peaches. We sat at a long counter, and were served by a waitress whom Tom called Larraine. She was about my age. So plump that her dress was pulled into streaked creases about the armpits, breasts, and waist, she was sober-faced and almost solemn in her bearing. She waited on us with a quick economy of movement which told of long experience, young as she was. As she leaned across the counter I could hear her breath expelled. It was intimately physical. About her there was a sort of misty warmth—not quite sweat but redolent of it—suggesting ardor, which she seemed to deny out of melancholy propriety. She wouldn't look directly at me. Tom—if he had ever been young he left it to others to remember this—preserved an oblivious courtesy toward her which made her in effect invisible to him. But I saw how in her round face deep dimples appeared when she smiled in response to Tom's short greeting. When she walked to the cook's window behind the counter, her knees were close together, and her body swayed to a rhythm which made the rolling flesh of her buttocks rise and fall in a two-part pumping motion at each side like thrusts of a soft little machine. Her eyes were a bluish gray, her eyebrows were golden brown. She wore a little curl in front of each ear, and piled the rest of her heavy bounty of pale-red hair in a high spiral which resembled a cone of cotton candy. Under her eyes were pale-brown hollows which seemed older than the rest of her fleshy face. Her hands were small, and her wrists had bracelets of creases where her plump hands met her rounded forearms. Pedantically, "Rubens," I said to myself, trying to fix the quality which made her a personage in her own anonymous right in that long narrow café where window shades were torn and the scarred floor and specked walls reflected lost hope. As we ate, she stood away from us, affecting indifference, though I thought she was making an examination of me, the newcomer. Presently she came dutifully to us again with her coffee pot. Her high full breasts jellied at every step.

"More cowffee?" she asked. I smiled at her but she ignored this. Her voice was rich and throaty, low in pitch, the one beautiful detail of her whole being, and reflected a curious, dainty, unspoken pride. I wondered if she was unhappy. She seemed tired. Perhaps she had been at work since five o'clock, when Magdalena began to stir in the morning. How long every day must she work? It was a lost life, so I thought.

"Well, sir," said Tom, suddenly rising. "Time t'go. —Put it all in the book, Miss Larraine," he said with a plainsman's courtesy. She nodded, reaching for her charge-account ledger, and we went out to the Ford. Tom, with a gesture, told me to crank the car while he sat at the wheel working the gas and spark levers.

We drove to the old stone store, which seemed a block long, with its sign *General Merchandise* painted on the irregular surface above narrow windows. As we went, he asked without looking at me,

"What for you so interested in that girl?"

I was startled at having been watched, and I said vaguely,

"Well, there's something about her."

"You look out."

"What do you mean?"

He shrugged and said nothing, but with a sideways jerk of his head told me to get out and go with him, while he shopped for items on Concha's list.

She was at the WZL headquarters with her husband, had little to do, wanted some yards of stuff for embroidery, and if they had colored yarns she was going to make a set of small rugs, and she had seen a set of madonna-blue drinking glasses from Mexico which she wanted: he shopped for the whole list which took three quarters of an hour, until he could say, "Well, that's about everythin but the blue glasses, which went and got sold yest'day"—for there were just enough families left in Magdalena to make a town with an occasional want for touches of life from elsewhere to lend grace in a land of hard terms and gritty substance.

By half past nine we were heading west on a gravel and dirt road with deep ruts dried after hard, infrequent rain. The ruts often turned the steering wheel within Tom Agee's grasp. In the countryman's certainty of his own need of others, and of their need of him in all he could give, Tom talked without pause. His pace was so unhurried that you could see the end of his sentence long before he spoke it, and you silently begged him to hurry up. His gestures were crabbed but eloquent, and his subject was his life up to the present moment. He seemed like a creature of the desert and mountain wilderness singing the song of its life in response to the beating sunlight.

"Well, I get tired of it. Who don't get tired of theirself and their life now and then?"

He stared at me in challenge. I nodded satisfactorily and he resumed the road. His face was like a piece of miniature landscape such as we were bumping over, with its gullies, buttes, ragged brush, pittings, sunned to a brick color. Every slow word from his dust-whitened lips was matched by his slow gestures. Every word, however simple, became weighty because of his authority of experience in matters however trivial. His pale eyes were folded over at the corners by slants of flesh after a lifetime against the sun. Until he'd made his point, his humor was stone-faced; then it broke open, and you knew you must laugh. Life with animals and their mute contrariness had hardened his sinews; the work of survival in the ungiving land had sharpened his values. He was marginally literate except in referring to the Bible, and then he expertly echoed its style. Talk was his medium. In this he had dignity, which came from the belief that his days and his world were of as much interest to everyone as to himself. He must have been handsome in his youth, like a crag seen from a distance. Now in his years he was impressive as an earth feature seen close to. A curious childlike sweetness lay about his light eyes in the form of heavy dark lashes. His hands were like roots of an old tree, and to make a point he would elevate them with spread fingers, and a sideways jerk at the air, where invisibly his ideas seemed to loom for him.

"For as the Lord telleth, then must man abide by the telling and bow his head unto the orders of the Lord," he remarked, with his right hand hanging up between us.

He said he knew the whole country from the Mississippi west to the copper camps of Arizona and from the Rio Grande to those nests of hell's eagles in the shack towns of the Colorado Rocky mines. Oh, and he knew the cities, where corruption burned like sulphur at every corner. How did he know? He knew because the real work of his life, now behind him, was that of a revival preacher. If he did say it, nobody in the whole West could bang the Good Book down on the lectern harder than himself. There was that time when he had three singers traveling with him, and a trombonist, and two young men drawn to God who managed the collections, and the transportation of the tent, and the folding chairs, and the Coleman lanterns, and who loaded the melodeon onto the flatbed wagon he owned to carry the freight. Them was the days of the Lord. How he loved it when he saw the next town slowly come into his gaze far ahead as his party of wagons and his flatbed drawn by mules went along the dusty roads which often paralleled the single tracks of the railroad, where the telegraph wires sang and picked up the sunlight against the sky like threads of silver. Ho, yes. He would see low clumps of trees and a water tower shining high, and a steeple or two, and mebbe a courthouse dome; and he knew people was there a-waitin, and here he went, a-comin, and Lordy! they was all gon meet the next evenin. It was blessed work just to get the tent set up and the chairs in rows in the orange-colored shade by day, and by night the lanterns hung a-hissin on the tent poles, and some outside, usually from big trees, cottonwoods mostly, throwing their light around in bright circles so men, women, and children could see their way down to the Lord's bench in front.

Well, he always stayed at least one week, sometimes two, mebbe three, if the harvest of souls was plentiful enough; and you wouldn't know it now, from his husky old voice, but he would hoot and cry night after night, and pray with his eyes shut, and his arms up, so clear and strong so's't they could hear him blocks away, even as far as the courthouse square, from his revival lot which he set up mostly on the edge of town after getting permission from the town clerk or mebbe the mayor himself.

The people. His people and the Lord's. How they listened, first, and then spoke back to him, like lambs all a-cryin at once, Praise the Lord, praise Jesus, oh, Lord, I know, I know. And when the Spir't came down on them, the Holy Spir't, so's't they were out of their-self, all callin and cryin to be saved, and their tears flowin like unto Jordan itself, and the singers' voices and the trombone risin, and the fine young men bendin over the sinners feelin of their flesh and urgin them to go down to meet Jesus, and him liftin his voice over them all like the Patriarch over his flock, why, then he sometimes felt so powerful he believed he could work mir'cles, and sometimes, too, he felt like the great breed bull, for the power to breed was in him, but it was for the good, not the bad, but the flesh rose up like a tower in the strength it had, and he gave the strength to all, for all was purified.

"And I tell you, young man, there was the Lord's work bein done, and I done it s'long as He called me to do it until it happened."

There was a silence of a rough mile or two. I felt I should not ask what happened, for I knew he would tell me, and soon he said that one year he heard his voice growing feeble, and he thought he must have strained it for the Lord, for he had never spared it, and it was that power which brought thousands down to the bench to find salvation; and it soon came about by the Lord's will that he had no more voice than I heard this minute, and his days of travelin and shoutin the glory of God was over. Oh, he repined bitterly at times, for he was but a weak vessel of flesh, but there was nothin to do but go on the best way he could. He had been before the public for nigh on twenty years. He knew what he just might do then.

As I listened for mile upon mile, hearing the voice of the land I was gazing at, I saw mountains to the west ghostly in the blanching sunlight. There were foothills like crouching old lions. On the horizon—how far away? it seemed like infinity—were strange pyramids of perfect shape, and even farther, green-blue mountains under opalescent veils of light and distance. In the universal light, clouds floated in flocks and cast their shadows over the rise and fall of the earth, and made new shapes of what they traveled over. Never had I felt so dislocated in place or time, or even in my own character, as on that ride across that unknown country, and even in what came later. I heard the voice of the land with its rude poetry, its animal nature, and its blind acceptance. My father, my mother, the friends I knew at college, seemed lost forever to me as we advanced through the dust and the light into the hard, alien country, which yet had its own little easements, for I saw wild white poppies by the road, and purple, white, and yellow verbena.

Midway in Tom's soliloquy we came to a view of land which made me exclaim. He waved a hand at it and identified it as the Plains of San Agustín. It was like a lake of light, reaching endlessly away to the south. Faint, far mountains seemed only to emphasize its isolation and superb vacancy. It was like a mirror of an empty sky. What lived there? What *could* live there? Was there courage enough in the human world to know that land? An odd exaltation possessed me. I resolved that man was equal to anything—and the corollary to this, that man was capable of anything, was to come to me later.

The sight of the plains made me impatient to ask Tom Agee about the Wenzel ranch, but his steady, slow emission of what must be told any stranger kept me silent.

"So I said—this was in West Texas, where I was at the time, asking the Lord what to do now that I could not but bow my head under the silence He had put upon me—so I said to myself, Tom Agee, I said, you're goin to run for county judge and bring the justice of the Lord to people under the law."

The fissure of his mouth closed in stern triumph for a second, and then its irregular seam opened and the stream went on. There was a fall election. He ran, but was defeated by the evil forces of Six-sixty-six. It was the Mark of the Beast itself, he said, and the Devil had managed the whole thing. Tom had sold his revival equipment to the handsome young men of his troupe and they went and made a shady business out of it, reaping money, not souls, and, so he heard, they also took their fill of women whom they first drove blind with holy emotion. Did I know one thing? They had learned their trade under him, and then they *per*-verted it. Oh, Job. Job's suffering remained his example and con-*so*-lation. His wife died, his sons were growed up and gone, he was alone. He worked his way across New Mexico till he got a job as a ranch hand, and after a few years, dad-burned if he waddn't the ranch foreman for old man Wenzel at the WZL; and there he was to this day.

"What is it like at the ranch?"

He sketched a random design in the air with his cracked spread old hand as if to show me the picture he had in his head. Then he said it was real pretty. Old lady Wenzel—he meant Don Elizario's first wife—loved flowers and trees. She planted and tended them all day long. There was two long brakes of salt cedar, nigh unto twenty feet high by now, and over the house was a mighty stand of cottonwoods. The old man had rigged up running ditches to the flowers and trees from the windmill tank out back beyond the salt cedars, and he, Tom, had never seen so many roses when the season was ripe. But that was before.

"Before?"

"This new Miz Wenzel let the roses go to rack and ruin, for she said they was nobody out there to come and see them." The house? It was one-story, made of stone, and it had a new part out back built for the young wife, and it had wooden porches front and back covered with trumpet vines. Inside, it was sure enough beautiful. Old man Wenzel was never one to spare money givin his wimmin what they wanted. It was a sorry time when his first wife died. Before then everything seemed so happy. He paused and nodded grimly ahead at the alkali dust of the road. Times changed. He made me think of how recently I had come to this conclusion for myself.

"I met them in Albuquerque," I said. "I mean Don Elizario and his new wife."

"I know. I know. We're supposed to work you so hard you'll get some tough meat on you. Time I was your age I could rope and throw a bull caif and sit own him in nine and a half seconds. —I was raised up own a ranch, though, and you wasn't."

"She's a beautiful girl. What does she find to do out there all alone?"

"All alone." He mused quietly for a moment. Then, "I sure feel sorry for that child. He treats her nice, but she sure is lonesome. Fact is, she don't do anythin, all day long. He won't let her talk to any of the men. She means no harm. I'll tell you what." He turned and looked squarely at me. "She's plain hungry."

"Hungry?"

"Now don't you go to askin me questions, for I ain't sayin ary another word about it. If you don't know what I mean, then keep your own counsel."

He frowned as though I had offended him. To change the subject, I asked,

"What is going on now at the ranch?"

Well. They's just about done shearing the sheep, and the wool was being bagged for shipment to Magdalena and Socorro and Chicago in the empty railroad cars that came up during the night. Then they would start in a few days with the dipping.

—How was that?

—Didn't know what sheep dipping was?

—No, sir.

Well. They taken and get the sheep in one corral, and they's a runway that slopes sharp downward and the sheep are driven down it into a long cement trough filled with the dip, and they have to swim to pass through it, for the trough is deeper than they could stand up in, and more than three feet wide, with straight walls so they can't take and scramble out, so they have to swim mebbe seventy-five feet to get out of the trough at the other end, where they's another corral they finally jump up a ramp to get to. As the sheep swim along, yelling like Beelzebub, the men on each side of the dip along the way push them under, head and all, and they come up shakin their heads and crying and blowin, but they have to be got under to be sure all the ticks and scabs and burrs is killed or loosened.

"Ticks."

Ticks that got buried under the wool and bored in the skin, and if they waddn't killed and sores and scabs treated, the next coat of wool would be poorly because of patches of dead hide underneath. They had to do it for every crop of wool. Hot work. Hard work. The smell was enough to stink a dog off a gut wagon. But to see it done right, old man Wenzel was there, and so was Tom Agee. They always took on a few extra hands, some from Mexico, some from the sheep camps south of the ranch, and that was why I was comin, and why that sorry no-good stranger from El Paso was hired, who had answered an ad in the El Paso *Herald Post,* and that was all they knew about him. The good Lord only knew what had become of him and where they'd get another this late.

"*Breach of contract,*" pronounced Tom, and added, "Sometimes people still call me *Judge* though I never did fill that office."

"I see. —Where do the fellows live?"

There were two bunkhouses, one big one, where Tom Agee had a separate room at one end. The other, smaller one had room for two. That was where I would be put, along with the other new man if he should ever appear.

"It's a right nice layout, the whole place. —You a college boy?" he

[149]

suddenly asked with a ferocity half-curious, half-scornful. I said, "Yes." He nodded silently, and then putting his jaw forward grimly, he said, "Well, we'll take care of that."

"Well, Mr Agee, don't let it prey on your mind. I just did what the good Lord in His wisdom set me to do."

"You mockin me, young man?" But he suppressed a twitching smile that betrayed satisfaction at my cheeky answer, and waving jerkily off to the far northwest ahead of us, he said, "That's the Gallina Mountains. We'll be turnin off right soon. And don't you go to calling me Mister. My name's Tom."

I began to notice that the country to the north of us—we were traveling due west—slowly changed in character. Scrub piñon and other pine trees dotted the hills and darkened the distant land. To our south, the Plains of San Agustín faded into the distance as low rises of land began also to show scattered vegetation. It was those plains, now behind us, which gave me my image of how far I was, how alienated, from any world I knew; and lying awake on that first night, it was the plains which shone so brightly behind my closed eyelids in the dark. When we left them behind I felt we had crossed a boundary. I wished I was already at the ranch, familiar with it, and without qualms and questions.

"What is Don Elizario really like?" I asked Tom. "I know Concha—I had a long talk with her in Albuquerque. He went off to talk on the phone."

"You call her Concha?" asked Tom sharply.

"No, no, I don't call her anything. But that's how everybody refers to her."

"They do, eh? Who's everybody?"

"Everybody talks about her in Albuquerque."

"They do, eh? Well, just you be careful what you call her. She's Miz Wenzel and don't you forget it. And don't go near the house. Nobody gets there."

"Why?"

"Why! Why, because they're all men, that's why."

"I see. But I think she would like to have parties."

"Heh. Now about him. He's different."

—Different this year from last. He was older. He seemed more careful. What about? About everything. He was hard-working and he worked everybody hard, and he was fair, but he stood for no nonsense from anybody, and he liked to come out after supper and sit around the cowffee fire with the men for a while, but he seemed tired. That is, tired inside. He made like he finally give up to something. Mebbe it was just bein old. But you wouldn't think he was old during the day, workin. Didn't know.

"I don't know. If I was still before the public doin the Lord's work, I'd get him down on his knees, Cathlick or no, and pray with him and find out what's holdin down his soul. I b'lieve I know but I can't say 'thout I am certain and *then* I wouldn't say. I did always respect him. But now I feel a little bit sorry for him. He'd have my hide if he knew that. But some way, I got the feelin I want to comfort him. —Now you stay away from that house, hear?"

"I was just going to call and pay my respects."

"Just don't you do it. He'll know right off that you're there and why. As for her, she's none of your business. —There's the gate. Get out."

He waved to a turnoff leading toward a barbed-wire fence in which a gate of wire strands was rigged between two posts and held at one end by loops of wire which could be lifted and lowered. Tom expected me to open the gate. I went to the post with the wire loops and tried to lift off the top one. It did not give. The tension of the wire was so great that I could not free the moveable gate post from its top loop and the other one at the bottom in which it was footed. I looked at Tom. He showed no interest. I struggled with the gate again. He let me, but at last he ambled out of the car, pushed me aside, wrapped his left arm around the moveable gate post, threw his weight toward the fixed post, the other one yielded, the top loop came free, and then the bottom one. With scornful silence more searing than profanity, he threw the whole gate aside so the car could pass through. He drove through and stopped the car to wait for me. I ran to get in. He blew a sigh like a bull and declared,

"Don't you know *innythin? Close* the gate. In this country, you never open a gate 'thout you close it. Git."

My initiation had begun. I went to the gate and, after many tries at imitating Tom's method of using arm, shoulder, and body against the stretching of the wires, got the gate in place again.

We rode silently and slowly along a road worse than the one we had left. We were heading north over earth which showed pale brick red now, and far off the Gallina Mountains had turned dark under cloud shadow. Here and there a red gully lay, dry, ravaged by past cloudbursts. In the bushes of pine which we passed the song of cicadas rose like the scream of machine metal. Presently Tom spoke again, shouting to be heard. Though I did not hear all he said, I was relieved that no trace remained of the scorn he had shown me at the gate. I heard scattered phrases.

"But it's a good life—hard—the old man—let him make the move —I remember him—then mighty handsome—prize bull—people had ought to think before they—"

He interrupted his broken monologue and pointed ahead with a finger like a big dried twisted carrot. The ranch headquarters slowly came into view.

First we saw the windmill. It was not turning, but its vanes were so set that they caught the full white midday sun and they blazed like a source of the sun itself. The galvanized-iron roof of the house also gave back the sky in a hot white glare over two of the long rooms. The house had several angles, indicating rooms facing differently. A huge cluster of old cottonwoods stood behind the house and by afternoon would shade it. On each side but somewhat removed stood the breathless brakes of salt cedar. The old wife, Rosario

[152]

Wenzel, had planted them as protection from the winds of dust in their season. There was a faint brown blur of outbuildings and penciled lines of corral fences, and lesser structures of obscure purpose, in one of which I would probably live. The ground rose slightly and the track of our path ahead wavered crazily, according to the ruts, in a long and diminishing scratch of pale-orange dust.

"Nigh there," observed Tom.

※

Sooner than I had expected we had come through another barbed-wire gate. I heard the subdued bleat of sheep, which sounded to me like the onset of collective nausea.

Tom brought me to the upper corral, above the house to the north, where men were shearing. Beyond a glance or a lifted chin gesture, nobody acknowledged me as Tom handed me a long-tined rake and pantomimed how I was to collect the shorn wool falling from the heavy clippers. As a sheep was worked on, it was held down by the shearers, who bent over their job in their big hats, which shaded their faces from me. The dust rose breast high and hung there. The heat was under the skin. Tom disappeared. I swept wool with my rake. As the piles grew higher, a middle-aged Mexican hauled them away into lesser piles to be bagged. Sweat ran from us all and dust made a little skin plaster with it. The sheep exuded a smell of dried feces mixed with dust, and the rankness of desert grass, and sour decay of stuff caught in the wool which once wet by rain or urine dried rancidly. Raking away, and breathing as shallowly as I could to avoid taking into my lungs all the foulness suspended in the air, I felt blisters spring up on my hands as they gripped and slid on the rake when it dragged the filth-heavied wool.

[153]

After time which I did not measure, the work was suddenly interrupted when a clanging summons came from the chuck wagon, which stood among the outbuildings. It was the cook calling us to the evening meal at a little past five o'clock. The men straightened up and stretched. Some—there were about seven or eight in all—looked at me with hard curiosity as we all started toward the chuck wagon, which stood at an angle to the cookhouse. Tom reappeared and, vaguely waving first at me and then the rest, spoke my name in introduction.

By his supper fire built in a U-shaped brick fire hole in the open, the cook, a small thin man wearing an apron, and beating a huge spoon against a tin plate, kept up a wordless cry with his face turned upward like a coyote in a performance which he seemed to enjoy for its own sake. It was his ritual invitation to us to eat. He had gray whiskers standing out like the face fur of a lynx and—to me an incongruity—he wore a pair of tin spectacles at a crazy angle far down on his nose.

We lined up to take plates and load them from the small vats and trays where his food was to be spooned out—beans, beef in hunks and stew, biscuits like lumpy fists, and at the end, a bushel basket full of bruised apples and a huge enameled coffee pot much battered and surrounded by tin cups. The sun was still hot, still a while from setting, and we all drifted to the shade of a few cottonwoods, which brought us within fifty yards of the house. We settled down on the ground in silence.

Nobody spoke when Don Elizario came out of the house and ambled toward us. He seemed not so tall as I remembered him in his elaborate house in town. He walked with a slight lurch to the left at every other step. Hatless, he showed his white hair, which was mussed forward over his brow like a boy's. His gray-yellow mustaches were slightly raised in a friendly smile, and as he came closer he said a few words—"*Amigos—qué colór, qué no?*"—and nodding around the scattered group, some of whom lifted a chin to him, he came over to me and put out his hand, squatted down beside me with a blown breath of effort before I could stand up in respect.

"Welcome," he said with a husky little laugh, which referred to the conditions of this meeting so different from our last. "You will have to work twice as much now that the other *hombre* never showed up."

I was too tired to do more than smile back at him. He gave me a grave, long look, then, as though to read my whole nature and make a judgment. Uneasily I looked back into his narrowed stare, which revealed only a little drop of light in each of his eyes. The others watched this inspection silently, and then one or two nodded, as if they knew what it was about. Abruptly Don Elizario rose and waved his hand around over the other men, a patriarchal gesture, then slowly returned to the house.

The sun went behind some horizon clouds as it fell. The cook whacked his tin dish again to signal for the return of utensils to be rinsed in a common tub of hot water. Tom came beside me and asked if I wanted to see where I was going to live. After I rinsed my plate, cup, and big spoon, he led me off to the little bunkhouse, which stood thirty or forty feet from the big one. He kicked open the door and nodded at the interior. It had one small window at the far end. He said the door was left open all night for ventilation, and that bein the case, it was a right good idea to keep an eye out every morning for critters such as scorpions, tarantulas, and rattlers, which had been known to settle in on some ole night or other. The room had a bunk along each wall. Between them was a space five or six feet wide. Two nails for clothes were fixed opposite each other on the raw walls. There was a table with one chair under the window. On the table was a coal oil lamp.

"Which bunk?" he asked.

I pointed to the one on the left as we faced it. He said I could take my suitcase from the car and settle it under my bunk, which made that territory mine,

"You can wash outside with your basin"—he pointed to it on a shelf above my bunk—"or you can get yourself over to the windmill tank. There's a pipe where you can stand for a bath if you're willin to wait long enough, or you can bring a can of water over here. You'll find the outdoor privy for yourself. Anythin else?"

I shook my head. I did not say that I had expected the Wenzels to ask me into their house on my first evening.

"Sometimes the hands set round the fire after supper and sometimes somebody sings a song, or tells a story, and you can have a cup of cowffee till bedtime."

He left me. I was ready to drop into bed. But tired as I was, it was almost morning before I slept with all that behind my eyes.

❦

At half past five Tom woke me by kicking the bottom of my open door. He set a tin bucket of water on the floor and said, "I won't be bringin this every morning," and added that breakfast would be there to be taken in ten minutes and work would start at six o'clock. He watched me to be sure I was awake and upright, then went off to get the other men to the chuck wagon.

Stepping outside, I splashed myself and dressed, aching. The morning at that hour was like balm. Above the Magdalena mountains the sun was coming up and its golden sky merged overhead with the palest blue. Shadows were long toward the west. A cool little wind passed over us but stirred no dust. Our grove of trees was like some enameled marvel, sparkling with freshness. It was a morning new under creation, so delicate and precisely formed were all objects, so perfectly lighted and shadowed by the rising sun.

But an hour later, again in the corral, we already felt the heat of the day, and it seemed to me that our humanity disappeared, merged, into the character of the creatures we worked upon. Once during a brief rest we heard a distant sound over the flat, short-grassed land. It was the combined bleatings of another herd of sheep being driven from the other Wenzel ranch far to our south. They were being brought for shearing and dipping. Their herders walked beside the sheep, whose course was kept in line by two black-and-tan sheep dogs who ran back and forth, barking at the edges of the little dusty procession. The sheep, with their knock-kneed walk, their sharp little hooves, their white eyelashes and half-dropped lids, their Assyrian noses and self-satisfied mouths, took on an anthropomorphic character for me; and I reflected that like much of humanity, having no idea of what was in store for them, they came on their way with crowded and witless good nature. They were soon driven through the corral gate in struggling eagerness, making their vomit-like noise, and in turn came to us where we worked.

My right hand was swollen and burning from burst blisters. I tied a handkerchief around my hand. Nobody offered to trade jobs. I could see why, for the shearing took practice and skill, and when now and then the shearing blades nicked the skin of a sheep and drew blood, the man who had let it happen was jeered amiably by the others. It would be easy to injure the animals—they struggled at being held down. My heaps of sheared wool grew bigger and bigger, and it was clear that we needed another man to haul them away to be bagged. The missing ranch hand made his absence felt.

At noon Ira—the cook—set up his clamor for chow, or grub: words which the men used naturally but which because they carried for me the professional cant of cowboy fiction I thought false. Once again Don Elizario came to join us, this time to eat. He sat on the ground with us, asked questions about the work, talking mostly to Tom, though he spoke also, in Spanish, to the Mexicans in the crew. When he was done with his plate, he stood, sighed a belch of repleteness, and came over to me.

"This evening, eh?" he said. "You come and have supper at the house? Six o'clock, eh?"

I thanked him, he nodded, and then, with droll sweeping motions, sent us back to work.

❦

It was mid-afternoon when one of the Mexicans cried, "¡MIRA!" and pointed. We quit work and turned to see.

Up the rutted dusty road just beyond the eastern clump of salt cedar came a figure. He had a canvas bag slung over one shoulder. He walked with a swinging gait, as though his single smallness were equal to the whole land. Tom Agee sat back on his heels to watch him approach. It was a young man, perhaps twenty-two years old. Coming to us, he smiled in full confidence of a good reception. He pulled off his hat, which was sweat-stained and trough-shaped at its brim by the clutch of his hand. He was covered with dust and spotted with sweat. His clothes—a red-checkered shirt, trousers of dark striped material, and Western boots all scuffed at the feet and brightly stitched in fancy designs at the sides—were shabby. At the corral rails, he threw down his bag, which looked heavy, and leaned on the middle rail, smiling genially. Tom was not disposed to smile back.

"Just who might you be?" he asked while everyone listened.

"I'm the new hand."

"You was supposed to be the new hand yesterday."

"I know. I got delayed by unforeseen circumstances."

"Never mind talkin fancy. How'd you get here?"

"I got the Springerville stage out of Magdalena this morning, and got him to drop me off at your gate on the highway. Then I walked. Pleased to meet you-all."

Tom hesitated. He was offended by this cheerful composure, and for a moment seemed to consider turning him away; but we needed help, and at last, he said,

"Just what do you think you can do?"

"Well"—looking at the work interrupted—"I can shear."

"Well, oh, Lord, I guess—well, get on in here and get to shearin over there with that set in the corner."

"I'm sort of hongry, you know. It was a long walk and the stage had no place to stop for dinner."

"Get on it or get on your way," said Tom, and nodded to us to resume work.

The newcomer climbed the rails and went to work in the far corner of the corral. As he passed me, he said, "Hi," and gave a short laugh, as if to say that he saw at once how different he and I were from the rest. I had the irrational superiority of the predecessor, even if by only one day, and I merely nodded back at him. But I watched him get down to work and saw, as everyone did, that he was expert at the job; and the air was alive with combined respect, speculation, and dislike for him.

Dislike: for in that company of work-graven men, older, resigned, scornful of ways not their own, he was by his looks alone an offense. Despite sweat and dust he looked clean. After his long walk he radiated energy. In the midst of hard, clamorous work he shed good will with smiling indifference. Most offensive of all, he was like an allegory of all-knowing innocence in the midst of ignorant experience. He bore himself as if he could turn his hand equally well to any task, and as if any task were hardly worth doing. His confidence came from his good looks. He had no right, when the rest of us were runneled with distorting wet dirt, to look not only comfortable but handsome. He was not tall, but the proportions of his body, the harmony of its parts, shone right out. He had the look, and the quickness of reflex with sharp, continual turns of the head, wary and keen and interested, of a lion cub; his lean frame covered with the finest pelt—golden tan; light hair. His face was younger than his body, and as unmarked as a child's, with small features so regular and color so high that somebody, in disguised envy and resentment, yelled at him,

[159]

"How you doin, Babyface?"

To this nickname, which was commonly used from then on, he merrily made an obscene gesture, and got on with his work.

When I went at suppertime to wash off the day's fetid residue, I saw him tearing at his food like a dog. There was more than hunger to it; there was the power of all appetite. He paused long enough to call out, "See you later," for he had been told he was to share the small bunkhouse with me, and now he viewed me with a conspiratorial attitude: two young men of superior style amidst that small simple mob of sheep shearers, herdsmen, and ranch hands. With a short nod I rejected his assumption and made ready to dine with Don Elizario and Concha. As I changed into cleaner clothes I resented having to share my quarters. How could I read my Mencken and the other voguish book I had brought—the *Tertium Organum?* I moved the table and the coal oil lamp closer to my bed to establish from the first that by right of prior claim they were more mine than any newcomer's. I doubted complacently that he had any such thing as a book in his bag. I decided to endure him merely as a specimen to observe for my notebook entries.

※

The ranch house of gray stucco was half hidden by heavy trumpet vines and the tamarisk brake which separated the bunkhouses from it. The front door had two panels of frosted glass etched with a design of flowers through which someone within could have a slim glimpse of anyone outside. All that could be seen from the porch was a vague, still presence, as though someone inside were deciding whether or not to open the door in response to my knock. Then suddenly it opened.

"Yes, come in," said Don Elizario, standing aside ceremoniously for me. He brought me into a parlor which was left as his first wife had furnished it with pieces from Mexico—stiff chairs covered in prickly red plush, and a center table draped to the floor with an embroidered Spanish shawl heavily fringed. The house was stifling, though the air outside had begun to cool with the lowering sun. On the walls were oval portraits of earlier Wenzels covered with convex glass. In faded sepias the fathers and grandfathers looked out above stiff high collars and high-buttoned, thick black coats and sweeping mustaches and heavy-looped gold watch chains, while mothers and grandmothers stood behind their men with timid hands wristed with ruffles resting on broadcloth shoulders. The women wore high pompadours and frozen expressions of chaste calm. Their faces were supported by boned net collars and their bosoms looked as if carved out of shining wood with no hint of fleshly shapes beneath. Propriety denied passion, even simple feeling, in all the portraits; and sitting with me, Don Elizario, as the issue of such ancestry, was an image of the same impassive convention.

"My wife is getting our supper," he said. He sat with his knees apart, leaning a little forward in the faded refinement of the parlor. He was in shirt sleeves, without collar. A collar button gleamed on his neckband. "You are satisfied here?" His Mexican accent sounded in all he said.

"I hardly know yet—the work is hard, but I can get used to it."

"We are not what you are used to," he said, meaning not the place, or the work, but the men.

I did not know how to speak to this without sounding superior or rude. I replied,

"It is good of you to let me spend some time here."

"If I were younger—" He sighed, and the inarticulate love of the hard life reached through the plushy dusk. The rank animal male society, the animals themselves, their natural smells, ways, perversities, and innocence, their brute powers to be overcome, their instinctive cautions and fears to be outwitted—these were the burdens of life in which he was most at home.

In the depths of the house we could hear kitchen sounds. He

turned toward them and then to me proudly, as if in them he saw Concha.

"She is a good cook," he said.

"She is very beautiful, sir. You are a fortunate man."

To my surprise, he frowned, leaning a little nearer to me with a strange appraising squint.

"You have seen her again?"

"No—only that day at your house, and then, too, far away when she drove by several times when I was out on my bicycle."

He leaned back.

Was it possible that this reassured him? I could not imagine—and then I could: he was jealous of how any other man saw her, and with anguish he imagined them as a pair. This notion went sharper for me when he asked, almost pleading below controlled calm,

"You are Catholic?"

"Yes."

"Yes. —A good one? You go to Mass?"

"Yes."

He was not yet satisfied.

"You go to Communion?"

"Yes," I said a little stiffly.

"Every Sunday?" he insisted.

I nodded, preferring not to speak further about a private matter. If I was impolite, he did not notice.

He was eased. My conscience, then, would be his ally, if I should be drawn to his beautiful girl. I was uneasy at the pathetic bareness of his concern. Burdens seemed to fall away from him. With his knuckles he wiped his eyes, where ready feeling—relief, in this case—brought a start of moisture.

"You write to your *madre?*"

"Yes. —I don't know how often I can, from here."

He waved his hand. I need not worry. I must write to my *madre* often, and my mail would be taken to Magdalena by the ranch car, which went to town every few days for supplies. I could count on my letters coming and going. In fact, sometimes, if I wanted to, and if they could spare me at the corrals, I could take the car myself. All I had to do was ask. Don Elizario was more than jovial—he became merry.

"One moment."

He went to the next room and returned with a bottle of José Cuervo tequila and two small glasses, and poured drinks which with a silent toast to each other we took in one toss and swallow. In answer to a question I had not spoken, he said.

"She does not drink."

In a moment, Concha appeared in the parlor doorway. In the dim room her vividness was subdued, and so was her temperament, but her gray eyes gave light. She greeted me silently, letting me press her inert hand, and then with bowed head she led us to the dining room which her husband had built for her. Between the old parlor and the new dining room was a narrow unlighted hallway. On its wall was a telephone in an oaken box with a small hand crank and a cradled receiver on its side. The mouthpiece stood out from the rest at the end of a long brass bracket. As we moved past it to supper, Don Elizario indicated the phone with complacency:

"We are *moderno* out here at the ranch, also."

"Unless," ventured Concha, "there is thunder and lightning"—she shuddered—"and then we cannot hear anything."

"Yes, yes, the wire. There is a wire connecting us with the line from Magdalena to Datil. Sometimes we can see the *electricidad* on it."

He laughed gently at belonging to such a proud trick of science and nature.

In the dining room, suddenly all was bright, garish. In her own part of the house, Concha had had her way. Excess and expense were everywhere visible—the heaviest silver, the most profuse cut glass, the brightest curtains and rug and wallpaper. Above the table

[163]

hung a cluster of electric lights twined about with glass grapes and vine leaves. The electricity came unsteadily from a dynamo run by the windmill. As we sat down, Don Elizario said to me, as if testing my credentials and good faith,

"You will say grace, eh?"

I recited the common Catholic grace, ending with *"Per Dominum Jesum Christum in vitam aeternam, Amen,"* to give a priestly turn for his reassurance. He gave a wan little laugh of appreciation.

It was a heavy meal, almost unseasoned except for a paste of *guacamole,* which was fiery with red chili powder and seeds. There was almost no conversation. Concha kept her eyes lowered as though still in her convent school. Her husband ate with great sweeps of a big spoon which he used instead of a fork. His napkin was tucked in above the collar button. Once he paused to ask me,

"¿Más tequila?"

"No, thank you."

"Es muy bueno para la digestión."

"No, thank you. I don't really drink."

He sighed with comfort.

"This is delicious," I said to Concha.

"Thank you," she replied without looking at me. She was enacting her husband's view of her role.

Concha took away the dishes and in the kitchen readied our dessert—a bowl of mangos awash with juice. Before she returned, Don Elizario asked me how I liked "the big city" of Magdalena—a joke.

I should have seen it, he declared, years ago, when the mines were working full time, and the hotel was filled day and night, and the railroad siding was crowded with the private cars of Eastern capitalists. Many a time he had dined on board one or the other of these, talking investments with those New York bankers. They listened to him. He knew what he was talking about. He was not as rich as they were, but he was rich enough for their respect, and before the mines began to give out, and the town to fade with them, he got enough money buying and selling shares—more, in some cases, than the bankers themselves. What times they used to have at the Marigold Hotel! One time the secretary of President Díaz of Mexico came to talk investment, and Don Elizario himself was the host, and when the secretary went back with useful information, the President sent a letter and a medal. Between the words, Don Eli was telling me what a great man he used to be.

"In those days, they used to call me Mr Magdalena. I knew everything that went on there. Even right now, there is someone who tells me everything that goes on there."

He wheezed a little contented laugh.

After supper he sighed with contentment, and said he had to go out to see how the men were doing, as he did every night. He left me with Concha.

She led me to the new sitting room which her husband had built for her. It was like a movie set of the vamp period—satin draperies, two floor lamps with pagoda-like shades hung with long silk tassels, a fur rug on a deep sofa, pierced brass lanterns shedding a patterned soft light, many cushions on furniture and floor, and on a velvet ottoman an almost life-sized toy of a leopard with green glass eyes.

Here she became animated. She now felt it her duty to entertain, and like a child, the only way she knew how to do this was to bring out things to show.

"Now I can show you my wedding pictures. I brought them along from town."

We sat side by side, though not dangerously near, as she opened her albums of white imitation leather. She photographed superbly. In only one or two pictures her diffidence at being a bride showed through all the lace, tulle, the waxen tuberoses of her wreath, the enormous bouquet of lilies she held. For the rest, she posed expertly, even in the joint pictures with Don Elizario, who was resplendent in stiff evening dress as they stood in full sunlight outside the church of San Felipe de Neri in Old Town, Albuquerque. She looked up at him with lustrous gaze. Her freshness in years was lovely, and to it she added the statuesque allure which she had learned from afternoon hours in the dreaming darkness of the Central Avenue movie houses at home. After half an hour of slowly turning the pictures, where I saw also her impassive parents and relatives, her four flower girls, her train bearer (a little male cousin) and her ring bearer (another), and the parish priest in his jubilee vestments, I said,

"The camera suits you, Concha."

"Don't let my husband hear you call me that, Richard."

"Mrs Wenzel."

By her use of my first name, though, she put us in some sort of league. Starving for any connection with anyone, she abandoned her impersonation of a grown-up, submissive, but important wife. She said, hopelessly,

"Movie star."

"You could have been."

The past tense made her gaze at me with a dispirited sigh. But it was true. In the silent films, conventionally directed, she might have captured audiences with her beauty alone, while her actions and lips went through the accepted signals of movie passion. A little tuck in her smooth brow reflected her resignation now. She looked around at the terms of her luxury, which represented a prison she had entered almost without thinking.

"He is very good to you. He worships you."

She nodded impatiently as if to dismiss an irrelevancy.

"I worry about him, you know," she said.

This, coupled with her misery, touched me. I asked why.

"You know—you should not tell this to anyone, he does not want them to know—you know, he is not well."

"No? He looks like a robust old man."

"Old man, yes. —Yes, he has something wrong here." She gracefully indicated her heart. "Pecta-something."

[166]

"Angina pectoris?"

"Yes. That." She shivered. "Sometimes at night I am afraid, will I wake up next to him and he will be dead? Or—"

Or herself in his dead arms? occurred to me as she halted her thought.

I had not before seen in mind so vividly the image of them together in bed, like any man and wife.

"And then," she continued, "I am even more afraid when I wake up at night and he is gone."

"Gone?"

"Yes, late at night he often gets up and goes outside. He says he looks at the stars, and listens for the cows, if they are all right, and there he stands, looking and listening, I don't know what for, until he gets cold, in his old nightgown, and then he comes in again, to me—"

—To get warm of her lovely body, after being alone and silent in the starry darkness, taking stock of his world, and perhaps wondering how much longer he would be able to see it?

If I had felt sympathy for her, now I had pity for him. His fears were now doubly poignant when I saw them in light of hers. For a moment, an even further notion of what their marriage might lack lighted and then went out in my mind. I must spare them (who in their ways so mutely asked for reassurances) any speculation. They must be allowed the dignity of what they chose to show the world.

Setting her albums aside, she said,

"Your hands. They are all raw."

"Yes. That rake."

"You see?" she said, commenting on the expert management she immediately decided upon. She went and fetched a bottle of liniment and some bits of cotton. Sitting beside me again, she began to bathe my blisters with the soaked cotton, holding my hands in turn. I was watching her face so intently, and she my hands, that we did not hear or see Don Elizario come in. He must have stood for a long moment; and then, scraping his steps, went back to the hallway and returned at once with a pair of old cracked leather work gloves. Concha was by then across the room from me, holding her liniment bottle to her breasts as though in self-protection. Don Elizario ignored her. To me, giving me the gloves, he said,

"These will help you. So, good night. Come to see us whenever you like." His voice hardened a little. "My wife gets lonely."

At this she put her hand over her mouth, wondering at him. What did he mean? But I thought that his bestowing sanction upon my welcome in her name robbed her of a last independent pleasure in imagined variations of her days.

※

The light in the small bunkhouse was still burning and I was sorry if it meant that Babyface was still awake. But he was asleep, so exhausted that even facing the lamp did not bother him. If he had been waiting for me, he had been unable to keep his eyes open. He was bare to the waist, with his blanket thrown across his legs. He looked more than ever like a large child. He had been too tired to wash before throwing himself down on his bunk. The dust of the day paled his skin and darkened his cap of light hair, which was like thick short fur. His head was on his doubled-up right arm and his left arm hung straight off the bunk almost to the floor. Around his neck rested a thin tarnished brass chain which vanished into the shadow of his pillowing arm.

Resenting the loss of privacy, I undressed as quietly as I could, hoping I would not awaken him. As the lamp was still lighted, I decided that I must establish my prior right to read as late as I liked, and that it was my habit to read every night before sleeping. I opened my volume of Mencken, which Lyle had given me, and turned to the essay on "The Husbandman," which made such hilarious if extravagant fun of the farmer—"the lonely companion of

Bos Taurus" who renounced "Babylon to guard the horned cattle of the hills," but than whom "no more grasping, selfish and dishonest mammal, indeed, is known to students of the Anthropoidea," the living reason for "saddling the rest of us with oppressive and idiotic laws, all hatched on the farm. There, where the cows low through the still night, and the jug of Peruna stands behind the stove, and bathing begins, as at Biarritz, with the vernal equinox, there is the reservoir of all the nonsensical legislation which now makes the United States a buffoon among the great nations. . . ." I was suppressing impulses to laugh out loud at such passages when in turning a page I saw that my bunkhouse mate was watching me.

He was grinning. The lamplight showed me his face closely for the first time. It seemed open and guileless, but it was difficult to see into his eyes; for in the right eye there was a curious disfigurement. It was a wedge of light in the circle of the iris which gave his stare an elusive direction, though I knew he was looking straight at me. It was something not visible at a little distance. Close to, it seemed to put him into a different dimension of space from anyone he looked at. Evidently he had no loss of vision. The effect was strangely powerful, for while it made you hesitate to look directly at him, it forced you to do so.

He said genially,

"I don't have any of that c-r-u-u-d."

"That what?"

"The book, and that."

It was my introduction to his habit of talk. He was more foul-mouthed than anybody I ever heard, even in my army years later in the Hitler war.

"I read before going to sleep every night."

"Oh, I can read, sure enough. I just am not interested. I have enough to fill my days. And my nights."

He gave a comradely laugh at this reference to his prowess at night. He was now wide awake and in a mood to talk.

"My name is J. Buswell Rennison, but everybody calls me Buz—

have ever since I was a crawlin baby in south Texas by the Rio Grande."

I told him my name.

"Where're you from, Richie?"

"Albuquerque"—thinking any of my history further back need not concern him.

"Come on. They tell me your daddy's governor of New York."

I was then forced to say a little more to correct the news about me which probably beginning with Don Elizario had been enlarged throughout the sheep camp.

He took this as an invitation to sit up and listen with sociable interest. As he did so, his neck chain swung around upon his tight-muscled chest and I saw a metal disk hanging from it. It was the size of a half dollar. He saw me looking at it and pulled the chain over his head and handed it to me.

It was colored with bright cheap enamel. Around the rim it read ATLANTIC CITY BATHING BEAUTY. In the center was a bossed figure of a young woman in a striped bathing suit. Her head was tilted in flirtation, and across her middle she held a lettered ribbon which said, A LUCKY PIECE. Her left knee was laid provocatively against her right thigh.

"My lucky *piece,*" he said as I handed it back to him. "I got it in a hock shop in Mexico. I call it my ice breaker. I let it slide out of my shirt, and I can tell by the way they look at it the first time what it will or won't do for me." He fondled the amulet and chain and added, "It's a mighty handy little thing to have around. Not that I've needed it too often—my personality generally does the work."

He was amiably settled for a ramble though autobiography, which he undertook with pleasure in himself. For a few minutes I held my book open to suggest that I meant to return to it; but I finally gave up, closed it, put it on the table, and let him go on. His voice was light, his mood candid, and he laced almost every sentence with smiling obscenities. (I exactly quote only a few which carried

[170]

meaning in moments of high feeling.) He was so certain of the interest of his life, because it was his, and he someone of well-confirmed excellence in all he undertook, that I was soon far beyond my pose as a collector of specimens.

As he talked, sitting up and gesturing freely, I never knew exactly where his flawed gaze rested whenever he turned toward me; but with genial power, he made me see with almost a familiar eye much of what he talked about. Presuming a universal lack of reticence in others, he invaded my attention with exuberant candor as though he had known me from boyhood. His experience was limited to the physical; and yet he had acquired a sharpness of mind and an ease of expression, however crude, such as I had not heard equaled among even the best of my fellow students of that time. On that night, as well as on many later occasions, he spoke of his life. Here I have assembled in one place the gist of many notes recorded at odd times. By the rift of light in his eye, and the working of his mind behind it, I wondered how much of what he told was true and how much fantasy; but what he invented—if invent he did—told as much about him, I thought, as what might be fact. He said he remembered everything that had ever happened to him, and it flowed out of him like a stream.

His family were fruit growers on the lower Rio Grande in Texas. He had worked in the orange groves ever since he could remember. How a water moccasin had actually chased him in the river when he was nothing but a tiny boy, pecker-high on a pickaninny. How he used to shuck himself buck-naked with the other boys and spend all day Sunday swimming and messing around—"you know how kids do each other"—in the shallow brown river. How they used to take their BB guns and hide in the grass in the banker's orchard where his horses grazed and shoot them in the rump to see them jump and hear them holler. What they did to a naked sissy boy one time in the school basement with a bottle of Dynashine shoe polish and then when he went and snitched on them, what they did to him after that with lighted cigarettes. The way it felt when the young wife of a fruit trucker showed him and the boys everything and let them in all the way. He was the leader of the gang because he already knew about that, and he was leader for three years, until he had to run away at fifteen for getting the daughter of the leading chiropractor in Harlingen, Texas, pregnant. That was the best thing he ever did—running away, not the other thing, there was nothing that special about her, but he always had his mind on bettering himself and how could you do that at home? He had never been back since, but he never had trouble finding jobs, on ranches or in towns, and someday when he and I were off on a long trip together, hitching rides on freight trains or autos, he would tell me about some of them. He learned more about human nature by the time he was eighteen than any old man he ever saw. Did I know what the best rule was? It was not to give a flying frig about anybody else's feelings, for you could never know what those were anyway, and all that mattered was what you felt yourself, and you know that what you felt the most was right down there, where he was pointing. He got East as far as Chicago, and Northwest as far Vancouver, and then he gradually came down the coast to San Francisco. There as a bellhop he made more money on the side (he particularized at doing what for old widows and married women after hours) than he ever saw until he got to Los Angeles. That was where the rainbow began and ended, with him in the middle, as someone told him. One day they took one look at him and said he belonged in pictures, if only he would get dressed up to be somebody else, like a cowboy, or a tango dancer, or an international prince in disguise who was on his way to claiming his rightful kingdom. It sounded mighty inviting to him. A number of people had the same idea about him, but it seemed a long time before he got anywhere nearer a movie camera than somebody's bed. Not but what he didn't enjoy it, with the stuff they gave him, that he could sell, or when he couldn't stand the others for a while, that he could give away in turn to someone young when he wanted them for his own personal enjoyment. They did not care, out there, what they did. It was wild and mighty nice, and he had to admit that he still enjoyed being the leader of the gang by natural right, and if they thought they had done it all, they had another think coming at the things he showed them. One of them—he spoke a famous name—tried to kill theirself when he told her he wouldn't be back. But that about being a movie star—he finally insisted, one day, and they got him to have a screen test, and that did it. It was all over. That thing in his right eye made him look blind on the screen. He saw it himself, and they said they couldn't have a movie star who showed only his left side all the time. He could see the sense in this, and they had him back where he was before, in and out of their big cars and swimming pools and fancy bedrooms, until one night he was having such a good time with several people that somebody got hurt sure enough, she had to have the ambulance, and he lit out for Mexico. He stayed there for a year and he never heard if she died or not, though he certainly hoped she didn't, but he thought he should not go back to Holly-wood, even when his money gave out and he had to sell all the little gold things they had given him back then. The next thing he knew, he had a full beard. It was blond, like his head, and he got a job as night clerk in the hotel at Avanzada, Mexico, where tourists who talked English kept coming down from Arizona. He was known there as the former assistant manager of the Palace Hotel in San Francisco. Messican women certainly went for blond-bearded gringos. It was a fine job, but the hotel burned down one night when a bunch of bandits rode into town and had a battle with the local army garrison. So everything he had in the world including his hidden wallet of new savings that he meant to better himself with burned also. He headed for Agua Prieta, across the border from Douglas, Arizona, but there wasn't any work in either place, and he got on over to El Paso. He thought the beard wasn't needed any longer. He shaved it off and slept several nights at the Salvation Army. Then he saw an ad in the paper for a job. He answered it, and made a date to be in Magdalena, New Mexico, to get a ride to the ranch and [here his affability became almost boisterous] what did he do but miss the date.

"But I'm not sorry," he added. "I had me a time in Magdalena."

He arrived there a day before he was supposed to and went to have a cup of coffee in the café of the hotel. That did it. There was that girl, the waitress, and he knew before he said anything about a "lucky piece" that she was one.

"Larraine?" I said—that downcast, tired, plump young woman?

"That's her."

They went upstairs to her room at the far end of the corridor of the Marigold Hotel in the afternoon. She had been given a bottle of bootleg corn by a friend. They got drunk—he ve-ry drunk, and except for when she had to go downstairs to work at suppertime, they stayed up there, because she couldn't get enough of what he had to give. She swore she had never known anything like it. Maybe she was just saying it to make him feel good. Anyway.

"That doesn't sound like her," I protested, I suppose in a haze of chivalry. "I saw her the next day when I had breakfast. She was not like that at all. She was quiet, hardly looked at anyone. You must have been with somebody else."

"Not at all. She was just hung over."

So was he—so badly that he had to stay upstairs to sleep it off, which was how he happened to miss Tom Agee and me for the drive out to the ranch the next morning. In the afternoon, when he felt a little better, she took him around to see some friends of hers, a girl and her young man who were going to be married. They were making plans. Larraine was asked to the wedding. She asked whether she might bring Buz, if he could get back to town for it. They agreed.

"Look, let's you and me go together," he said with animation. "You'd sure like Larraine. We'd have us a high ol time."

Everybody always got horny at a wedding, he declared. He knew he could fix me up. He sounded like a boy aching with possessive happiness over a new jitney—innocent and jubilant. My silence seemed like assent to him. He was sure we could manage to get to town somehow on the wedding day, which was a Saturday. If nothing else, we could walk the eleven miles to the highway and flag the Magdalena-Springerville stage. Or maybe we could just appropriate the ranch Ford and be gone before anybody would know it. I then made a mistake.

"The boss says I can borrow it if I want to go to town to mail my letters."

"Then it's all settled," he cried, rocking back and forth with physical satisfaction in how things fell right for him. "You and I are going to hit it off, Richie. I can always tell."

Why had I listened to him so attentively, after all? He had the invaluable knack of holding your interest, whether by his sheer vitality, self-loving confidence, exotic information, I didn't know. But I had never known anyone like him who showed such encompassing good will coupled with a startling lack of moral sense, and I was fascinated by the smooth mix of those opposites. Perhaps I felt envy at his unrestrained life, even as I wondered how much of what he told might be only romances and lies in which to see himself. But in these as well as in truth lay much of his essential self.

I was now sleepier than he was. He would have talked all night if I had not been overwhelmed by engulfing yawns. He laughed forgivingly and huddled himself down into his blanket. The night was turning cool, we had to be up at half past five for the first day of dipping the sheep.

"Douse it," said Buz, his voice thick with comfort. I turned out the oil lamp. In a few minutes I could see the stars through the open door. "A high ol time," he murmured. "It's no fun havin it alone."

How much he took for granted. The frontier American must have been like him—his sociableness so confident that he could not imagine reticence in others. Always on the move, he had no roots. Always encountering and leaving strangers, he had to make the

[175]

most of whatever contact he had with them. His assumption that every life was like his made it only friendly to trade lives as soon and as fully as possible. Sophisticated travelers on the early frontier were always amazed by the garrulity and curiosity of the plainsman, and also by the appeal of the individual man who felt himself equal to the joys and hazards of a whole wilderness.

※

I see my own work of that summer of a half century ago as though the years were a deep physical distance away. Everything stands in miniature though distinct detail lighted by halations of memory, watched from a height looking down at the swarming creatures, men and animals, at their hard tasks; and somewhere in the midst of it all at my various jobs is my young self.

The figures are tiny, seen from so long ago, but brightly lighted. I have the feeling of an illicit observer, an eavesdropper, for they do not know I am looking and listening. Years and distance away, they seem to create a harmony now out of the confusions of that far time. Even as I remember those, I taste the foulness of the task they are doing. Their colors are brilliant, they throw shadows like spilled ink, for the sun is furious. This little group seems to stand as all humanity at timeless purpose and act, and they forge again a link in the human chain reaching from antiquity, so that their commonness becomes a marvel of discovery about man's enduring habitude. A dimly remembered passage from the third of Vergil's *Georgics* in Dryden's translation tells me again of the persistence of human ways in the parallels between the Roman shepherd's husbandry and mine, as a youth:

Good shepherds, after shearing, drench their sheep.
And their flock's father (forced from high to leap)

Swims down the stream, and plunges in the deep.
They oint their naked limbs with mothered oil;
Or, from the founts where living sulphurs boil,
They mix a Med'cine to foment their limbs,
With scum that on the molten silver swims:
Fat pitch, and black bitumen, add to these,
Beside the waxen labor of the bees,
And hellebore, and squills deep-rooted in the seas . . .

I hear the mixed noises of the job—the shouted orders of the men, the sound of hammering huge nails repairing timber work, the chorus of cries from the sheep, and I know again the stenches rising from the various acts of work, cooked to a sickening intensity by the blaze of the heat from the sun and the fires.

For there, between the corrals, they are hauling logs and building fires to heat a mixture in two huge tanks of galvanized iron with open tops. These are supported on iron trestles, braced with timbers, and the fires are set beneath. Men are driving burros to bring kegs of water from the windmill tank. They lift and pour the water into the iron vats, where it is mixed with gallon upon gallon of a dark-gray, lumpy mass consisting mostly of a powerful disinfectant called Black Leaf 40. This gives off a stench like vomit mixed with creosote, released into the air through a bubbling scum. Many of the men wear kerchiefs tied around their faces under broad shadowing hats.

On platforms by the vats, one man at each keeps stirring the mixture as more water and disinfectant are added. The fires are constantly fed. In the day's heat the fires have become almost unbearable, and the men who have to come to them, shielding their faces, and in their faded colors and crouching haste, resemble details taken from vast old paintings of catastrophe. Other men are driving sheep in the upper corral toward one corner of it, where a cleated incline awaits them. At their head is the emperor ram who going first will have all the others blindly follow. At the end of the incline is a solid wooden gate like that of a sluice which can be raised in grooves; and when the time comes, the shorn sheep will be driven up the incline and through the gate, and down a slippery slide into the cement trough which has been filled by feeder pipes from the high vats with the thick, hot, stinking mix.

Their cries are wild as they slide into the trough, which is four feet wide. They must swim to live, all seventy-five feet of its length. They cannot scramble out of the dip over the sides, which are sheer, and eight feet deep. Struggling to keep their heads above the surface of the foul dip, the sheep make a continuous bleat. Their shorn legs lash, they survive by sheer terror and instinct. But not an inch of their skins is spared the treatment of the dip, for men with long poles which end in Y-shaped prongs are stationed at intervals on each side of the dip, and with their prongs, the men push every animal under the surface as it passes them. The sheep struggle against each other, tightly packed, choking and crying, lashing the dip mixture to spray which scatters upon the men. At the end of the long trough, its floor rises with cleats. The sheep scramble up it, and a timber alley fences them in and directs them in all their foul crowding into the lower corral, where they shake themselves, and cry and cry at the terror they have been through. A sluice carries their drippings back to the trough. Overhead, low and circling, a network of buzzards cast their exact shadows over the creatures of the ground.

The old hands are ready for the job to be done every summer, but a newcomer can hardly work at first for nausea at the sight, sound, and smell of the dip. The old man is at hand throughout much of every day until all the sheep have been treated for ticks, lice, and other parasites. He does not handle a pronged pole, but his eye is everywhere, governing the timing of the sheep in their approach, their slide, their passage through the hot slime, their emergence at the other end; the feeding of the log fires under the vats; the replenishment of the tanks; the rhythm of the men at their work of submerging the sheep and the skill with which they time it so that as few sheep as possible may drown—though now and then one does, and its body must be probed for and hauled out and burned, adding a new stench to the air.

If a wind comes up, and dust stirs, the sounds and smells of the work drift everywhere, even to the ranch house, where invisible and alone the old man's young wife is awake and dreaming of affairs far away from the brute world at her doorstep. Other creatures do their duty at the work: running up and down the corral barriers and the length of the dip are the sheep dogs, barking with excitement and concern. Now and then they turn aside for a quick rough caress from a worker, and feeling their duty approved they seem to smile with their tongues hanging out; and wagging their handsome tails, they return to their charges. The shorn wool already bagged is on a flatbed, horse-drawn dray which leaves for the highway and Magdalena, where the wool will be loaded in the railroad cars and taken to the rail junction at Socorro, and be on its way to the markets of Kansas City and Chicago. The hard work hidden by the unmarked distance is brought into the organized commerce of the cities and the world. Never under the summer sun has work seemed harder, and men closer in their anonymous part of it to the very nature of the animals they tend. The marvel is that with means so primitive, and with relatively so few men, and with animals so frantically self-protective, a degree of efficiency is reached, a job done in its annual cycle for a space of days; and at the end of work, an exhausted and at moments even a rude lyrical humanity returns in the evening to those who have borne the burden of the day.

꽃

At the end of the first day of dipping, Don Elizario came from the house after supper as we were all sitting or lying around the coals of the fire where the cook's big enameled coffee pot kept his brew steaming for our tin cups. The sky was washed with the last rosy light of the west. Our aching bodies sought ease and cool. It was time for sociability.

Don Elizario made a point in such evenings of joining his men, to give them his comradeship as unspoken gratitude for their work. If we were to have entertainment, we must make it for ourselves; and he must do his share. Anyone who could sing a song, or tell a story, or dance a jig, was called on to do so. We left a little clearing between us and the campfire for anyone who would perform by the faint glow, like stage light cast upward. Don Eli sat on an upturned bucket, as his legs were too stiff to let him get down to the ground and up with comfort.

On our first evening festival, Ira the cook—the men called him Irene for their view of him as female in his role as cook, and because of a way he had of shrilling and shooing like a woman when anyone tried to steal anything from his stores of food—usually began the show as someone cried for his fiddle and his dance.

Irene ran to his wagon. He slept there rather than in the bunk-house and guarded all his possessions in neatness. In a moment he returned with his violin. Making a great act of tuning it, listening critically with the box close to his ear among his wild but sparse tufts of hair, he created anticipation as by an overture to a play. Finally, satisfied, he pushed his crooked spectacles up on his nose, slapped the ground twice with his right foot to announce rhythm, and began to play with a scratchy thin tone a repetitious piece like a tune from a square dance. After one stanza played standing still, he began with the next one to shuffle and stamp and turn to his own music. Turning one way, he was the man, crazily gallant and stiff; the other, he was the woman responding, mincing in exaggerated gentility. Soon we were all clapping hands and whistling encouragement to his music. At this, he would flare his eyes at his audience like a flirt, and then toss his head at our impertinence and beat away at the dusty ground while his mosquito noise kept up with perfect, insane regularity. It was growing dark. Someone threw wood on the fire and light blazed up, throwing the footlight glow over Irene in his greasy rags. He scorned, dominated, and wooed his audience like a great star. Finishing his performance, he slowed it down, and, at the very end, made a deep, rickety, but splendid bow, holding his fiddle and his stick of horsehair widely apart. He created the illusion of a large theater, transforming our enthusiastic but sparse applause into an ovation.

There was a moment of satisfied quiet. Don Elizario nodded his approval of the show, which he had seen many times. His presence among us was so at home and so easy, yet so sure of its authority, that we were all sure of it too. Nobody was immediately moved to follow the cook with an act, and so, clearing his throat, making rusty little sounds, Don Elizario grandly brushed his profuse mustaches upward with the knuckles of both hands and said,

"I will tell you a little story."

Nodding and smiling faintly, he slowly told in his mild old voice a story about a certain Saint Jerónimo—not the famous Saint Jerónimo, but another less well-known but a saint just the same.

"Did you ever hear of the Devil himself making a saint out of anybody?"

Well, that was exactly what happened in the case of Saint Jerónimo. It seemed that Jerónimo was a ver' handsome young man who had his way with all the fine young beautiful girls in his town (this was somewhere in Spain a long time ago). There wasn't a girl who didn't lie down with him the minute he asked her to. When he made pusha-pusha, they cried out in joy, "Jerónimo, Jerónimo." All the other young men said he had the ver' Devil in him. He had to fight many duels, but he never lost one, and turned up fresh as ever to pick out a new girl.

The Devil got him all those girls, everyone said there were two thousand five hundred and nine of them—Don Elizario with a wheezy little laugh gave the signal for a general stir of carnal laughter, in which all joined—and when it came to number two thousand five hundred and *ten,* the Devil made a saint out of young Jerónimo; for when Jerónimo tried to make pusha-pusha with her, the Devil prevented his *verga* from rising, just exactly at the moment when it was needed. The young lady, who was the daughter of a king, and ver' used to having her own way, slapped Don Jerónimo in the face, saying, "You are good for nothing but being a monk," and went home to the king's palace.

And Don Jerónimo saw the Devil sitting over there on a tree stump with his own *verga* pointed like a carrot and jumping around like a goat's. The Devil was laughing and laughing. Don Jerónimo said, "Ver' well, I will become a monk." And so he became a monk, and lived a long life of good works, and his *verga* never tempted him again, and after he died, he performed many miracles and became a saint.

Everyone stirred. The subject had been raised which was most on their minds, far away from women, tired enough to believe or dream anything, and hungry for any expression of their desire which it was impossible to fulfill; and, too, the possibility of sanctity in any human predicament crossed their minds, however faintly, since everybody believed in goodness as well as evil.

Someone cried out,

"Hey, Irene, tell us about the last time you tried to get you a sheep, and what the ol ram did to you for it!"

The cook, in shadow beyond the firelight, tossed his head and waggled his tongue at the question. Everybody laughed at both the questioner and the questioned, and at the inevitable folk joke about those who work with sheep year in and year out. A sort of anonymous comradeship descended upon us all. Sanction, so mildly introduced by Don Elizario, was now rudely confirmed.

Just at that moment, out of the darkness between us and the house in its dome of cottonwoods silhouetted against the stars, Conchä came toward the firelight and entered its long rays, which stretched away on the ground between the shadows of the men.

Her husband stood up and said sharply,

"What are you doin here? You get back to the house!"

"There is a telephone call," she said. "The Datil operator is trying to get you—"

She turned to go, gathering herself in fear. As she turned, she saw Buz for an instant. He was staring at her with his mouth open. The firelight was on both their faces. The exchange of a look between them was like a bolt of feeling, as if a door had been thrown open and closed on a revelation. Everyone saw this—Don Elizario saw it. He lunged toward Concha and struck her on the buttocks to drive her to the house. They diminished away into the darkness.

"Jesus Christ!" exclaimed Buz softly. "Did you see that?" He asked me, "Who is that? His granddaughter?"

"His wife."

He exclaimed,

"Wife!" making the word obscene. He spat scornfully.

The others were all long aware of Don Elizario's marriage, and by now were indifferent to it. They saw no reason for the evening to come to a sudden end. Someone called out,

"All right, there, Babyface, now you just give us a song or a story."

This was said in a tone slightly menacing, and the others added their voices. In the air was a threat of hazing the latecomer if he should refuse. Buz shrugged and asked,

"Well, is there anybody got a *guit*ar here?"

One of the Mexican herders handed him one. Buz tuned it even more elaborately than Irene with his fiddle. As he strummed for his own satisfaction, he said,

"I'll sing you a song I made up myself."

Stolid silence met this. Finally, in an expert imitation of the show-business singers who broke their voices sentimentally on stressed words, he sang:

> *Oh, my darlin Bonnie Mae,*
> *I said goodbye to you today,*

And I wonder if I'll ever see you more.
With your hair so golden bright
And your eyes so full of light,
Oh, my darlin, wait for me I do implore!

Oh, no gal was ever sweeter,
If so, I'd like to meet her,
But my darlin Bonnie Mae need have no fear.
As long as stars are in the sky
Then my love will never die,
And my blue-eyed Bonnie Mae will be my dear.

Bonnie Mae so sweet and slender,
All her words so true and tender,
I will carry in my heart until the end.
Hand in hand we'll walk through life,
Oh, my darlin little wife,
And nothing from each other shall us rend.

Slow final chords. Silence. Then,

"She somebody real?" asked a voice longing to believe.

"Hell, yes," replied Buz. "Only her name was different."

"Did you marry her?"

"Hell, no. The sorry little bitch ran off with a horny circuit preacher. Them shoutin sons of bitches get all worked up with their Bible whackin, and then can't keep their pants buttoned."

Tom Agee half rose and hoarsely cried out in his weak voice,

"Now look here, you little squirt, you just keep some respect in your mouth for the good men who harvest for the Lord!"

"He was a preacher," I told Buz.

"Well, Reverend, no offense," said Buz. "They's all kinds."

But he grinned like a rosy satyr at those nearest him. There might have been a reply, but from the house dimly away came two sharp little screams. We looked at each other and most probably saw the same picture. Don Elizario, done with his phone call to Datil, which would connect his line with Socorro and Magdalena, had turned to Concha and beaten her to teach her a lesson, and, I thought, to chastise himself for what his jealousy had to remind him of.

There was an animal look on Buz's clear little face. If she had made a powerful impact on him, in their lightning-quick meeting of eyes, his excitement, and its nature, were now doubled by the idea of her being hurt physically on his account until she had had to cry out. Someone went to the coffee pot on the coals, which breathed now bright now dim on the light night wind. The pot was empty. It was clear that Don Elizario was not coming back. Tom stood up to signal the end of the campfire hour. Everyone drifted off to bed.

When we were alone in the bunkhouse, Buz asked,

"Did you mean what you said about him and her?"

I nodded.

He groaned.

"She's too beautiful to live—especially with *that*. If I could only—"

"You'd better not. He's crazy when it comes to her."

He locked his hands behind his head on the hard uncovered pillow and stared up at the rough beams of the ceiling.

"All my life I said I only wanted to get me a rich woman and settle her down and keep her pregnant and then, whoo! I'd be free to do for myself with anybody I wanted to. But when I see someone like that—what's her name?"

"Concha."

"Concha. I don't know. Did you see her lookin at me? —Oh me, oh my. I just bet she'd welcome the change . . . One more look, and it'd be all over."

I remembered Tom Agee's advice to me about Concha; but I did not repeat it now.

Buz had a new idea.

"They tell me you are the only one here who goes over to the house."

[185]

"I don't know. I *have* been there."

"You goin back?"

"Maybe."

"Yes, Richie. Take me with you! That way, I—"

"I couldn't."

"Sure you could. You could just say you brought your friend to play a game of Crazy Eights, or talk about the weather, it wouldn't matter what, just so I—"

"No. The old man wouldn't have it."

"Well, so how come you get to go there and not me?"

I explained how I happened to be at the WZL.

"Well, I don't have any society doctor to get me in where I belong, but I thought I had a *friend.*"

"You do. I just know how things are over there. You wait till the old man asks you. Then I'll take you."

"You sure are the prize gutless wonder!"

I picked up my book and began to read. It was like closing another door in his face. He could not endure being excluded. If he lost me, he lost everyone here. After a while he said,

"Where will you go after this job is done? We've got only a little while more."

"I'm staying on till September some time."

"What are you suppose to do here all that time?"

"Oh, odd jobs after the cattle come back and the range men come in, I suppose."

"I bet they aren't paying you anythin. I bet you are just a dude on vacation. *I* have to work for *my* living."

"No, they aren't paying me anything. They are doing me a favor, so they say."

"And you work your balls off for nothing?"

"Listen, I'm trying to read."

He most of all dreaded separateness. He went on,

"I get paid off at the end of the dipping. I don't know where I'll go." Expertly, he put pathos into his voice. "Listen, Richie. Why don't you go with me? We'll figger some place to go. Nobody ever turned ol Buz down yet, at anythin. With your brains and my guts—*you* know—why not?"

I remember the power of his confidence in himself, and the appeal this allowed him to exert. His energy was compelling. His color was high, his eyes sparkled, and the flaw in one of them seemed to evoke a vision of a world in which he was all-powerful. His light voice softened with the excitement of conspiracy.

"We'll show the sons a bitches," he said urgently, meaning the world at large.

I had to shake my head.

"But why? Why?"

Saying why took much time and wrangling; at the end of which he was deeply aggrieved, and I was sorry for him, angry with myself, and wondering how I could find a way to be his friend, in spite of everything.

¥

The next evening, Don Elizario was back with us as gently merry as though nothing too real in its revelation had happened the night before. He was ready again for imagined romance, and the rituals of comradely obscenity invoked by men isolated together. Don Elizario cleared his throat.

"I have a song tonight," he said as though to make us forget the night before. We became quiet. In a moment he began to sing. The sound was remote and clouded, in a quavering husk of a voice. I thought of the slowed song of some shelled desert creature—a cicada—created to celebrate the hot and empowering desert light, but now making its last salute to life and creation. That it came from a man full of present regret, and still lively ·longing, made it, instead of lusty and funny, as touching as shame for that which could not be controlled. He sang:

> *Darling, I am growing old,*
> *Silver threads among the gold*
> *Shine down there on me today;*
> *Life is fading fast away.*
>
> *Let me feel you everywhere,*
> *Where I'll find your golden hair.*
> *Let us mingle though I'm old*
> *Silver threads among the gold.*

Applause for the boss man was lively; but even before it died down, Buz, gleaming with hard high spirits, took the audience with a song which sounded like a direct reply to Don Elizario's gentle old obscenity. Whacking the box of Pancho's guitar for attention, Buz cried out like a comedian over a boisterous crowd, pressing the unspoken rivalry he dared to feel against Don Elizario:

> *H-o-o-oo,*
> *Will you love me when my batteries need re-chargin?*
> *Will you love me when my carburetor's dry?*
> *When my inner tubes have lost their self-respect?*
> *Will you be satisfied just to bill and coo?*
> *Or will you sit around all day and cry?*
> *H-o-o-o-,*
> *I'll drive that ol tin lizzie till I die!*

He sang it through again, to clapped hands. Don Elizario stood up When the stanza ended, he said sharply,

"*Mañana, mucho trabajo, amigos.* So now break it up, break i⁴ up."

The circle began to drift away. Don Eli called out,

"Bebbyface, you come here."

Buz paused, and then, with a mock-humble skip, went over to the old man, who held out a hand, slightly trembling, with forefinger pointed at Buz:

"You stay 'way from my wife, you hear?"

"Yessir. Me? I don't even *know* your wife, Mr Wenzel. Sure, sir. Anything you say."

But his smile contradicted his respectful promise. Don Elizario waved him off and turned homeward. Buz watched him go, then turned to me, expecting approval. But he saw in my face, apparently, that he had ended forever any chance of his being invited at last to come with me to the house on some fine evening.

"What the hell!" he said defiantly. "There's more'n one way to skin a cat—if you know that I mean."

※

Like most young people, I was not then fastidious—inclined more to endure what was about me. Through no choice of mine, Buz Rennison was a fixture of my days. In his deceptively slight, neat, clean body, there was something of the confident child, and if self-love and innocence were not the same thing, he made them seem so. He had the intuitive sense of a cat when it came to feeling the mood of another, and like the cat, if he felt himself momentarily rejected, he set out to win fond attention.

"Richie, I've been watching you and thinkin about you. I figger you can help me to find out how to better myself. I said to myself, How does a man get ahead? He don't get all the way there, where he wants to be, just by using his physical culture. I said to myself, No, I said; they have to use their brains. You use your brains all the time, even when you're alone, don't you? You're always readin in a book, or puttin things down in those little pocket books of yours."

"Yes."

"Well, I never went to college, hell, I never finished high school, even, but I've done a lot of livin, and I'm not so dumb. But I figger I've got a lot more to me than I know how to use."

"Everybody has."

"Don't turn me off like that. I want to make a *contribution.*"

He mixed pleading modesty with worthy ambition and I had no idea how much he meant any of it; but uncomfortable as I was under the implied flattery and envy of my state of life, I was touched by the other self he showed me, and I was depressed at not knowing how to guide him into ways he sought. It was impossible to tell anyone to begin at the beginning, all over again, and make a new life.

"Will you help me?" he asked.

"I'll have to think about how I can do it."

"Well, for now, that's good enough for me. I knew you would never let me down."

This made me more uncomfortable than ever. If I suffered his worst simply as features of a specimen, I found it more difficult to come to terms with his creature best. I was sure of only one thing about him—never had I seen anyone whose fullest expression was physical, the center of which was blatantly sexual. In act and response, even self-unaware, he revealed this. You'd never see in him any of the humble proprieties of "simple" people. He rarely modified his behavior but enacted his impulses directly. His physical life was intense—even to the way he slept, breathing heartily. Sometimes he kept me awake with this.

One night I had enough of it. Stealthily I got up and pulled on my blue jeans and went out into the cool calm darkness.

The night yielded a waft of wind which slowly turned the wind mill, whose gong-like sound drifted over the ranch. The ground wa pebbly, prickly, and I was without boots. I walked with wincing care toward the salt cedar grove between me and the house. There was joy in being alone. The waning moon was still so bright that the stars were paled. The day's ungrateful ground became the night's pale velvet. Over the house the cottonwoods were modeled like sculpture—clusters of soft light in relief against caverns of deep shadow. I savored the natural world so fully that a youthful kind of ecstasy lifted me out of myself, until the great mosaic of the stars, and the moon in its decline, united for me the urgency of man's concerns with the vast impersonal glory of the abiding universe. Despite promises and longings, I did not know where I was meant to go in life. And yet there I stood, myself in the center of the visible world, possessed in my own thought and feeling which united all; I the vessel of dimensions I could never measure. It was one of those moments of mystery—or was it revelation?—which came to the young in terms sublimely dislocating, all the more marvelous because it was beyond the asking.

It was therefore jarring suddenly to see a figure emerging from the moonshade of the salt cedars into the moonlight, and to hear a voice come huskily calling,

"¿Quién es?—who's there?"

I was not used to night vision, but he was: it was Don Elizario. I replied softly,

"Richard."

I could hear him come toward me, and in a low murmur of relief, he said, "Ah, ah." When we came to stand near each other, he said,

"You are night owl, like me?"

"No, I was just awake. I felt like going out to look at the night."

"Yes," he replied, "yes, I too." He laughed gently. "And I always come outside by myself to make my water on the ground, you know? I grew up doing it. There is something about it, I don't know what."

[191]

He invoked antiquity in his natural act and pleasure. We stood looking at the sky. I could see him well now. He wore an old-fashioned nightshirt with his feet in shapeless masses which I took to be carpet slippers. With his fingers spread like elongated paw pads, he pointed in a lurching gesture at the sky and said,

"You know? I come out at night and I wonder why all that goes on"—the firmament—"and we pass away. If I can see it, and you can see it, we have it inside us. Why don't we last like the stars?" A pause. "Well, we are good, and we are bad, but the stars are nothing, they are just faithful and they are just beautiful, eh? There is no reason for them to die."

"Well, but they do, sir, you know? After billions and billions of years, some stars do die."

Again his wheezy mild laugh.

"It might just as well be forever, then, eh? —How old are you, *chico?*"

I told him.

"Aa-ha. When I was your age—" He stopped, muted by his memories, and so was I, whatever they might be. Presently, "I was married a year younger than you are now. I was a ver' handsome man. Many girls. All I knew was the land, from my *papá*. He told me once, *The land will either kill you or you will make it serve you.* I have made it mine." He waved at the horizon, and the south, where his other ranch lay so far away out of sight. "My sons. There were four. Two are living. They are like me. They live for the work. We are rich and we still work hard. I come out and look up there, and I say I have done all a man is made for." He faced toward me. The immense night had induced in him an impersonal intimacy. "When you have done all you can do—" His voice fell away. The wind stroked the slow turning blades of the windmill. A sheep dog barked once, remotely, loyally. The softest stir went through the salt cedar shadows. His world was speaking to us. His silence was melancholy, but seemed also to carry the content of acceptance. He shivered. He crossed his arms as if to seek warmth. He asked,

"You are happy here?"

"Yes, sir."

"Here is where I belong," he said as though to set happiness aside for himself as irrelevant, if he was where he belonged. "Go to bed, *joven,* much work tomorrow. Good night, good night—" He was moving away and his voice faded with him. *"Buenas noches."* My heart came into my throat, why I could not say, as I watched him taken into the shadows of the brake.

❦

It was a measure of how lost and tired I was in my new world of hard work and rude life that I thought so little about my own world of parents and home. It was doubly shocking to be reminded of all I had left when Tom came back from a turn-around trip to Magdalena bringing a parcel for Concha and mail for me.

Her parcel was what the p'ione call had been about on that earlier evening: it contained a bright-red silk dress which Don Elizario had ordered for her from Daniels and Fisher in Denver as a second-anniversary surprise. The postmaster at Magdalena had been watching for it, and when it came, he had placed that phone call with the news by way of the Datil exchange. I saw the dress on its first evening when the Wenzels again asked me to supper to celebrate the wedding anniversary. Tom Agee was there also. At the proper moment he rose and made a courtly toast with his water glass. We answered with our glasses of champagne, which the host had ordered from Juárez. Concha wore her dress with joy, showing it off with seductive passes of her hands along her beautifully posed body. Her husband watched her with pride, and looked at Tom and me for the approval which we could both give without alarming him.

"It is my favorite color," said Concha. She kissed her husband on

[193]

the cheek and he put his heavy arms around her for a moment and then dropped them and turned away.

At the end of supper, he said,

"Aah, I almost forgot. Tom brought some letters for you. The Socorro paper, too, if you want it."

He gave these to me as I left. The men were at the campfire. I went alone to my bunk and by the light of my oil lamp opened my mail. The newspaper lay on the table, and before I read the letters my eye caught a headline over a brief item in a lower corner of the *Socorro Defender* which read: IMPEACHMENT PROCEEDINGS, NEW YORK GOVERNOR CHARGED. There were only a few wire service lines. I read them at once. A motion to impeach Governor Pelzer had been made on the floor of the assembly. Evidence of improper influence and financial peculation was reported to a committee appointed by the assembly to investigate, and the assembly had now voted overwhelmingly to send a bill of impeachment to the state senate.

My mother's letter, which I read next, said,

"—and you can imagine the effect this has had on your father. His fever went up, I had Dr Birch in, who told him he must positively stop fretting, but all Daddy would say over and over was, *To think, at such a time, I have to be out of the picture*. But the doctor told him that he would be able to come back into the picture all the sooner if he now put the whole affair out of his mind. But of course he can't and I know how he suffers. Sam arrived here two days ago with the news before it broke out in public. He brought Daddy all the documents, and all the talk behind the scenes. Oh, how shall I ever stand it, to see him tormented in mind as well as body"—and then she went on with questions about my welfare, my work, and added, "Don't get into any trouble with those cowboys, and don't worry about us, I'll let you know if we should ever need you in a hurry." This was like her—the imprecisely ominous references which went with her kind of motherhood. I smiled at this, but my heart was beating fast for the turn of events, and my disquiet was increased by a letter from Sam.

He had no doubt that the senate would find Pelzer guilty. The trial there would be ugly and protracted. Sam was bitter at the irony inherent in my father's absence at exactly the moment which might make him governor; and once governor, who knew how far my father would go later? Sam had every belief that Washington would follow in some form or other after, say, two terms in the governor's mansion. His own plans had been always predicated on my father's running for the United States Senate, with himself as chief legislative secretary. Sam, in his loyal conviction, believed that would be only another beginning, though he never actually dared name any office higher still. And now, having resigned as lieutenant-governor, my father was not eligible to succeed Pelzer, even if his health should permit this.

"What I believe," wrote Sam, "is that the greatest medicine your father could have had would have been actually to become governor when Albany is at last through with Judge (and Mo). I have done some reading about t.b. and I gather the mental element is at least as powerful and in some cases more so than the physical. I think your father would almost literally take up his bed and walk, and then throw it away, if he had the chance to go on to what should rightfully be his. It is a staggering irony that honor, ability, and opportunity should all be at hand, and yet all now be powerless. I won't conceal from you that your father is much depressed. I knew he would be; and that is why I came right back out here the minute I saw how affairs are sure to end. The Eastern papers have all taken notice of the fact that only a matter of weeks ago the lieutenant-governor resigned for health reasons, and they all deplore it more than ever. The clippings (your father insisted on seeing them all) make bitter reading for him. I have tried to set him going again with the W.W. material (he has actually written two chapters, lovely stuff) but he is too real to settle for a deliberate distraction, and he is also working hard to obey Dr Birch and keep the Albany affair out of mind, which only makes it more incessantly obsessive. As you may gather, I am myself in a howling rage at this maddening convergence of events. I'm afraid I'm not much help to your parents since I'm no good ever at concealing my state of mind and opinion. But I am staying on, for a little while, anyhow (though Joanna, having refused to come with me, now threatens to come and fetch me home). I suppose I can be useful in a few little things, such as protecting your father from reporters (the *Journal* here asked for an interview following a query from the AP), and taking him for afternoon drives, when the country shows its greatest splendor, but even this makes him rueful, with things as they are. And I am certainly useful in reminding Lillian not to heave her great sighs, keening over what might have been, etc. etc. She is a devoted fool, but a fool nevertheless, though her mere presence is of some comfort to your mother in managing the household and your father in handling office matters relayed from Dorchester, and who can be ungrateful for loyalty, anyhow? Are you a rancher by now? Lyle Pryor was cackling over the indignities you must be putting up with. I hope you have learned to say *Go to hell* with passion—it was all that saved me in the army among my physical superiors, bantamweight that I am, before I became a lieutenant. I'll keep you informed."

I was scarcely done with my news from home when Buz returned from the campfire. Giving up on my hope of being alone, I spoke to him. He did not answer. Turned away from me, he threw off his clothes, and in every line of his figure I could read a sense of self-righteous anger. I said something again to him, and again he ignored me. But it was I who had wanted to do the ignoring, and now in a perverse turnabout, I disliked being snubbed by him. We lived too closely together to indulge a continuing animosity. I knew what was bothering him—I had gone again, and without him, to supper at the house where Concha was to be seen. Nothing I could say would convince him that I could never have managed to get him into that house. He was unreasonable. This angered me in my turn. Pulling the lamp closer, I consigned him to hell, and settled down to write letters to my parents and to Sam. Perhaps Lyle was right: what was I enduring among the people around me? But as I wrote, my description of the life at the WZL was full of praise for everyone and everything.

❧

The weekend halted our work at Saturday noon. I went to Don Elizario.

"I have to send some letters home, very important, about things that have happened there. Do you think I could borrow the Ford to go to Magdalena to mail them?"

"No bad news, eh?"

"Not good."

"Eh, eh. Yes, then, take the Ford this afternoon, but be sure you get back by Sunday evening."

"Yes, sir. Rennison wants to go with me, to attend a wedding in town. Would that be all right?"

He smiled and spat.

"You take him as far as you can and lose him, as far as I am concerned. —No, bring him back, too, we have to finish up next week."

"Thank you, sir."

"You know? Nobody else regularly calls me *sir*."

He laughed breathily and, like the head of a family, waved me on my way with the effect of a blessing.

Buz was lying on his bunk staring at nothing, still disdaining my presence. I was sure he was bored with his self-imposed loneliness, but he knew of no way to break out of it with dignity. I said, rather stiffly,

"I'll be driving to town this afternoon in the Ford, if you'd like to come along."

He sprang to his feet like a cat. He swung a hard blow at my upper arm in exuberance, and said,

"Boy, you are somethin. I knew we would be partners. Let's go! We'll make that weddin after all."

He said he would let me drive out of the ranch gate, and then when we reached the highway, he would take the wheel, as he had covered the whole West in a Ford in his time, and if you could ride a horse, you could drive a Ford on those rutted roads, with their chuckholes and juts of gypsum. All he hoped for was that it wouldn't rain, for when a car got stuck in that red and white dirt, all you could do was wait and dry out.

"Why are you goin to town?" he asked.

"To mail some letters home."

"I never write any letters. I never get any, either." Not entirely with humor, he added, "Nobody knows I'm alive except just where I am."

But the prospect awaiting him in town—and me, he generously made clear—had raised his spirits until, driving the car sitting partly sideways, and hiking up exaggeratedly with the bumps as if riding an animal, he let out an exultant yell on general principles.

He had plans all made. First we would run by the post box near the tracks and get rid of my letters, as he put it, dismissing my whole life at home; then we would go to the Marigold Hotel and get up to Larraine's room and wash up. There was a rusty old leaky shower down the hall. Then when Larraine got off work, she was to get herself prettied up, and then we all three were goin to the weddin of her friends. She would be surprised to see us, especially me, as she knew nothin about me, but she'd do innythang he told her to. I would see later on how true that was. And we would help make that weddin somethin *they* wouldn't forget in a hurry.

He spent a few miles in repeating his repertory of bride-and-groom jokes. His mood was so merry and his anticipated enjoyment so frankly indecent that my initial squeamishness gave way to his vitality, and I saw him as a phenomenon instead of as an alien in my world of manners. I paid him the honor of speculating whether modesty was a matter of shame, or an attitude protective of what was so precious to the making of human life itself. I was much concerned just then with life, and death, its complement; and the more Buz rattled on with his obscenities delivered in his light voice and his features illuminated by a boy's glee, the more I began to welcome a sense of deliverance from troubles at home about which I was powerless to do anything. I began to feel anonymous through his presence, and the immense land we were riding through raising a long plume of dust added to this feeling. The plains sweeping away in every direction toward scattered mountains far away, the short parched grasses, the scrubby trees and bushes widely apart dotting the land made a country where you could be lost, perhaps forever, perhaps until accidentally found. Dimly, out of the very sympathies I felt so keenly, and yet could not act upon, I wanted to be someone else; to be myself lost.

Magdalena began to show in the distance—a low straggle. The only two-story building was the brick Marigold Hotel. As we came among the dusty streets and unpainted houses, all looked deserted, but here and there a tended yard, a watered tree, a window with curtains, a yard of chickens, and a dog or a cat spoke of the remote and essential life which still clung together to make a town.

We posted my letters in a box at the one-room railroad station by its black wooden water tank where the stubby locomotives of the branch line took on water. Then we returned to the main street, and Buz, lounging over his wheel, made a speeding run of four blocks to the corner where we must turn to the Marigold. The Ford rattled along and flapped its exhaust pipe. It was a sporting passage through town and a few people came to their store fronts to watch in amazement. I expected a local constable to stop us; but we scraped to a halt by the café end of the Marigold. Buz threw himself out the door of the car and, knowing I would follow, crashed his way into the restaurant to confront Larraine.

She remembered me. Her eyes asked Buz what I was doing there.

"He's goin to the weddin with us and afterward we're goin to have us a time, all three."

I spoke to her. She smiled with her face lowered, but with her eyes meeting mine. She looked prettier than I remembered. My new knowledge of her may have shown in my face, for she suddenly blushed and turned away down her counter at some improvised work. Buz gave me a jab in the side and whispered loudly,

"She likes you. They always do that when they like somebody and don't want to admit it to theirself. Come on."

He called to her that we were going up to her room to get ready. When would she follow?

"I get off work at four o'clock. You better be out of there before then," she said. "The wedding's at four-thirty."

"We've got our car," he replied. "You just show us the church and we'll all go and c-r-r-y our eyes out."

She blurted a laugh as though unwilling to belong to him in any way, but also with a hint of an admission that he had made her his when with his boisterous lust he had entered into her lonely life earlier that summer.

❦

"Two blocks over and one up" from the Marigold, as Larraine directed, the First Pentecostal Church of Christ Kingdom Come stood on a gravelly corner. It was a plain box of pebbly stucco with a squat, slatted tower covered in black tar paper and surmounted by a short wooden spike. The interior was stained in yellow calcimine, and a raised platform at the far end supported a box-like lectern.

Friends of the bride had decorated the bleak stage with gallon cans covered by white paper and filled with already wilted wildflowers. The afternoon was stifling hot. The packed benches sent up a steamy atmosphere composed of excitement and sweat. The minister—a rangy man in a black suit with a white necktie—sat on his chair at one side of the platform waiting for the wedding party. Small noises, dimmed for the sake of propriety, came out of a room opening out of the—so I thought of it—sacristy.

There was no place to sit when we arrived. We stood against the rear wall. Out in front only a few cars were parked at random. Most people had walked, though evidently a handful had ridden, for five saddled horses were tethered to a weathered telephone pole at the corner. Expectancy and a sense of what was fitting kept the little throng in the church in a fixed stillness. Their daily selves were stricken with a sense of serious occasion. Now and then someone could not help turning to discover whether anything could be seen at the door. But all knew that the signal would be given when the schoolteacher who sat at the abused piano which stood under the right front window would sound the first note of "Here Comes the Bride."

At last it came. To jangled chords the bridegroom stepped out of the sacristy and across the platform to await his bride. He was a tall, thickly built young man of the country whose face was pale under his sun- and windburn. He was trembling a little. He licked his white lips. Under dark brows, his eyes were glazed and fixed. He was soberly dressed, and so was his best man, who came to stand beside him. This one was a smaller, gleeful fellow, who peered with mischief at friends in the congregation, making silent references to what his friend, ol Cecil, was about to experience, now, and especially, afterward. Cecil saw nobody. He was the one person in the event who showed a detached solemnity. When the pianist with soulful restraint went on with the march, he did not turn to watch his girl come up the aisle.

She was small. She trembled even more than he. Her head was

topped by a veil which was crowned with a spray of artificial lilies of the valley. They shook with her emotion. She carried a bunch of white carnations which everybody later said had been brought on ice from Socorro. Her dress was white with a long train—the product of weeks of work by local housewives who told each other afterward at the reception that they had never seen a finer. Set off by her wiry gold hair, which stood away in curls from her thin little face, her cheeks were rosy. In her feeling, suppressed for the sake of the sacred vows which all had gathered to witness, she brought a pang to many an observer, as to me. However mean the surroundings, and meagerly pretentious the preparations, an ancient debt was being paid to itself by life: ceremony given as due to the means by which life would be renewed.

The minister rose and came forward to receive the bride at the platform, the music stopped, the young rancher took his bride's hand, and they stood, he stalwart and suddenly at ease, she with her head raised in pride, both staring straight ahead. The minister said,

"Now here we stand in the presence of the Holy Spert, to join this man and this wumman together in the holy bonds of wed-*lock* which is ordained by the Lard that no man nor wumman shall put asunder, so help them God."

By his loud, hooting voice, and his hands spread above the bride and groom, and by his head thrown back with his eyes closed, he invoked the invisible powers of which he was the spokesman. An almost palpable shiver of communion went through the congregation. How often was there occasion in that lost little town, and among the prisoners of that immense land, for a lofting of feeling which would deliver them from their common lot? Their emotion was contagious, and as the ceremony proceeded with homily, vows, and an interminable blessing with the minister's hands spread wider, he invoked the whole world's sanction upon this man and this wumman as they did now enter solemnly into the holy wedded state. There was an inarticulate beauty in what all believed in at that moment. In a silent prayer I added my blessing to that shared one beating in the hearts of those gathered there. I heard a small sound beside me and glanced down. Larraine was weeping in subdued gusts which raised and lowered her shoulders convulsively. She saw a self which could never be reached, I thought. Beyond her, Buz made a slight thumbing motion at her and above her head winked at me, sharing his comic scorn for all which everyone else took solemnly, and which he knew could not last.

It was true that when the end came, and the teacher began to pound away at her recessional with ecstatic inaccuracy, the assembled mood changed as if a cloud had gone off the sun. With bent heads the young couple ran down the aisle, everyone laughed and applauded, and on his planks the minister trumpeted out repeatedly, "Ho, yo, yo, glory be!" in a laughing roar which sounded above all else, and all left for the wedding reception, which would be held at the home of the bride's father, who was the rich cattle-feed merchant of the town.

Smiling through her tears, Larraine took a moment to powder her face. Then with a radiance which had something wanton in it, she said, "Here we go, boys," and Buz drove us, bucking the car, around the corner and down the dirt street for four blocks to a gray cement one-storied house with a deep porch whose short stone pillars were covered with sweet pea vine. Behind the house rose olive-gray foothills, in one of which an abandoned mine entrance with fallen timbers spoke of the prosperous past. Guests crowded after us. Cecil and his bride, Allie Sue, received them in the front room to shake hands. The parents of both stood with them. Decorum prevailed in the front room; but out in back of the house, as Buz discovered immediately, several young men were drinking bootleg corn whiskey while they carried out a rite as old as the wedding itself. They were imposing lewd mockery on the greatest joy of the animal creation in its human form.

Cecil's own Ford touring car was waiting at the back door for the

moment when the newlyweds would run out to it under a shower
of rice and catcalls, to drive away for their honeymoon in El Paso.
Cecil's friends were at work. A pair of them at the back of the car
were tying tin cans to the rear axle with long strands of baling wire.
Two others, one to each side of the car, in rutting hilarity, were
painting words on the car body. Buz joined them, drinking of the
jug which was passed around. The young men were drunk on
whiskey and prurience. They slapped with their brushes:

GRAND OPENING TONIGHT

CHERRY, CHERRY, WHO GETS THE CHERRY

SHE GOT HIM TODAY HE'LL GET HER TONIGHT

Buz seized a brush from one of the young satyrs and across the rear
of the car, he painted:

WHAT WAS THAT, SHE HOLLERD

which brought a roaring cheer from the others.

A flushed young man began to festoon the car with toilet-paper
streamers. There was intensity to all their work. They got drunker
and drunker, and so did Buz, and so did I. The final touch was
given the car when the best man put a jug of whiskey behind the
driver's seat. It was labeled *Love Tonic*.

Now everyone went into the house to join the crowd. Decorum
had begun to break down there, too, though no liquor was being
served. But wives were remembering, and husbands were speculating enviously and full of laughing pity for what ol Cecil had got
hisself into. Erotic feeling was running through the guests, as earlier

in church all had been taken by the holiness of the ceremonial sanction.

Buz came to me at a lace-curtained bay window. He was drunker than anyone, yet his ready talk was not blurred. In his strange slit of light his eye contained something wild. He half turned his head and gave me his well-rehearsed smile, which had done so much for him around the world. He took hold of my heavy belt buckle and tugged at it to pull my attention and tell his power. Working it up and down, he put his other hand behind my neck and jerked at me there. With great confidence, in a burry voice thick with appeal, he said, while his eyelids drooped and opened with the sleepiness of drunken affection,

"You son of a bitch, you know what I'm goin to do from now on with you?"

"No. Let go of me."

He did not let go, but went on, earnestly close to my face,

"I'm goin to be just like you. I'm goin to read a book every time I can get me one. I'm goin to look at everybody the way you do and make them wonder what I think of them. I'm goin to fix it so's I know anythin they ask me. I'm goin to better myself and make you proud of me. We're goin to be a real team. You son of a bitch."

"You're drunk."

"So're you. So let's get drunk. Ol Richie and Buz."

Just then Allie Sue came out of the back room dressed for travel. A shout went up. Cecil took her arm. They struggled through the crowded rooms to the back door. Running down the back steps with lowered heads, they tried to enter the car as though unseen. But Cecil saw some of the poor jokes on his car. His neck turned an angry red. He made two or three swipes at the drying white paint with his fine new Stetson hat, and even brushed at the car with his shiny new sleeve. He knew the folk custom which mixed obscenity with marriage. But something he now knew in a new way was being demeaned. Allie Sue tugged at him. In her face turned to him there was radiant satisfaction at how every single element of a proper wedding—even to these painted words—had come to them. *Everybody did everything just like they always did:* the joy of this was in her face. Her husband's outrage seemed to her ungrateful. He finally thrust her into the car, ran around to the driver's seat, and jumped into the car, which his best man cranked for him after several young guests tried to prevent it, and scowling like a cloud shadow, Cecil drove off, spurning gravel and dust while all cheered. Allie Sue's mother stood in the back door, waving and weeping. No matter what the terms, she saw the universal in her child's ordeals, past, present, and to come.

❦

Larraine had to return to work at the Marigold café until after nine o'clock.

"We'll meet you upstairs at ten, hon," said Buz, "and then! *zowie!* if you know what I mean!"

She knew. In her familiar gesture, she lowered her face, but her breath caught in her throat, and her bounteous breasts rose and fell with a gust of excitement. Looking like a modest high school girl, with her delicate hands, shadowed eyes, and sweetly plump cheeks, she wore shyness over a nature whose ardor Buz was able to arouse by the simplest suggestion.

We followed a couple of the young men from the wedding to houses where they knew a drink was to be had, and a ·good story. Though he grew drunker as ten o'clock approached, Buz never lost his power to dominate and cozen with his talk, but only became more confidentially eloquent. More susceptible to liquor than he, I heard only part of what went on as we ranged the town.

In one house we sat with a middle-aged couple who had three

children—all small boys. The father was as sun-cured as saddle leather. His face was creased like old mine tailings gullied by rain. Hard work and joylessness marked him. His wife was made up for the wedding like a burlesque show girl. Under all her blue and red and white color, and her fiery dyed hair, she looked used-up to exhaustion, and her weariness was caught in the hard edge to her voice. They both put on company manners for us at first, until we drank with them. It did not matter that we were strangers. They had just had a taste of conviviality outside their crowded shack, and they hated to let go of it. Soon the father sighed with comfort and pulled off his boots. When the three little boys, a year apart in age, with the oldest about seven, looked around the door jamb like curious small cats, I was almost sobered by the contrast between the inquiring wary sweetness of these cubs and their worn, life-tried parents. The children had caps of burnished gold hair. Their big eyes were light sapphire blue with thick dark lashes which shadowed their tawny cheeks. They held their chiseled, delicate mouths open, the better to hear what was going on where we sat in the kitchen. Their little pointed chins and short noses and small nostrils looked as though carved by the most innocent of sculptors. Children! I wished they were mine and I wished for my own. Would life do to those children what it had done to the rasping woman and the disgusted man who had given them life? With drunken lucidity I had thoughts about the stages of life which I had never thought before. The idea of purposeless purity as it gazed at us in timid hunger from the doorway made me half rise from my chair to go to the children, as though they were mine.

This was a mistake, for the father, who had not seen them, followed my look, sat up, took one of his sweat-and-mud-roughened boots, and threw it at the children, roaring,

"Get the fuck out of here, you sneaking little sons of bitches!"

They ducked swiftly out of sight while their mother shrieked after them,

"And see that you get to sleep, or I'll whup the shit outen you!"

"So, as I was sayin," remarked Buz, as though the family tumult had never happened, going on with a story to which I did not listen, but which our hosts found arresting, for they watched his lips and feasted on his energetic presence, which brought them a world away.

Later, out on the gravelly walk, I said,

"What will ever become of those little boys!"

"Whoof. What do you care? They'll just grow up. All kids do. Look at me."

"What about you?"

"My daddy beat the livin tar out of me day in day out because my mother liked me more'n she did him. He worked in the lumber yard sometimes and he had a great collection of boards to slap me with." He laughed as though his boyhood was now a good joke. "But I had me enough and I just ran off and I never been back or had a word since."

"But what about the doctor's daughter?"

"Sh't! Anybody of us did it to her all the time. She used to meet us for it."

He mused genially over his history, and after a few steps, he said,

" 'V'you ever played around with more'n one at the same time?"

It took me a while to read his meaning, but he flung his arm around my neck to press his question and free my memory, and I said,

"No."

"Son, ain't livin."

Larraine knew what was comin—he had told her, and she let on she didn't believe him. But she knew, for he had told her the time he first met her about the things they used to do out on the coast, and she got all excited about it, and asked him to tell her more. Tell her? Buddy boy, tonight we were not goin to tell her, we were goin to show her. How about it?

My head throbbed in the bright overcast light of a dusty sky as we left the Marigold Hotel on Sunday morning.

Slumped at an angle in the driver's seat, Buz drove with his wrist hanging over the wheel. After several miles, he asked,

"What the hell's the matter 'th *you*?"

I shrugged silently and looked aside at the blurred hills. He persisted.

"Why'd you leave us?"

"I'd had enough—" in meanings lost on him.

For those hours in the pit of night, Buz by his elated example worked to make me over in his own likeness, to the joy of Larräine. He cheered me on like a trainer taking credit for his player. He was happiest when he shared his pleasures. I went after my own, in my turn, drunkenly intent and persistent. At one moment Larraine shed a few tears, saying she was a lonely person, and was glad of us. But as the loveless night began to fade, along with my fill of bootleg corn, I began to see not only Buz and Larraine but myself.

As my father said, in every life there was something, great or small, to be ashamed of. Where would last night ever fit into the comforts and graces of our life at home?

"You were pretty rough with her, you know," I said.

"So that's it," he replied. "Well, they all love it. You better learn."

I now faced two ways—one, toward the inner self where my father still reigned; the other, toward a world of knowing which, good or evil, I must see for myself, and judge and use.

Buz felt no concern. Envying him, I dwelt on mine.

❈

To exhaust memory, I worked harder every day of the following week. The dipping would be ended by Friday and the flocks driven southward. Whenever he could, Buz tried to talk about our night with Larraine, as though endlessly reviving it in words would make it more exciting than the event itself. He still expected to excite me with this, as he excited himself, and he was honestly injured when I evaded the subject.

"You sure are sore about somethin, after the good times I set up for you," he would say in a baffled sulk. I had no answer for him. Facing his simple zest, I was ashamed of my shame.

There was another consequence more puzzling. Concha sent word by Irene that I was to come for supper to tell her every detail about the wedding. Within an hour of this invitation, Don Eli ordered me aside and said,

"No supper. You will stay away from my house from now on." He stared without expression, and after he spoke his jaw was set jutting forward under his whiskers like that of an old lion. When I made a bewildered gesture, he went on, "Never mind, I know about you and that girl and Bebbyface, that *cabrón*. I have people in Magdalena who tell me everything. I did not think that you—" Turning away, he motioned me back to work at the dip. Here was a judgment against me, on top of my own. I wanted to blame Buz. But could I?

I watched him now and then with Don Elizario in the working background. Between them continued a truce, baleful on one side, cheerfully wary on the other. When I caught one glancing at the other, I wondered whether the silent game between them would have further moves.

I knew for certain on a late afternoon when the declining sun was changing color from white to pale gold, and the coming evening seemed as perfect and fragile as an eggshell.

❊

Foul from work at the dip, I went to my bunkhouse for a shirt which I had washed and hung out in the morning. After a shower I would put it on before supper—"dressing for dinner," I said sourly to myself. Buz was not in the bunkhouse. I found my shirt, a towel, and some lava soap to use with the hard alkaline water pumped slowly forth into the windmill tank. A pipe with a valve provided the shower bath. To the valve a rope was attached, and when with one hand you pulled the rope, the pipe let forth a cold thin stream, while you soaped and rinsed with the other hand. The work at the nauseous dip made you blench at your own smell; but of all the workers only Buz and I regularly used the shower at the end of the day. Whenever he stood under the cold stream, he made a great show of shock, yelling and capering. His presence there, even unseen, could be known by his howls, which sometimes turned into song.

To reach the windmill I had to go toward the ranch house until I came to the westernmost brake of salt cedars; and there I would take a path which put the brake between me and the house. The windmill stood beyond. Its eight-foot galvanized-metal tank was hidden from the house if you looked from the porch, but the salt cedars, though tall and fully plumed at the top, grew more sparsely at the stems. If you stood near to them, you could see through their cluster to the mill, the tank, the shower, and the long waver of the plains beyond.

I passed the large bunkhouse and saw Don Elizario conferring with Tom Agee. They were resting on their haunches close to the earth. Tom was evidently working out with his boss some plan for work. He would take up a little clod of earth and place it nicely, pointing to it as if to say that this represented one thing; then with another he would establish a different thing; and finally, with a twig, draw a line making a conclusion with the two, while Don Elizario gravely watched and nodded in agreement. Their conference was absorbing and leisurely. Neither glanced up as I passed a few yards away. It was a companionable hour. From the chuck wagon came petulant noises and a scrap of wailing song where Irene was getting supper. The stillness otherwise was broken only by the drifting rankle of chains and the airy chime of the windmill slowly turning. All was at peace and nothing called for my attention until I came around the end of the brake, from which I could see both mill and house. But then my eye was struck by color as though I saw the streak of a cardinal bird which would be gone if I looked directly.

I turned to look and stood stock still. At the mill, after bathing, Buz was dressing—pulling on his boots, tucking in his shirt. His pale hair was plastered down on his neat skull. In a moment he shook it off his brow and out of his eyes, and in doing so, he saw what else I saw, the flash of scarlet behind the brake.

There stood Concha watching him through a little gap in the salt cedars. How long had she watched—a young Susanna reversing the whole scene of the desirous elders? She was wearing her red dress, the anniversary silk dress, and her body was fixed in a stillness of desire which took Buz with her whole being.

When he saw the red dress, he looked quickly around, saw nobody else, and in a few running bounds he was at the brake, through its barrier, and had her in his arms. She thrust him away, she tried to keep her dress from getting wet from his dripping hair, but he held her fast, devouring her mouth and face as though she were Larraine. In a moment, laughing, he let her go free. His face was gleeful and he knew she would reach for him. She did. He took her again, but now she was terrified less of his assault than of her longing; and she pushed him off balance. He grasped her red silk at the shoulder. It tore, a visible betrayal. She felt for her bare shoulder, and in terror, she began to run to the house with one hand over her mouth, while with the other she crossed herself three times. Her heavy black hair fell like a veil over her face. She reached the porch and safely disappeared within. Laughing silently, Buz let himself with caution back through the brake and returned to take up his towel at the shower.

I went forward. He said,

"You sure missed some fun."

"I saw."

He looked startled.

"Did anyone else—*you* know?"

"No. I left him talking to Tom. But you're a damned fool to take a chance like that."

"No, no, son. *She* was. He can't do *me* anythin, but he can *her*. —And what was she doin there in the first place?"

He capered in delight, presenting the self which drew Concha toward what she desired most, and most disastrously.

"Don't you *ever* think of what *might* happen?" I asked.

"I do, and I did, and *it did*, and it will again! It's just a matter of time. Oh me, oh my."

"I don't mean that—I mean the trouble you could cause?"

"Oh. That. —No, because it may never come, and you can lose a lot of things if you go to thinkin that way. I hate to think of everythin you've missed all your life till the other night. —Here. You take the water now."

He slowly ran off like an athlete in a long training exercise, down the path, and around to the chuck wagon, where he enjoyed deviling Irene.

When in my turn I left the tank, I looked toward the ranch house and saw Concha on the porch steps, framed by the blowsy trumpet vines. She was safe in a different dress—white—leaning against a porch post. Anyone would think she was at peace, taking in the immense evening as the day's great event. The eastern horizon was softening with what looked like a rise of pale smoke, and the first stars were beginning to show. But what a tempest must bewilder her mind and heart, I thought; and how commonly, wonderfully strange that none of this showed in her lovely form. She might seem only weary and content. What can ever be really known, I thought with a sort of desolating fellow feeling, of what really troubled, pleased, or concerned anyone; and, with that unknown, how was it possible for one human being ever to judge another? Even one most alien? Even J. Buswell Rennison?

✻

His excitement of the afternoon lasted into the night. He would not let me sleep. He did not know exactly when, but he knew for sure now, that he would have her. He had known all along that she wanted him. It was something he could tell with any wumman. He wadn't even surprised this afternoon when he happened to turn and see her through the stalks of the hedge. She must have been there all the time he was havin his shower. Well, then, she had an eyeful. It wadn't that far away—ten, fifteen feet—but what she could get a real good look at him. He was satisfied with what she saw, and he bet she was too. Like to drive her crazy. Plenty of others had been—and so he was off on detailed accounts of adventures, real or mythical, which I had not yet heard. He was so vain about his body that he sometimes seemed to be talking about that of somebody else, both aggressive and narcissistic in an admiring way. But by his elaborate confidences he was inviting mine; for if he could not be enacting his joys, the next best thing was to be talking about them, and those of anyone else who would respond in kind. I had nothing I wanted to tell him. My earliest love was the briefest of initiations, and if I told him of it, he would make remarks about it whose happy foulness would lead to violence between us. Finally, he would have been puzzled at the complications of purity, desire, and the single-mindedness of an idealized love.

"Oh, ah," he mused, lying back luxuriously with one hand behind his head and the other briefly answering to his loins, "I needed only a few more minutes there today. You know what? You don't know what I know, and that is, they all have got it on their mind just as much as I have, and once you know that, there's no stoppin anythin, with any of them."

He gave me an oblique smile, and that odd transfiguring chip of light in his right eye seemed to give out a shaft of energy, even while it seemed to avoid seeing me directly. He had a habit of hugging himself in self-pleasure, and he did it now—the very image of a healthy child physically happy, with blooming cheeks and no need of life at the moment but the plumbing sense of well-being.

"All I know is," he said at last, when I reached to turn down and out the wick of the coal oil lamp, "I'll go crazy if I don't get her."

"You never will," I said in the darkness.

I could hear him rise up on his elbow to face me.

"What's to prevent?"

"The old man. Her fear."

"What's she afraid of?"

"Well, apart from him, she's afraid of committing a sin. She's very religious. There is such a thing, you know, as all that."

"Oh me, oh my, Richie, what you don't *know*. Religion always comes *afterward,* don't you know that? I found that out long time ago from lots of *them*."

"All right: you know why she ran away from you this afternoon? —She crossed herself three times while she was running away. I saw it, you didn't."

"But just's I say: *afterward*."

He made a soft breathy laugh and fell back to his hard pillow and the sleep of the justified.

❈

In midweek under the searing August sky we were nearing the end of our Vergilian job of dipping the sheep. There was little enough classic lyricism about it. The hot winds blew the breath of the vat fires toward us. The sheep raised a fearful din as they were driven after their rams into the slide, which then threw them into the deep and stinking trough of the thick dip with its thickening film of scabs off the sheep and the excrement of their panic and the rubbery clots of creosote and Black Leaf 40 which had not dissolved. We stood, four or five on each side of the trough, with our long poles, which had the curved iron Y's at the end with which we pushed each animal under the surface, holding it just long enough to be sure the drench had reached its every part, and just short of drowning it. When we let it up, the sheep struggled to the surface and frantically swam in the only direction possible—ahead, bumping against the thickly packed flock fighting to reach the far end of the trough, go free, and live. Finally, choking and yelling on a sustained bleat, the sheep hoofed its way up the cleated incline, shaking and coughing, to join the roiling massed circle of its flock mates in the corral from which the return to the far pastures would be made.

It was too hot to leave off our shirts—for all but one of us. Buz worked bare from the waist up, taking pride in his dark biscuit tan, against which his lucky piece swung and winked in the sun. We all wore work gloves which were caked and stiff with dried dip. Don Elizario wandered along one side of the trough from end to end, watching, advising, nodding at the importance and efficiency of the job which he had performed hundreds of times. He knew how in itself it was nasty work, but he knew it had to be done, and how to demand of his men that it be done properly. Tom Agee matched him by overseeing the opposite side of the trough.

By mid-morning, we had been at the job for nearly five hours. The strangling clamor of the sheep, their endless choking and coughing and crying as they rose from their submersions, came to seem like part of the natural day, in its blazing monotony. In the white sky, the great hawks with their undersides reflecting the sandy

color of the plains flew low above us, and above them, slowly spiral-
ing, the black buzzards kept watch for carnal prey and cast their
slow shadows over us far below as they sailed.

I was opposite Buz at the trough. Tom Agee was next to him.

At a moment, I happened to glance over at Buz, and saw a look
of tight-jawed delight in his face. Then I saw that as his next sheep
came along, he pushed it under the opaque slime, as we all did with
ours; but he did not release it as soon as he should. At first, nobody
saw that he was trying to drown the animal. His body was bent like
a tensed bow. His face was lighted by excitement. When the sheep
fought to come up, he pressed it down again as though running a
spear into a victim. I waved to him to let go. He did not see me. But
Tom Agee, following my gesture, turned to Buz next to him and
saw what he was doing.

"Let it go!" bellowed Tom in as loud a voice as he could use.

Buz faced him with a mischievous grin and then turned back to
press the rod against the drowning sheep.

"I said—" shouted Tom, and then, with no more time for words,
swung his huge hand and heavy arm at Buz, knocking him down.
Buz's sheep prod flew into the air. The sheep came to the surface
and began to sink again until two of the men held it with their poles
against the densely packed bodies of the other sheep. Weakly it
strove for breath and began to find it. It was not dead after all,
however zestfully Buz had tried to kill it.

He sprang up from the ground and swung to hit Tom, who held
him off with his long, bony arms. Buz shouted at Tom with words
that snapped like bullets from his mouth fixed in a hard muzzle.

"Aw, you God damn ol Bible-whackin, pants-pissin, chickenshit,
son of a bitch!"

Rage in another can cause fear and nervous laughter. We all
started laughing when Tom, with his face whitened in shock,
knocked him down again as if with a length of two-by-four. Leaving him on the ground, Tom went toward Don Elizario at the other

end of the trough. But the old man had heard the commotion and was already treading across a plank at the end of the trough to see the trouble.

"He tried to drownd a sheep!" yelled Tom hoarsely, pointing at Buz with a trembling hand.

"I never!" shouted Buz.

"I saw him," Tom continued, "and so did everybody else—?" He turned to inquire with a look at the other men if he were not right. Several nodded. "Don Eli, you got to fire the no-good runt."

Don Elizario seemed not to hear him. Keeping his eyes on Buz, he motioned to the rest of us not to slow down the work, for the sheep kept coming. Then he said to Tom,

"No, we need him till we're done. But a little lesson, *qué no?*"

With that, in a suddenly revived surge of virile power, he astonished Buz and the rest of us. He picked him up bodily and threw him with a mighty heave into the struggling stream of the tightly packed sheep as they went past in the slime. Don Elizario then stood with his hands on his hips and looked impassively at each of us in turn, and the world, having shown what a man can do when he must.

Buz clambered against the sheep. He did not sink into the trough, but like the bodies which flailed all about him, he was soaked with the hot dip. Stinking like one of them, he hauled himself out of the trough and took a few steps toward Don Elizario and shouted,

"I quit!"

"No," said Don Elizario in the mild voice of a man who has shown his strength. *"Oiga, cabrón,* you pologize to Tom *muy pronto!* Then you get back to work."

There was an irresolute pause.

But power lay with the old man, and need with the young.

"Well, then," muttered Buz with his head down, "I take it back."

We looked at Tom. He decided this was enough of repentance. He picked up Buz's pole, threw it to him, and Buz went back to work like the rest of us. The whole matter took a very few minutes; but it had been so charged with feeling that we were all subdued. Three passions had been so powerfully exposed against each other that, instead of jeering and hazing the loser, none of us felt like looking at him, or at each other. As the wet muck on his clothes quickly dried into a crust, his humiliation was complete, and a current of sympathy could be felt among the dipping crew.

When it was time for Irene's noon dinner, Buz did not come near the chuck wagon. He went to his bunk and found a change of clothes in his vagrant's bag. While we ate more or less in silence, he was at the tank, trying to wash off the filth and stench of the trough. When he was done, he brought his fouled clothes to the vat fire and threw them into the coals.

That night, as though in answer to my strong but unspoken question about why he did not quit after all, he said, with fatalistic simplicity,

"I need the pay."

Now I understood how the other men, poor in their rough, all-enclosing world, must have felt pity and fellow feeling for him, which they could not openly show, even if they might condemn his cruelty. The power if not the right lay always where the money came from; and after all, what was a sheep? Only an animal, worth so much a pound for its wool and its mutton. Anyhow, many a sheep died out on the pastures from weather or distemper, and what did it matter?

"Richie?"

"What now?"

"When this is all over, let's you and me really team up. How about it? You never answered me about this."

I tried to dodge again, saying,

"Well, where are you going from here?"

"I don't know. Do you?"

"Yes."

"Well, how about it?"

"No, you see, thanks, but I have to get back."

"Well, go to hell! You're just like the rest of them. The ol bastard thinks he can do anythin he likes to Buz Rennison. Well, he'll find out. Th'ain't anybody livin can do what he did to me and get off like nothin ever happened!"

I did not answer. His anger, like that of a hurt child, soon gave way to ruefulness. He sighed.

"No, you've been a real friend. I don't have any other real friends. Nobody stays my friend for very long. I keep wonderin why."

"Oh, nonsense. People will always admire you, no matter what"— but if I sounded bored, he did not notice it.

"You think so?"

"I do."

"Well, I've done all right so far, seein that I have never wanted to settle down."

There was relief in his voice; some note which meant that he thought he might have lost me, and was now glad that he could think this wasn't so.

The next morning (it was the last of the long days of dipping) work was taken up again as though nothing out of the ordinary had happened the day before.

❉

All day Friday we saw nothing of Don Elizario. Several times Tom Agee went to the house and returned. He said the old man was resting: seemed like he might have strained something yesterday when he threw that foul-talkin Babyface into the dip. Inny-how—and Tom as foreman went about finishing the work of the past days. The men would be paid off at the end of the day. Early the next morning before the day's heat began to grow the flocks would be set on the trail for the lower ranch. Irene and his cook's wagon would go with them. One man would be picked by Don Elizario to stay behind to help Tom and me empty and scour the vat, skim and bail out the trough. The Wenzels might remain at the ranch for a little while to see things closed up, and then return to Albuquerque in their big car.

Throughout Friday Buz worked with zeal at his last day of dipping. There was anxiety in his labor. He worked hard to re-establish himself sociably among his fellows and with Tom. Tom ignored this. But by evening, when the job at the dip was done, Buz had everyone else restored to him in comradeship; and when we came to the firelight with our tin cups, there were calls for him to entertain us. He responded with winning modesty.

He had an instinctive sense of what an audience would like. On this final evening, the mood was sentimental. These men were sorry to separate from each other now, for they had known a bond in their work, and now that the work was over, if there was nothing else to keep them together, simple habit ruled their feelings. Each had his own vision of sentiment, and Buz touched it with songs he sang that night.

He played the guitar with tenderness instead of the slapping bravado of his earlier shows. He sang what the men thought of as songs of the range, the rude poetry of their hard lives. Their horses were loved and mourned as their best friends. The sheep and cattle they tended were given loving nicknames. The comradeship of the ranges and the pastures was celebrated as something they would never forget, even as in turn they would ride up the Last Trail, which led to Glory Up Yonder. It was a quiet little crowd that listened. Buz's voice was light and true. He seemed like someone incapable of a low thought or an evil act. With the purity of his playing and singing, he told us that if no man was either all good or all bad, every one of us no matter what his faults believed most in

[221]

the good. Few fellows got what they deserved in this life; but every one of us could be sure of one thing—no matter where our work might take us, we would always know there was someone to come home to; and he sang his song of Bonnie Mae again, to state this comforting illusion, and this time, he let her remain real for us, a vision of purity and constancy we all believed in as we believed in our right to carouse when the spert moved us. Just now, we were as ready to be wise and virtuous men as at another time we might let ourselves go to hell-raisin. When Buz fell silent, bending his head like a juvenile innocent, I was as glad as the rest when someone called out,

"Just one more!"

He remained quiet with a showman's instinct until the listeners wondered. Then with a few gentle chords he began the song, "I Dream of Jeanie with the Light Brown Hair"; and under the pleading sweetness of his true young voice, that lone little society thought of itself at its best, in the chaste celebration of absent love.

The fire was low when he finished singing. The men were unwilling to rise and go to their bunks. They talked now in easy comfort about what they would do next—who would stay on the lower ranch, who would move on to other itinerant jobs, who had families to go home to, who would go back across the Rio Grande to Mexico, where they lived.

During this murmur of farewells, Don Elizario slowly came out of the shadows into the dying firelight to be with his men once more. Despite his inescapable power as the man who paid them they revered him for what he was. They hoped to come back next summer when the time came. He took his due as patriarch so simply that when a few half rose to greet him, he absently put them down with his thick old hand, and with aching difficulty let himself down to be with them on the ground. He had little to say at first. He traveled the circle with his gaze, nodding his thanks and his good wishes to them all, even Buz, who ducked his head as though humbly before the old man's steady look.

Silence, full of companionship and respect, waited on Don Elizario. We could all see him as our eyes got used to the loss of the firelight, for the moon was nearly full—would be full tomorrow night. In that lucent silver pour he seemed almost a monumental figure. His great head was bare and his white hair shone in the moonlight. The heavy locks of his brow, lying as if roughly fingered there, made his head seem boyish in silhouette. Heavily his body breathed at rest. He seemed now to believe in his old age, for he was tired. When at last he said a few words, his voice was thin and husky. Where was the strong old man of the days of work who had been equal to most tasks that had to be done? At home, my father's illness had always made the daily present seem precarious, and we had always veiled our own uncertain future in hope. But something in Don Elizario's presence that night gave me my first intimations of how precarious, also, was any future.

"Well," said Don Elizario, "we have done good work. *Muchas gracias a todos*. Every year. Every year, we must do the same thing at the same time. There is something good in this. Eh? You are all younger than I am, some of you much younger. Do you know? If you have to go on a long walk with the flocks over the range, you watch for landmarks. You know where you have been and next time how far to go. Now I look at my life that way. You will some day." He sighed with acceptance. *"Bendito sea Diós*. Yes. *Sí, cantamos,"* and then in a quavering tone he sang the line from the favorite Mexican hymn which used the same words—"Blessed be God." Some of the Mexican men picked up the tune and the text and sang with him.

> *Bendito, bendito,*
> *Bendito sea Diós,*
> *Los ángeles cantan*
> *Y alaban a Diós,*
> *Los ángeles cantan*
> *Y alaban a Diós.*

At the end of this impromptu act of familiar piety, we all felt blessed. Without any further words of benediction and farewell, Don Elizario came painfully to stand and, waving his heavy old hand at us, turned to go.

Buz stepped after him and said,

"Sir? Mr Wenzel?"

The old man paused. Their figures were edged with moonlight.

"¿Qué tal?"

"Sir, I sure am sorry about yesterday, and I'm wonderin if I could just stay on to do the extra work after the others have gone? I need the pay and I don't know where I'm goin next. I sure would appreciate it."

There was a little pulse of urgency in his voice. The last thing I had come to expect was compunction of any sort. The cock of the walk now acted forlorn.

"Well, well," said Don Elizario in a soft marveling voice. "Bebby-face is sorry. So. *Pues,* all right, you can stay, work with Richard, but you will have to work on Sunday, and you will have to be done as soon as you can. *El Tom* will pay you. My wife and I are going to Albuquerque. You can stay with Richard. Tom knows the work that is to do. —Irene"—he raised his voice for the cook—"leave food for these two. They will have to feed their own selves."

With nothing further to say, he went off to his house, where no light showed, and to his wife, who waited in darkness.

The gathering began to break up. Irene produced a Jew's harp from his pocket and gave a tuneless buzzing twang to which he took exaggerated steps away to his wagon, two at a time, pausing to strike an attitude of disdainful elegance; and then again he advanced and paused, over and over, making a stylized exit from the company, the place, and the occupations of the past days.

When we saw a light come on inside the canvas wall of his wagon, Buz and I went to him to draw our rations. He received us with a social air, and then shrewdly calculated the least amount of food on which we could live for four more days.

"Four days will do for *you*," he said, sassing us with word and gesture. "I'm not going to empty *my* shelves for two no-good gold-brickers."

He stuffed a burlap sack with our supplies. When Buz reached for a box of potato chips, Irene slapped him on the hand with petulant grace and cried,

"No, sir! Not in a *million years! Those* are for myself. You think I'd serve delicacies to common ranch hands? Not on your life. *Stealing*. The idea. In the *Marines* we'd know how to handle an uppity pup like you"—for he always claimed that he had served as a Marine in the recent Great War.

"Oh, Miss Irene," said Buz with mock humility, "I'm just so sorry, dear!"

"And I'll have you know my name is *Ira*," snapped the cook, handing me the sack and slapping the air to drive us out of the wagon.

"Yes, Irene," answered Buz as we left, and we heard the cook exclaim to the indifferent world,

"Oh, why was I ever—!"

Later, Buz took a long time to go to sleep. He tossed and grunted until I called out to him,

"Why don't you settle down, over there? You're keeping me awake. There's a lot to do tomorrow."

He exhaled noisily.

"Boy, I sure have got it bad tonight. —It isn't fair."

"What?"

"They're leavin and I haven't seen her again."

"I think they're going to see a doctor about the old man. He has you to thank for that. It took a lot out of him to handle you that way."

"So it's my fault? The old fool. He'd better not get in my way again!"

"In your way! You got what was coming to you. He's been good to you, letting you stay on."

"Come on, Richie. If he'd done *that* to you, you wouldn't forget it in a hurry. *I* never will!"

"You said you were sorry."

"Sorry? I've never been sorry or ashamed for anythin I ever did in my whole life. But now I don't care if I stay or go."

"I thought you needed the pay."

"I could use it. But there's more to life than pay. You notice he's taking her away early and that's why he's lettin me stay on. I don't owe him any thanks." His voice grew edgy. "Just the opposite, if you ask me."

His temper was rising. He was ready to enlarge his grievance. I blew a yawn, turned over, and went to sleep.

The next thing I heard was the rankle of gear and the disturbed bleating of the flocks, and the distant voices of the men, before sunrise, as the southward drive began over the range to the lower ranch.

※

We worked all day with Tom. There was no sign of life at the house. In the silence of the ranch the noises we made seemed even greater than they were, after the days of yelling sheep, shouted orders.

First we dug a trench leading from the far end of the trough down a low slope which led to the arroyo. Into the trench we would bail the settled brew of the dip, using five-gallon buckets. Eventually, the stuff, with all its scabs and clots and stench, would slowly edge down the incline and into the arroyo, where we would cover it with loose dirt. We would then go to the vat and scour it with iron scrapers and coarse steel wool until, said Tom with stern satisfaction, our hands, even in their cracked gloves, would turn raw. We would haul leftover firewood back to the piles beyond the corral from which it had been taken.

As the hours passed on Saturday at our work, Buz began to appreciate the irony behind Don Elizario's kindness in letting him stay. I saw Tom Agee read Buz's face with righteous pleasure as the demands of the job in time and effort came clear. Tom was used to the work. He worked steadily, in a long-sustained rhythm, and as the day went by, Buz and I saw that this was both more effective and less racking than our fits and starts. We seemed to make little progress. The trough seemed almost as full at quitting time as when we began.

When evening came, with it came the rise of the full moon over the Magdalena mountains. It was at first a deep orange-rose as it lifted into the earth's haze; and then as the sky darkened above, the moon color changed into an unearthly yellow. Tom observed it. Speaking generally in order to avoid addressing Buz, he said,

"Now you look at that. Now you look backward over your shoulder to the west. They's some weather workin up." Over the Datil mountains hung a long straight bank of clouds. The mountains were an almost gemlike blue, but somber as well as clear. Between clouds and mountains there was a long, even gap of open sky. Its color was ominous—a strange deep yellow. "That kind of a sky means change. I believe we goin to see some rain mebbe tomorrow. If that rain had o' come before we was all done with the dippin, why, we'd a been days more gettin done. Fires out, sheep ornery, dip all thinned out. I tell you. When it comes, it sure does come. I've been marooned here days at a time in these August rains. This red clay."

I felt a weight in the pit of my stomach. Would I be marooned here? When would I get home? What was happening there? What would they say when they saw me? Did I look any different? Would they see me inside out? I had made sport of the virtue of my father and mother. What was I going to do with myself? They needed me. How could I save anybody?

※

After the heaviest day's work I had yet known, I fell asleep before the moon, now so clear and white that no stars could show near it, reached its height, and I did not stir all night. With the habit of dawn, I awoke but for a last moment of luxury kept my eyes shut. It was Sunday, but the job had to go on, and if I'd known any way to manage it, I would have risen and gone to Magdalena, Socorro, and home.

But without hope of that, I opened my eyes and turned to wake Buz. He was not in his bunk. He must be outside getting breakfast. I dressed and went out into the morning twilight. At first I did not see anyone, and then I saw him, between the house and the campfire place. He was bent over, swinging his foot across the sharp grass, closely searching the ground for something. I called out to him. He straightened up sharply as though to deny that he was looking for anything; and then he trotted waggishly over to me and said we ought to get ourself busy over a fire and a coffee pot and a frying pan.

"You're out early," I said.

"You cert'n'y were sleepin."

We built a little fire. Its smoke drifted toward the main bunk-house and brought Tom out for the day. He joined us for breakfast, which we made out of Irene's rations—coffee, stale cold biscuits to warm over, fried eggs and bacon. The early sun was now hidden by a general overcast. Tom looked up.

"I told you, didn't I?"

"It ain't rainin yet," declared Buz.

"I did'n say it was," replied Tom, to me.

We had the rest of the meal in silence. At the end, Tom, slapping his gaunt thighs, got up and said,

"Let's get to it before that sky opens up on us."

We went to the trough. Tom handed each of us a long-tined rake from the edge of the trough.

"We'll get it all out quicker if we scrape off the top of the slime," he said. "Yesterday, the buckets didn't get ver' much."

So we were right—we had not made much progress, so far.

"Why didn't you think of this yesterday, dad?" asked Buz.

"Fer your information, buster, I spent half the night tryin to locate these rakes. Somebody put them away after the shearin and I didn't find them till nigh midnight, out back of the feed house. Then I threw them down here. Now pick up your rakes and you get on it."

We all three dragged the rakes across the thick wet crust of the dip, pulling the hardest and largest lumps out over the edge along the length of the trough.

After an hour or so Buz went to Tom. There was a strenuous air of new respect about him.

"Mr Agee, sir," he said, "I got some urgent business in Magdalena. And I just wish I could borrow the Ford and run into town and tend to it, and then come right back?"

Tom leaned on his rake and scowled as if to destroy him with God's lightning, of which His minister was the wielder.

"I know your kind of business in Magdalena, Master Rennison, and I don't like the nature of it. The answer is no. Now you get on back to your rakin."

Buz turned white. In a pleading voice I had never heard him use before, he went on.

"No, sure enough, sir, this is mighty important and it ain't what you may be thinkin it is. I wouldn't ask you if it wadn't. I just beg you, Mr Agee."

[229]

"You haven't earned any favors around here, young man. You get back there now, right quick!"

Tom made himself larger in wrath. He could whip Buz with one hand and both knew it. Buz turned away and looked at me with the breaking face of a boy almost ready to cry. Then, wiping his eyes on the back of his hand, he went slackly along the trough to his rake and his station near the far end. As if harvesting a new crop, Tom returned to his long, slow, rhythmic sweep with his rake, and where I worked between him and Buz, I imitated him.

It must have been almost at once that Tom cried out in a cracked hoot,

"Oh, my gret God Ammighty! Richard! You come right quick!"

There was such horror in his voice that I ran to him. Bending all his weight on his rake handle against the trough edge, he was holding up something half revealed from the dip. He nodded for me to see it. "Gret God Ammighty!" he said again, now in a hush.

On the wet end of his rake he was supporting in much strain the body of Don Elizario. The face and shoulders and one arm were visible, glistening in a coat of the gray clotted dip.

"Quick," cried Tom, "we must get him out! Go get your rake and he'p me lift him out! Hurry now!"

His first shock gave way to urgent efficiency. I ran to my rake, and as I ran I saw Buz staring at me.

"Buz! Come and help! Something terrible—"

I didn't wait for him to answer, but took up my rake and ran back to Tom. I set it under the lower part of the body and together we drew it to the edge of the trough, and when Tom said, "Now!" we knelt quickly and grasped Don Elizario and brought him out to lie on the ground. The creosote and Black Leaf 40 flowed slowly from his face. One arm was twisted above his head with fist clenched. The other lay beside him. In the gray muck which was upon him he looked like a wet statue of himself in a posture of torment, molded in his clotted nightgown.

I felt a shadow over me and turned to see Buz, leaning over us to look at what we had found.

"Oh my, oh my," grieved Tom, "isn't this the worst pitiful thing ever you did see!"

The sorrow in his voice had a hard lifetime behind it. He shook his head heavily, looking back and forth over the whole length of the old man.

Then abruptly, noticing something barely visible in the clenched fist, he said, "What's this?" and leaned to find out. He picked the rigid fingers apart and released the slide of a thin brass chain, and when the whole hand was opened, there all plain was Buz's lucky piece, with its "Atlantic City Bathing Beauty." Tom held it up, and when he saw its face revealed as the wet dripped off it, he shouted,

"Where did this damnation thing come from?"

Then he remembered where he had seen it almost daily at work with Buz and the rest of us. He heaved to stand and reached for Buz. Buz wildly looked about for somewhere to go. There was nowhere to go on the endless land under the sky darkening with its bated storm. He looked to the house. His body tightened with the same bolt of energy I had seen when he caught his first sight of Concha. In a second he twisted just out of Tom's reach and ran to the house and up to the porch and began to beat at the door. He threw himself against it and beat and beat. The door was locked. There was no answer. His face was turned so his cheek was pressed with the rest of his body against the old white wood panels. His eyes were shut, his mouth working silently open.

Tom ran after him, whipping off his belt as he went. Taking the porch in one jump, he pulled Buz away, threw him down, and tied his hands behind him with the belt. He walked him roughly and fast past me to the main bunkhouse. As they went by, Tom said to me,

"You get on in to Miz Wenzel and you tell her the best way you can. You tell her to wait inside a while."

I went to the house and knocked gently, and waited. Silence. I called her name. No reply. Dread, and the memory of Don Eli's law, kept me from trying the door. The curtains were all closed. I tapped at a window. The house was silent.

I went back to the porch steps and sat down to listen for any sounds from within. I crossed my arms on my knees and put my face down on them to hide from that morning.

❊

In a little while Tom returned alone.

"You tell her?"

I shook my head and explained why.

"I'll go own in," he said. "I have to get to the telephone operator and get to the law at Socorro. She must be sleepin mighty deep."

He went up on the porch just as raindrops as heavy as spent bullets began slowly to fall on the tin roof, making sounds that rang separately. In another moment the sky opened and a cloudburst was upon us. I ran on to the porch and then I looked back at where Don Elizario lay where we had left him in his befoulment, and I made as though to go to protect his body from the downpour. Tom detained me.

"It's a mercy," he declared. "He must be washed clean before she gets to see him. —In all my years—"

The deluge suddenly increasing drowned out his words. He unlocked the door and went inside. I stood behind the screen of vines on which the rain beat as if to destroy what it would end by slaking.

❊

The storm, said Tom, interfered mightily with the telephone lines. Thunder and lightning came with the deluge, and the connection to Socorro by way of Datil was blanked out time and again. Tom said—and I thought of suppressing this detail for fear of playing too close to allegory—the tremendous crashes after the lightning which tore the sky were the wrath of gret God Ammighty at the foulest crime there could be.

He finally saw Concha. With her husband somewhere out in the day, she had locked the front door and gone to her bath deep in the house. When the thunder broke, she came to hide in the middle passageway of the house, where there were no windows. She remembered how dangerous it was to be in water during thunder and lightning. No, she had heard no one knocking.

"Did you tell her?"

He did. She crossed herself and backed away from him at his news. Then fell to her knees and, wailing in a passion of grief, said it was her fault, and began to pray aloud in Spanish. How was it her fault? Tom asked, and she replied that she should never have let her husband wander around outdoors alone at night that way. He couldn't see very well at night, he had been feeling faint in the last day or two. It would be so easy to fall into the dip and drown. She wept into her hands and kept saying, Oh, God, oh, God, in Spanish.

"No," said Tom, "that boy had something to do with it."

She screamed and hid her face in her arm. The harm of the world was now human instead of abstract in the will of God.

Tom told her then we would all have to go to town as soon as things could be arranged. I would help him. Please, she would please go to her room and stay there until we called her. She ran away and shut the bedroom door. Tom let her be.

I helped him bring Don Elizario to the house, where we did what we could with tubs full of water to clean away what the storm had not. We cut away his nightgown and sponged his body. He seemed diminished out of life, and a noble strangeness lay across his face. As we worked, I was "much possessed by death," and there were moments when I thought I could not continue; but Tom Agee's angry, sorrowful strength put something in me which let me go on, even when, using our sponges, we cleaned away from the old man's body the last film of the dip and saw what lay revealed. Tom looked up at me and silently pointed to the bruised, torn marks on Don Elizario's heavy old breast. Spaced precisely, they were cuts, violently made, by the tines of a rake, such as we had used at the trough.

Tom sat back on his heels and held his silence as though he could not speak to anyone of what he now knew for certain. But after a while he looked at me and said,

"I *thought* he was lyin. Now I know it."

He had taken Buz to the bunkhouse and had tied him to a stanchion of one of the double-decker beds. He showed Buz the amulet and asked formally if it was his. Buz, after a panting silence, admitted that it was.

"That was what I saw him looking for in the grass early this morning," I said.

Then Tom asked him, you did it? No, not exactly, Buz answered. He had never meant to. The old man was wandering around and Buz was restless—he did not say for what—and when he saw Don Eli he went toward him just to be sociable, but the old man swore at him and demanded to know what he was doing out, like that, near the house, and ordered him back to bed. Buz said he had no cause to talk to him like that, and refused to turn and go. The old man took a step toward him and hit him—oh, not very hard—on the side of the head. Buz pushed him back. The old man lost his balance and grabbed at him. Buz pushed him off. To recover himself, the old man leaned toward Buz again with his arms whirling around. He reached for Buz again and caught Buz's neck chain. Buz stepped away, the little chain broke, the old man staggered backward, lost his balance again, and fell into the sheep dip.

Tom asked him what he did then.

"Do you know what that ornery little devil said?" Tom asked me with awed disgust. "He said he just walked off and left the old man in the dip. He said, 'He threw me in, didn't he? *I* got out, didn't I?' "

Tom said to him,

"You pushed him."

"I never."

"Did you push him under?"

"No. I never."

Then what did he do? asked Tom.

Buz said he just walked away.

And him an old man? exclaimed Tom, and Buz replied that that wasn't *his* fault.

Tom said to me,

"To the shame of my hand and my faith, I hauled off and smote him as hard as I could across the face, and I left him. I was ashamed because he was tied up and he was scared and saying the first thing that come to mind. But now I see those rake wounds, I'm not ashamed any more."

❧

The law, at the county seat, Socorro, when all was finally understood over the storm-troubled telephone line, told Tom to head out toward Magdalena with the body, the prisoner, and whoever else might be there at the ranch. Two deputies would start out from Magdalena to meet him, soon's they could get going.

The ranch would be deserted when we left. Tom locked what could be locked. Our procession formed shortly after noon on that Sunday. We laid Don Elizario wrapped within blankets which concealed him entirely on the back seat of Concha's big yellow car, which Tom would drive. Buz, with his hands tightly tied behind his back, sat next to Tom in the front seat. I drove Concha in the Ford.

We started out in the downpour. Tom sent me ahead, in case I got stuck in the red clay of the road which by now was deep mud. His orders were to go as slowly as I could, and drive on the tufted grass between the ruts and on the roadside, where my wheels would have better traction.

The early afternoon was like deep twilight. I leaned forward over my wheel to peer through the rain. I would turn my lights on and then at once turn them off, for their beams only made the huge individual streams of rain more dazzling, and further hid the im-mediate distance. I remember how my heart was beating—not actu-ally fast, but in heavy blows. In our two cars we made a procession of sorrow, with the killer and the dead following me and the widowed girl through the downpour. Now and then I felt my nerve begin to falter in a sudden, weakening tingle throughout my flesh; and I managed to hold on by forcing my will to fight the mud sucking at my wheels. If I glanced now and then at Concha, it was only to be sure she was in control of herself. She was silent. Her face was gray-white, her eyes were circled by hollows the color of dark ash, her lips were pressed tight as if to suppress shock and sickness. In her lap her fingers ceaselessly climbed in and out of a tense pattern. She was not even praying now. She was oddly removed from all that had happened. She was somewhere else in her mind, far away, where she would rather be, now and hereafter. We did not speak.

It took us until mid-afternoon to pass the few miles to the high-way gate. I opened it and stood in the rain until Tom had brought the large car through. As it passed me, Buz lifted his chin at me and smiled in a comradely greeting—old friends, weren't we?—and he winked as though to promise something we could share when "all this" was over and done with. He was desperate in his refusal to believe what was real to other people.

The land began to slope gently toward the east as we edged our way along the dirt highway now. Here the rain ran off more swiftly. Where there were lifts and then falls of the contours, the red water collected in wide pools obscuring the track we were following. When we came to the western edge of the Plains of San Agustín, the road was like a slow river, flowing eastward. Under the opaque red surface, the ruts held their shape, and suddenly my wheels slid into them, the power was wrenched from my hands, and the Ford sank into the grip of the mud and came to a halt.

Tom was fifty feet behind me. He saw me try to rock the Ford back and forth to come free. Spinning the wheels only threw up mud and dug the car in deeper. When I could not move the car, Tom halted his at a safe distance behind me and ran to me.

"Here," he yelled against the rain, "you get back there! I'll get this car out. Go on, quick, he's alone! You guard him!"

He handed me his rifle, pushed me toward the big car, and took my place at the wheel of the Ford. I heard him race the engine as I ran through the water to the yellow Cadillac. My mind was not on the prisoner—in heavy dread it was on the blanket-wrapped figure in the back seat.

Soaked through, I reached the big car and ducked behind the wheel and slammed the door. My teeth were chattering. The rain was cold, like my vitals.

"Boy," said Buz genially, "you look a sight."

Catching my breath, I did not answer him. The air suddenly lightened as the curtain of rain opened briefly. The Plains of San Agustín showed. I saw the sky-colored vacancy, and then the curtain closed again and we were as if nowhere.

"Lissen," said Buz in a hissing whisper. He glanced over his shoulder in case the still form of Don Elizario might hear. "Richie! Now's my chance! He'p me get these ropes off!"

I scowled at him, completely puzzled.

"I mean, *listen,* Richie, you can let me go free, ol Tom is busy up there, he won't see or hear, give me the gun, and I'll just hop out and get lost over there in the plains. Nobody'd ever find me there! I'll get me on down to Messico. Richie!"

I held the gun away from him. I stared at him. I felt like someone else. If I let him go free, could he make his way from bush to bush, gully to gully, in the Plains of San Agustín, and in that lake of light, day after day, could he disappear? If he could use the land like an animal, might he come to the border far to the south, cross the Rio Grande, and be free? Or would he only be a prisoner, not of men, but of the country itself?

"God damn it, Richie, hurry up!" He had no doubt at all of my willing complicity. "There iddn't all that much time. Come on, my buddy—" with all the sentiment of his sweetest songs.

"Buz, you know I can't. Now cut it out!"

He rubbed his chin on my shoulder like a cat and said,

"These ropes sure do hurt."

"I said, cut it out, Buz! This is no fooling, you know." I lifted the rifle an inch or two. "After what you did!"

"He p'voked me! —I'm not foolin. Don't you remember the good times we had?"

He called up a whole imaginary history of us together. Even though his hands were tied behind him, he tried to draw his shoulders forward in his old gesture of cuddling himself to remind the world of his appeal, which had always got him what he wanted, and must always do so, because he believed in it.

I was scared by his unreality. At the same time, I was sickened by the power of any human being over another; captivity: restraint as upon an animal: any measure of indignity performed upon any individual by any body of people, for any reason. Though he was in custody for the worst of crimes, I was even so pulled by a sense of our common humanity and its general sorrows. At once, this sentiment angered me for its softness. He was a gross criminal. He deserved all he would get. But I was even angrier at the thought that if I were in his place, I too would look irrationally to anyone for help. I could give no help. I felt a perverse share in his guilt because I was so free of his trouble. How long ago, really, had it begun? Staring at him I had a view of him so impersonal that for a moment it seemed to suggest man's common lot—the newborn infant drawn with wet head and blind wrinkled shocked face from his mother's womb; the child growing with who knew what hopes and blessings over him, or what maltreatments, by those who had given him life; the boy learning how much? how little? beyond animal ways; the youth making the self which brought the young man to this; the man shackled by fellow men and helplessly subject to them.

"You hurry now, boy, hear?"

I shook my head but my mind was hot and senseless. I said, holding my sympathy where it had to be,

"But he's dead."

"That's right, so nothin can he'p him. But you can he'p me, Richie. Let me go. This is ol Buz, you ol son of a bitch"—his voice mellowed—"you can't forget that night at the Marigold, can you? Richie, come on, come on, just the plains, there, and I'll get me down to Messico."

What to do with a maimed creature but let it go?—as I could not. Something in my face must have changed, looked to him like promise, freedom, Mexico.

"That's ol Richie! Quick now!"

He turned to give me his back and the shackled arms.

But just then Tom came walking heavily like a giant through water. I saw now that he had coaxed the Ford free, and that it stood a little higher.

At my failure to act, Buz turned, saw Tom, and knew then that the Plains of San Agustín were forever beyond him. He half rose in rage from his seat and fell back again, shouting,

"A-a-h, you're all shittin sons a bitches!"

Tom looked keenly first at me and then at Buz. What had he

prevented?—this notion went across his face; but he had no time for imaginings, and roughly he gestured to me to get out, go to the other car, and start forward again, while he took the rifle and climbed in beside Buz and put the big car in gear.

"Keep your front wheels turned a mite to the left, till we get out of this here little lake," he said. "Go own, now. It's gettin darker."

I went to the Ford.

A few miles and a long while later, Concha said,

"Are you sure he did it?"

I could not speak of the proof clutched to the death in Don Elizario's hand, and the rake slashes on his breast.

"Yes, even though he says he did not mean to do it."

She fell silent, though she shivered, almost with the effect of clattering, as if she were at last coming awake to knowledge that had numbed her.

Passing the whole stretch of the Plains of San Agustín, I shook my head over the notion that any sort of freedom could ever lie that way, or any other, for Buz. Escape, but not freedom.

Shortly before evening the rain thinned.

Soon I thought I saw lights through the rain; then I was sure. The lights of two other cars were showing, coming to meet us, as the Magdalena mountains began to clear and fade and loom again way ahead through the varying rain.

❀

We reached Magdalena at nightfall with the rain still falling. There we were to be detained until the sheriff of Socorro County arrived. Tom took us to the Marigold Hotel, where he found rooms for us all. Concha wanted nothing but sleep, sleep. Tom and I went downstairs late in the evening to drink coffee and eat what we could. I wondered what to say to Larraine if she should ask me about Buz; but she was gone. Another waitress said Larraine had left, talking about a job in Lamesa, Texas, which she had heard of.

"She said she don't stay long in any one place. —Would you wish the regular dinner?"

The next morning, the sheriff was waiting for us in the lobby. He swore Tom in as a deputy to form part of the escort when we went by train to Socorro, where Buz was put in jail and all of us were questioned in turn. Tom and I knew what we knew and told it.

The whole town had the story by noon and the press by evening. It made a great sensation. Don Elizario belonged to the whole region as its great man. A mob gathered outside the Socorro County jail at the end of the street, south of the plaza. They were ready to lynch the murderer. Armed deputies stood them off until time for the evening train, when under an order issued by the county judge, the prisoner was bound over under a change of venue to Santa Fe County, there to await trial.

Again we were all together—Concha, Tom, Buz, myself, and Don Elizario—northbound by the same train to Albuquerque. From there Tom and another deputy took Buz to Santa Fe. Concha went home to her family and I to mine.

CHAPTER V

🦋

Prayers for the Dying

"LET ME LOOK AT YOU, my darling! What you have been through!
Hideous nightmare, from all that we've read. Murder! Oh, and"—
my mother shifted gaily into one of her little irrelevancies—"so
much about *you* in the papers, your picture on the front page, a
horrid picture, all full of mud, and those clothes, but we *did* recognize you. To think of it all!"

I felt her shudder and also her loving satisfaction at my brief
notoriety as she held my shoulders and looked into my face, searching for the child she knew so well in the man who with every year
was becoming someone else. But never much inclined to pursue the
"shadow side" of human nature—so I thought—my mother went
on,

"But how well you look, how brown. Did they work you so hard?
You look like a sailor, all ropy muscles after a voyage. Tell me, what
was the food like?"

She was being busy and merry to make a great event of my
return; but she seemed older. Her formerly occasional habit of
winking both eyes against distraction or emotion was now incessant.
Her life had turned inward to one purpose—my father's hourly need
of reassurance.

"And oh!" she exclaimed, "I know now what you went through giving those hypos to Daddy—I've been doing it every day, and when I make him bite his lips, I could die. I'm so glad you'll be doing it again, won't you?"

It seems to me now that I came home readier to deal with pain than before. I came home from a land which gave space to my vision, and loss to my youthful conviction that virtue controlled all. Now I knew that virtue had to be salvaged as best it could out of every human situation. The sacred and the profane had previously been separated for me. Now they had blurred edges where they met. Even so, I was home again in my native moral climate.

"It was crude and monotonous, but after a while, we never cared," I said. Then, to justify myself in a matter about which she would never know, I added sharply, "Distraction of any sort was welcome for the moment."

"I suppose so. Well, it agreed with you. Come, your father is waiting to see you and hear all you have to tell."

He said, when I found him in the patio,

"You've had quite a finale to your own fresh-air cure, Doc."

He was expert in the hectic humor of the tubercular. There were pink spots at his cheeks, whose bones threw a deeper shadow now. Under his scowl, his eyes were brilliant and carried a strong mixture—peculiar to the Irish, I suppose—of strong sympathy and self-protective gaiety. He was lying in the sunshine, wearing a cap, with a steamer rug over his long frame. His hands looked sculptured, with an unearthly pallid cleanliness about them. In his voice there was a strong, new grain, and his movements were abrupt and vigorous. He meant to show the world—and me—that he was not being consumed with corrosive thoughts about his condition, and the loss of what at any moment now might have been his proper office as governor of the state of New York.

But once our greetings and idle solicitudes were done with, it was the one topic he could not stay away from.

"Sam tells me not to keep going on about it," said my father drolly, "but it's the only interesting thing I know at the moment."

"Where is Sam?"

"Down at the telegraph office picking up telegrams. We get several a day with all the play-by-play news—the senate trial is in process."

"And the Pelzers?"

"You know, the strangest thing"—his eyes took on the fire of malice—"Mo Pelzer actually telegraphed asking for a deposition from me as a *character witness* for the defense. I was stricken with admiration for the boundless nerve of that family. There *are* people who never see themselves at all, don't you think?"

Indeed I do, I said to myself, and there are others who see too much of themselves. I said,

"How did you handle that?"

"Superbly. I had Sam wire back to say that my attending physicians—we made it plural—advised against any emotional concerns at this time."

He laughed, laughing made him cough, his eyes brimmed with merriment, he waved his white hands at me to express what his breath would not permit, and then I had to laugh at his high spirits. As his cough subsided, he put up one finger to hold the conversation until he could speak, and then he said,

"Do you remember that day during the campaign when we were at the Fort Schuyler Club in Utica when Judge took me aside for a brief conference?"

"Yes."

"I never told you what it was about. Well. Now. This: would I agree to lead the action in the senate to get the lenient tax laws passed in favor of the Chippewa Shipping and Steel people? If I would do so, behind the scenes of course, would I be satisfied with a payoff: he called it a donation to my campaign chest, if you please: of a hundred and fifty thousand dollars? When I stood numbed by amazement, not greed, he misread me and hastened to add that he thought he could get them to go to two hundred thousand. His share, he admitted with an air of honest good fellowship, would be considerably more, but he was sure I would agree that that was only proper, as he was the designer of the whole progressive concept, as he called it; and also, he stood to lose more than anyone else if anything should go wrong. *Should go wrong!*"

"Is that why you were so furious when you came out to me?"

"Of course."

"What did you tell him?"

"To go to hell, naturally, and moreover, I told him that if I was ever asked under oath, I would quote the whole interview verbatim. You should have seen his face. He looked like a vulture in shock. He could have killed me with his beak."

"Have they asked you for the story?"

"Not yet. Sam is sure they will."

"Will you have to go to Albany?"

"Ask my attending physicians. —No, probably not, but I am beginning to believe I could do it. A deposition will answer, I suppose."

"Bombshell?"

"Bombshell, with patriotic flares. —Are you all right, Doc?"

"Yes. Why?"

"Oh, I don't know. You look sort of:"

He shrugged.

※

At five minutes before ten the next morning, the bells in the two towers of San Felipe de Neri in Old Town began to toll for the Requiem High Mass of Don Elizario Wenzel. My strongest wish was to stay away. But I also wanted to join in the general absolution over him in the Mass. The old church, with its paper flowers and pink-washed walls, baroque white and gold wooden altar, leaning dim old sacred paintings, was crowded breathless.

In the middle aisle, before the sanctuary, lay the purple-draped coffin of the old man, flanked by three towering candelabra on each side. I stood in the rear of the church, where many Mexican men were also standing. I saw local officials—the mayor, the police chief, leading businessmen, both Anglo and Mexican, and reporters, including Lyle Pryor, who would write a serious column in place of his usual cranky little paragraphs about "lungers," local politics, and Congress. The city, the whole state, were angrily moved at the circumstances of the murder. In ranching country, most people knew what sheep dip was like.

There was a long wait in stifling propriety before Concha arrived with her old father and mother and a long string of family connections. She was all veiled, but her face was dimly beautiful in its pallor and stupefied by endurance. They went into black-festooned pews at the front of the church. Soon afterward, another group arrived, two men in black suits, with their women, who wore black shawls over their heads. The men were middle-aged, heavy, frowning likenesses of Don Elizario—his two surviving sons by his earlier marriage. They sat across the aisle from Concha and her people. They stared straight ahead, ignoring her. An almost palpable enmity was in the air between the two families. People nudged each other to call attention to this, and so crowded was the church that finally I felt the nudge as it traveled back along the pews, accompanied by little murmurs. Everybody knew that there was a matter here of a fortune which must be divided by death as once before it had been divided by marriage portions. When speculative stir subsided, as if a swarm of bees had collected itself and droned away, the celebrants of the Mass, three Jesuit priests in black and silver vestments, entered from the sacristy, and the last act of Don Elizario's history began.

The tension was extreme. I felt it in my vitals. For those more openly susceptible, it soon became too great to bear without response. A muffled shriek came from the front pew—Concha. Her tiny mother, who looked as though grief and endurance were woman's natural state, bent to comfort her; but the outcry was a signal for others of the family to honor the occasion, and a chorus of wailing women paid tribute to the young widow. Why can't they shut up, I said to myself, but the truth was that my decorum was not so much offended as that my nerves were caught up in a contagion of feeling. Something in me longed to let itself go free in some sort of expression. I felt the gathered emotion grow in the whole church. It seized me, tempting me, until I began to feel like someone else. The heavy air, hot with August and thick with incense and hysteria, seemed unbreathable. But it was more than that hour in San Felipe which was working in me. It was the focused effect of the weeks beyond Magdalena, and their culmination; and roughly, hardly knowing myself, I pushed my way to the door, through the thick crowd of standing men, away from the presence of God and general guilt, and across the street to the plaza. There I fell down, shaking, upon a bench near the weathered bandstand in the center of the park. From there I could dimly hear the chanting and the dutiful screams through the open door of the church, about which children clustered, peering and climbing against each other like a litter of puppies, trying to be part of what was happening within. After I had subdued my shakes, I went to my river glade, fell down on the fine sand, and with my arm covering my eyes against the light, the troubles of days past and of that morning, and others which I saw but did not want to see in days ahead, I sought sleep.

❦

The others left the dinner table to move into the long, glass-enclosed gallery at one side of the patio where the card tables were set up. Sam and I stayed behind with coffee and brandy. He had a little habit of looking keenly at me and then dropping his gaze and then looking keenly again. He did not ask me directly, only with his eyes, about my weeks away. He was closest to me in age of anyone in the house and I longed to lighten my thoughts by telling him every detail of the summer. But his strong intelligence was lodged in a rectitude which, while it would make no judgments in the case of a friend, would still hold to a fastidiousness which I could not put to a strain.

"It must be an extraordinary matter, to be close to a murder. And such a one!" he said, with an air of disposing of the painful topic for me.

I refused his tact.

"Is there strong feeling here about the case?" I asked, to bypass my own feeling.

"Oh, yes, terribly. They tell me no case has made as much outcry since the territorial days, when the frontier was still pretty close."

"You know law. What will happen to Rennison?"

"I think even if he changes his plea to not guilty, he will be convicted. Everyone I have talked to is sure he will be executed."

"You know, he will be killed for what he *is*, as much as for what he did."

The lowered and raised look again.

"You knew him very well?"

"Very well."

"Did you get along with him?"

"He always thought so, I thought so only at times. There is something appealing about him, but he is a fool. He doesn't see things like anyone else. He is unable to help it."

"You saw it coming?"

"Not exactly. But neither was I entirely astonished, though appalled, of course."

"I suppose you will have to testify."

"I suppose so. I don't like the idea."

"You have a certain sympathy for him?"

"I suppose I have, in the abstract. No—even personally."

"Why?"

"I suppose— I think probably because I have never known so clearly how events, combined with somebody's big inner world, can so entirely overwhelm any one creature, however much he may deserve what may follow."

"Yes, it is even more ironic and final when the events are of the creature's making, isn't it?"

"You mean, one really ought to imagine all possible consequences before taking action at any time?"

"Yes, but without becoming paralyzed. There are choices, after all."

"Yes, I know," I said, meaning more than I would ever tell him. He felt my reservations and quickly moved on to a topic we could equally share. He said,

"Governor Pelzer, for example."

He went on to tell of the senate trial in process at Albany. They were still hearing witnesses. Damaging evidence was being forced out of hiding day by day. The press was given a running digest of the proceedings. By direct telegram and by ravenous consumption of the newspapers, both local and imported—*The New York Times, The Albany Times-Union*—my father followed the trial, seeing himself as he might have been but for his removal and resignation.

"Do you think," I asked Sam, "that Pelzer made my father resign because he saw this coming? What good would it do him to have my father officially out of the way, if he was already exiled across the continent?"

"Thieves' honor, I suppose. Pelzer wanted to prove to the Chippewa people that he was doing everything possible to keep his commitments. Three more reasons. One: because he can't match your father's mind, style, and above all, decency, he hates and fears him, out of vanity. Two: with your father firmly out of the way, the tax swindle might squeak through the legislature. Three: if worse came to worst—as it has—then he could feel justified in asking the Chippewa people to get him off by strategic 'contributions,' *videlicet* bribes, to susceptible legislators, which would not be possible if your father had any position left."

"It sounds fatally unrealistic."

"A definition of most politics. Things of the sort have been pulled off at every level of our government—town, county, state, federal."

"Will it work now?"

"I think not, not with all the publicity so far. It's been incredible. But even so, a strong partisan fight is developing which will delay matters some. The party is being idiotic."

"How is Father taking it?"

Sam made a little circle in the air with his brandy glass.

"Some days it seems to get up his Irish, so that he wants to fight; and on other days, he knows he hasn't got the physical fight in him yet, and he goes into absolutely abstract Gaelic gloom, when we almost tiptoe around the house and want to be cross with each other. Lillian, the poor dolt, weeps so much that she powders her eyes before coming to the table, and you want to laugh because her moon face looks like a clown's, where the brimming eyes wash away the powder, and then you want to pat her arm and say 'There, there,' which is what your mother usually does. And then Lillian *really* lets go, rivers run over her cheeks through the talcum." He sighed. "I'm only glad Joanna didn't come out with me, after all. She'd say unlucky things in this atmosphere."

"Are you—?"

"No date set yet, but we think October."

"Good. I think you've had enough of us and our goings-on."

"Rubbidge"—a word of my father's—"we're not done yet, you know."

He looked grim, an expression which made you forget that he was a small man. In his fine neatness, his chiseled look of breeding, and his keen wits under polite control, Sam gave me heart. Abruptly he stood up and said we should go in to see what the others were up to—"as if we didn't know." It was one of those game evenings. In the early days of my return, I welcomed their wasteful distractions.

❧

They had just finished a round, and when they saw Sam and me, they gave up to gossip. Eleanor Saxby, Count, Lyle, and Serena Sage were at the bridge table. At another, Percy Sage and my mother were playing Russian bank. My father had gone to bed. As we came in, Lyle in his bawling nasal voice cried out at me,

"Well, kid, it did the trick, eh? Look how he's changed. My God, youth snaps back and forth, don't it? We sent him lily-white and drooping, and here he is, bronzed and tough. How do you like the real world?"

"Don't talk nonsense."

"You're right. *All things* belong to the real world. But finding out more of them is what I'm talking about. I expect murder is rather maturing, eh?"

"Oh, Lyle," said my mother, "it is nothing to make fun of. You can't make fun of *everything*."

"What else do you suppose keeps me alive?"

"No, he's right," said Percy with a lift of his left shoulder—an expression of disdain too mild to be offensive. "He has no real *center* to his life."

"Bingo," answered Lyle. "You've said it. You're luckier. You have your money."

"What a peefectly extraordinary remark," said Serena, who thought noticing money was vulgar if you didn't have it, but not if you did have it.

[251]

"Yes, money, you know," said Count eagerly. "Do you know about the Wenzel money?"

"The Wenzel—" cried Eleanor Saxby, gathering her full breasts together like possessions to be cherished by her gemmed fingers.

"But let me tell you!" exclaimed Count. "I have the, but *the* whole story!"

First of all, nobody knew where Concha was for several days in her early widowhood, but Count had found out from one of his downtown sources that she had gone to the Loretto nuns at her old school, Saint Vincent's Academy. They had taken her in. In those few days, much had been done.

"You can be sure of that," interrupted Eleanor. "I know what they—"

But Count quelled her with a fierce glance and went on. The two Wenzel sons, so much older than their young stepmother, Concha, and hating her so much, had arranged to buy, after the probate court action should be concluded, the Magdalena ranch and animals from her for a great sum: about half a million: and thus gain control of all of Don Elizario's real property, never to deal with Concha again. But his will, in addition to leaving the ranch to her, had left her all the remainder of his estate in stocks and cash, and she was now *"en*-hormously," said Count, "but *en*-hormously rich, *millones y millones. ¿Cuánto? Creo que,* I think, t'ree, four, millions dollars."

"Really!" exclaimed Percy with new respect.

"But she won't have the faintest idea of what to do with it all, will she," observed Serena.

"Well, *I* know," said Eleanor with her most worldly confidence. "Those nuns got hold of her and they will get the money too. I used to be a Catholic, and my brother is a priest in Milwaukee, and there isn't anything I don't know about how those people get their money and what they do with it."

"What *do* they do with it?" asked Percy. "Aside from running

[252]

industrial schools where they teach indigent youths how to make crutches to be thrown away at shrines."

Varying degrees of laughter met this, but Eleanor was not to be robbed of her initiative.

"Well," she said, "half of it goes for all those well-stocked rectories, and the other half goes to Rome. The Vatican owns the six largest banks in Europe. Did you know the Pope is a Jew?" she added as both heretic and anti-Semite.

"Eleanor!" exclaimed my mother chidingly, on both counts.

"No, really. It is the best-kept secret in the world, but a cardinal told my brother in Rome once, and then put him under automatic excommunication if he ever told a soul. Well, when he got home, he told me, and then went to Confession. —Why do I make up such nonsense?" She laughed, self-forgivingly.

"I know," said Lyle.

"Why?"

"Because it is in your nature to do so, madam."

"Oh," said my mother, "I keep thinking of that poor girl. She is probably trying to think out her own life, after what she's been through."

"I might go through it for four million dollars," wheezed Eleanor. She turned to me. "Wouldn't you like to marry a rich widow?"

Sam saved me from replying, for he saw that I would be rude.

"Do you mean yourself, Mrs Saxby, or Mrs Wenzel?"

She laughed, tacitly admitting that she had been talking nonsense, and that what she most enjoyed was the sound of her voice, heavy with cigarettes, experience of sex in happier days, scarred lungs, bourbon whiskey, and genial malice.

At the time, I saw and heard all this with confused dislike. What arc could ever connect the world of these people with the life of the earth and its labor, the blind needs of the animal creation, the sorrow of evil and savage death which I had come home from? Moreover, I had briefly become a snob of the bucolic. Now I see

[253]

them all without scorn or laughter, but only with memory of their various postponements of the fatality which held them in thrall, to their full and anxious awareness.

They were ready to resume their games. Sam went to the library at the other end of the house where on my father's worktable lay the folders of notes for the next chapter—it was still only chapter 3—of *Woodrow Wilson's Theory of Government,* to which Sam, in off-hand tact, hoped daily to return my father. On my way to bed, I paused at my father's door. No light showed under it; but he heard me, and he called huskily,

"Come in, Doc."

I opened the door. The hall lamp made a triangular plane of light across the room and reflected dimly on the bed, revealing my father. I stood beside the bed.

"What do you think you should do this fall?" he asked—for we were near to the end of August and we had never made plans for the coming academic year.

"It depends on several things."

"Yes. For one thing, it now seems likely that we won't be returning to Dorchester this year." He seemed healthier for having accepted the idea. "We'll still be pretty far away, won't we?"—and he meant from each other, if I returned to Aldersgate University in New England.

"No," I said, "as long as you stay here, I am going to stay too, and I will apply at the university here, if you approve, and then we can all go home together when the time comes. And that will be fine. Sam has careful plans about things for you there when you're well again."

"He has?"—but he knew it.

"Yes. And I believe him."

"We'll see," he replied, with an impersonation of a judicious attitude; but I heard through his measured words that same energetic belief and joy in public position coupled with honorable ambition which had brought him so swiftly to prominence in the city and the state where he had spent himself so prodigally. "Thank you, Doc, and good night." I started to go. He added, "I want you to be a happy man. I have been. I hope you discover how to be, for yourself, while you are still young."

We said good night. He always made me feel more than he said. Did I now seem unhappy to him? How did parents know things never mentioned?

❧

"Who is calling, please?" I heard Lillian ask in the blithe office voice she used on the telephone. In a moment she came rapidly and heavily to me and whispered as though the telephone could hear, "It is Sister Mary Aquinas, the superior of Saint Vincent's Academy! She wants *you*, Richard!"

"Hello?"

"This is Sister Aquinas at Saint Vincent's. Will you please to come here this afternoon at three o'clock?"

Her voice was cool, commanding, polite, with sibilants exaggerated by the telephone.

I agreed.

"Thank you," she replied. "It seems rather important—" with a hint of suppressed and impatient skepticism, but mannerly.

"Yes, Sister."

I was prompt. The academy sat on a corner lot on the north side of town. It was a pale-red brick building out of the nineteenth century, with windows rounded at the top, half shuttered within, and surrounded by a little procession of thin evergreen trees. I was shown by a novice all in white with downcast eyes into a corner parlor where the daylight scarcely entered through heavy lace

[255]

curtains above the lower half of closed indoor shutters. On the wall was an enlarged, thinly tinted photograph of old Archbishop Lamy, in whose time the school had been founded by the Loretto sisters, who came originally from Kentucky.

Sister Aquinas did not keep me waiting. She came through the door and closed it, all in a single gesture, while gazing at me with an analytical smile which never left her firm, pallid face.

"Please to sit down." She made an ample but delicate sweep of her long, strong hands, and then chose a chair close to me at right angles. For a silent moment, leaning rigidly forward, she continued her probing inspection of me; and then, for discretion, she cast a habitual glance to right and left, which required her to turn her whole body because of her deep, starched hood, and said,

"There is someone here who desires to see you. I wanted to see you first. She does not yet know that you are here in the house. You know of whom I speak."

"Yes. I think so. —How is she?"

Sister Aquinas glanced upward, leaning slightly back, and shut her eyes up to heaven for a second. Then, recovered,

"You will see. But I have consented to send for you on condition that nothing is said or done to upset her further."

"Upset? I don't wonder."

"I believe you were present at the time of the tragedy?"

"I was."

"And you have not seen her since?"

"Not to talk to. I saw her at the funeral."

"You will keep this visit confidential entirely?"

"Yes, since you ask it."

"There is excellent reason. You will not see her again."

"She is going away?"

"I have not said so."

"No. I see. I will of course never speak of today at all."

"To give scandal is a grave sin. I believe you are to be trusted." In the habit of command, she put her white hand on my sleeve and squeezed my arm with remarkable strength, as if sacredly binding me in duty. "Wait here, Richard. Thank you for coming. Our Blessed Mother will reward you for it so long as you do not betray Her."

She rose. Her full folds and heavy cincture and long rosary swung regally about as she turned and left me, again shutting the door.

In the door were two frosted glass panels. About ten minutes later I saw a blur on their other side and then the door opened slowly and Concha came in. Full of feeling, I called her name and started toward her. She put up her hand to halt me. She was thin and colorless. Her gray eyes were paler for the dark hollows below them. They had found clothes for her which made her look like a grown-up convent girl—a middy blouse, blue serge skirt, black stockings, and buttoned slippers. She seemed years older, yet years more beautiful despite her spiritless bearing. She took the chair of Sister Aquinas and I resumed mine, leaning toward her to let her read my feeling.

There was a long pause. We could hear the academy clock ticking slowly outside in the narrow hall, where it hung on the wall high above the black and gray tessellated slate floor. Finally, we both started to say something at the same time. I fell silent, to hear her.

"—ever seen him since?"

I shook my head.

"Have you prayed for him?"

"No." It had never occurred to me.

"Will you promise me to?"

"After what he—?"

She nodded and two huge tears came and went in her eyes. Repeatedly she played her fingers together and apart as she had done in that rain-blurred ride from the ranch to Magdalena. Having now made a resolve, she took a deep breath and faced squarely toward me. She told me what could hardly be told and—I now knew why—was never to be repeated.

"That night? You know? After it happened to my husband? He

came to the house. The door was unlocked. I thought it was my husband. I was in bed, I woke up, in the dark. I said, *Are you all right?* but there was no answer and then, and then, he was-he was at me."

With the fewest words she made me know what had been done to her in her terror, and against her will. In my knowledge left over from the Marigold Hotel I remembered how that must have been.

She fought. He almost smothered her to death with her pillow. She screamed unheard. Forcing his way, he hurt her. It was like storm raging upon her. If only she could be dead, then. She was almost dead and at the same time alive, as though out of her head.

"When he discovered how I was— That-that I was a—"

She could not say the word, but when he found that she was a virgin,

"He went wild."

She put her fingers to her eyes as though to keep me from seeing her.

Nobody knew now but the sisters and me.

Her emotional artlessness in wanting to tell me moved me as much as the facts themselves. The usual murmurs of sympathy would have said little. I took her hand. She let it lie in mine limply. It was damp and cold, half alive. She was incapable of physical response of any sort. After a while, staring toward the old archbishop's portrait but not seeing it, or anything else, she said,

"The sisters have places to send people like me. They still like me just like before. They know it wasn't my fault. Nothing like-like it has ever happened to them, but they seem to understand all about it better than I do. They know how to take care of me, and when the baby comes"—she looked away. I tightened my hold on her hand but there was no response. "They know how to take care of it and they have a place to keep it to grow up and all like that. Two of the sisters are going away with me tomorrow. One was my old dramatics teacher." Now she looked at me again. "Sister Superior said I could see you after she met you if she thought it was all right then."

She withdrew her hand and put it across her mouth to muffle a sob. She said,

"I just had to say goodbye to *someone*."

"Concha!"

"Thank you for coming. You—"

There was a blur of a figure at the ground glass, and a discreet sound at the door—the turn of the knob, but no opening of the door, to mark the proper end of the interview. With propriety, she stood up.

"Goodbye, Richard. You were the only one to treat me like a lady."

She approached the door, which opened silently before her. She passed through it to join the one who waited outside. Steps retreated up the slate hallway, turned a corner, and were gone. Concha receded uncritically into whatever her life must be. I was left alone with the open door, and the slow, walking tick-tock of the academy clock. After waiting a moment for someone to come and tell me to go, and no one coming, I let myself out.

What I had heard needed an outburst, in act or thought. What came to me was a mental tirade against Eleanor Saxby. I said to her, "Well, you're right, they've got her, and thank God; and yes, people like you are sometimes right; but for the wrong reasons."

⁂

Sam woke me up with the news that Governor Pelzer had just been found guilty in the New York state senate trial for his impeachment. Before the day was over he would be out of office, and indictments for perjury, violation of election laws, malfeasance in office, and bribery were waiting for him. In the absence of the lieutenant-governor, the senate would vote within twenty-four hours on a successor who would serve for three months while a special election would be readied to bring a new governor to Albany for the balance of the vacated term—a period of some fifteen months.

"The pressure is on," said Sam.

"For what?"

A spokesman had telephoned the news that if my father would consent, he would be nominated by the Democratic Party to run for governor in the special interim election.

"But don't they understand?"

Oh, they listened, but they were blinded by enthusiasm. Sam had reported faithfully my father's health. Even so, a delegation, chosen from the legislature and my father's original supporters in Dorchester, were talking of coming West immediately to see my father, consult with his physician, and urge the great purgation of the disgrace laid upon the party and the Commonwealth of New York State.

"What does my father say?"

"You'll be amazed. He seemed to lose years of age and all preoccupation with illness when I talked to him half an hour ago. He hedges the issue round with every possible objection, but you can see by the light in his eye that he asks to be overruled, and that he has been given a remarkable second chance."

"But Dr Birch?"

We knew what the answer would be to that question. Later in the day he came to the house and listened to the whole exciting story. He then made a general examination of my father, and ended by saying dryly,

"Not *quite* yet."

My father assured him buoyantly that he felt ever so much better since the news had come. Imagine what this could mean to him: you see, he would accept the call only if he were not forced to endure the rigors of campaigning. He would make it a condition that he would respond only to a genuine draft. Then, once elected (for there was no doubt that he would be elected, even if Mr Coolidge's people should try to intervene from Washington) he would continue to rest for a greater portion of every day. Why, he knew exactly which men in the legislature would carry on most of the work for him . . .

"Delusion," remarked Dr Birch. "As for the decision, I recognize of course that as yours alone."

He departed without saying goodbye. My father looked at Sam. Sam said,

"Another opinion?"

It was a straw. My father clutched at it; and as messages flew back and forth between Albany, Dorchester, and the Rio Grande road, the plan for the visiting delegation grew rapidly, now to include, at enormous expense underwritten by an anonymous backer, sending Dr Morton Frawley with members of Our Crowd from Dorchester. He would consult with Dr Birch, hoping to establish a contrary medical opinion. The delegation would come by the California Limited, stay at the Alvarado, and hold political and medical consultations at the Casa del Rio.

The household seemed to glow with new purpose and optimism. My father was like a boy after a great prize, eager to do more than was asked of him in good behavior. He rested for longer hours each day, slept more every night, took his own pulse and temperature less often than usual to prove that these could tell little of interest, and even wondered if my daily hypodermic injections were really necessary (though he continued to receive them stoically). He delighted us all with his high spirits.

"But not a word," said Sam, warning us all, "to anyone of what is going on. We need the value of one stunning surprise announcement. Nobody should know about our visitors until they have left, when we'll make the news release."

But as Lillian O'Rourke heard these instructions, her proprietary pride in my father and his golden future—for once elected, nobody doubted that he would be re-elected to the full term—betrayed her. Before the delegation arrived, she encountered Serena Sage one day in a shop and under vows of holy secrecy told her what was impending.

*

My mother, though compliant, was restrained in her view of all the hurried optimistic plans at home. No prize of ambition or obligation to public service meant more to her than her husband's health. Such as she had seen of political life seemed to her more farcical than rational, and founded on a system of expedient treason. How could we be sure—my father, Sam, even myself—that the mighty powers which had supported Pelzer might not throw overwhelming opposition against my father if he consented to run? And how could anyone expect to limit himself in any performance of public duties? She remembered well enough the dreadful campaign summer under which my father had broken down. She had to agree that my father seemed noticeably improved in his condition, but the local lore of what Lyle called the lungers was full of cases of those who had gone home too soon, believing themselves cured, only to collapse again in their return to active life.

"I'll show them how much better I am," my father would protest.

"How? Nothing is worth it if there is any risk at all!"

*

Unwittingly, out of their social sense, Serena and Percy Sage provided an opportunity for my father to prove himself to the delegation.

They came one day to propose that they entertain our visitors.

"Visitors! What visitors?" asked Sam vehemently.

"Ah," said Serena archly, "a little beed told me."

"What little bird?"

Sam guessed soon enough. But the point was, the Sages would give a superb picnic for our guests. They knew a peefectly heavenly spot for a picnic which would give the Easterners a maavelous taste of Western life. It was a little canyon made of ancient lava at the foot of the volcanoes on the horizon west of town across the Rio Grande. We would go in motorcars through the dunes until the sand was too soft and heavy, and then we would walk the rest of the way, perhaps a quarter of a mile, while their "couple" would bring all the hampers, ice buckets, drinks, cushions, and steamer rugs for the picnic lunch. The Sages needed to know only how many guests to expect. How few chances there were "out here" for any fresh events! Always the same faces, the same gossip, the same hectic hopes! And how amusing it would be to start, right here, way out in New Mexico, the campaign for the next governor of New York!

Percy, though a North Shore Republican, said he was *"intrigué"* to be, as it were, sponsoring a Democrat. Back home, politics to him had always been a matter of appearing occasionally at outings with shirt sleeves rolled up, a hot dog in one hand, a handshake in the other, a candidate's name on the hatband of his straw boater, and a general air of having descended from the great house of the neighborhood to exhibit three timely virtues: democracy in action at the lowest level, virility, and highly bred good nature. Even resorting to the chewing of gum, he was the patrician accepting this revolting duty every two years. If his endorsement weighed less with voters than he believed, giving it vested him with a fine eighteenth-century sense of doing a squire's duty—really, he said, a constitutional *privilege* which made him a citizen simple as any other. As for Serena, she was *enchantée* by the idea of the picnic.

To our amazement, my father agreed to it.

My mother shook her head and gave in. But not Lillian. She

advised against the whole venture. Her familiar mood of sustained "gladness" at anything we did gave way to one of her rare stubborn fits. It was possible that she felt remorse for having gossiped to Serena Sage about the political visitation, thus setting off the plans leading up to the picnic. She thought my mother agreed with her about the hazards for my father in any unusual exertion. When my mother sided with him, Lillian felt snubbed and retired into a wounded gloom which was as Irish as her other mood of teary, smiling worship: Her very appearance changed. Despite her heavy flesh, she managed to look haglike, curling her lip in silent foreboding, glaring sideways at the contrary world.

"Oh, Lillian," exclaimed my mother, "for heaven's sake, let the clouds lift."

"Insult me all you please," replied Lillian. "I will stay home and pray. *Some*body has to."

Despite her use of piety to punish others, no plans were changed to mollify her.

"Nobody is to mention this whole thing to Birch," decreed my father.

"No, we know what he would say," said my mother. "I insist upon one thing. Morton Frawley is to come with us to the picnic."

"Naturally. He is a guest, like the others."

※

Dr Frawley was one of those people who are always referred to by their full names. Both tribute and intimacy were established by this for those who liked attachment to eminence, and who enjoyed both names together, provided they were euphonious. Personality added weight to the tradition. Morton Frawley, M.D., was a rather short man whom I had hardly glimpsed in Dorchester. He was trimly built except for a slight thickening about the waist which admirable tailoring almost concealed. His dark hair was thin but brushed so well that it revealed only a brilliant shine instead of a glimpse of pink scalp. He wore thick, rimless glasses which greatly enlarged his eyes to liquid brilliance above his excellent, short, straight nose. He removed his glasses to read. His dark mustache was trimmed to accent his full, ruddy lips. All his patients swore by him, which sometimes meant that they liked him not so much for his skill as for his reassuring charm, which lit up his round face, gave brightness to his cheeks, and made his glance merry. He looked to me like an idealized man of medicine wearing a white coat in an advertisement while holding a test tube up to the light.

With the delegation, he arrived one afternoon on the California Limited. The usual local crowd was gathered nearby to see the great train make its half-hour pause. Who on board for California might take a constitutional along the brick walk by the tracks? Any movie stars? There was sure to be a wheelchair or two for arriving invalids. Worlds away came, paused, and departed with the train.

When the delegation alighted, the Albuquerqueans observed a group of obviously substantial newcomers; and when they saw my father go forward to greet them, a few knew who he was and waved on general principles. He leaned on my arm until he was within a dozen feet of the visitors; then he straightened up, and with his high good nature as evident as ever, his "public" animation at its best, he gave hearty handshakes all around. In the style of his great days, he was dressed in his cutaway coat and all its accoutrements, including a high silk hat, even though they might be out of place in the desert. He knew how well all this became him, for if he had a single visible vanity, it was for dressing up to the nines. Clearly, he made a brilliant impression on his visitors, who had no idea of how much of an invalid to expect.

Dr Frawley was fully indoctrinated about his mission. My father's friends from Dorchester and two from the Albany legislature—one from the senate, one from the assembly—had assured Morton Frawley that provided his medical findings were favorable he would be professionally occupied with the Next Governor of the Empire State. Under expressed concern for my father's welfare, this carried a lively hint of professional prestige by which Morton Frawley (such was his reputation) might be moved. He knew my father's case— had sent him West in the first place, an invalid on a stretcher. Straightway, he would see his old friend and classmate Dr Birch, study X rays, discuss the prognosis exhaustively, and then himself examine the patient. As a professional man, after all, he refused to promise anything before having all evidence before him. Meanwhile, he promised that he would enjoy his first journey to the West, where he had sent so many patients from the icy or steaming, frozen or boiling, climate of Dorchester.

The Albany legislators were substantial men, given to appraising glances, and heavy with paunches, watch chains, and clouds of cigar smoke. My father's friends from Dorchester—the two representatives of Our Crowd—were keen in another way. They had known me since my childhood, and I was supposed to call one of them "Uncle" as a courtesy. They were leaders of their city, they believed what they had sworn to on the watch they had given my father, and they had adopted his reform policies so righteously that their indignation at the Albany scandals concealed any self-interest they might have retained. Though I did not question their real affection for my father, their present anxiety and hope were too visible to be met with comfort. I let Sam play host. They all knew him from the earlier campaign days.

When the two doctors held their conference, nobody else was present. After it was over, Frawley came to the house and spent half a day alone with my father. Escaping the event, I only heard my mother say, "Dan, here is Morton Frawley to see you," and my father reply heartily, and then Frawley exclaim, "Well, you're looking like a very different man from when I saw you last," and then doors closed.

"Iffy."

Morton Frawley was quoted as having given this judgment to the delegation after considering my father's case and the wisdom of going after the election. But he went on to say that, under well-understood and agreed-upon restrictions, the whole notion of a return to politics at present was, actually, not *altogether,* in his opinion, out of the question. His qualified statements were given with what Sam called moist charm. We were told that Our Crowd and the lawgivers were jubilant at this ruling. Everything moved cheerfully toward the day of the picnic at the volcanoes.

※

The whole land lay a mile high, and to this altitude was added the further grand upsweeps of the mountains at every point of the compass. The mountain air was over all, and at times, taken with a deep breath, it was so light and pure that it made you feel giddy for a moment, in a pang of conscious well-being.

Through miles of diamond-clear light the volcanoes to the west rising from a long, half-buried crust of black lava lay against the far horizon like those man-made deities of Egypt which seemed to become natural earth forms. The volcanoes had been dormant for centuries. Lyle, who fancied local history, said their active time must have been coincident with the prehistoric general volcanic upheaval in northern and central New Mexico, which was remembered with awe in the spoken lore of the Pueblo Indians.

Percy and Serena had found their picturesque picnic spot during Percy's third year at Albuquerque, when he was declared an arrested case for whom it was safe to go exploring the country all about. Not many people went across the river to the entirely vacant sand shelf which stretched far north and south in the foreground of the volcanoes. It was for just this reason that the Sages liked the place. Once, having driven too far into the dunes, their car had been stuck in the scarcely marked sandy road. Now they knew just where to leave the car and walk to the black lava wall where the sand ended, and where a little canyon opened which could not be seen from a distance.

When I said I did not want to go to the picnic, I was overruled: I would be needed to drive one of the cars, and to help fetch and carry picnic supplies—rugs, hampers, ice buckets, along with large, festive standing umbrellas to be opened against the beating heat of the sun. Too, Percy's portable phonograph with its hand crank and his case of records—jazz, which he had lately discovered and was "simply dippy" about, and so should we be, he promised, when we heard Paul Whiteman or Bessie Smith, who was "peefectly killing."

It was a large party, for it included not only our household, the visitors, and the hosts but also Mrs Saxby, Count, and Lyle Pryor (who gave his word not to report the event even confidentially to his newspaper).

With poor grace, I took part in the day, for since returning home, I did not want to see much of anybody.

We drove out in three cars, crossing the wooden bridge over the Rio Grande at Barelas. In my car were Eleanor Saxby, Lyle, Sam, a member of Our Crowd, and Dr Frawley. As we crossed the sandy riverbed, the doctor exclaimed,

"But where is the water? I thought the Rio Grande was an enormous river!"

"Look how wide it is," replied Lyle.

"But it's two thirds dry sandy bottom!"

"So it is. But its flow and depth are not to be seen here," said Lyle irritably. Like many new residents, he had become proprietary about the Southwest.

"Then where?"

"In history. The river itself has never been as deep as its name."

"What on earth are you two palavering about?" exclaimed Mrs Saxby, who had other plans for herself and Dr Frawley which had nothing to do with local history. At her most confident, if over-blown, femininity, she appropriated her new friend Morton Frawley with an opening move in the game of important mutual friends, and in five minutes, she had brought him to acknowledge four persons, all of whom, carefully chosen for mention, were prominent in one or another way, but chiefly through wealth. Of these, her triumph, acknowledged by Dr Frawley with a frank new appraisal of her, was her establishment of intimacy with the Ramson family of Dorchester ("steel") on whose Great Lakes steam yacht, the *Marianna,* she had been a guest.

"Oh, yes, Teddy and Marianna Ramson are great friends of mine," said Dr Frawley, comfortably continuing the game.

The caravan was led by Percy and Serena in their seven-passenger touring car. Percy drove with the top down for the sake of the bronze sunburn which gave him his cosmetic health. Heading toward the sands, his car carried his wife, my father and mother, the other member of Our Crowd, and the New York state legislators. The last car of the column contained the picnic ingredients and the Sage servants—the only "couple" in domestic service in Albuquerque—and Count, who carried an oddly shaped leather case.

High spirits animated the expedition, which Percy called an "outing." We drove for about fourteen miles, and then, at a signal with lifted arm from Percy in the leading car, we halted in the heavy sand of the road, which faded into the dunes.

"Everybody out!" he called gaily. "It's shanks' mare from here on!"

I glanced at Dr Frawley.

"How far?" he asked, thinking, as I was, of my father—could he safely walk under the blazing zenith through sand which would drag at every step we took?

"Percy Sage says no one can drive all the way. Cars get stuck in the sand," I said, "but he says his little picnic place is much less than half a mile farther."

Frawley frowned.

"You and I," said Mrs Saxby, flaring her nostrils like a fine thoroughbred mare retired from the track, "will walk with Dan and take care of him."

"You'd make a gorgeous nurse," replied the doctor, flirting on the sort of reflex which had gained him the reputation of being a *dashing bachelor* and *fast*. The compliment did not entirely please Eleanor for the social level it assigned to her.

※

When I was a very small boy I used to imagine the nearest and most common of conditions or events as tremendous. A certain thicket of rose bushes in our garden I was able to transform, thanks to fairy tales, into a dense forest filled with hidden rewards and thorned menace. The little lake in the park faced by the museums near which we lived became the Atlantic Ocean, where I could rehearse odysseys already traced with a finger on the globe which stood in its tripod by my father's library desk. The Alps on occasion were no greater than the sierras of not yet muddy snow piled up along the streets of Dorchester by snowplows the day after one of our Great Lakes blizzards.

Now, in my state of mind, the walk through the dunes on that early September day became for me a crossing of a desert. Time was suspended, distance was measureless. With all the others I toiled, conscious of every step through the sand. My breath came shorter because of exertion in that altitude. The sand dragged heavily at our feet, but how heavily I did not know until ahead of me my father faltered for a moment and put his hand to his side. Eleanor and Frawley leaned sharply toward him. I heard the doctor say, "Perhaps a few minutes' rest?" but my father shook his head and ground his jaw forward and immediately resumed his trudging against the sand. The others were all ahead of us. No one else saw the incident. The official future was intact. I saw our file as little moving dots on a horizonless tableland of an undiscovered continent.

At last, and suddenly, over the crest of a dune, we came to the pitted sloping face of the old lava flow, and there before us was a narrow cleft leading into deep shade, which we gratefully entered. The little canyon opened out as we went farther. One wall was in shadow, the other in sunlight. The canyon floor was sandy and irregular, and Percy halted us at a spot where separate hunks of lava lay about, close to each other like furniture placed at regular intervals.

"I call this place Stonehenge or the Henge for short," he cried, as though it was his creation. "Isn't it scrumptious?"

The couple began disposing steamer rugs over the rocks and on the sandy floor, and Percy himself set up a long folding table of aluminum, which was soon covered with a pink linen cloth. Rows of food and drink began to appear there. The organization was flawless. The mood of the laborious walk was transformed into a festive air. My father, glistening with sweat from the walk, was animated and outgoing, as he always used to be when surrounded by people for whose comfort and pleasure he assumed responsibility whenever they had assembled for his sake.

"Isn't it remarkable!" exclaimed my mother when I came to her with an iced drink. "He really can *do anything,* can't he, when he thinks others depend on him!" But this was as much a plea for reassurance as an admission of a marvel.

The party settled down.

"How do you like my Henge?" demanded Percy.

"You buy it," said Lyle, "and build a grand hotel *and* a paved road, and a fine restaurant and a bootleg bar, and I'll manage it for you."

But he was still panting and pale from the walk.

"I could never," replied Percy, opening a hamper of deviled eggs and caviar, "have anything to do with a business which catered to people's *appetites* in any way." He shuddered. "People become *beasts* if anything goes wrong when they order drink or food or beds."

Mrs Saxby gave one of her coughing laughs and spoke through cigarette smoke.

"You're so right, Percy. There's only one appetite that can give satisfaction just about every time." She wheeled her prominent gaze on Morton Frawley and added, "That is best managed by ladies of the profession, one at a time."

"You tell 'em, kid," said Lyle. He was breathing easier. "Have you ever tried it?"

Mrs Saxby took this as so preposterous as to amount to a racy compliment. She turned the sexual reference into a full-bosomed blandishment, once again in the direction of Dr Frawley, who gave her a ribald gleam which made her blush.

"My God, I'm blushing," she declaimed hoarsely. It was her policy to draw attention openly, even at her own expense.

Percy waved the company to serve themselves at the picnic table. Nobody hurried to move, but Frawley, after an inquiring look about at everyone lounging on cushions and rugs, said, "I am famished, it must be the altitude," and under polite control, he went to the table, took up his plate, and, leaning forward over the delicious array, he inspected the dishes from one end to the other. His lips worked as he rehearsed the flavor of each dish before him. He moved his sleek head in pleasure as he looked closely from one to another platter or bowl or slicing board. His whole body was tensed with appetite. He seemed to postpone the delight of choice as he let his fork hover above now this, now that, enticing dish. He swallowed once or twice as the juices of taste began to run in his mouth. He made me think of a fastidious buyer shopping for exactly the article he had come to find. At last, darting his fork at a succession of dishes, he became the brilliant surgeon who knew his work so well that he never wasted a movement. When his plate was full, he turned and saw that we were all watching him. Sweeping his fork over us all, he inquired in well-managed surprise, "Am I the first?" and without further delay sat on a rock and began to eat. Percy ordered the champagne opened. Frawley had bestowed well-being upon everyone by his frank and jolly response to the food. The picnic was already a success, and was given democratic sanction when Percy unbuttoned his starkly plain gold cuff links and rolled up his shirt sleeves. My father and his visitors drew aside by un-spoken agreement and ate their lunch as a separate little group, talk-ing politics. Sam was with them. The rest of us subsided into the usual banter. My mother almost never took her eyes off my father, at the same time helping to keep alive the gaiety required by the event. I berated myself for not being able to add to it.

"Cheer up, kid," said Lyle, "nothing lasts forever."

※

While the political conference went on in deep shadow several rocks away, Count brought out the odd oblong leather case which he had carried to the picnic. It showed many scars in spite of much polishing. From it he produced a narrow, flat, stringed instrument— a really old vihuela, the ancestor of the more familiar guitar.

"To entertain," he said, watching himself with coy modesty as he began tuning his pegs. "I will sing for you." Another minstrel of that summer.

"Why, Count!" exclaimed Eleanor. "You never told us. You are talented!"

The rest of us reclined in the hot shadow of the little canyon wall. Lighted as in a theater by the upward reflected glare from the sand where Count now stood in full sunlight, we made a random pattern of shape and color as we waited in stillness. Count struck an elegant, sloping attitude. In his straw boater, his old striped blazer, his yellowed white flannels, he impersonated a juvenile leading actor. I could imagine theatrical make-up on his narrow face, with his eyebrows darkened and raised to give an expression of sad innocence.

With his ancient, sparsely strung bow, he scratched a few long chords; and then in an astonishing tenor voice with a rapid bleating pulse to it, he sang an elaborately ornamented melody after the flamenco style:

> *Sierras de Gra-na——da,*
> *Montes de Ara——gón,*
> *Campos de mi pa——tria,*
> *Para siempre adiós, adiós,*
> *Para siempre adiós . . .*

The vihuela despite his scratchings had a mellow sound. He contrived a throbbing emotion with the unlikeliest means—his middle-aged imitation of a fine, youthful singer, his intense but unmusical voice, his swaying posture. Lost in what he sang, he was a Count we had never seen. Far from entertaining us, he was rapt in lament as old as the history of his province in Spain.

"How curious," murmured Serena.

"He makes me nervous, what's he saying?" whispered Eleanor to me, refusing to allow real feeling to reach her.

"He is saying goodbye to the mountains and plains of his homeland," I whispered back. "It is a song by Enrique Granados."

"I don't care who it's by, have him stop!" and she put her hands over her ears.

Luckily, Count was so carried away that he heard and saw none of the embarrassment which his performance put upon us all. As music, it was so excruciating, as feeling, it was so powerfully forlorn, that we all knew we were in the presence of the real creature behind the daily gloss of a desire to ingratiate with his elegance of manner. The light bore upon us upward from the brilliant sand. The desert stretched away, the distant mountains and the day's far-gathering thunderheads made us all small in the wilderness, and Count smallest of all, yet the only one of us at the moment to assert his ultimate solitariness openly, like a lone locust energized by the boundless heat of space.

＊

By four o'clock we were back home at the Rio Grande house, where my father retired to rest. The visitors would return for dinner—all but Morton Frawley, who had been captured by Eleanor Saxby for the evening. She had access to a raffish speakeasy at the mouth of Tijeras Canyon in the mountains twelve miles east of the city. She promised him a glimpse there of what was left of the frontier spirit in Albuquerque. She would call for him at the Alvarado Hotel in her *tin lizzie,* and they would set out on an evening and—who knew?—perhaps a night of adventure.

"She is a masterpiece of self-protective ambiguity," said Sam to me, for we both heard these arrangements being made. "She leaves it to Frawley to turn the adventure either way for the night. I promise you, he will be safely tucked away in his hotel room by ten o'clock. I would venture that the overpowering Eleanor is not his type."

"What happened at the picnic conference?" I asked him.

"Well: first of all, it was a reunion—it gave them all honest pleasure to be with the Governor again. A little small talk, and a few glances exchanged over the problem of how to get to the point. But your father dug them out of their diffidence by saying they must be quite certain that they had no other candidate in mind. No, no, they said, there was now less than three months' time until the special election—under the state constitution, you know—and there was not time to build up another candidate, and in any case, they didn't want anyone else. Your father's campaign for lieutenant-governor was recent enough so that every voter knew who he was, and why he was elected with such a wide margin on the Democratic ticket."

"Was there any health talk?"

"Of course. But they insisted that such a short time was to his advantage, for the reason that it would not tax him with a long, drawn-out campaign. Furthermore, they would even so make certain that he was spared every possible exertion."

"So?"

"He gave them each his steady, blue, keen look with his head slightly lowered, you know the look, and then he said briskly, Very well, he would run, provided—and here he had a moment's fun, for he held them up with a finger until they got uneasy—provided he could name his own lieutenant-governor. Oh, if that was all, they said; certainly; and did he have anyone in mind? Yes, he said, he had, but he would not say who just yet. They nodded modestly. None of them presumed to guess *he* might be the one, but you could absolutely see the thought cross some of the faces. It was a clever move, and then it wasn't long before we began to think of names for the usual committees. The Dorchester crowd said they knew where they could get plenty of clean money. The Albany types said they could speak with authority for overwhelming support in the State House. I put in my oar by saying that we would have 90 percent of the press with us. We all got agreeably carried away and saw a landslide as inevitable."

"Are you for it?"

How orderly Sam looked when he was direct and serious—his dark gleam of gaze through his spectacles, which oddly made him look handsomer than he was. Intelligence was visible in every feature of his finely carved face.

"Well, you know," he replied. "I'd rather see the Governor *write that book,* just to be absolutely safe about the physical thing, and then try the political thing next time round. But he has decided to 'go,' and I'll work my hide off for him. He knows I'd gladly make a career out of serving him all the way, and I don't think there's any limit to how far he can go. Some people are born to play second lead with distinction. I'm one. —You've had a good life with him, haven't you?"

"With both of them"—my parents. "I think I've been selfish and clumsy, never to let them know how much I feel for them."

"Do you want to help them now?"

"Of course. Why?"

"Well, if you don't mind, I'll risk a word of avuncular advice." He made a comic gleam through his glasses.

"Go ahead. You're all of eight years older than I."

"Thank you. You've been pretty depressed lately. Whatever happened during the summer, do try to shake yourself free and get back to your old outgoing self. You probably never saw it, but I've seen it many times, the look on your father's or mother's face when they used to see you coming back to them any old time. It made them happy simply to look at you if you were happy. I'd like to see that look on their faces again. —D'you mind?"

He was in no way asking for confidences. He was posing a case for civilized behavior, and the power of love. He struck home in a way which released me from the self-absorbing ache left over from the events of the summer.

"I know," continued Sam, "that nobody can be happy on command. But for the sake of others, you can impersonate it. And habit, you know, has its own power. —I know something about this, or I wouldn't harangue you about it."

Without adding a word, then, he alluded to his coming marriage, and the deliberate concessions it required of him in order to give Joanna the possessive certainty she sought. He knew when to desist now. I needed no more advice.

"I've got some wires to send about today's conference," he added.

"There will be interesting speculative stories from a confidential source in tomorrow's *New York Times*. See you at dinner. There will be a windup conference afterward in the library."

For the first time since I had come home I was able to take a full, deep breath.

※

After dinner I sat alone with my mother in the patio, while deep in the house the political visitors, Sam, and my father worked on the text of an official announcement to be released in Albany on the following Monday.

"I will allow them five more minutes," said my mother. "He is much more tired than he admits."

There was a little while of thoughtful silence. Then she said, roaming aloud in her thought,

"I keep thinking of poor Mo Pelzer. Isn't it dreadful to climb up over someone else's disgrace!"

"I thought you didn't like the Past Grand Orphic Sibyl."

"I don't. But I feel sorry for her—and for Governor Pelzer, I suppose, though that strains Christian charity."

"But he's a crook, and she's an overdressed pineapple."

My mother laughed in spite of herself.

"You're dreadful."

"We've always known that," and then, under my new policy, I said, "But what a fine day we had."

"Yes, in some ways."

She reached for my hand and held it. Presently she said, with some odd mixture of sadness and love,

"Do you really know the man he is?"

"Oh, yes."

"You will know it even more when you are married yourself, and know what it is to make one life out of two."

"Of three."

"Yes, three. It has been three, hasn't it, darling?"

She let my hand go and reached her arms toward the amazing stars and the idea of heaven. My feeling rushed up in me so fully that I was afraid to show it. I stood up.

"I think I'll turn in, Mother."

"Sleep well, dear.".

I started to go. She suddenly called, strangely urgent,

"But I wonder . . ."

"Yes?"

A sigh, then,

"Nothing, *nichts*. Good night, dear heart."

I lingered a moment, for when something troubled her, she often refused it to us at first, only to change her mind and speak out. But she kept silent now, and I left her alone.

※

How strange, when I felt before I heard great disturbance of the night in the far end of the long house. When I heard my mother cry out, I sat up wondering. There were doors, and there were steps running. Then came knocking on my door, and before I reached it Sam, calm and desperate, threw it open, saying,

"Hurry, Richard, quickly as you can, get to the car and drive like hell and bring Frawley here. He's much nearer than Birch. Hurry, for God's sake. The Governor is hemorrhaging. I have called an ambulance. Frawley must ride to the san with him and do what he can. I've talked to him, he cannot get a taxi this late. Your mother is holding on. Please, now, Richard."

He ran back to the other end of the house. By now I was enough dressed. I ran out to the car and wild in my gut drove to the hotel where they told me Frawley's room number, not detaining me because I looked as I did. I ran up the tiled stairway to the second floor. He was waiting with his door open. He had thrown a light topcoat over his pajamas and he wore his bedroom slippers. He ran to the car with me while the night clerk stared at us. At the curb a Mexican motorcycle policeman was standing by my car with its lights on and its engine running as I'd left it. When he began to ask questions, I shouted "Emergency," and, pointing to Frawley, "Doctor!" and at the policeman himself, "Help! Run ahead of us, please, we have to go fast, the old Wenzel place out on the Rio Grande road!" We raced through the city. It was empty and faintly lighted. A few forlorn night figures stood still to watch us tear by. As we came to the river road we threw up dust and gravel and at last reached the house, where all the lights were on. Lillian in her blue flannel bathrobe stood in the open front door waiting for us with her hands clasped to her breast like the Madonna, her dun-yellow hair falling around her shoulders. Her silent terror made her impressive for the first time. We raced past her into the house and down the corridor to the far bedroom, where in my mother's arms my father was leaning half upward while the blood of his life was choked forth on the towel she held to his lips. In his stare we read everything he knew now to be true. My mother ever so gently gave way to Frawley and came to stand with me, trembling within my arm. Her face was white as this paper, her eyes pouring with light amidst the sunken shadows of her cheeks. When Frawley said over his shoulder, "A bowl of ice," it was she who freed herself from my grasp and went to fetch it. Frawley made a pack with the ice in a towel and placed it about my father's neck and over his chest and slowly eased him to lie flat, keeping his hand on my father's forehead for reassurance. My mother held my father's right hand from the other side of the bed. Lillian came in and knelt at the foot of the bed, praying her rosary into her thumbs, her eyes blind with tears. I felt myself growing cold, seeing everything as happening to strangers while every feeling went dead within me; for I was saving myself by noting specifically every detail of the scene with a recording eye and ear, so that when the ambulance came, making noise on the gravel of the driveway, and Sam went to show the orderlies in with their stretcher, I could not make a move to help in any way but watched them take up my father and lay him on the pallet and carry him out to the ambulance. Frawley followed to ride with them to Saint Anthony's. He beckoned my mother to come with him, at the same time conveying to the rest of us to follow in our car. Sam telephoned the hospital once more to say we were now coming and they were to have a room prepared and people waiting in the emergency entrance where the nurse and intern on duty remembered my father and acted rapidly to do everything needed. So it was done by the time Sam and Lillian and I arrived and were told which room on which floor. We went up in the grindingly slow elevator to step into the long corridor, which was sibilant with distant hollow sounds and terrible with pale-yellow electric light making watery reflections in the polished brown linoleum of the hospital floor which led us to the door of the emergency operating room, where nurses came and went. From inside the wide door held ajar came obscure sounds, and the mystery of them brought me a stifling return of feeling so great that I said to myself, "My father," and "Oh, my God, I am heartily sorry for all my sins," as if by a crisscross of facts I were guilty of bringing my father to die that night in Saint Anthony's. But he did not die. By the earliest daylight limning the mountains he was still with us. My mother came from his side into the corridor, reaching quietly for us like an old woman for whom there is nothing more to know, and said,

"Morton Frawley says we must get some rest. There is no immediate danger now. Richard, will you take me home?"

My father, as I knew him, never left Saint Anthony's again.

Their farewells were in every detail correct, but it was plain that the delegation departed in rueful bitterness. Their hopes fell disastrously with my father's. The lesson was all too plain. Dr. Frawley had more address than the others, and took a little time, holding my mother's hand, to explain what his clinical practice had taught him.

"Yes, you see, there is an odd correlation—I have seen it so often before—between tuberculosis and optimism. I am afraid that it sometimes marks an approaching downturn for the patient; but meantime he feels almost visionary. Undue euphoria, you know. In your husband's case, it took the form of a revival of his ambition and the belief that he would again be equal to its pursuit."

My mother was less theoretical.

"Oh!" she cried, roughly fingering the tears which came to her eyes, "I could kill Percy Sage for making him walk all that way in all that sand . . ."

"Yes, that concerned me gravely," said Dr Frawley. "I myself was conscious of temporary fatigue when we finished crossing the dunes."

"But why did you let him do it?"

He gently touched her arm and replied,

"Ah, but there were many other factors. T.b. is full of surprises. It was a combination of events. I am afraid we have to look chiefly to your husband's hopes to explain his setback."

"Setback! Dr Birch thinks he is very gravely ill!"

"I have seen Jamie Birch this morning. We agree. But I am hopeful that lost ground can be regained."

"You mean that Dr Birch does not think so?"

"I do not speak for him."

Morton Frawley said this with a slight wryness, for evidently Birch had quarreled with him over his leniency in the case, and they had parted with coolness, in spite of which Frawley had prevailed on Birch to continue in charge of my father's cure. Dr Frawley smiled winningly. His hair, glasses, and bright cheeks shone together.

"You must bear with Jamie Birch. At Cornell Medical we all used to call him Jamie Grouch."

"Well, I wish we had borne with him day before yesterday," said my mother, rising to end the farewell interview. I was allowed to take Frawley to the door, where Mrs Saxby was waiting to drive him to the station. There, until the eastbound California Limited arrived, she could fill his every social cavity with impacted messages for the Ramsons and "all that crowd."

As they drove away, a delivery car arrived with a huge box of flowers for my mother. Lillian brought it to her in the patio gallery, where we were waiting for the time of our daily visit to Saint Anthony's.

"Do open it for me, Lillian dear," said my mother.

Lillian tore away the wrappings and found a card which she held up and read aloud:

Dreadfully sorry to hear the unfortunate news, and sure all will be well, much love, Percy and Serena.

Lillian gasped.

"*Dreadfully sorry!*" she repeated. "They'd better be—*and so should you!*" she added in a shriek to my mother.

"*Lillian!*"

"Don't *Lillian* me!" She threw the enormous flower box to the floor and trampled it. Her face went white and red in patches. Tears seemed not to be dropped but flung from her eyes into the air. Her huge throat quaked in spasms as she tried to make the words which her grief kept choking off. What she was trying to say was that my mother was guilty of criminal neglect: that poor darling of a man: to be dragged out of bed to go off on a crazy spree like that: what was she thinking of: nobody who really loved him would ever have—

"Shut up, Lillian!" I shouted.

"Lillian, *dear,*" said my mother, going to her.

Lillian backed away, throwing her arms about.

"Don't touch me! Nobody knows what I've been through all these years, and now to see him—"

My mother gave me a look. *How she loves him!* it said, after "all these years" when we had made a comfortable joke about Lillian's slavish and satisfying service to my father.

My mother could always prevail. She held her arms out to Lillian and said mildly,

"I know it is mostly my fault, and may God forgive me, Lillian, and he needs you now more than ever, and so do I, so do I!"

With that, Lillian went hugely soft and collapsed against my mother, weeping now in remorse upon the shoulder of the wife of the man she adored and mourned. Her ugliness in grief hardened my heart; but not my mother's.

"I know, I know," she said, leading Lillian off down the gallery at the patio side. I picked up the box of flowers and took them to a garbage can on the back porch. Half an hour later, when I happened through the house again, I saw remnants of the flowers arranged in two huge vases, one at each end of the library table.

❦

It seemed almost like his decision—my father's swift descent to inert invalidism. Daily his resources, visible and invisible, diminished. When we went to see him at Saint Anthony's, either together, my mother and I and Lillian, or any of us alone, we sat for the most part in silence to spare his replying. We had our separate styles of encouragement.

My mother, using her little habit of rapidly blinking both eyes at once as she smiled against any mournful aspect, always prepared herself with a few bits of news, and even, when desperate, made some up. Then she would read to him until he signaled that she might rest for a while. Now and then he would use a single word to ask for a report—"University?" and she would tell him how matters went with me in my enrollment and classes at the university on the mesa. I went there now to give a semblance of a future to our time in New Mexico. He nodded on his pillow at the good manners, if not the good sense, of this. My mother never played nurse—pulling at pillows or window shades or asking if he wanted any special delicacies to interest his appetite. She was real with him, never implying anything but the truth about his condition, but never, either, relinquishing the future for them together, which she refused to give up. He hungered for her every time she had to obey hours and leave him. I thought I could see a whole vision of their past in his eyes. He held her hand with his, which now consisted of veins and bones; and the beauty in his face with all its new hollows and shadows was something to enrage me for what it could not enact. And then, almost within a step or two of the door closed behind us, my mother would let her courage falter, and she would show her terror and her love, almost feverishly. Sometimes we would encounter Dr Birch in the corridors alone; and he would show her a sort of deathly tenderness.

Lillian, on the other hand, when she was with my father, thought it proper to make her full face long, subdue her voice, tiptoe, and cause her soft, occupying presence to totter a little as she strove to force her sympathy into polite acceptance of disaster. Her Celtic taste for broken hearts and the infinite mercy of God gave us a delicate problem, for it became necessary to invent reasons why she should not come as often, or stay as long, as she wanted to, since her presence depressed my father until all he could do was pretend to fall asleep when she came; and then he had to listen to her massive tiptoeing and clever rearranging of objects in the hospital room as she worked at leaving little surprises for him when she should be gone and he should awaken.

On the morning after he had been hurried to Saint Anthony's she began a series of novenas to Saint Jude in the Church of the Immaculate Conception on Sixth Street, where Father Agostini, the old Italian Jesuit who had come as a youth under Archbishop Lamy fifty years before, gave her communion, and crossly tried to conceal his awareness of her tears, which were like those in plaster relief on the face of the Madonna-at-the-Foot-of-the-Cross to whom she prayed so barrenly.

There was no office work for her to do now, for all matters were being handled by the manager of the Dorchester office; and Sam—Sam, at my father's insistence, had left us to go East to Joanna. We soon received engraved cards (made by Shreve, Crump and Low) announcing their imminent marriage. At almost the same time came a letter from Sam announcing his appointment as dean of James Monroe College, the century-old institution with its special style in northern New York State which would suit him like an inconspicuously good garment. It also had a certain social cachet which would bring pleasant opportunities to Joanna. Since my father was done with politics, so was Samuel Dickinson.

And I: I watched the man born for great affairs see them recede from him, until he seemed to hear of them as in a dream. When his strength allowed, he would ask me in his husky whisper what the news was, and I assumed Sam's role of keeping him informed of how matters went at home, until the special election was over, and the Speaker of the Assembly had been elected to fill out the unexpired term which had held so much power over our family affairs. After that matter was done with, my father's interest waned, though now and then, when a flicker of his old humor and scorn managed to rise through the melancholy which had him gazing at nothing by the hour, he would ask me for news of "Mr Coolidge," and he would speak of him as "heir to our national Pelzer." I hardly ever heard him swear or resort to ugly language (my education in this art reached new heights under J. Buswell Rennison), but one day when I had to inform him that Judge Pelzer had been taken to Ossining, my father murmured, "Poor bastard." The sincerity of thi effort, with all its crowding reminders of failure, sent him off to sleep. His head rolled slightly to one side, so that the light caught it in a slanting caress, making the bony structure both brighter and more deeply shadowed.

As the afternoon light failed, I sat for a long time looking at him, both through memory and a desire to find some analogy of experience ample enough to contain a sense of his life in a dimension of the heroic. In this I was looking also for an image of human life at large, and, I suppose, I was combining both visions as a response to youth's search for metaphors, in the absence of reasons.

The vast lake with its oceanic and common waters obeyed the wonderful physical law which caused it to seek always a lower level toward the all-accepting sea. So, as it narrowed at one end, and the altitude of the land gradually fell, the lake was channeled into a river. Out of the nowhere of the great lake came a new form, contained and defined by banks. Flowing placidly but with vigor, it was beautiful between its groves. For as far as you could see, the river's course was unimpeded, consistent, purposeful. It could even be governed by those who knew how. But presently, in its long serene progress, the river flow encountered obstacles. Rocks below the surface revealed changes in its bed. Hazardous rapids made ruffles of white water and sudden sweeps of emerald sheen as the current swept around rocky sluices. And then far ahead the air was increasingly filled with a roar of tumbling waters and clouds of mist flying upward. Almost before warning, the level flow, pressed by the volume of the lake far behind, and the confining riverbanks, lost the supporting bed of the land, and then, beyond suddenness, the waters fell fearsomely and gorgeously downward, so that anyone watching was lost in the hypnotic pull of that vast fateful tumble. I remembered myself throughout my childhood and after, in the groves, on the banks, and at the brink of the Niagara, where I had obeyed the need to keep life; and there, too, loomed my father and his whole course, from the illimitable reservoir of past humanity to his narrow lifetime, and his fall.

One day I brought him the mail. One of the envelopes held a little weighty bulk, and he looked at it for a long moment before opening it. I had noticed that it came from one of the most intimate members of Our Crowd. Ever since the time of the picnic, my father had now and then shown a depressed concern over his failure to justify the eager hopes they had all had of him. He had "let them down." They must think pretty poorly of him now. It was a sorry thing to lose lifelong friends. I had heard enough of this to assume that such thought was running in his mind now, for he was wearing the deliberately empty face which he assumed when his deepest emotion was at work. This all changed when he opened the envelope and out fell a little packet wrapped in tissue paper which yielded up a gold watch chain with a round gold pendant. On the pendant was an engraved message. He leaned toward the light with it and his face broke into the first full smile since he had re-entered Saint Anthony's. Too moved to speak, he silently handed the gold chain and medallion to me. I read the inscription: *Representing the chain of our friendship you have wrought so well.*

He had not let them down. If a man could wear a watch he still had time to live. This is what his friends were telling him. He was grateful. But he was also responsible and real in his knowledge. He said to me, trying to let some extra resonance into his breathy voice,

"Richard, will you do something for me now?"

"Of course, Father."

"Do you remember the key?"

"The key?"

He showed a sad impatience by shaking his head on the pillow.

"Yes, yes, the bank key I gave you and told you to keep for me!"

"Oh, yes. I have it in my room—the key I used to put that portfolio into the safety deposit."

He rested his breath for a moment, then said,

"Go to the bank and take out the leather envelope. You will find two sets of letters inside."

His excitement was rising. Trying to save him effort by anticipating him, I said,

"I see. You want me to bring them to you?"

"No, no"—irritably—"I want you to burn them all."

"Oh."

He thought for a moment; then,

"One is a set of letters written by me. I think I want you to read those. The other set I want you to burn without reading them. Is that clear?"

"Yes."

"You may be shocked, but if you think less of me afterward, you are not yet the man I expect you to be."

"I see."

"No, you don't. But you will. —When you have the letters, the box will be empty. Pay off the rent and return the key to the bank. We have no more use for it."

"Do you want me to do this right away?"

"Now. Today. I want to know it has been done, while I have time to know."

I made a gesture to deny his meaning, but he rejected my loving fakery, and said,

"We all know what we know. —What time is it?"

I told him.

"The bank is still open. Go now, Richard, and thank you, boysie" —using a nursery name I had not heard for almost twenty years.

I hurried to the bank, made my transaction, and then went to my river glade. The afternoon was coming in rays through the broken vaultings of my trees. A few feet away the little river sounds gave life to the stillness. I unlocked the leather envelope. I recognized my father's handwriting on a bundle of perhaps three dozen letters. But I recognized also the hand, in violet ink, on the top envelope of the other bundle, which was tied with a little ribbon of the violet velvet with which florists used to tie Parma violets in a little bunch, such as my mother, and her friends, in the fashion of their time, would pin to their waists indoors, or, if festively going out into the deep white winters of Dorchester, to their furs.

❦

The letters in violet ink were written by the woman who was the first passionate love of my life—that person of grace, realism, and unhappiness who was the closest friend of our household. At the edge of my adolescence I called her Aunt Bunch, though we were not related. She was in her middle thirties, I was twelve or thirteen, but with playful charm she erased the distance between our ages and let me live seriously in my love for her, while she returned my feeling tenderly and with lovely absence of mockery, ignoring the amused condescension with which all others watched our affair. She was married to a much older man, dry, rich, finicky, who had never given her a child. She saw me, I knew later, as her child as well as her chaste lover. Perhaps all women so see their truly loved men. Her eyes were violet-blue, her hair was heavy and pale golden. She wore it rather loosely gathered about her softly modeled face, whose complexion made me think of white and pink peonies. I called her Aunt Bunch from childhood because she habitually wore or carried a bunch of Parma violets, which went so wonderfully with her eyes, as I once heard my father tell her, and I recognized the truth of this, which I had not seen for myself. It was a discovery of the harmony of color and style as they expressed an innate nature. I loved her awake and dreaming, with only the remotest stirrings of sex, until the day came when at a certain age I unintentionally saw her making love with my father's business partner, a young officer just before he was to go overseas with the army in the 1914 war. My world crashed, and so perhaps did hers. But our worlds were mended for us both before too long—I began growing up, and she helped me by denying nothing of her unfaithfulness. Her beauty and her indulgence of my fantasy about her had made me think of her as virtue itself. Years later, as I read the letters which were to be burned while my father still lived, to be sure they were destroyed, I saw her as she was, exalted by making the gift of her love. She gave it to my father, who found it too precious to refuse. They were lovers.

His letters told me this and more. He suffered for betrayal. Weak before his secret desire, he was anguished in his love for my mother, which did not lessen, as his letters made clear. How could this be? Yet it was. The lovers had hopes which called from afar, impossibilities which could only be held away by brief fulfillments with no promises for the future. When her husband died, it seems that Aunt Bunch wondered if perhaps—but no, no, there could be no thought of my father's ever leaving us for her. He loved my mother, he loved me, and yet passionately he told Aunt Bunch she must never leave him.

What prodigies of skill they summoned to keep their affair secret. What private delights in their very secrecy. Qualms of hypocrisy came now and then to them both. My mother was her best friend— how could she do this to her? And yet she did, and could be forgiven only in his arms. When he expressed his own feelings of untrustworthiness, he, a leading figure in the blameless life of the community leader, the husband brilliant in his happy marriage, what velvety reassurance she gave him with her love, for apparently she promised that she would die before ever endangering his position either in his family or before the public.

I read on, page after page, seeing my father turning and turning in a new light; and between little surges of anger on my mother's behalf, and even of irrational jealousy on my own, I felt a mingling of exaltation and pity for this buried life shared by two people whom I loved so greatly.

[291]

My father's letters spared me nothing. How could it have been otherwise, with a man so handsome, so full of blue fire in the eye, piercing charm in the character, excellence of the body, who followed so hotly upon life?

Like little shutters opening upon memory, moments came back to me. I thought of the time when I overheard my father say to her at our house that she had never looked so beautiful in her life and that—he laughed delightedly—he supposed she couldn't help it. I saw, but could not then read, the look she returned to him—one so wishful and yet so hopeless that if I had been older I might have known what must one day follow.

I wanted to take down passages of the letters, for the lovers were so eloquent—my father explicitly so in his, Aunt Bunch by what he reflected and responded to in hers—so direct in their frankness, unable to resist rehearsing their most recent time together, that they must live it over again in words. But my mission was to erase all record of that love; and only a few phrases remain in my general memory of how they wrote to each other. "Oh, my darling, my marvel," he wrote, "whenever was there such an hour as yesterday? I scarcely knew myself." After their encounters he would move around as though in a dream: he felt he came and went about the world like a great Cheshire cat, a disembodied smile of delight. He found himself looking at every female with something that made her shrink a little, accusingly, as if he meant to rape her. He did not mean to be crude—he was only trying to express what was still with him every time he left her. There was evidently to be a time to meet in New York. "Oh, God, forgive me, when I think of my hands lost in your heavy gold hair and your eyes open like violets."

There were calendars of where and how to meet and for how long, and records of gifts exchanged, and vows of joy in the clandestine masquerade which could never be resolved in their open union short of calamities which neither of them wanted to visit upon anyone else. They had no idea of what would either save them or destroy them. When it finally came, their love was fired up more greatly than ever, for they both saw what must happen, though Aunt Bunch saw it before he did.

When he was first approached with demands that he run for public office, she told him he must do it, but evidently she also said that it must be the end for them. He had wondered in previous letters what could ever be the outcome of their union; but neither had expected what actually came.

What her simple realism cost her I could read in his anguished protests, and what he quoted of her words. They had managed very well so far, he was sure they need not part if they were especially clever about their continued plans. She said he must not be naïve— the political opposition would watch him day and night, hoping for private flaws to make public. She told him that a man's life was not the same as a woman's. He must have more than love to meet his full worth. She loved him so well that she would let him go to that full worth. Here were all his letters to her. He must destroy them, and all her letters to him. In his last letter he acknowledged their return; and in it I thought I read a note of the most delicate relief that the most dangerous passage of his life was about to end. At the same time he protested with loving fury her decision to "travel abroad" for an indefinite period, as she had the means, and she could always say she needed a change from Dorchester. Wasn't it ridiculous? She had always seen herself living in Paris, anyway. An invisible fabric had held two lives together. The letters gave me the sensation of hearing the fabric ripped apart.

He tied their letters in separate bundles. Where had the violet ribbon come from? Perhaps on some snowy afternoon he took her a bunch of violets tied with it, and then kept it because its scent reminded him of her. Or—more prosaically—perhaps he retrieved it from a wastebasket at home when nobody was looking, and in doing so, made an uneasy link in his thought between my mother and his mistress. He kept the bundles at some peril, always no doubt planning to dispose of them, yet unwilling to; until he made me his guardian and confidant when he was too ill to destroy the evidence himself.

The sun was falling lower beyond the willow and cottonwood leaves. I gathered dry twigs and leaves and made a bonfire. One by one I fed the letters into the little flames, holding back only one envelope with the violet writing. I took the ashes and let them sift through my fingers into the brown current of the river. My father and my love and my fear for him sifted through my thoughts. He had entrusted me with his whole life, now, in the evidence of his fallible and powerful humanity, with its pathos and the flawed beauty of its secret fulfillment. I was proud of his confidence; and I felt that unknowingly he had given me a measure of absolution for the folly and squalor of the Petronian night in Magdalena, and for the shame I had felt ever since. Not that I compared my drunken excesses with the grace of the love which had possessed my father and Aunt Bunch beyond their power to resist. But there were degrees of betrayal to be known, and perhaps judged, in both cases; and if my upright father could sin, then, however sordidly, so might his son. Knowing his secret now, I could forget mine.

In my notebook I copied the return address from the last envelope. The day would come when I would want to use it.

As I went home in the long, brilliant twilight, I brought to mind other matters which the letters revealed to me. I knew now what had given so much reckless energy to my father's campaign. How we raced together back and forth across the state for his rallies and speeches. How he would fall suddenly exhausted and unapproachable for hours at a time. How he was, then, throwing himself into a new life as much to escape the loss of his love as to purify the state of New York and gratify his supporters. Giving her up, running away, making love to a whole public took more strength than his emotions left to him. Lyle Pryor's cruel realism about what would soon kill Carlton Gracey returned to me now. Life's denials and ambitions, more or less equally mixed, played a great part in tuberculosis. It was possible now to recognize despairing alternatives in the histories of both Carlton Gracey and my father.

The next day, in my visit alone to Saint Anthony's, I answered the inquiry in my father's eyes by showing him a pinch of ashes I had saved. I said,

"This is all that is left."

With his eyes he asked what I thought.

"I read them."

"All of them?"

"Yes. That is, only yours. Thank you, Father."

He closed his eyes and pressed his lips together to contain his feeling of relief on several counts. Peace came into his face. In a moment he added,

"Your mother must not know."

"Oh, never! Nor anyone else."

He sighed. It was a comment of wonder at how he could have done what would have hurt my mother to know. He lay quiet. He was gathering strength to say something further to me. His closed eyelids quivered a little with his thought, and then opening them, he seemed to come fully awake in his mind. He began to speak in the rapid, uninflected way he used now to consume as little strength as possible. I leaned closer to hear him clearly.

He said there was something else on his mind.

"Yes?"

He hoped I could promise him something without having to go against my own wish.

"Yes. Surely. What is it?"

He said he knew what I eventually wanted—to write books—but he asked me to promise to finish medical school no matter what.

Then he waited, and so did I, for a moment.

I did what had to be done. I put my hand over his as it lay white on the white sheet, and said,

"Yes, I promise, Father. I will go ahead."

"God bless you, then, Doc," and he smiled at the nickname which would turn real.

❧

In the echoing corridor where we all waited, Dr Birch came out of the room and softly shut the door after him.

"I think, now, yes," he said to my mother.

"You mean to send for Father Agostini?"—the parish priest who served also as hospital chaplain.

She nodded to Lillian to hurry to the telephone.

"Is he awake?"

"I'd say, he is aware. Just."

"Should we go in?"

"The nurse will call you. Sister Mary Vincent is also with him."

"We'll wait here."

"Yes. —I'll return soon."

Lillian hurried back to us, trying for my mother's sake not to cry. She sat down next to my mother on the leather couch against the wall and took my mother's hand. They held to each other.

In a quarter of an hour we heard the hard rustle of his cassock before we saw Father Agostini come around a corner at the end of the hall. He walked, leaning a trifle backward and to one side, as if his great weight were unevenly distributed. He was old and rheumatic, abrupt, and impassive. Putting a narrow purple silk stole about his neck, he bowed to my mother but did not pause before entering my father's room.

Sister Mary Vincent and the nurse came out, leaving the priest alone with my father.

In a little while he emerged and the women returned to the bedside. Now, without haste, he came to us and sat down beside my mother.

"All is well," he said in his burry Italian accent, and he meant, not for now, but forever. He had to leave us. We stayed all evening, and far into the night before the door opened and Mary Vincent put out both her hands to us in silence, and with a consoling smile drew us in to know my father and be known by him in his hour.

❧

All too soon, then, our duties became plain. I went to the county courthouse at Albuquerque to explain my difficulty. I was listened to with the contained face which the law assumed in weighty matters; but it was presently arranged that I would be allowed to go to Sante Fe immediately to make a deposition in the district court there instead of waiting to testify at the Rennison trial, "by reason of the death of the witness's father, and family obligations in connection therewith, necessitating immediate travel to New York State for funeral services and interment of the deceased"—but I must return if called as a witness. (The call never came.)

❧

Other disposals, large and small, filled the hours before we left. Lyle Pryor saw to all the travel arrangements for us—reservations, tickets, a car to meet us in Chicago. Lillian managed the flood of telegrams and long-distance calls. Eleanor Saxby's best-loved view of herself was that of the "good scout," and with reassuring good sense, she relieved us of all decisions about closing the house, shipping home what belonged to us, dealing with the real-estate agency, and selling our little car. She filled our house with her confident, well-argued proposals, coughing explosively through her cigarette smoke, and holding her whiskey glass against her shoulder between sips. She was happy to have something worthwhile to do, and in unspoken ways kept reminding my mother what it was to be a widow,

[297]

since she herself was one. We could count on her to keep us informed back home when she had anything to report. When she said, more than once, "Just leave everything to me, my dear," my mother would say, "Eleanor is such a dear, she is being wonderful." When it was time to be taken to the eastbound Limited, Percy and Serena had their big car waiting for us with their chauffeur. As they were sure we would rather be alone, they would not come to the station with us, but would be thinking of us, and meantime hoped this little hamper of nibbles would help to make the train journey more bearable. "They are so thoughtful," said my mother, in that state of contained grief—the very condition which let her accept on their own terms all expressions of sympathy.

My last act in the Rio Grande house was to send, without a note, a clipping from the local paper about my father's death to the address in Paris I had copied at my riverside bonfire. My envelope carried no return address or name.

⁂

Escorting my father's coffin home to Dorchester, we, as a family, were traveling in our own history through a moment which would last all our lives. I thought of Lincoln's funeral train, and the catafalque in the historical museum at home which I had often visited in awe as a boy.

On the night before the California Limited drew into Chicago, where we must change trains, I had dinner with my mother in her compartment. I wanted to be alone with her. Lillian and I each had a lower berth in another part of the car.

We dined well on trains in those days, and I persuaded my mother to drink some fine Liebfraumilch which Lyle Pryor had brought us wrapped in a newspaper as we said goodbye at the Albuquerque station. Handing it to me, Lyle said,

"I hope we meet again. If we do, I'll never again call you 'kid.'"

We never met again.

Under other circumstances, the soft-shaded Pullman lights, and the privacy, and the wine would have made the event seem like a little celebration. Now we were silent for a long time, until, looking out through the dark at the lights of isolated houses and little towns made innocent by distance, my mother said, against her palm, with her forehead resting against the cool window of the compartment,

"My poor dear."

The words settled some sort of resolve for her; for she turned to me and said,

"There is something I keep thinking of, about him, among all the other things. But I shouldn't, now."

"Not now?"

She shook her head and for the first time began to cry. I came around the table between us and sat next to her to put my arm around her. She wept against my shoulder, unable to speak just yet against the memory which engulfed her.

"What is it, Mother?"

"No, no," she replied, coming slowly to the calm of speech. "I don't know if I should ever tell you. Oh: I am so ashamed."

"Ashamed?"

"Yes. I did something I should not have done, but I could not help myself, though I believed it would make me miserable."

And she told me her story.

One day a batch of forwarded mail arrived at the Rio Grande house from the office in Dorchester. Lillian went through it, picked out the letters she thought my father ought to see, and gave them to my mother, who would take them along the next time she went to the hospital. Among them was a letter from Paris, addressed in violet handwriting which my mother knew well. She singled it out and put it in her bureau drawer. It was from Aunt Bunch. But why was it addressed only to my father, and sent to his Dorchester office, instead of directly to the house, either at Dorchester or Albuquerque? My mother was torn by qualms of heart and conscience. For years she had had thoughts which she had tried to dismiss as unworthy about my father and her best friend—there were inadvertent signals between them which she could not help noticing, and moods in my father which she had thought it wise not to comment upon.

"But I knew."

"Knew what?"—but I understood.

"Yes. I knew in my heart, but I had no proof; and anyhow, anyhow—"

She pressed her fingers against her tears. In muffled words she made me know that no matter what was going on to make my father happy, she felt it ought not to be turned into something ugly, whatever it might cost her to keep the secret. There was anguish in her tenderness as she spoke of this.

"You've no idea of the depth and power of his feeling for her, really turmoil, and for the longest time I thought it was all for me, all for me, and sometimes I scolded myself for thinking anything else."

The letter: she knew she ought to take it immediately to Saint Anthony's without comment; but for a day she held it back, wondering what to do. At the same time, she knew that if she did not deliver it immediately, she would never do so without reading it. Two more days went by while she was tormented by a need to know for certain, and by shame at what she was doing. Finally, after another day, she did what she had often smiled at in novels. She steamed open the envelope. The thin French glue responded easily. She read the letter. It told her all she had tried not to believe. It was a second farewell in which Aunt Bunch agonized over the impossibility of coming to help my father return to health. She raged at the obstacles between them, and she even said that the worst was this—that they both loved my mother so much that the thought of hurting her was unbearable. No longer deceived, with life and death now filling her days and nights, my mother felt a devouring rise of pity for the man whom she had loved singly and dearly for so many years.

With rueful self-knowledge, she now said to me,

"If he had not been so sick, I might not have been so unselfish."

She resealed the envelope, and when the next letters came from home, she shuffled it among them and with light indifference gave the packet to Lillian to take to my father. He would never know that the letter had been seen by anyone else.

"I suppose he could not help it. Perhaps I failed him in some way. Don't think harshly of him."

Knowing even more than she knew, I touched her hand in reassurance. She continued,

"So much happens to people. Mostly they remain the same people. If you love them—you know? To believe the world through each other? He was such a beautiful man. Nobody knew this as I did. I saw him hurt and downcast as well as happy and strong and *head*-strong—then: then: the way he would turn to me: trust: need—"

She let silence say in weariness that if you loved anyone, nothing much else could matter. She saw tears appear and recede in my eyes, and she added,

"No, no. Richard, Richard, he was dear, and he was good. You must never think anything else."

But I could not tell her that I had a few days ago made peace with the idea of seeing my father whole, as a fallible man. I thought of what that final letter might have meant to him. He must have managed to destroy it by himself.

"Do you know?" mused my mother, "when she left him to live abroad, I sometimes wondered if he drove himself so all that summer in the campaign in order to make himself put it all away for good. He used to come home so tired he could hardly speak. But you know—the harder you try to forget something sometimes, the harder it is. If he was fighting two things at the same time—no wonder he broke down."

"Do you think Father ever suspected that you knew, then?"

"Sometimes I thought so. He said once or twice, 'Rose, what are you looking like that for!' I would just shrug and change the subject. —What power it must have had for him!"

"Do you hate Aunt Bunch?"

"No. I do not hate her. But I hope I shall never have to see her again."

"What a fool Lillian is!" I said angrily. "Why couldn't she just take the mail directly to him? All of it? She is such a fool."

"Yes," said my mother, now placidly, "she is. But like the rest of us, she must be taken as she is. Anyhow," she added, with a hint of her sweetly defiant energy, which showed when she defended herself in any matter, "I did what I did, and I'm sorry I did it, and perhaps I should never have told you anything."

"No, I'm grateful."

"You had to grow up, anyway, didn't you? This summer must have seen to that."

※

Whenever I think of the weeks which followed, it is to remember the white marble Cathedral of the Holy Angels, where my father's solemn Requiem High Mass was held. As I watched with carefully reserved feeling the black and silver figures of the bishop of Dorchester and his deacons at the altar, behind which lay the marble sarcophagi of earlier bishops, I knew myself again as the small boy who had hidden for a whole night in the cathedral hoping for a miraculous visitation from the Enfant de Prague. The glories and fears of that night were part of my secret sensations now, and they made me smile in a sort of desperate protection against present emotion.

Lillian and the Dickinsons were with my mother and me. Lillian kept turning to see the immense throng which filled the cathedral. With tears flowing down her swollen face, she wore a look of bridling satisfaction at the honors paid to my father by his city; for as she said so often later, "Everyone was there," including Our Crowd, some of whose members served as pallbearers. The mercy of impersonality had descended upon my mother. She bore herself too proudly to show feeling—"Like a queen," as Lillian remarked to everyone so often that finally no one listened, "I said, *like a queen*."

Snow was falling, whiter than the white of the cathedral stone. Sounds in snow are different from those heard in clear weather. The passing bell began to toll as we left the church. Its sound, coming through the marble louvers so high above the scene in which everything was black and white, seemed to fall and settle upon us like the snow itself.

*

In those days of finality, Sam was once again our salvation. After examining all our material affairs, including my father's will, he set about doing what was needed. He found a buyer for our house, leased a modest, pleasant apartment for my mother in the Lenox Hotel, where she would not need her own cook or housemaid, set up a fund just ample enough to see me through college and medical school, and finally negotiated a scheme by which my father's business partner bought out the controlling interest in their joint affairs, which provided lifetime incomes for my mother and Lillian. Lillian would go into retirement, as the partner could not be expected to endure years of her reminders that things at the office were done differently in my father's day.

The Dickinsons stayed with us until my mother left our house. Sam advised me to telephone my dean at Aldersgate University to ask for readmission at the start of the mid-year semester. This was granted, I wrote my roommate that I would be back; and with a little thread of happiness weaving itself into settling emotions, I looked ahead to entering again into the student world where there would be—as yet—no lifelong tragedies for anyone. I would return in a stage of maturity far ahead of that of my classmates. I would be already a new Richard, a "harder" Richard, among those friends who were still in the process of learning how to be "hard"—the ideal of that generation. My mother urged me to go. I was not to think of her, living alone. She had many friends. Her favorite household possessions went to surround her in her new apartment. Now displaced, they would never mean together what they once had meant. I would be with her for my college vacations. I was not to worry about her. She was already "taking an interest." In this she was aided by Joanna Dickinson, who, safe now in her own marriage, and newly filled with assurance as the wife of a college dean, was at ease, and able to reveal a lightly comic view of life which was useful to us all. We actually missed her when, happy in the seemly belongings of her world, including Sam, she went home with him to their own lives.

❦

As for the more recent past, Eleanor Saxby wrote a running account of J. Buswell Rennison's trial at Santa Fe, which she attended with zest. When he was found guilty and sentenced to die, she sent, without comment, a clipping from the *Albuquerque Journal,* giving the facts, including a reference to the electric chair.

The day I read that, I went to walk along the edge of Dorchester harbor and out to the end of the reaching breakwater. Already shielded against the new winter was a great fleet of the long ore and wheat freight boats, which again made a still colony of black idleness against the pale-gray sky. I took it all to myself to match my mood, and stared at the horizonless lake way out past the breakwater toward invisible Canada. Under the ice, Lake Erie sent its ever-renewed vastness toward the river and the sea. I felt the necessary detachment of the survivor.

EPILOGUE

❊

The Logic of Wishes

WHEN MANY YEARS LATER the Hitler war came, the sense of life for those in uniform was one entirely of chance and coincidence. There were dangers both to one's secret self and to adequate performance of duties in thinking in any other way.

❊

At the headquarters in Grosvenor Square, the young English orderly announced,

"Your driver is waiting, name of Lance Corporal Cromleigh, sir."

"Thank you. I'll be right down."

I took up the sealed portfolio which I had brought to London from Washington, signed out, and went down to the street. It was a cold autumn day with a pewter-colored sky. In the air I still noticed what had struck me the day before on coming from Hendon airfield—the smell of dead fire exhaled by burned-out ruins left by Nazi bombs.

Standing by the jeep waiting for me was a trim, smartly uniformed English girl.

"Lance Corporal Cromleigh, sir. I have your trip ticket to Fairford Air Force Base."

"Thank you. How long will it take us to get there?"

"If we don't strike fog, we should be there in under two hours."

"Good. My business should not take long, though one never knows. In any case, I must be back this evening for a morning flight to Prestwick and back to Washington."

She drove expertly out of London by the Cromwell Road and to the west. We spoke little, but when she answered my occasional question, her voice was light, clear, and beautifully cultivated. She held her small head high. The profile line from her brow to her short nose, purely chiseled lips, chin, and slender throat was almost laughably beautiful seen in the context of her rough British army cloth. Her color was high; pink cheeks against severely brushed gold hair. In impersonal military habit she did not look at me when she spoke, but I could see that her eyes were blue. There was some air about her which made me want to bridge the officer gap. I said,

"Excuse me, but I have to review my notes as we go."

"Of course, sir."

I took out my pocket notebook and looked at my obscure scratches—not precisely a code, but a set of references which meant something only to me, in preparation for the staff meeting I was to attend at Fairford.

❦

There was a representative of each service in the Allied Command at the meeting in the base commander's office. My Pentagon portfolio was broken open by the general in command at Fairford and the discussion began. It had seemed to me that a half hour's work would be enough to produce the requisite initials and release me for my return to London; but it was late afternoon before the matter was resolved, the portfolio resealed, and handshakes and salutes exchanged. As I came out of the office whose windows were permanently blacked out with plywood, it was to find a late day blind with fog. Lance Corporal Cromleigh and her jeep were invisible until I came to within a dozen feet. She started the engine as soon as she was able to recognize me in the thick air. I climbed in and said,

"This will be slow going, won't it?"

"If any," she replied lightly.

"I suppose we ought to try, though."

"Yes, Hendon, Prestwick, Washington, of course." But she was leaning forward tensely and moving the car very slowly. We were feeling the narrow road from the base back to the village of Fairford, and, if possible, beyond.

"Lights?" I asked.

"Worse with, sir."

The earth-held cloud was coming at us in slow, thickening billows, and night was falling upon us with them. As we came to what seemed a tunnel of dirty fleece, the lance corporal declared this to be a street of the town, and driving even as slowly as she was, she saw a thick figure directly before us only in time to swerve and halt. An old angry voice demanded to know why we did not watch where we were going. This made the lance corporal laugh. Swept by the dense air, she turned toward me and said,

"I wish we knew!"

"No," I said, "this won't do. —Perhaps it will lift presently?"

"May or may not."

"Well, is there any place where we might wait it out a while?"

"There is a nice old inn, the Bull, if we can find it."

"We'll try. —Were you given any lunch, waiting? We can have some tea now, anyhow."

"If you think it suitable, sir," she said with an allusion to our difference in rank which was a brilliant mixture of military respect and mockery of it.

※

We were given tea in the parlor of the Bull, where I received a dimly lit impression of a room lined with sooty lace and old carpet. In a little grate burned two lumps of cannel coal. Lance Corporal Cromleigh took off her stiffly visored cap and shook her hair free. We were served by the stout, wheezing old landlady herself, who explained that all three of her housemaids were off in war work. We exchanged gloomy sentiments about the fog and she left us. The tea was comforting.

Suddenly Lance Corporal Cromleigh sat up listening with her face turned. She heard before I did the growing thunder of many hundred bombers overhead. She looked at the ceiling as though to see them.

"They are trying to feel their way home to the base from a mission," she said. "Oh, God, the poor darlings. In this."

She put her hands to cover her ears. She said,

"One never gets used to it, that tremendous sound in the sky. It always makes me think of something quite mad, when I was very small—the roaring of the Niagara Falls when you are close to them."

"You've been there?"

"Oh, yes. I hated it. We were all going out to Alberta and stopped to see the falls and my darling little twin brother—we must have been five or six years old—nearly jumped over the barrier into the falls out of sheer excitement, but a young man there caught him just in time. I was screaming like a banshee and the nanny didn't help matters much. —Odd what idiocies one does remember, from the worst times. I had on a little pair of new brogans I was proud of, and the spray was getting them all wet, and I shrieked and shrieked that I didn't want to go any closer to the river, but I couldn't manage to tell them why."

❦

Pamela. She looked into the coals. By their reflection I saw Christopher in her face. The situation was as unlikely as it was true. I had a powerful impulse to keep the secret of my part in that day by the cataract long ago. A silence continued upon us, so long that she finally turned toward me with inquiry unsaid. In her face was the light of amused and yet longing memory. I finally said,

"How is Christopher?"

"But you know his name!"

"You will not believe this, but I was the young man who held him back from the brink."

"Dear God."

❦

If it is the logic of wishes that they come true in unexpected ways, that one of mine which I had thought of now and then through the years was granted—what had ever become of the St Brides family?

Marveling can go on only so long. We soon had enough of it, though, to let us come into the feeling of a lifelong friendship. Pamela put her hand on my sleeve for a moment and said,

"Oh, we thought of it so often!" She spoke with fond humor and an undertone of sadness. "My brother went on for years with his heroic story. You were his hero. He kept a postcard of Niagara Falls to show everybody until we shrieked at him not to be such a bore." She looked at me drolly. "I was sure if I ever saw you again I must recognize you from Christopher's grand description of his savior. —Sorry to say, I did not."

"No. —But I can see you now, after all, as I did the first time."

"What a little wretch I was."

"Oh, no."

"Oh, yes. —But Christopher? You asked? Navy. He was lost in the Saint Nazaire commando raid. Bravely, we were told. He held back for a wounded man and then had no time to join the boat before it pulled away and the shots came. They always say it about twins, but I was absolutely cut in two, I was really half a life, for so long, afterward, even though I was already married."

The old landlady came into our almost dark parlor and asked if we might not want a nice bite of supper, "such as it was."

We followed her upstairs to the dining room. A few old people and children were already at small tables. Going there was a lucky, small distraction. I had no moment to speak what Pamela must have known in my thought—my picture of her exuberant brother in his golden childhood, and a distant turn of pain for his end.

It was a time of everybody's story of loss. She had come to terms with hers and could tell it simply and briefly. Her father had been in the War Office, on non-combat duty after a wound in France. The loss of his heir really, she thought, killed him, though he did not die until pneumonia seized him some months later. His nephew, a don at Oxford before the war, succeeded. Pamela and her mother left St Brides's Abbey, though urged to think of it as theirs, which was in any case pointless just now, as it was soon lent to the government for a convalescent hospital. She made me see the place because of how lovingly she spoke of it—a large house in two styles, one wing Elizabethan with a ruined Gothic arch, the other Georgian, with a moat on which two black swans and two white lived, all set in a vast lawn bounded by a woods on three sides. When you took a walk along the grassy edge of the moat, the swans, with an effect of taking the air with you, sailed slowly beside you on their still water. Pamela's mother had a job on Charles Street with the English-Speaking Union by day, and by night was a fire warden in Eaton Square. Major Adrian Cromleigh—an archaeologist whose name I knew—was in Africa with Alexander. He promised to bring Pamela back there after the war. They had no children, but hoped to have a large family, oh, yes, a *large* family, as Adrian said, "to restore the earth" after this wretched affair was over.

Ah, well. Enough about her. What about me?

Soon enough told—a graduate in medicine, a writer of books, married, with a son nine years old. I was diffident about adding, but I did add,

"Baptized Christopher."

"For him?"

"Yes, partly."

"How sweet."

She turned away to hide what she felt. I rose from the table. I said, "I'd better have a look at the weather," and went downstairs and out into the street. The fog was heavier than ever.

※

"No, sir, you'll be going nowhere tonight," said the landlady at her high counter in the musty old hall. Yes, she had a room each for the young lady and me, and she agreed to set a clock to wake herself and let us out at five in the morning as we must leave in plenty of time to get to London on official matters. To be sure we were awake she would knock on our doors. Lance Corporal Cromleigh agreed that there was nothing else to do. In due course, we said good night and went to our damp, icy rooms.

❦

All correctly, Lance Corporal Cromleigh returned me to London in the clearing daylight next morning. By nightfall I was far out over the Atlantic bound for Santa Maria in the Azores, Stephenville in Newfoundland, and Washington. There were many hours for some long thoughts. Failings, wishes, willed and unwilled circumstance. I remembered how, until she died, I would go to visit my mother and become her hero of occasions; and how one time, when with a familiar sense of guilt I had to return to my small, happy family and leave her to her loneliness, she said,

"Wouldn't it be wonderful not to have to make the best of things?"

❦   ❦

❦

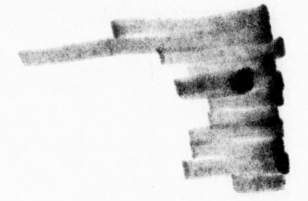

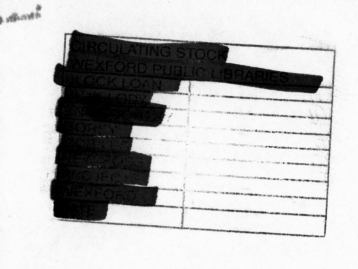